THE TWO LIVES OF EDDIE KOVACS

A NOVEL

MIKE NEMETH

The Two Lives of Eddie Kovacs

Copyright © 2022 by Nemo Writes, LLC

All rights reserved. No part of this publication may be reproduced, distributed, or transmitted in any form or by any means, including photocopying, recording or other electronic or mechanical methods, without the prior written permission of the author, except in the case of brief quotations embodied in reviews and certain other non-commercial uses permitted by copyright law.

This is a work of fiction. Any characters, businesses, places, events, and incidents are either the products of the author's imagination or used in a fictitious manner. Any resemblance to actual persons, living or dead, or actual events is purely coincidental.

Printed in the United States of America
Paperback ISBN: 978-1-956019-99-5
Ebook ISBN: 978-1-959096-00-9
Library of Congress Control Number: 2022945407

DartFrog Plus is a division of DartFrog Books
4697 Main Street
Manchester Center, VT 05255

For Angie, as always. She inspires me as she tolerates my compulsion to write stories.

Author's Note

Palm Haven is a figment of my imagination, although many similar places dot the coastal landscape. The north shore of Tybee Island is as pristine and protected as ever.

The Special Forces/Montagnard camp I called Vu Dong is also a figment of my imagination, although many such camps existed in the Centrals Highlands near the Cambodian and Laotian borders, including Tan Canh, Dak To II, Ben Het, Dak Seang, and Dak Pek. The subjugation of the Montagnard tribes by the Vietnamese is factual. Although they had been promised sovereign territory by both the French and the Americans, they were displaced by North Vietnamese refugees, prompting their migration to Laos and Cambodia, where they were systematically annihilated. Only some four hundred of their number escaped to America after the war.

During the war, America walked a fine line between arming our most effective ally—the Montagnards—and satisfying the Vietnamese, who feared a Montagnard revolt. The South lost the war in large part because it couldn't stop North Vietnamese infiltration into the Central Highlands via the Ho Chi Minh Trail.

American Green Berets who served in the Highlands camps will recognize some scenes in this book as having been inspired by true events.

"The world breaks everyone and afterward many are strong at the broken places. But those that will not break it kills. It kills the very good and the very gentle and the very brave impartially. If you are none of these you can be sure it will break you too but there will be no special hurry."
—*Ernest Hemingway*

"Only the dead have seen the end of war."
—*Plato*

CHAPTER ONE

Tybee Island, Georgia, Present Day

Eddie Kovacs didn't need a GPS to find the Palm Haven Condominium—it stuck out like a black eye in a family portrait. A massive structure constructed of white masonry topped by a chocolate brown Mediterranean tile roof, the luxury condo community looked as though it had been plucked from the Amalfi Coast in Italy and plunked down on the formerly pristine beach on the northern tip of Tybee Island. The building's two eight-story wings angled away from a four-story main building, as though they were the swept wings of a jet fighter. According to Sheriff Lance Carlyle, the locals wished the monstrosity would fly back to Italy and take all the rich assholes with it.

"No one wanted the damn thing to ruin the beach, but the developers promised jobs and greased enough palms to make it happen," Lance said. "It's like the island became South Florida overnight."

Eddie took a left onto the last street inland from the ocean and drove parallel to the backside of Palm Haven's sprawl. A few hundred yards along, a paved road to the right ran past a row of Leyland cypress trees that hid the loading dock and rear entrance from the prying eyes of residents and islanders. Halfway down the road, cars rested in numbered spaces under the parking lot's corrugated tin roofing. The entry and exit gate arms were down, so he took a roll of electrical tape from his glove compartment, tore off two short lengths, and walked to the exit gate. Unlike the key-card-operated entry gate, the exit gate operated automatically when an optical cell sensed an approaching car. He taped a black plus sign over the eye and the gate rose.

He drove his aged but pampered Ford Bronco in the out lane and parked it in slot 202. He went back to the gate and removed the tape and the gate arm dropped into place. From his rear storage compartment, he retrieved a rolling suitcase and a leather duffle bag. The strap of a canvas satchel, his substitute for a briefcase, went around his neck.

Acting as though he owned the place, he sauntered toward the rear entrance where an ambulance, lights flashing but no siren, was backed up to the loading dock. He climbed the ramp and peered around double entrance doors that had been propped open. In the vestibule, elevator doors marked "Staff Only" were closing to his left. Beyond a matching elevator on the right wall of the corridor, an alcove led to restrooms. He rolled his luggage into the alcove and watched as the elevator doors opened to reveal a gurney on which lay a body draped from head to toe by a white sheet. The paramedics wheeled the gurney into the hallway followed by a young woman dressed in green nurse's scrubs and an older gentleman wearing a white lab coat. They exchanged a few indistinct words, then the older gentleman and the nurse got back into the elevator.

When the elevator doors closed, Eddie shuffled out of his hiding place, shoulders hunched forward like a decrepit old man, and yelled, "Hey! Is that my buddy Steve?"

The tall paramedic at the head of the gurney said, "Go away, geezer."

Eddie shuffled closer.

The shorter, younger man at the back of the gurney held up a hand asking Eddie to stop. Eddie stopped.

"C'mon Dickie," the tall man said.

Dickie, the young guy, flipped up the sheet and read the toe tag. "Not your buddy. Guy named Jacob Hoffman."

"Ah, Jacob," Eddie said, as though saddened by the news. "Another opioid overdose was it?"

"Don't look like an overdose to me," Dickie said. "Guy's all dressed up in a suit. Clean as a whistle."

The tall paramedic yanked on the gurney pulling it toward the open double doors. "Let's go, Dickie."

"Thanks," Eddie said.

"No problem," Dickie responded. "Have a good day."

The paramedics swiftly rolled the gurney through the loading dock doors and into the ambulance.

Eddie straightened and dragged his luggage down a corridor lined with administrative offices and past up-and-down escalators into a lobby that gave him the impression he had just entered a four-star hotel. Several well-dressed people awaited help from a concierge. In the center of the spacious lobby, a gaggle of people relaxed on a cluster of plump white leather sofas. A minion in the Palm Haven uniform of white jacket and black slacks spotted him and hurried up to say, "Did you come in the back way?"

"Sure. I parked out back and walked in."

"You parked out back?" The nice-looking young guy sounded incredulous.

"Looked like your parking lot to me."

"Sir, we have valet parking only. You bring your car to the front, and we take care of parking. When you want your car, just call 1-0-0-1 and we'll get it for you."

"Handy. Thanks."

"Can I have your keys, please? Do you remember the number on the parking space?"

"Sure, I do. I'm in slot 312." He handed the anxious young man the spare keys to the Mercedes sport coupe his wife, Sam, had owned. Sam hadn't been able to drive for a long time, but Eddie couldn't bear to part with the flashy red car that was so reflective of Sam's personality.

The young man looked relieved. "Leave your luggage with me and check in over there." The bellhop pointed across the lobby to a counter above which hung a sign that read "Reception" in foot-tall letters.

Eddie thought the sign should say, "God's Waiting Room." He relinquished his luggage but held onto his canvas satchel and stepped up to the reception desk where a young woman in the ubiquitous white uniform jacket gave him the counterfeit smile of an airline stewardess.

"Checking in. Kovacs, Edward C."

"Ah," she said when she found him on the computer. "You came all the way from Wisconsin. Why here and not Florida?"

"Too many old farts down there."

A peal of laughter shot out of her, then she cupped a hand over her mouth in case he wasn't being sarcastic.

He gave her a smile to indicate he was kidding.

"Is your wife with you?" She craned her neck to look around him.

"No, it's just me now," he said.

Her smile morphed from cheerful to sympathetic. "I'm sorry, Mr. Kovacs. I hope you'll be happy here." She handed him a thick portfolio. "Everything you need to know is in there, including a map of the grounds and facilities, so you don't get lost."

"I'm pretty good at finding my way around."

"Of course, sir. We have you in guest apartment number 103, first floor of the independent living wing, just past the pool and the gym." She pointed over his shoulder to the other side of the lobby. "It's that way. The apartment is fully furnished but let us know if you need anything else. Apartment 410 is reserved for you when your household goods arrive. There's a thirty-day limit on guest apartment stays."

He nodded. "That's all I'll need."

He headed for his apartment and noted that there was only one way in and one way out. Not ideal.

The guest apartment was a replica of a suite at a long stay motel—one bedroom, one bath, a sitting area, a cramped kitchen, a round pine dining table with four chairs. He unpacked the suitcase, which contained enough clothes for a month-long stay, and then the leather duffle. On the dresser, he placed a squat plastic jar and a framed 8x10 photo of Sam. In the top drawer of the dresser, he placed six eyeglass cases containing aviator sunglasses. He had silver frames and gold frames with yellow, blue, black, green, and mirrored lenses. Sam had often chided him for his obsession with the aviators which were for him, a signal to other Vietnam vets that he was one of them.

Then he looked for a hiding place. Using his P-38—an Army issue miniature screwdriver and can opener that hung from his keychain—he unscrewed the cover of the air conditioning return vent in the kitchen and placed his badge, a thick wad of used bills, and his six-shot revolver in the ductwork. Eddie preferred revolvers because they never jammed, and they didn't leave casings behind.

At the table, he spread the facility map and studied it closely. In the central building, the communal dining room occupied the ocean end of the second floor it shared with the ballroom. He noted that the elevators in the vestibule at the back of the central building serviced all eight floors of each wing. He could understand how dead bodies rolling through the reception area to the grand entrance might have a deleterious effect on resident morale.

He opened the vertical blinds on what he expected were sliding glass doors leading to a patio and found instead a sealed window through which he saw the outdoor pool and its Tiki Bar. At this hour, a dozen residents lounged around the pool to catch the last of the sun's rays. The people on his list could be just outside his window but he hadn't been given physical descriptions. All he saw was slack skin, pouchy bellies, and sun-damaged faces.

Eddie had accepted the sheriff's invitation to discuss an *opportunity* as an excuse to revisit the city in which he and Sam had met and fallen in love. During an afternoon of nostalgic browsing, he found that Savannah had resisted change, confident in its charm and its leisurely pace. The citizens of Savannah revered the past and that produced a sense of stability that comforted Eddie. He had walked northwest on Broad Street, under a canopy of trees dripping Spanish moss, to Forrest Gump's bus stop at Chippewa Square, where he rested for a moment. Unbeknownst to the giggling tourists who took selfies while sitting on the benches scattered around the square, Forrest Gump's authentic bench had been shipped to a movie museum years ago.

Moving southwesterly toward Forsyth Park, he admired the restored townhouses on Savannah's famous squares, and two blocks west of the park on Gwinnett Street he found the house in which he and Sam had lived as newlyweds. Once a white Colonial, the house had been renovated and painted a happy shade of yellow. Standing in front of it, he mourned the life he had abandoned to secure the life he had lived.

Now the sentimentality faded under the weight of his seventy years and the folly of accepting this assignment. Did he think he could make up for Vietnam, repay his debt to the sheriff's family, and prove a District Attorney wrong for firing him by solving one last case? He had to try.

He cranked the blinds closed and said, "Time to go to work."

After a shower, he brushed his unruly gray hair—silver bullets his barber called them—and dressed in tan linen slacks, a French blue button-down shirt, penny loafers, and a brown twill sports jacket. He had promised himself never to wear rubber nurses' shoes or sports jackets in the powder blue or salmon colors the old farts favored. No Hawaiian shirts, either. He had no paunch to hide.

Satisfied that he looked like a rich old codger, he shook the jar for good luck and two jagged pieces of metal rattled around inside.

✳ ✳ ✳

When the escalator reached the second floor, he discovered that the dining room wasn't a room at all. No walls enclosed the sumptuous ivory carpet and—he counted them—twenty-four round tables covered in black linen tablecloths. The tables, each of them with six place settings, dotted the carpet like pepper on white gravy. Nearly every seat was occupied—ninety percent white, seventy percent female, and eighty percent retirees—dressed in the sports coats and summer dresses they had worn to country clubs.

Eddie understood now what the sheriff meant when he said, "We gave it a try, but my guys weren't, ah, the right age for the job. The residents clammed up."

There was no hostess stand, no maître d'. A passing waitress, balancing a tray of wine and cocktail glasses, said, "Sit wherever you like. We'll find you and take your order."

"I hope senility isn't contagious," he muttered.

She laughed over her shoulder as she hurried away.

He felt like a bird, waiting its turn for a perch at the feeder, but the liberal flow of alcohol pleased him. He had feared he'd be stuck with teetotalers in the Bible belt. These well-lubricated residents produced an alcohol-fueled cacophony of laughter and vibrant conversation.

He spotted four women in their eighties, all resembling the British Queen with their tightly permed gray hair, at a table with two empty seats. Its position against the left-hand wall was a perfect spot from which to observe the room. He headed that way, acknowledging the unabashed inspections of his fellow residents with unselfconscious nods. During high school summers spent caddying at an exclusive country club, he had learned how the upper class dressed and spoke and behaved and he had adopted their customs. Later, his one extravagance was membership at a golf club where he fit in because the members thought his job in the DA's office meant he was a lawyer. Playing a role was second nature for Eddie.

He stopped beside the table he had targeted and bowed slightly. "Ladies. May I?" He gestured to a vacant chair.

The women stared at him as though he had spoken a foreign language.

"I'm Eddie Kovacs. Just checked in today."

The apparent leader of the group said, "Nice to meet you, Mr. Kovacs," and nodded her consent.

He sat with his back to the wall, shook out his black napkin, and laid it across his lap.

The ladies resumed their conversation and ignored him. A waitress soon arrived to offer him garden salad with raspberry vinaigrette or lentil soup as a starter, Pasta Primavera or broiled salmon or baked free-range chicken with an assortment of steamed vegetables. He selected the soup and the pasta and asked for a beer.

While the ladies finished their meal, whispering among themselves, he sipped his beer and scanned his surroundings. Through a fifty-foot expanse of floor-to-ceiling glass, he could see the building's shadow inching toward the ocean while the horizon crept toward the beach where the two phenomena would merge into darkness when the sun set.

Residents in wheelchairs or using walkers occupied about a third of the tables. The people on his list lived in the assisted living wing and he regretted not finding a seat at one of the assisted living tables.

Two women circulated the room, stopping to exchange a few words before moving along, like butterflies pollinating flowers. When his soup arrived, so did social butterfly number one—a tall and slender, green-eyed woman of indeterminate age with brittle blond hair and high, hard breasts. He thought her surgically tightened facial skin might tear if she smiled.

"Who do we have here?" she asked him.

He tried to stand to introduce himself, but the woman placed a hand on his shoulder to hold him down and took the open seat beside him.

"I'm Eddie Kovacs, just checked in today."

"Well, you'll love it here." She placed a hand on his arm and leaned closer. "I'm Karen Wykowski and I'm pleased to make your acquaintance."

A whiff of sharp perfume shot up his nose like Chinese mustard, and he stifled a cough. "Likewise."

The table boss interrupted the introduction. "Welcome to Palm Haven, Mr. Kovacs. Do take some pains to find a regular table." The four elderly ladies dabbed their lips and excused themselves. With noses and chins pointed toward the ceiling, they shuffled away.

"Guess they couldn't stand the competition," Eddie said.

Karen laughed and crossed her legs to show him knobby knees. "You're fun." She asked him the usual introductory questions and feigned interest in his bland answers as she rubbed his calf with her foot. He had begun to turn the questions toward Karen and Palm Haven when social butterfly number two arrived at their table. Shorter and riper than Karen, sloe-eyed with thick chestnut hair and an apple dumpling-cheeked face, she wore a purple and gold dress that reached her feet. A glossy, white smile erupted above a pouty lower lip as she said, "I see you found him, Karen. Sorry, but there's someone who wants to meet him."

She lifted Eddie out of his chair by his elbow and slipped her arm through his.

"You're such a bitch, Madeleine," Karen spat. "Meet me later, Eddie. In the bar."

Before they could move away, the waitress appeared with Eddie's entree.

"Bring it to my table," Madeleine told the waitress.

As they eased between tables, she said, "What's your name, Cowboy?"

He told her.

"I'm Madeleine. Believe me, you'll thank me for rescuing you."

Madeleine's table sat next to and precisely in the middle of the huge window, obviously a table of honor. Four people at the table watched them approach: a willowy woman, a bald heavyset white man, a dignified Black man, and the man Eddie recognized as the doctor who had escorted the dead body out of an assisted living elevator. Madeleine sat Eddie in the one open seat, between herself and the other woman, and the waitress set his food in front of him.

"This is Eddie Kovacs," Madeleine announced. "Brand spanking new. Stole him from Crazy Karen."

The bald man whose thick pecs were losing the battle with gravity, interjected, "She's made of so much plastic she'll melt if she gets too close to a candle."

Everyone laughed and Madeleine shook her finger at him.

Madeleine pointed to each tablemate and named them. Susan Claiborne sat to Eddie's left and to her left sat her brash husband, Bobby. Next to Bobby, Donald McCabe gave Eddie an acknowledging nod. Michael Cevert, the doctor, occupied the last seat to Madeleine's right.

"Welcome to happily ever after," Susan said to Eddie, sarcasm tainting her Southern drawl. Susan, who didn't bother to style her long gray hair, had the look of a lost soul, someone who awoke this morning wondering how she had gotten here, how the years had slipped away. He labeled her a disillusioned former hippie.

"Which apartment are you in?" Madeleine asked.

"I'm in a guest apartment now, but apartment 410 will be my home when my household goods arrive," Eddie said.

"The pool view is nice if you like cellulite," Bobby said to chuckles.

Eddie felt he had to defend himself, as though he were back in grammar school. "That's all that was available."

"Ocean view condos become available all the time," Madeleine said.

"When the locals hear a siren, they say, 'There's another condo for sale,'" Bobby said.

"Michael has asked the ambulances to come without sirens now," Madeleine said.

Like the one that snuck up to the back door to whisk away a dead body today, Eddie thought. "I imagine that's a regular occurrence, ambulances carrying people away."

"Residents get taken to the hospital from time to time." Cevert gave Eddie a one-shouldered shrug.

"Usually, they croak in the hospital," Bobby said. "Jacob was the first to die here in what? Six months?"

Cevert glared at Bobby. "We lost Jacob Hoffman today," Cevert explained for Eddie. "Sudden heart attack."

"I imagine heart attacks and opioid overdoses are common at a place like this," Eddie said.

Cevert examined Eddie's face as though he were examining a blood sample under a microscope. "I'm not aware of any opioid overdoses here," Cevert said finally.

"That's a coal-country problem. Appalachia, right?" Bobby said.

Before Eddie could ask his follow-up question, two women, perhaps late seventies, sidled up to the table and did a poor job of disguising their interest in Eddie. The one with the plump, jovial face smelled of lilacs. She bent to place a comforting hand on Madeleine's shoulder. "We're so sorry for your loss," she said.

"Thank you," Madeleine said. "You're very kind."

The other woman had a long, slender nose, thin fire engine red lips, and a sharply jutting chin. "Maybe it was a blessing," she said. "Now you can't torture him with barbaric treatments." Pointing a finger at Dr. Cevert, Lipstick Lady added, "A hundred years from now, people will laugh at what you call medicine today."

"I'm not an oncologist, Phyllis," Cevert said patiently.

"Were you with him when it happened?" Lilac Lady asked Madeleine.

Madeleine hesitated and Eddie sensed she was carefully composing her response. "Yes, we were just coming down for lunch."

"His usual spot was in your chair, Eddie," Susan said.

Sitting in the dead man's seat, as cold as the cadaver, made Eddie shiver.

"Are you going to introduce us?" Lipstick Lady said to Madeleine, pointing a gnarled finger at Eddie.

Madeleine performed the introductions. Phyllis Candler—Lipstick Lady—was related to the Atlanta Candler clan that founded Coca-Cola, and Bernice MacMillan—Lilac Lady—had been married to a Florida timber baron.

"They're both loaded," Bobby said.

Madeleine swept a hand toward Eddie.

"I owned a string of dry cleaning stores in Wisconsin," he said. "My wife, Samantha, recently passed away after a struggle with breast cancer."

Madeleine patted his shoulder and told him how sorry she was.

As though he weren't sitting right in front of her, Phyllis said to Madeleine, "Put a hat on that face and he'd look like he just stepped off a ranch and rode in here on his horse."

"That's why I call him 'Cowboy,'" Madeleine said.

The two women tittered.

Eddie flinched. With his white two-day stubble beard on his weathered brown face, he didn't look like a man who spent his winters in Wisconsin. The beguiled women would be amused, he thought, to see a picture of him as a twelve-year old altar boy, black hair parted on the left and pasted to his scalp with Brylcream.

"If you play bridge, come up to the card room and join us," Bernice said.

"I do play. Thanks for the invite," Eddie said with a shy smile.

The two visitors took their leave.

"Watch out, Eddie," Bobby said. "There's just one man for every two women at Palm Haven, so the competition for male companions is fierce. The women will cook meals for you, fetch your dry cleaning, do your laundry and ironing. Hell, they'll do a lot more if you want them to."

"You make it sound like a whorehouse, Bobby," Susan said.

"Which it's not," Madeleine said. She acted as master of ceremonies, leading everyone through a brief biography. The movement of Madeleine's puffy lower lip distracted Eddie. As she spoke, it rolled down and quivered seductively.

Donald went first and proudly said he had been a trial lawyer in Atlanta.

"Made a ton of money offa all the black crime up there," Bobby said. "Just one wife, smart enough to leave him."

Donald flashed a smile at Eddie and said, "Bobby is so jealous."

Cevert admitted to being a retired internist and surgeon, also from Atlanta.

"Doctor to the wealthy Jews," Bobby added. "Several wives and a bunch of kids, but he can afford them."

Cevert, with a pinched face and a wisp of black hair remaining from a sad combover, seemed distracted as he fiddled with his wire-rimmed glasses.

"And you?" Eddie asked Bobby.

"We have a lot in common. I owned three Radio Shack stores in Savannah."

Eddie knew that Radio Shack stores had evaporated years ago, but he wanted to ingratiate himself with Bobby. "We'll have to trade war stories."

"Susan here was a teacher. Retired early," Bobby said.

"Bobby never appreciated the stress level," Susan said.

"Can I have some cheese with that whine?" Bobby asked.

Embarrassed, Eddie turned to his hostess. "Your turn, Madeleine."

"My husband was a developer, coastal property in South Carolina."

"Filthy rich and single again," Bobby said.

"Madeleine and Jacob were an item," Susan explained.

Nervously changing the subject, Madeleine said, "I've been single forever. My husband died of a heart attack a decade ago. Michael and Donald are lucky enough to have ex-wives and children who visit. Of course, Susan is luckiest of all as Bobby is here with her."

"Every day is her lucky day," Bobby said.

Susan gave him an obligatory smile.

"Bobby likes to stir up trouble. Each night, he brings us a controversial topic to discuss," Madeleine said. "It's fun."

"Left wing politicians want to push us toward Socialism and away from Capitalism," Bobby said with a gleam in his eye. "I'll go first. Socialism breeds mediocrity."

Bobby folded his arms across his chest as though there were nothing more to say, but his wife, Susan wasn't shy about her position.

"What you call mediocrity is equality and you hate that because you want to be superior. Socialism provides equal access to healthcare and eliminates poverty."

"Socialism encourages corruption at the high end of the scale and enables freeloading at the bottom of society," Michael said, as though the worn-out subject bored him.

"Isn't that what we already have?" Susan asked.

"Socialism is a fantasy sold to the poor to buy their votes," Michael said. "And who do you think will fund the socialist programs?"

"We'll get the money from the rich. I mean, not us, but the billionaires."

"The top one percent of income earners already pay forty-three-point-six percent of all taxes," Michael said. "Hate them if you wish, but they are as important to the economy as predators are to the animal ecosystem. They will be protected no matter which party is in power. The bottom sixty percent of Americans pay just thirteen-point-four percent of all taxes, so the money will come from us, the well-to-do in the middle."

"If I have the math right, the middle class is thirty-nine percent of the population and pays forty-three percent of the taxes. Our fair share," Madeleine said.

"That's right. Socialism is a war on the middle class."

Donald cleared his throat dramatically and won the table's attention. "Y'all are misinterpreting the numbers. Late-stage capitalism has produced an extreme wealth gap. That sixty percent of Americans pay only thirteen percent of the taxes means more than half of our people are poor. When the disparity between rich and poor becomes too large, the poor will revolt and we'll have a repeat of the French Revolution."

"I've got a solution for that," Bobby said, as he made a pistol with his hand and shot Donald.

"What do you think, Eddie?" Madeleine asked.

None of these people were on Eddie's list, but they could be valuable networking connections, so he didn't want to offend any of them. "Capitalism is efficient because it appeals to our avaricious, materialistic nature. We all want big screen TVs and the newest smartphones."

"Hell, yeah," Bobby agreed. "Capitalism is aligned with freedom. The poor are free to move up to the middle class."

"If only it were that easy," Donald said.

"You've had your fun for tonight, Bobby," Madeleine said, bringing the discussion to an end.

"We're going upstairs for a nightcap, aren't we, honey?" Bobby said while looking at his wife, Susan. She returned a blank stare.

Donald scooted his chair back and said, "I've had enough for one night. I can feel a headache coming on. Welcome to the table, Eddie."

"Come along," Susan said to Eddie. "Bobby has so much more to say."

"I'll take a rain check," Eddie said. "Long drive from Wisconsin."

Bobby, Susan, and Cevert drifted away, but Madeleine lingered. "Well, Cowboy, what did you think of our dinner discussion?"

What he thought was that Madeleine's group of friends provided him with perfect cover for his job. He felt the familiar tingle of excitement in his fingers—he knew what he was up to and they didn't. "It was fun, like you promised."

"The topics are usually more contentious. Join us for dinner tomorrow night and you'll see more fireworks."

"I'm always up for a debate," he said.

She squeezed his arm and he felt her warmth through his jacket and shirt. They moved to the escalators where she went up and he went down.

The long drive from St. Petersburg, Florida had fatigued him, but he maintained the nightly ritual he began the day Sam passed. He poured himself two fingers of bourbon, lifted the picture of his wife off the dresser, and talked to it as he shuffled around the cramped spaces of his apartment sipping his nightcap.

"It feels good to be back in the saddle, Sam." He chortled. Had he chosen that metaphor because Madeleine had called him "Cowboy?" He cleared his throat and started over. "I mean this place is like a circus. Tonight, I met the clowns and the carnival barkers. Tomorrow I'll go under the big top to meet the performers."

"Don't feed peanuts to the elephants," she said. "They're too rich for them. And stay away from the trapeze artists. They're too rich for you."

He scoffed. "You don't have to worry about me, Sweetheart."

"I'm worried about why you took this job," she said.

He took the job because it brought him full circle to Savannah for one last shot at redemption. Redemption had been placed on hold when Sam got sick.

Caring for Sam had consumed his every waking minute for three years, but taking care of her was the easy part. The repetition of optimism followed by disappointment was the hard part. First a lumpectomy, then chemo and radiation that seemed promising, then a mastectomy, and yet the cancer kept coming back.

When she passed, friends comforted him by saying, "Well, she's not in pain anymore."

He appreciated the condolences but he would never outlive the pain.

Since her passing he had time to reflect, time to evaluate his life and weigh achievements against failures. Despite a long, heralded, seemingly glamorous, sometimes notorious, career, the humiliating end to his career four years ago had become his legacy. He had gotten it wrong only twice, but they were whoppers.

"It's a chance to end my career with a win."

"Ah, the hero rides off into the sunset in a blaze of glory."

"Something like that."

"You're holding out on me, Eddie. You did the right thing in Florida and you know it. Is this about Vietnam?"

"I don't think about Vietnam anymore."

"Don't lie to me, Eddie. I don't think you've told me the truth about Vietnam, why it haunts you to this day."

He took his glass into the kitchen and poured another shot of Bourbon. He leaned against the counter and drained the glass. He had never told anyone the unadulterated truth about Vietnam. Like his dad's generation before him, his generation spoke of Vietnam only with those who had shared the experience. No one else would understand.

"I've never lied to you about Vietnam but I've never told you the whole story."

"Don't you think it's about time? Tell me now."

"To understand Vietnam, I have to tell you what happened before. You know I screwed up my brother's life when I was a teenager."

"You saved him from the Vietnam draft."

"And it ruined his life. My dad's, too. Tore the family apart. But I got what I wanted—four years at a boys' boarding school. I wasn't punished. When I got drafted, I thought I would gladly pay for my sins."

"So, this is about Catholic guilt."

"It's more like survivor guilt."

CHAPTER TWO

... 1970

I wasn't bitter but I was scared. Like my brother before me, I tried everything imaginable to wiggle off the Army hook. An Air Force recruiter told me how to cheat on the Armed Forces Qualification Test so he could pluck me off the reject pile and save me from the Army, so I tried it. We got caught. I got caught. I was saddled with a score so low that I only qualified to drive a tank through the Vietnamese jungles. It was my penance for coercing my brother Danny into evading the draft in 1966. He didn't have to serve and it ruined his life. My Dad's, too.

So, I was shipped off to basic training at Fort Leonard Wood, Missouri, and it wasn't as bad as I had feared. The cool fall weather was a blessing as we began each day with a one mile run, in formation, wearing combat boots and fatigues. As we ran we chanted silly rhymes about "Jody" stealing our girlfriend back home. After the run, we lined up for breakfast. Outside the door to the mess hall, a set of elevated parallel bars, about fifteen feet start to finish, were the last obstacle to food. Out-of-shape, overweight kids had trouble traversing the bars and dropped to the ground before reaching the mess hall door. Drill sergeants screamed at these kids and ridiculed them. Sometimes the fat kids were sent to the back of the chow line to drown in anxiety before their next attempt, and sometimes, a drill sergeant yelled, "Drop and give me ten," meaning pushups.

I had learned that the trick to navigating the bars was to approach them with a lot of forward momentum, to jump toward the bars, and to maintain the momentum as I swing ape-like from bar to bar. At the door, each kid shouted his serial number to a soldier with a clipboard who put a checkmark beside your name. That was how they determined if anyone had gone AWOL overnight. My number was and is 56454965, an indelible etching on my brain.

Within a few days my drill instructor, a buck sergeant named Byrd who was neither white nor black and possessed of a melodious Caribbean Island voice so unlike the coarse barking of the other sergeants, promoted me to squad leader and gave me an armband with two yellow stripes to denote my position as a "Candy Striper." He said he recognized my intelligence and leadership qualities. It felt as though I was a trustee at a prison, or a collaborator with an occupying force.

The position came with privileges, including no KP, and a weekly trip to the PX and Commissary to shop for the toiletries and sundries my squad members needed. On one such trip, I removed my armband, thinking I would blend in with other troops, took a seat in the cafeteria, and ordered a burger and a beer. A pair of MP's dragged me out of the Commissary like a crook arrested for home invasion. They took me to Sergeant Byrd who stripped me of my candy stripes.

Most of our training was conducted outdoors and consisted of double-timing, wearing a helmet and a backpack, and carrying the heavy, obsolete M-14 rifle, while fall rains added to the discomfort. We took intermittent ten minute breaks when Byrd yelled, "Smoke 'em if you've got 'em." I learned to nap during the breaks, using my helmet as a pillow.

On one exercise, we walked single-file on both sides of a one-lane road. We had been briefed to expect an ambush and that when we were "fired" upon, we should charge the shooters because the sneaky Commie snipers wanted to chase us toward their larger force on the other side of the road. Instinctively, I ran away from the initial shots, and was captured by the bad guys.

Byrd yanked me aside and said, "You're just not cut out to be a soldier, are you? I'll see what I can do about that."

Our final weapons qualification took place in a snowstorm that left frozen snowflakes in my gunsights. Street smart trainees had advised me to barely qualify so that I wouldn't be shifted to the infantry. I didn't have to fake it; I barely qualified.

With graduation approaching, Byrd dragged me into his small office at the back of the barracks and closed the door.

"This whole group of trainees will go to Fort Polk for infantry training but I don't want that to happen to you."

"At the induction center they told me I'd be driving a tank."

Byrd scoffed. "Those buffoons don't have the power to decide your assignment."

More lies. "I sure as hell don't want to be a rifleman."

"You're different, Kovacs. You have a gentle soul like an altar boy."

"I was an altar boy and studied for the priesthood for a while."

He bounced to his feet and spread his arms like that statue in Brazil. "See! I knew it. I'm Catholic, Kovacs, and I can spot one a mile away. I want you in a school that's appropriate for a kid with your intelligence."

I had been offered a school at the induction center in exchange for a third year of active duty. At the time, my calculation was two years driving a tank was better than three years as a cook or mechanic. But then the scales tipped; there would be no tank, just an M-16.

"I've been through the catalog, Sergeant, and I didn't see anything worth three years in the Army."

"You only got to see the courses they could offer with your low score on the entrance exam. There's another test called a GT test, General Technical, which measures skills and associates them with military occupations. Good courses, long courses, tough courses. Take the test, get a score of 110 or better, and you can go to the school of your choice."

I knew there'd be a quid pro quo. "I'll have to sign up for a third year."

"Yes. I won't kid you. But I'm not lying about the infantry."

I took the test and scored 132. Byrd was delighted. Then I chose an eight week course for Depot Supply Specialists at Ft. Lee, Virginia. Depots are behind the front lines, right?

"That's a good one," he said with a smile.

For the second time I raised my hand in front of an officer and swore the oath of a regular Army soldier.

With a fair-haired Scandinavian kid from Minnesota, a kid whose declarative sentences seemed always to end with a question mark, I rode an Army bus to Lambert Field in St. Louis, where I marveled at the Spirit of St. Louis, Charles Lindbergh's plane, hanging from the ceiling, before boarding a twin-engine prop plane for a flight to Richmond, Virginia. Over West Virginia we encountered violent weather that bounced our small craft around like a dinghy on ocean waves. The Minnesota kid used the paper barf bag and the cabin reeked of the rancid, gag-inducing smell of vomit. How ironic would it have been to elude the infantry only to perish on my very first airplane flight?

We didn't crash. My new buddy and I were taken to the bus station in an Army three-quarter-ton truck where we had breakfast before boarding another bus to Petersburg. When my sausage and fried eggs were delivered, they sat-by-side with some white soupy stuff with a pat of butter melting on top. I pointed to the mysterious stuff and told the waitress I had not ordered anything but eggs and sausage. "Them's grits, baby," she said. "Come free with ever' breakfast order." I was careful to separate the real food from the grits.

On the bus ride to Petersburg and Fort Robert E. Lee, we passed several Civil War battlefields and road signs directing traffic to Confederate Monuments and museums.

"I thought we won that war," I said to the kid from Minnesota.

"It's like we're in a foreign country," the kid said.

After basic training, Depot Supply School was a breeze. The Army was on the forefront of computer adoption and had automated the entire supply chain from manufacturers to depots to operational units. Using the computers, depot supply specialists requisitioned equipment, maintained inventory, and allocated equipment to authorized end users. The process was interesting, somewhat challenging, and absent any weapons.

On weekend passes, I often took a bus to Washington, D.C. to stay with my aunt and her husband, a retired Air Force Officer. I slept in the frilly pink bed of a cousin who was away at college. My aunt and uncle took me to the Smithsonian and the Lincoln Memorial, the Capital and the White House, and fancy restaurants. They regaled me with funny stories about Dad's antics in the Navy. He had gone to flight school but dropped out due to—get this—sensitive hearing that couldn't bear the noise. I imagined him casting about for something equally dangerous to do and settling on the submarine service because it offered so many ways to die for your country.

Along with my aunt, who was an Army civilian office clerk, and my uncle who was her flyboy boyfriend, Dad had been stationed at Pearl Harbor prior to the Japanese sneak attack. My aunt had been popular because she had a phonograph and a cook stove in her small apartment. Dad and his rowdy buddies picked up girls on the beach at Waikiki or at the big pink Imperial Hotel and took them to my aunt's place to dance and get drunk. During the attack on Pearl Harbor, Dad was on a firefighting gang and suffered shrapnel wounds from falling bombs. One piece of jagged Japanese metal lodged in his left bicep and doctors decided not to excise it for fear of damaging the muscle. They believed the shrapnel would work its way out of Dad's arm naturally, but his muscle embraced the shrapnel like a prize in a trophy case, and it's still there today, a permanent testament to his bravery.

He survived five years of Pacific warfare on three submarines and would have made the Navy a career were it not for my mother's me-or-the-Navy ultimatum. Never again would his life match the purpose and excitement of his wartime experience.

My aunt and uncle showed me a different side of Dad BM—Before Mom—but it didn't change my opinion of Dad AM—After Mom.

"Our family did suffer one casualty in the war," my aunt said, her eyes downcast, her voice soft. "You're named after your uncle Edward, your dad's and my youngest brother. Terrible waste. His patrol boat sank in a storm off the coast of Alaska when the war was nearly over in 1945. Did you know that?"

I did know that my namesake uncle died in the war. My other namesake uncle, my mother's brother, Edward, had drowned as a boy. I was named after two dead uncles.

"I didn't know the circumstances."

From our student barracks at Fort Lee, we had a good view of the Officer Candidate School parade ground. As the candidates marched in their pressed utilities and painted helmet liners, my buddy from Minnesota said, "Look at those egotistical assholes. They think they are better than us ordinary Joes, but the life expectancy of a Second Lieutenant in 'Nam is about ninety seconds."

Sergeant Horner at the induction center had told me it was two weeks.

"Meanwhile we'll have our feet up on our desk in some air conditioned depot," my friend concluded.

I acknowledged how smart we were, but my ego was telling me I should have been with the OCS guys and not the ordinary Joes.

Most members of our class received orders for Long Binh or Cam Ranh Bay or Da Nang, the huge logistics centers in Vietnam. Perhaps as a reward for finishing first in my class, I received a weird stateside assignment to an artillery brigade at Ft. Bliss in El Paso, Texas. Maybe I *was* smart.

Texas is big, everyone knows that, but just how big wasn't apparent until I flew from Richmond to St. Louis to Dallas and on to El Paso. Turns out, El Paso is as far from Dallas as Dallas is from St. Louis. El Paso sits on a little bit of land that juts under New Mexico like a wood sliver under your fingernail. The tail end of the Rocky Mountain chain sits to the west and the Rio Grande River and the Mexican border are to the immediate south. Upon my arrival at Ft. Bliss, I was given a bed and a locker in a dorm-like barracks and told to report to the processing center after reveille tomorrow.

We stand in formation, the sun an angry explosion in the east, as a commercial jetliner ascends over the Texas wasteland. "That's the Freedom Bird, going to Dallas," the soldier next to me says. "I'm short, twenty-six and a wakeup, and then I'll have a seat on that baby."

"I just got here."

"You won't be here long. Fuckin' place is 'Nam's back door. All you need to know while you're here is, Una cerveza, por favor."

So my reward for finishing first in class may be a short vacation before joining everyone else in Vietnam.

At the processing center I join a queue that snakes out the front entrance onto the sidewalk.

"We in the Army, man. Hurry up and wait," the Black Private behind me says.

The line moves steadily toward six clerks at gray steel government issue desks. At the head of the line, an NCO reviews each soldier's paperwork and directs them to the appropriate clerk. He opens my 201 file, scans my orders, pulls me out of the line and stands me against the wall. "Wait here for the clerk at the far end."

As the Black kid passed me, he said, "Don't *ever* want to be singled out in the Army."

I waited nervously for my assigned clerk to become free, then approached his desk. He held out a hand for my file and waived me into the seat in front of his desk. When he opened the file, he looked at me and laughed.

Oh, oh. "Something wrong?"

He tapped the name strip on his right breast. It read: Kovacs. I chanced a smile.

"You're Hungarian, like me, with a big head and broad, cheekbones." He smiled. I had always thought the men in my family looked Slavic with an Asian tilt to the eyes. After all, we're descended from Atilla the Hun.

"Where you from, Kovacs?"

"Wisconsin."

"I'm from Aliquippa, western P-A. Lots of Hungarians in the coal mines."

"Yeah, my grandfather started in those mines when he came from Hungary. Didn't like it. When the Spanish Flu hit, he moved to a light bulb factory in Chicago, saved his money and bought some land in Iowa and became a pig farmer. After World War II my father was discharged from the Navy training base at Manitowoc, Wisconsin, met my mother, and settled in the area." I felt like I had offered too much information, but this Kovacs just nodded patiently.

"We could be related, in P-A or maybe back in the old country."

"Could be." Kovacs is a common Hungarian name, meaning "smith," as in blacksmith.

"Steve," he said.

He held out a hand and I shook it. "Eddie."

He studied my orders and frowned. "You've been assigned to an anti-aircraft brigade—Nike Hawk and Nike Hercules missiles that shoot down enemy planes."

I'm confused. "Do they have a depot? My MOS is depot supply."

Steve chuckled. "There's no depot. Somebody thought they were doing you a favor by not sending you to Vietnam but you do not want to join this brigade."

"No?"

"No. The brigade is stationed at White Sands Missile Range in the New Mexico desert where they can play with their missiles without hurting anyone. They live in tents with the snakes and scorpions."

"Oh."

He paged through my 201 file and talked to himself as he read my records. "You have a great GT test score. You finished first in your depot supply class."

He closed the file, leaned back in his chair and gave me a thoughtful look. "Can you type?"

"Yes, of course."

He rapped the eraser end of his pencil on my file. "Your orders are a mistake. We can find someone else for White Sands. Bright guy like you belongs in personnel, here at Fort Bliss. How would you like that?"

That sounded blissful. "That would be great."

"Enjoy it while you can. Sooner or later someone at the Pentagon will wake up and notice that a soldier on a three-year hitch hasn't been to Vietnam."

∗∗∗

Steve and I weren't exactly buddies—he was my boss—but we had an occasional beer. We never nailed down a specific family linkage, but we felt a form of ethnic kinship.

Most of the guys in the barracks were Hispanic or Native Americans from the surrounding area. I befriended a guy named Hector Cruz and he became my tour guide. We avoided the GI bars in El Paso, went to the clubs the locals frequented and met "nice" girls. He took me to Juarez for a bull fight, walked me down the banks of the Rio Grande to watch illegal immigration. The Mexican families stripped naked and waded across with their bundle of clothes held over their heads. Then they dried off, dressed, and entered the promised land. We laughed at the border guards, two hundred yards upriver at the checkpoint on the walking bridge, oblivious to what was happening under their noses.

He introduced me to Margaritas and taught me the differences between Tex-Mex, Central Mexican and west coast Mexican cuisines.

Two months later, Steve waved me outside, away from the other clerks, with a sheaf of papers in his hand.

"What's the secret?"

"Troop levy," he said, flashing the papers at me.

Oh shit. "Did I get orders?"

"Not by name. It's for your MOS, 76P, for a depot in a place called Korat, Thailand. The depot is on an Air Force base, one-hundred-and-sixty kilometers northeast of Bangkok. I could ignore the levy or I could look around the post for another 76P." He paused, then grinned. "Or I could ship your lucky ass to Thailand."

"Thailand. How far from Vietnam?"

"Can't be far. Our fighters fly from Thailand to bomb North Vietnam."

"Is it dangerous?"

"Not as dangerous as Vietnam but you get credit for a Vietnam tour by serving in Thailand."

Credit for a Vietnam combat tour without going to Vietnam.

"Sign me up."

About a week later, he gave me the official orders and bought me a send-off beer.

You see how this was going, Sam? I had been on a coming-of-age adventure and I had paid no penance for my sins. God was laughing at me, mocking my feeble attempt at atonement. What, other than Divine Intervention, could explain a Drill Sergeant arranging a GT test and getting me into Depot Supply school? What else could explain a random meeting with a man who shared my family name and could send me to exotic Siam rather than war-torn Vietnam?

Each time God presented a way to avoid my penance, I yielded to the temptation.

I finished my third shot of Bourbon. That's enough for tonight, Sam. I'm tired. I'll tell you more each night I'm on this case. The twists and turns begin with the next chapter. Good night, Sam.

CHAPTER THREE

... Now

Eddie opened the blinds on an overcast day. For the moment, the residents would likely be indoors and that suited him. Dressed in khaki slacks, a medium blue collared shirt, a sports jacket, and tassel loafers, he checked himself in the bathroom mirror and remembered Sam saying, "The sixties called and they want your clothes back." No matter what Sam suggested, Eddie resisted her attempts to modernize his wardrobe. "The classic look never goes out of style," he told her.

He walked through the lobby, past the pharmacy, and beyond a large red arrow with the words "Medical Clinic" in bright white pointing down a hallway to his left. He rode the public elevator to the seventh floor of the assisted living wing. The elevator doors opened on a half-moon-shaped nurses' station manned by two busy women in black scrubs. The walk-up counter in front of an eight-foot-high wall faced the long hallway. Patients, nurses, and orderlies funneled through spaces to either side of the station. Behind the counter, a panel displayed lights representing the twenty resident rooms on the floor. Active call lights were lit and matched a flashing red light above the appropriate room door. He gave one of the nurses three names and was told that none of the three people lived on the seventh floor.

None of the three people lived on the sixth floor, but Donna Roberts had a room on the fifth floor, and a nurse directed him to the lounge at the far end of the hallway. He noted as he ambled down the corridor that conditions were sanitary, pristine even. He had expected the assisted living wing to smell like his grandma's house, but the disinfected air had been freshened with a woodsy scent, the black and white tile floors waxed, the light gray walls recently painted.

To qualify for an apartment in the independent living wing, Eddie had filled a form confirming he could perform the six Activities of Daily Living—bathing, dressing, eating, toileting, continence, and unassisted ambulation. The folks in the assisted living wing were incapable of one or more of the activities.

As he passed open doors, he noted that most of the residents had lost their mobility, which likely meant they needed help bathing and toileting as well. *This is what it feels like to die*, he thought. *Not the last gasps for breath as you pass, but the relentless deterioration of physical capability.*

Next to the lounge Eddie noted a door to a back stairwell. In the lounge, two women with walkers sat on a couch facing a TV on which a soap opera played. In the very center of the room, the pump in an aquarium filled with brightly colored fish made a gurgling sound. To his right, a shrunken little woman dressed for church, including a pillbox hat, argued with a male orderly.

Eddie walked up to them and said, "Is this Donna Roberts?"

"Who's asking?" the man said.

"I live in the other wing. Her son worked for me and asked that I keep an eye on her."

"Have you come to take me to the lobby?" Ms. Roberts asked Eddie.

"Didn't know she had a son. He never visits," the orderly said.

"Johnny is coming to take me out today," Ms. Roberts said.

The orderly patted the little woman on her shoulder. "He'll be here soon." The orderly stepped close to Eddie and whispered in his ear, "Did you know her husband, Johnny?"

"No," Eddie said. "Never met him."

"Probably because he's been dead for years."

"Will Johnny find me up here? I should go to the lobby to wait for him."

"You just wait right here with this nice man, and I'll be back with a wheelchair. Okay?"

Ms. Roberts nodded.

"Do you mind?" the orderly asked Eddie. "I'll be right back."

Eddie didn't mind. It would give him a chance to ask his questions in private. "I'm just here to help," he lied.

Eddie sat on the couch beside Ms. Roberts. "Are you getting your medications?"

She turned to look at him with tears in her eyes. "They never let me see Johnny. He's going to give them hell."

"I need to know if you're getting your drugs and if you're taking any opioids."

She wrinkled her nose as though she had detected a foul smell. "I don't like the night nurses. They're mean, but I get to sleep quickly after they give me my night pills."

Eddie had more questions, but the orderly—his name tag said Joey—returned with a wheelchair. "I'm going to take you down now," he said to Ms. Roberts as he helped her into the chair.

He took Eddie by the arm and led him into the hallway. "I'll give her a quick ride through the garden, and she'll forget all about Johnny. This has become a daily problem. She belongs in the Memory Care Unit, but we never see that son of hers. Tell him to come see me."

"I will," Eddie said.

Disappointed that he'd have to make a return trip to ask Donna questions she probably couldn't answer, he moved to the fourth floor and located Lucy Griffin in a room that overlooked the parking lot. He knocked on her closed door. Someone shouted, "Come in," so he eased the door open. Cheery yellow walls welcomed him into a carbon copy of his temporary apartment.

A woman young enough to be his daughter leaned against the doorjamb to the bedroom, anger painted brightly on her makeup-free face. Her dishwater blond hair had been shaved above her ears, but her ponytail stuck through the vent at the back of her baseball hat. She wore an Atlanta Braves T-shirt, gym shorts, and running shoes. Her legs were heavy, her chest thick, her arms well-muscled.

"Who are you?" she asked Eddie, her accent a pronounced South Georgia twang.

"I was asked to look in on your, ah, mother?"

"Aunt. Get your damned facts straight."

"Sorry, no one warned me about the attack dog guarding the door. Can I do my job?" He motioned to the bedroom doorway.

Slightly abashed, she said, "It's about time," and she stepped aside.

In Eddie's experience, three smells were impossible to cleanse from his olfactory lobes: a baby's soiled diapers, a dead body, and a neglected elderly shut in. On the bed lay a woman, tall and rawboned, in a flannel nightgown. She hadn't been bathed or dressed. When she saw Eddie, she said, "Don't you touch me!"

"Why is your aunt in the assisted living wing? She looks strong. Does she have a disability?" Eddie asked the younger woman.

"Hell no. She's strong as an ox and ornery as a mule. I need help with her because she won't take care of herself."

"Why hasn't anyone helped her today?"

"You tell me. They expect me to do it, but I ain't getting paid to be no nurse."

"Is she under the bed?" the elderly woman asked.

"No, Lucy, she's gone." Turning to Eddie, the younger woman said, "She hates that Black nurse, Roundtree."

"Who's that?" Ms. Griffin asked, pointing to Eddie.

"The man who's going to fix it."

"Baloney!"

Eddie thought "ornery" might be an understatement. "I'm Eddie," he said to the niece.

"Janice. I pay an arm and a leg for this place, and they still won't do their jobs. I file complaints and nothing changes."

Eddie moved to Ms. Griffin's bedside table where a cluster of medication vials sat beside an empty plastic pill organizer able to hold four dosing times for a seven-day week.

"Why are these drug vials in your aunt's room?" Eddie asked. "Don't the nurses fill the pill organizer at their station?" Eddie had prepared for his stay at the facility by reading the regulations for patients able to self-administer medications.

"Lucy won't take them unless I tell her to, so Roundtree brings the vials and lets me load the organizer. The bitch will be back for the pill bottles."

Janice's coarse language surprised Eddie. He read the labels on the vials. A certain Doctor Arjun Banerjee had prescribed the drugs. "Who's this Dr. Banerjee? Is he in the Medical Clinic downstairs?"

"What? No. Banerjee is the dot head from Savannah who writes all the prescriptions the nurses ask for. Shouldn't you know that?"

"Yes, they should have told me."

"I don't know why she's getting all these pills. She's healthy, so you should check it out."

He didn't need to check it out—he knew by sight that there were no opioids among Lucy's medications—but to maintain the ruse, Eddie noted all the prescriptions and doses in his little Joe Friday notebook. "Let me check it out."

"You do that."

Eddie walked back to the nurses' station and tracked down nurse Roundtree, a flustered and frazzled woman in her thirties with high cheekbones and flat black eyes that might have been borrowed from a ragdoll.

"What's the deal with Lucy Griffin?" he asked her.

"Deal? Who are you?"

"I'm her attorney." Eddie handed her a card naming him an associate of the firm Wilke, Miles & Stovall.

"Oh, it's come to that?" Roundtree glanced at the card and tossed it on her desk.

"Just acting as a friend of the family for now."

"Wouldn't have guessed those Crackers had friends. The deal is she won't let me touch her. Calls me 'nigger.' So does the niece. I asked the niece to help, but she refuses. We offered her a Memory Care room, but the niece won't pay the upcharge. I'm trying my best to get the old bitty kicked out," Roundtree said, her feet spread, hands on her hips, and a scowl on her face. "Anything else you want to know?"

"Just one more thing: she's confused about who is her personal physician now. Is it Dr. Banerjee?"

"I've explained this to her thick-headed niece a hundred times. Most of the residents have come from far away, so they don't typically see their former doctors. If she wants to go to Waycross—that's where she's from—and see some doctor there, that's her privilege. But she doesn't, so Dr. Banerjee manages her medications. He performs the service for most residents."

"Couldn't she see the doctors in the clinic?"

"She's prejudiced against Indians, too?"

Eddie shrugged.

"No, this ain't no nursing home. The volunteer doctors in the clinic only see residents for daily sick call issues: colds, headaches, sore joints, that sort of thing. Urgent care."

"Okay, I'll explain it to the niece."

"Appreciate it."

Eddie didn't return to Lucy Griffin's room. He had to find one more person, so he took the back staircase down to the third floor. He cracked the door and surveyed a chaotic scene that reminded him of a busy hospital—nurses and orderlies in black scrubs and volunteers wearing vests like Walmart greeters pushed wheelchairs and assisted residents in and out of rooms and up and down the corridor. He asked the nurse at the station for Gerald Matthews.

"You family?" A plump, brown-haired woman in her forties didn't look up from her paperwork. Her name tag read "Sandy."

"Yes, a cousin, Sandy. Our mothers were sisters."

"Close but no cigar. He's designated as memory care now, so it's immediate family only."

She continued to ignore him. From behind the station, a male orderly pushed a resident in a wheelchair. Eddie glanced around the side of the station and noted the elevator marked "Staff Service Only." Beyond the nurses' station, on the left side of the corridor, he saw a nameplate on a closed door that read: "Dr. Michael Cevert." He wondered why Cevert would have a room in the assisted living wing.

Switching his attention back to Sandy, he said, "So, Gerald has moved downstairs?"

She looked up. "Not yet. We're waiting for a room to come available down there."

"But he's gotten worse?"

"What's your name?"

"Eddie. I live in the other wing and just wanted to check on him."

"Well, Eddie"—hands on hips—"I'm not qualified to distinguish normal senility from dementia, so Dr. Cevert helps us with that. But in my estimation, half of the people in assisted living belong in memory care. Of course, the other half belong in a nursing home, but rich folks won't go to a nursing home, so they pretend they live in Downton Abbey and we're their servants."

"Okay, I'll speak to Dr. Cevert about seeing Gerald."

"You do that."

Sandy gave him half a smile and returned her attention to her paperwork, so he went back to the elevator bank. Instead of riding down to the lobby, he went back to the fourth floor. As he walked past the nurses' station, he told Roundtree he was going to have a word with Lucy Griffin's niece.

"Appreciate it," she said again.

He didn't stop at Ms. Griffin's room. He trotted down the back staircase to the third floor and took his time looking for Gerald Matthews. He found one room with a paper sign written in red magic marker on its door—Memory Care—but Eddie didn't step inside.

Near the nurses' station, Eddie tried Dr. Cevert's door and found it locked. He rapped lightly and the door burst open.

Sandy, her arms full of files and documents, barged into him and things fell to the floor. "What the hell are you doing?"

Startled, Eddie stooped to pick up files and a pad of blank prescription scripts. He handed the mess to Sandy. "Sorry, thought I'd look in on my friend Dr. Cevert."

"The doctor's not in. Get off my floor!"

Eddie held his hands up in surrender. "No problem. I'll see Dr. Cevert at dinner and let him know his office is well-protected."

Eddie held the elevator open as he watched Sandy return Cevert's office key to a lockbox on the backside of the nurses' station. He rode the elevator to the ground floor. A steady, light rain now dripped from a low sky, trapping the residents indoors. The hallway to his room smelled of chlorine escaping from the indoor pool, where water exercise classes were being conducted. Through the gym windows on the other side of the hallway, he saw a well-attended Pilates class.

In his room, Eddie ate a room service breakfast of Raisin Bran and two percent milk garnished with a sliced banana. On his laptop, he Googled the medications that had been prescribed for Lucy Griffin. Dr. Banerjee had not prescribed any opioids for Lucy, but he had prescribed a nightly pill that won him a place on Eddie's list of suspects.

✳ ✳ ✳

As he wound his way through the packed dining room tables, Madeleine noticed his approach and patted the empty chair beside her seat. Tonight, she wore the same dress style as last night—a floor-length shift—except in red with silver trim and squiggly designs. Already in their seats, all his tablemates sipped wine or cocktails, except for Donald who clutched a tall glass of tomato juice.

"Thanks for saving me a seat," Eddie said to Madeleine. To the table, he said, "Hope I'm not late."

"We're just getting started," Bobby said.

A waitress appeared and Eddie asked, "What's for dinner?"

"Wok stir-fried vegetables, poached Chilean Sea Bass, or Chicken and Rice casserole."

Eddie frowned. He pointed through the window. "There's an ocean full of succulent shellfish just one hundred yards away, you know."

"Some people are allergic," the waitress said in defense of the menu.

"The Sea Bass is good for you," Susan said.

"I imagine it is," Eddie said. He ordered the casserole and a beer and asked the waitress to bring Tabasco sauce.

"Of course, sir," the waitress said and then retreated toward the kitchen.

"I'll take you to the Salt Island restaurant for lunch one day and you can gorge on shrimp and oysters," Madeleine said.

"I'd like that. Do you ever eat at the grill upstairs?"

"They don't have tables for six," Madeleine said.

Donald failed to stifle a coughing fit, covered his mouth with his handkerchief, and excused himself. Eddie watched him leave the dining area and head to the restrooms. "Is he okay?" Eddie asked no one in particular.

"Allergies, I suspect," Cevert said.

The waitress brought Eddie's beer and Tabasco.

Eddie marveled at how the lively conversations at the other tables produced a clamorous noise level that shielded individual conversations from eavesdropping. The restaurant effect, he called it, and the phenomenon gave him the freedom to question his companions.

"Do you still practice, Michael?" Eddie asked. "Here at Palm Haven."

"I see a handful of patients who are far from their previous homes and prefer me to finding a local physician."

"He's picky," Bobby said. "He sees Donald and Madeleine but refuses to see me."

"There's nothing wrong with you, Bobby."

"Except his personality," Susan said.

Eddie wondered if that meant Donald and Madeleine had medical issues. "Was Jacob Hoffman one of the privileged few?"

"Yes, he was a patient," Cevert said.

Eddie suppressed a reaction. He deduced that Hoffman had been pronounced dead in Cevert's third-floor office and that's why he came down to the loading dock in the staff service elevator. "How about Gerald Matthews?"

"No, no. I just consulted on his case. Sandy said you're a cousin of his?"

Sandy had already blabbed to Cevert. *Have to watch out for Sandy,* Eddie thought. "We were Army buddies, but I didn't think Army buddy was going to get me in the door."

"You shouldn't lie to nurses," Susan said.

"The nurses act like prison guards. You have to lie to get anywhere with them," Bobby said.

"It's immediate family only for memory care patients, I'm afraid," Cevert said. "It's a Palm Haven rule, not mine."

"But you made the diagnosis, so you could make an exception for me, couldn't you?"

"No, I can't, Eddie." Agitated, Cevert repeatedly pushed his glasses up his nose. "Like I told you. I merely confirmed his diagnosis and recommended to the administration here that he be moved to the Memory Care unit. Your Army buddy is so far gone he's forgotten how to tie his shoelaces."

"Were you in Vietnam together?" Bobby asked. "Is that where you got the scar?"

Bobby referred to the shiny, puckered tissue, white against Eddie's tanned skin, between his left eyebrow and his hairline. It resembled the letter C that had toppled over, the opening facing his eye.

"No, the scar is the result of a car accident. Gerry and I were stationed together here in Savannah," Eddie said. "I never got to 'Nam."

"I'm glad you didn't kill any innocent people over there," Susan said.

Donald returned to the table, bleary-eyed and still clearing his throat repeatedly. The waitress delivered their food. Eddie peppered his casserole with Tabasco sauce and still found the dish uninteresting.

"Do you know this Dr. Banerjee?" Eddie asked Cevert. "I have some prescriptions to be filled."

"I know him but not well. I'll fill your prescriptions if you like."

"That'd be very kind," Eddie said.

"Sure, take on the new guy when you won't do anything for me," Bobby said.

"Stop grousing, Bobby," Madeleine said. "What's the topic tonight?"

"Use your phones to Google: 'What percentage of Earth's atmosphere is greenhouse gasses.'" Bobby wore a shit-eating grin. "Read the NASA article."

Donald stared at his phone as though expecting it to do something on its own. Cevert grunted. Susan smirked. Eddie and Madeleine began typing.

"Come on, all of you. Just do it."

Reluctantly, the others complied, and soon, they had surprise in their eyes.

"I was under the impression that greenhouse gases were about to obliterate the atmosphere, but that's not what this says," Madeleine remarked.

"Let me break it down for you in a way that's easy to visualize," Bobby said. "Imagine the earth's atmosphere is a football field, one hundred yards long. The first seventy-eight yards would be nitrogen and the next twenty-one yards would be oxygen, which gets us to the one-yard line. The next two feet are an inert gas called argon. The last eleven inches—eleven inches, for God's sake—are the four greenhouse gases that have liberals' panties in a wad. Methane, nitrous oxide, ozone, and carbon dioxide *combined* are just eleven inches on that football field."

"There's got to be a scientific explanation," Madeleine said.

Bobby shrugged. "It's a government hoax."

"C'mon, Bobby, we just don't understand how the atmosphere works," Madeleine said. "Maybe eleven inches is all it takes to cause global warming."

"You don't have to be a scientist to understand what's going on here," Bobby insisted. "The fossil fuel industry is largely Republican while the renewable energy freaks are Democrats. It's about power, no pun intended."

Susan said, "You can't deny climate change, Bobby. There's empirical evidence of ice shrinkage at both poles and rising ocean levels. Weather patterns have changed dramatically all over the globe."

"I'm not denying climate change. I'm saying it's a natural phenomenon and not manmade."

Cevert took a moment to remove his glasses and polish the lenses with his napkin. "I just read a study by researchers at an Ivy League university. They've discovered that trees scrub carbon dioxide from the air, so they recommend that we start planting trees to delay climate change."

They all laughed.

"Did they discover that it would be faster to *stop* cutting trees down?" Donald asked.

Everyone laughed again.

When the laughter subsided, Eddie said, "I can't argue for or against climate change but I know one fact that makes me wonder if we're addressing the problem the right way. Methane has one hundred times the warming power of carbon dioxide. And the good news is that unlike carbon dioxide, methane dissipates in the atmosphere. Once it's gone, it's gone forever."

"Okay, I'll stop farting!" Bobby said.

Susan giggled.

"Shut up, Bobby. Where does it come from?" Madeleine asked.

"Agriculture, mostly," Michael said. "Cows."

"True," Eddie continued, "but one-third of today's warming is caused by leaks in the oil fields of the Permian Basin."

Cevert pursed his lips and slowly nodded in thought. Susan appeared startled.

"Where is the Permian Basin?" Madeleine asked. "The Middle East?"

"Texas and New Mexico, the largest oil field in America. The leaks are the result of sloppy oil drilling practices and lax regulation," Cevert said.

"So, there are ways to address the problem other than making us drive electric cars," Madeleine said.

"The argument has been co-opted by people with something to gain," Donald said, then he erupted into another coughing fit.

Two dinners at Madeleine's table had been sufficient for Eddie to map the personalities and roles of his new friends. Imagining them in middle school, Bobby would have been the playground bully, Susan the dreamy waif who wanted to escape the cruel world, Donald the pragmatic opportunist, Michael the sissified teacher's pet, and Madeleine the girl too pretty to be approachable. Decades later, they were the same people they had been as children.

Eddie waited for Donald to catch his breath. "Right now, about eighty percent of the electricity that charges electric car batteries is generated by fossil fuel plants so prioritizing cars is literally putting the cart ahead of the horse. The first step to save the planet should be converting power plants to nuclear fusion. Logically the second step should be an improved power grid so it could handle everyone driving an electric car. We're not ready for the future and approaching it backwards."

"Like I said, this war on gas-powered cars is a liberal scam," Bobby said.

"This is a fascinating discussion," Michael said, "but it's curtain time."

"*Cat on a Hot Tin Roof*," Susan said. "Residents are playing all the parts."

"I'm going to bed," Donald said.

"I saw the play on Broadway," Madeleine said.

"I've seen it, too," Eddie said. "Touring company, of course." He imagined the absurdity of one old fart playing Brick and an even older fart playing Big Daddy.

After the others left for the ballroom, Madeleine said, "Have you been to the third floor?"

Although he already knew from studying the facility map, Eddie said, "No, what's up there?"

"All the fun places." Madeleine urged Eddie to follow her to the escalator.

The third floor reminded Eddie of the food court at a mall. The barber shop and the beauty parlor were closed at this hour, but the ice cream parlor, the grill, and the bar were populated with noisy residents enjoying their evening. Madeleine led him into the dimly lit bar and to a small, cocktail table along a wall. Eddie flipped the switch on an electric candle in a glass vase and the meager glow cast alluring shadows on Madeleine's round face. Except for crow's feet at the corners of her eyes, her face was wrinkle-free, the skin supple and clear.

Madeleine ordered a Cosmo and Eddie a beer. When the waitress brought their drinks, they clinked glasses.

"How does Michael merit an office inside the facility?" Eddie asked.

"It's a trade. He's the night emergency doctor on duty. Same as cops getting a free apartment for serving as on-call security at apartment complexes."

"Makes sense. Takes too long for someone to get here from Savannah."

Madeleine took a sip of her Cosmo. "What's the dry cleaning business like?"

"Like any other business. I took care of the books, paid the bills, sourced the supplies, handled legal matters and other administrivia. From that perspective, all businesses are the same. My older brother, Danny, ran the stores. We had four of them."

She had a faraway look in her eyes for a moment. "Land development is such a dirty business. It starts with political payoffs and ends with shoddy construction. Developers can only make a profit if they cut corners. 'Contractor grade' material is a euphemism for low quality. Bruce was a bully and good at making money."

"A shame you had to endure being rich." He said it with a playful smile to imply sarcasm.

"Ah did suffer the guilt of the affluent," she said with an exaggerated Southern drawl. "I had the best life money could buy, just not a fairy-tale romance."

He wondered if Jacob Hoffman had been a fairy-tale romance. "Were you still married when he passed?"

"Oh, yes, I hung in there for thirty-five years." She gave him a wistful smile. "He liked me in the same way he'd like a sports car or a set of golf clubs. I was an excellent possession, but there was no emotional connection. I thought about divorce many times and then he dropped dead, and I no longer had to decide whether to divorce him."

"You really are over the mourning period. Any kids?"

"No." At the dinner table Madeleine was the cheerleader and shepherd of lost souls, but under her veneer of cheerfulness, he sensed a streak of regret.

"Me neither. We tried but it didn't happen for us."

"Did you get help? There are many ways to make it happen."

He leaned back and wiped condensation from his beer mug. "No, we accepted our situation. Never even got tested because we didn't want either of us to be to blame."

"You were kind and considerate toward each other. Sounds like a fairy-tale romance."

He considered the statement as he ordered another round of drinks. "We had plenty of emotional engagement. Sam was feisty, free-spirited, her own woman. Street-smart and ready to fight at the drop of a hat." Eddie remembered Sam saying that their disagreements were the Velcro that bound them together. Teflon marriages, she said, always ended in boredom. "We celebrated our fiftieth wedding anniversary several years early because she wasn't going to make it to fifty."

"She died of breast cancer, you said. You took care of her till the end?"

"Yeah. It dragged on for years. Chemo and radiation, a lumpectomy, mastectomy, reconstructive surgery. But a couple of years later, it appeared in her other breast and that meant another mastectomy. A year after that, we learned the cancer had metastasized. She never stopped fighting, no matter how many times her body disappointed her. Suffered in agony until her last breath."

She leaned across the table and covered his hand with hers. "You're a brave man, Eddie."

"This is a new beginning for me."

"You chose a good place for that," she said.

"I'm a little surprised by how old everyone is." Eddie estimated that twenty percent of the residents were under retirement age.

"It's just like South Florida, wealthy retirees gobble up most of the condos. But we're not too old to enjoy ourselves." She gave him a look he could have interpreted as flirtatious.

When they emerged from the bar, Eddie reflexively turned toward the escalators and elevator banks, but Madeleine turned in the opposite direction.

"I thought you were going to your apartment," Eddie said.

"I am." She turned into an alcove between the bar and the restaurant on the assisted living side of the building and Eddie followed her to a single elevator door.

Madeleine fished a key card from her Fendi bag and touched it to a wall-mounted reader to call the elevator. The most expensive penthouse suites, Eddie remembered from the facility map, were on the eighth floor in the assisted living wing and accessed by a private elevator. When the doors opened on an empty car, Madeleine reached for his hand and squeezed it. "See you tomorrow, Cowboy."

Before turning out the lights, Eddie briefed Sam. Graciously he called Donna Roberts and Lucy Griffin "unreliable sources of information." Equally as graciously, he described his dinner table friends as "interesting." However, he noted that two doctors had piqued his interest.

Sam said, "You've always had a 'thing' for doctors, Eddie. Doctors didn't kill me; the cancer did."

He wasn't sure about that. The curly-haired, exuberant oncologist who ushered Sam from blissful ignorance about her disease to an unspeakable death hadn't lost enough patients in his brief career to form a realistic prognosis. Sam's quality of life deteriorated as the doctor prescribed one pointless therapy after another. She was a dead woman the first day she walked into that doctor's office.

"If there are illegal opioids at Palm Haven, a doctor is involved somewhere along the line."

"I think you're enjoying another vacation, like the one you were on in the Army."

"Ah, yes, the Army vacation. Well, that lasts a bit longer, then the tables turn."

He poured himself a shot of Bourbon, his nightly sleeping pill, and resumed his story.

Chapter Four

... *1971*

"It's like breathing under water," the soldier standing next to me said.

We had landed before dawn at Don Muong airport on the outskirts of Bangkok and yet the humidity hovered around ninety percent, equal to the temperature. To our left, the terminal, crowded with small brown people, consisted of a ceiling and pillars, open to the crushing weight of the thick air. We watched a train rumble past the terminal, spewing red sparks into the night from its coal-fired engine.

An NCO approached our group with a smiling little man he introduced as our bus driver. "Follow him, stow your duffel bags, and climb on board."

We did as the sergeant asked, all of us bone-tired from the twenty-four-hour trip from Travis Air Force base in California, with stops in Hawaii and the Philippines. Most of the troops fell asleep on the bus, but I watched in awe as the countryside unfolded at sunrise. I had naively expected grass huts and stray livestock, but Bangkok was replete with skyscrapers, broad avenues, neon signs, and Japanese cars. The bus crossed the Chao Phrya River, so muddy and polluted it could make you stop eating fish, where sampans and floating market stalls had already begun a day of prosperous commerce.

After battling city traffic for half an hour, the bus turned north on a two-lane highway into the heart of the country. Dense jungle threatened to engulf the roadway and oxen-drawn carts slowed our progress. Deuce-and-a-half military trucks bullied their way past miniature pickup trucks and cars. We drove through villages and returned waves to farmers and shopkeepers. No one shot at us and that brought a smile to my lips.

Most of the troops were engineers who disembarked at a camp forty-four kilometers north of Bangkok. They would build roads and string power lines and telephone lines across Thailand in exchange for our use of the Thai air bases as launching pads for air strikes.

One hundred and sixty kilometers northeast of Bangkok, the bus stopped at the Korat Royal Thai Air Force Base to let me off. I had orders for the Army's 91st Field Depot, which shared the base with the American Air Force. The bus carried the unluckiest soldiers to bases on the Laotian border, closer to the action.

My best friend, a Mormon from Utah, sweated in the suffocating heat of the motor pool while I worked in the depot's air-conditioned offices where I managed the supply of trucks, jeeps, tanks, weapons, and so forth for a portfolio of units scattered around Thailand. I pushed the keys on a computer terminal and I had a Thai secretary to handle the typing and filing. I took exceptional pains to service a Special Forces A-team stationed at Nakhon Phanom on the Laotian border. From that base, "Jolly Green Giant" helicopters rescued downed flyers in Vietnam. On behalf of the Green Berets, I skirted Army regulations and tricked the computer system into expediting equipment deliveries and exchanges of new equipment for lost or damaged equipment without the usual red tape.

Because the Air Force guys flew combat missions over North Vietnam, Bob Hope's USO tour made a stop at our base so we could ogle Jill St. John and Miss World-USA. Canned beer at the NCO club cost $.10 and a night with a village girl cost $5.00. Each morning I walked to the "wire," the fencing around the base's perimeter, and bought fresh pineapples, bananas, and mangos for breakfast. This perfect environment had but one drawback: Before dawn on every good weather day, dozens of F-4

Phantom fighters lit their afterburners and took off with a load of bombs. Since we weren't bombing the North, I assumed the planes were bombing the Ho Chi Minh trail. Whatever. No one could sleep through that racket.

Ever since my grandmother bought me a transistor radio for my tenth birthday, I had fallen asleep with rock music blaring in my ears. I continued the practice by moving my cot beside our shared stereo system, plugging in a set of headphones, and queueing up a seven -hour tape of anti-establishment music—Chicago, The Doors, Buffalo Springfield, and Jefferson Airplane—and some mornings I slept through the racket.

On my first opportunity, I hopped a ride on the C-130 air taxi to the Don Muong airport/airbase in Bangkok. I toured the vibrant city and fell in love with the spicy cuisine. That night I ventured into the red-light district where G.I.s on R&R from Vietnam drank too much, fought too much, and too often, got arrested by the Thai police. I chose the California Bar, a less raucous place with a band covering American rock songs and took a seat at a table by myself. The waitresses were available for rent and as I declined their offers, they rotated, hoping I would find one of them acceptable.

I drank the local Singha beer and eavesdropped on the frightening stories the Viet vets told one another. I pitied the soldiers who tried to forget what they had seen, forget what they had done, forget what they would do again when they returned to the battlefield. Many of these kids would die in the jungle, a week of alcohol-fueled debauchery in Bangkok their last fond memory.

An hour later, an older woman, probably mid-thirties, ushered a young waitress dressed in pink to my table. "This is number one girl," she said. "Make you happy before you go back Vietnam."

"No, thank you. I'm stationed at Korat. Just down for the weekend."

Her eyes grew wide. She was voluptuous in a way uncommon for Thai women and dressed conservatively, not like the prostitutes. She dismissed the waitress and said, "You come all the time?"

I tried to imitate the great lovers in the movies. "I will if I can see you."

She tittered. "No can do. I am Mama-son for the girls." She swept her hand to encompass the room and all the pretty young waitresses.

"What time do you get off?" Still imitating the movies.

A thoughtful look crossed her face. "You come tomorrow, during day. We have lunch, okay?"

"Okay."

The next day, I met her at the bar around noon. She called herself Sunee and managed the California Bar for the Chinese owner, a rotund gentleman who unfortunately joined us for lunch. They had a proposition for me: buy cheap booze and cigarettes on the Air Force base and bring it to Bangkok to sell to the bar at a profit for me. They would resell it to the R&R G.I.s at a profit for themselves. Together we'd all get rich off the war. I told them I'd think about it.

Monthly, each soldier was issued a ration card to buy an authorized amount of cigarettes and booze. I found that most G.I.s did not use their ration cards fully and were willing to lend me their cards. I also found that my friend could furnish a jeep from the motor pool for a small fee. I could certainly smuggle booze and cigarettes into Bangkok if I wanted to.

So I did. I didn't do it for the money. I wanted an excuse to see Sunee. I piled cartons of cigarettes and cases of booze into a jeep and drove to Bangkok for a rendezvous with Sunee and her Chinese boss. They were delighted and asked that I make a trip down to their bar each month.

Sunee stopped by my table several times that night, ensuring I was being served properly. The waitresses did not solicit my business. Late that night, Sunee said, "You stay Chao Phrya?"

The Army had taken over Chao Phrya hotel to house officers in Bangkok on official business. "I'm not authorized."

She gave me a skeptical look, then shrugged. "Okay, you stay my house."

That night, I got to know Sunee very well. She wasn't shaped like a Thai because she wasn't a Thai by birth. Originally, her Muslim family had been herded out of India and forced to resettle in Pakistan, but as a young woman, Sunee had emigrated to Thailand and adopted Buddhism. Perhaps our shared quest for religious meaning helped forge an empathetic bond.

She had a nice little cottage surrounded by a garden with a religious shrine at which she burned incense. Her bed was hard as a rock. The commode was a porcelain hole in the ground over which you squatted to do your business. The shower was a short hose connected to a water spigot in the sink. Or, Thai-style, you could dip water from a barrel and pour it over your head. The lack of amenities did not deter me. I liked staying at Sunee's house.

My monthly activities became routine: gather up unused ration cards; rent a jeep at the motor pool; buy up a load of cigarettes and booze; drive to Bangkok; sell the contraband to the California Bar; drink for free; and stay at Sunee's house.

My father had served aboard submarines in World War II, dodging Japanese depth charges. For his generation, evading combat duty was shameful, but my generation felt no shame in evading Viet Cong bullets. The Greatest Generation, my ass. I loathed their fatalism. I was smart enough to stay out of harm's way.

My Thailand vacation lasted about six months.

✳ ✳ ✳

It didn't alarm me when Major Ralph Dabrowski summoned me to his office at the Depot; we had an easy working relationship. Thickset, with thinning blond hair, Dabrowski sat behind a government-issue metal desk and beneath a stylized photo of the Chicago skyline. The small, interior room seemed inappropriate for the man who controlled the movement of supplies around the country of Thailand until you realized it was the coolest room in the building. Dabrowski did not like to sweat. He returned my salute and told me to stand at ease.

I did a sort of parade rest thing and he said, "No, really, at rest."

I tried. The other guy in the room made me nervous—a fit man in starched jungle fatigues and jungle boots, with an odd rank insignia on his collar—a single white bar with four black stripes—and no name tag above his right breast. He relaxed in a side chair, one leg crossed over the other. He appeared to be tall, with closely cropped black hair and white sidewalls. He wore a sidearm, an officer's Colt .45 pistol. The weapon wasn't standard issue; it had pearl hand grips.

Guy must think he's General Patton.

"We were happy when you showed up here, Kovacs. Like a pro football team drafting an All-American quarterback in the first round. A real 76Papa is a rare thing." Dabrowski paused.

All the 76Papas are in Vietnam, I thought.

"Since you've been here, you've become my best portfolio manager. The way you've taken care of the engineers and the Green Berets has been a credit to this organization."

He paused again and I got the feeling he had laid a trap for me. I nodded my thanks for the compliment.

"Now CID has found evidence of serious anomalies in the supply chain for Special Forces units." Another pause.

Thoughts raced through my brain like slides on an overhead projector: *They know I've been cheating for the Green Berets; CID—Criminal Investigation Division—is the Army's version of the FBI; Stone Face over there is CID.*

I chanced a glance at the silent man and saw a twinkle in his eye. The cop had gotten his man.

"Sorry to hear that, sir." My voice sounded like sandpaper on dry wood.

"Don't worry, we'll get to the bottom of this with your help."

"With my help?" They wanted me to roll over on my Green Beret buddies.

Waving a hand at Stone Face, Dabrowski said, "This is Chief Warrant Officer Tucker Carlyle of the CID. You'll be his partner."

"Partner?"

"You're CID now," Carlyle said in a Southern drawl. From a breast pocket, he pulled a laminated ID card with all sorts of stars and watermarks on it. He tossed it to me, like a Frisbee, and I caught it. "Carry that at all times, flash it if you need permission to go somewhere or do something but otherwise tell no one that you're CID. Not your hootch mates, not your girlfriend, not your mama."

"What am I supposed to do?"

"Step one," Carlyle said, "is pull the computer records for the Special Forces A-teams and figure out how they're stockpiling more equipment than they're authorized."

Hell, I knew how I had cooked the books for the Green Berets. I did it because those guys were risking their lives and it wasn't fair to make them do it with their hands tied by Army regulations. It felt like surrender when I said, "It won't take long. I have all the records at my fingertips."

"Not the Green Berets here in Thailand," Dabrowski said. "The A- and B-teams in Vietnam."

"Oh. I don't handle those guys. I think the depot at Long Binh supplies them. You'd have to ask those guys what's going on."

"I'm not going to ask the crooks to spill their secrets, Kovacs," Carlyle said. "You're going to figure it out for me."

"Me? How?"

"The Green Beret units we're interested in train the Montagnards in the Central Highlands. After you analyze their computer records at Long Binh, we'll go up there, find the equipment, work back to how it got there, who gave it to them. Your supply training and knowledge of Special Forces units make you a great partner. Hell, you know their Table of Organization & Equipment by heart."

No! No! Not that place, that war. "But my tour here is half over."

Dabrowski chuckled. "Only way you can finish your tour here is in the stockade, Kovacs. CID confiscated twenty cases of Army-ration liquor and fifty cartons of Army-ration cigarettes at the California Bar in Bangkok last night. We know how it got there. You've danced to the music, now it's time to pay the piper."

"Help me solve this case," Carlyle said, "and I'll ship you straight stateside from Vietnam. Otherwise, it's back here to the stockade."

So, God would have the last laugh after all. Despite all the good fortune I had experienced, I'd still end up in Vietnam. "Yes, sir," I croaked.

Carlyle handed me a set of orders transferring me to a Military Police Company at Long Binh Vietnam. "Pack up your shit and be ready to move out tomorrow."

✳ ✳ ✳

Carlyle and I hopped a C-130 transport along with a motley collection of soldiers and airmen bound for Don Muang Airport in Bangkok. The passengers sat in webbed seats along either side of the fuselage, allowing cargo to be anchored down the center of the plane.

At Don Muang we found our gate for the commercial charter flight to Saigon. G.I.s returning to Vietnam after R&R in Bangkok milled about in random groups, most of them looking hungover. He dug a small square jewelry box out of his kit and handed it to me.

"What's this?" I started to open the box and he closed a hand over mine to stop me.

Standing close, he whispered, "Go into the latrine and put them on."

When I hesitated, he gave me a little shove. I found an empty stall and closed the door behind me. The box contained insignia like Carlyle's except with just one black stripe. I assumed they were Warrant Officer insignia. It took a moment to accept the idea that Carlyle wanted me to impersonate an officer, but CID had the power to do most anything it wanted, so I removed the Specialist Fifth Class insignia from my collars and replaced them with the fake insignia. I pinned a third bar to my baseball cap. I flushed the toilet, playing the undercover spy role as I had learned from reading John Le Carré novels.

"What's the deal?" I asked Carlyle.

"An enlisted man wouldn't be respected during this investigation. It's a temporary battlefield promotion to Warrant Officer First Class, but don't mention it to anyone." He gave me a conspiratorial smile. "They're an old set of mine." He fingered the insignia on his collar. "I'm a Chief Warrant Officer Fourth Class."

"What do I call you? What do I call myself?"

His eyebrows danced up his forehead. "Warrant Officers are referred to as Mister and a last name. Mister Carlyle and Mister Kovacs. In casual conversation people will call us Chief and enlisted men will call us Sir."

We boarded a dark red and bright yellow Boeing 727, operated by Braniff Airlines. The G.I.s heading back to war directed catcalls and whistles at the "round eye" American stewardesses. After takeoff, the raucous noise level and shouted demands for service made conversation impossible. I sat stiff and silent as a Mummy as the plane bore me irrevocably toward the fate Danny and I had sought so desperately to avoid. Vietnam. Death. Penance.

Unlike the gently sloping landing patterns of commercial airliners at U.S. airports, this 727 reached Ton Son Nhut airport at eight thousand feet and then spiraled to the ground like a vulture circling a rotting carcass.

"Minimizing the possibility of ground fire hitting us," Carlyle said. "The pilots on these charter flights are all ex-military, so they know how to do it."

After disembarking, MPs herded the other passengers to an area on the tarmac one hundred yards from the passenger terminal and ordered them to stay put until they had an armed escort.

"They don't want these drunk soldiers cavorting through a commercial passenger terminal. They'll make them wait for their units to pick them up. You see that graveyard beside the farthest runway?"

He pointed and I nodded.

"The 101st Airborne kicked Charlie's ass in that graveyard a couple of weeks ago."

Carlyle led me around the terminal and to the parking lot.

"I never go inside the terminal," he said. "During Tet, the VC put a rocket through the roof. They have it zeroed-in and I don't want to be there when they fire the next one."

I tossed my duffle bag into the backseat of his personal jeep and he drove northeast to the Long Binh Army base. On the twenty-one-mile trip we passed Colonial-era buildings, ornate pagodas, Buddhist temples, and open-air food stalls. The roads were clogged with scooters and motorcycles, Army trucks, gaudily decorated buses, and strolling women in So Dai—long, brightly colored, satiny dresses—who seemed to have already forgotten that there was a war in this country. The colors, the noise and the smell of open-fire cooking overwhelmed my senses. It wasn't what I expected a war to look like.

Carlyle made a right turn before reaching the main gate and entered the base through gate nine. An MP saluted us and asked for ID. I handed him the ID Carlyle had given me. That elicited a respectful nod.

Our route onto the base brought us through an area that resembled a stateside industrial park—long, metal buildings in neat rows interrupted by fenced storage areas holding fuel tanks and vehicles—and into a residential area of prefabricated aluminum hootches buttressed with sandbags stacked four feet tall. I estimated that each hootch could house a dozen men. The jeep stopped in front of what looked like a cheap motel. The wooden sign at the roadside read "Transit BOQ"—Bachelor Officer's Quarters.

"There's a room in your name—Chief Kovacs. Dump your bag and we'll get some chow."

I humped my duffel bag into the building. The Charge of Quarters, a kind of concierge for the billet, led me to a cell-like two-man room with a concrete floor and Army cots similar to the ones I had slept on in Thailand.

The sergeant informed me that the shared showers and latrine were down the hall. I had expected something a bit more luxurious for officers.

As the jeep jerked away from the curb, Carlyle gave me new instructions. "I'm just Tucker when we're among other junior officers, Kovacs. Don't call me sir. Just speak conversationally and for God's sake don't salute. Salutes are for senior officers. Got it?"

"Got it."

Carlyle drove down the perimeter road, past the billets of a light infantry brigade, and parked in front of a Quonset hut. Just one hundred yards away, a tall, wooden guard tower plucked from a prison movie hovered over the perimeter wire and commanded a three-hundred-sixty-degree view of the countryside. On either flank, firing bunkers stretched into the distance.

He fingered the insignia on his collar. "There are bigger O-clubs on base, but we won't run into any senior brass among these ground pounders. Just act like you belong."

So, we're hiding.

At the bar, Carlyle ordered a Crown Royal and ginger ale—a Presbyterian—and I asked for a beer. He led me to the farthest table, away from boisterous infantry lieutenants on barstools. He leaned back and rubbed his five o'clock shadow, which was dark and uniform. After a moment he leaned forward and said, "I've read your 201 file, but who are you, Kovacs?"

What do I say to that? A fallen Catholic? A kid fearing his short life might end in this third world country? I settled for, "Just a regular guy."

"Come on. I know you grew up in Wisconsin. Lots of snow?"

"No, we were above the snowbelt, often too cold to snow. Frozen tundra. I tobogganed and ice skated occasionally because that's how we met girls, but I didn't venture outdoors much until summer."

"Family?"

"Blue collar."

"Why didn't you go to college and avoid the Army?"

"No money."

Carlyle flagged down a diminutive Vietnamese waitress. He ordered a second round of drinks and a steak. I ordered a burger and fries.

"You can have a steak," he said. "My treat."

"I'm not really a steak guy. A burger and fries will seem more like home."

The waitress flipped a hand and said, "Steak better." She hurried away.

I tried to deflect the conversation away from my unremarkable past. During my time in the Army, I had learned to distinguish the accents of the soldiers I met. His voice didn't possess the soft, musical tones of Virginia or the rough-edged accent of Appalachia. "I'm good with accents, but I can't quite place yours. Maybe South Carolina."

"You're close—Savannah. But I went to school in South Carolina—The Citadel."

"So, the military is a career for you?"

"Maybe. My father and my younger brother, Beau, run a private detective agency in Savannah, and they want me to come home and work with them. They catch cheating husbands and that's not exciting enough for me." He gave me a rueful smile.

With a smile of her own, the waitress brought our drinks.

Carlyle leaned across the table and kept his voice down. "A little history lesson and then I'll tell you about our mission. The Montagnards are Vietnam's indigenous peoples living in the Central Highlands where the borders of Cambodia, Laos, and South Vietnam converge. They've been hunter-gatherers and farmers on those lands since long before the Vietnamese came from China and stole it."

"Stealing land from indigenous people's happened all over the world and thieves weren't only white European settlers."

"Correct. The Montagnards are oppressed, denied education and medical care. The Montagnards hate the Vietnamese, and the Vietnamese hate the 'Yards.' That's what they're called by Americans—Yards. The Vietnamese call them 'Moi,' which means savages."

"American settlers called the Indians 'savages.'"

He nodded. "The French had promised the Yards their own little country with full autonomy, but the French were driven from Vietnam at the battle of Dien Bien Phu in 1954 and the promises weren't kept. Sound familiar?"

I answered immediately. "We broke our treaties with American Indian tribes."

"Correct." He cleared his throat. "After the French were kicked out of the country, the Yards formed an organization called FULRO to unite the thirty-two distinct Montagnard tribes into a single fighting force to revolt against the South Vietnamese government."

"Native Americans tried that, but it didn't work."

"Hasn't worked for the Yards either. The problem is that the Central Highlands are the infiltration point for North Vietnam's troops and supplies. The Ho Chi Minh Trail runs down the Laotian and Cambodian borders just to the west of the Yards' territory. Before we ever knew there would be a full-scale war in Vietnam, Special Forces units were stationed in the area to organize the Yards to protect their villages and interdict the supply routes."

He glanced around the bar and verified that no one was paying us any attention. "The South Vietnamese have put limits on the kind of weaponry we can give to the Yards—Army surplus from World War II and Korea, no vehicles or tanks or artillery pieces—and the troops and supplies keep pouring in from North Vietnam. It's a conundrum: Arm the Yards and maybe we're helping them overthrow the South Vietnamese government; don't arm the Yards and maybe we're helping the North Vietnamese win the war."

"Why don't the South Vietnamese stop the incursions in the Central Highlands?"

"Now you're asking the right question, Kovacs. We had the 4th Infantry Division in the Central Highlands but we've pulled them out because of Vietnamization. We want the South Vietnamese to fight the North

Vietnamese but they don't want to. Now the South Vietnamese suspect that the Green Beanies are cheating, arming the Yards with more and better weapons, and the South Vietnamese want it stopped before the Yards have the capability to revolt."

"What a mess. What are we supposed to do about it?"

"Our only job is to verify that the cheating is happening and figure out how. It's up to General Abrams to decide what to do about it. MAC-V turned the problem over to CID and I was chosen to investigate. Then I chose you."

I knew the initials MAC-V stood for Military Assistance Command-Vietnam, the auspices under which we conducted an undeclared war in a foreign country's sovereign territory. "Terrific," was all I said.

The waitress returned with our food—steaks for both of us.

"Number One steak. You like."

She was right: the steaks were good.

Back at the BOQ, Carlyle dug into his kit and pulled out a sheet of paper and a map. "I've marked the units we're interested in on the map. Study them tonight so you know what you're looking for tomorrow. I'll pick you up right here at 0700 hours and we'll go to work."

"Yes, sir." I saluted him and he shook his head and snickered.

I spread the map out on the bed and referred to Carlyle's notes as I located the units. I found the major city of Pleiku in the middle of the country, then traced a highway north to Kon Tum City, the provincial capital of Kon Tum province—AKA, the Central Highlands. Following a secondary road northwest, I found Dak To, the location of the Green Beret headquarters unit for the region. Thick red lines denoting major roads became skinny black lines as I traced the roads north to Dak Seang and Dak Pek. Although those remote A-teams were in the serious boonies, the two camps that lay to the west, near the Laotian and Cambodian borders, gave me greater concern. Ben Het lay nine miles from Laos and Vu Dong sat eleven miles from Cambodia. I'd have been safer in the stockade in Thailand than at these border camps.

I wrote Mom a letter and told her I'd be out of touch for a while because I was on a special mission. I'd let her know when things were back to normal. I told her how much I appreciated her as a mother and how much I loved her. In case she never heard from me again. I did not mention Vietnam.

Although the BOQ in Vietnam was curiously quieter than my hootch in Thailand, I missed the stereo and the music. I tossed and turned for hours.

CHAPTER FIVE

... Now

"Hey! Stop!" Roundtree yelled at Eddie as he hurried around the fourth-floor nurses' station.

He stopped. "Good morning, Nurse Roundtree."

"My name is Letitia. I called the number on your business card. It's out of service." Her eyebrows climbed her forehead. A question.

"Sure. We're all retired now, and the firm is officially closed, but I still have a license. I should get new cards printed."

Roundtree leaned against the counter and thought about it. "What are you up to today?"

"Just making sure she's no trouble for you. Maybe I can get the niece to take her for a walk in the gardens. Get her out of your hair."

"If some damned lawsuit lands on my desk, I'll countersue for racial bias."

Eddie held up both hands in the surrender position. "No one wants a lawsuit."

She motioned with one hand for him to go on and turned back to her work.

Eddie ambled past open doors, loud televisions, residents being pushed in wheelchairs, nurses darting in and out of rooms. Several residents were in the lounge at the end of the hallway. Everyone had had their breakfast. He knocked on Lucy's door and heard a muffled, "Come in."

Janice sat on the couch, watching a soap opera. From the bedroom came Lucy's rhythmic blubbering. Eddie sat in a wood-railed side chair. Janice waited for him to say something.

"Does she always sleep this late?"

Janice swept hair off her forehead. "Some days she sleeps until noon, and I have to go to work before I can talk to her."

"How does she feel when she's awake?"

"She gets a lot of headaches and she's sick to her stomach all the time."

"Has trouble remembering things?"

"CRS—can't remember shit," Janice said, and she managed half a dejected smile.

"I checked on her meds. She's taking a powerful sedative called Rohypnol. It's ten times stronger than Valium."

"Does she need that?"

"She's being sedated to keep her from causing trouble."

"Those motherfuckers!" Janice bounced to her feet, ready for a fight.

Eddie waved her back into her seat. "Go to a drugstore and buy an over-the-counter sleep aid. I'll be back later to help you make the change. Got it?"

"Are you a doctor?"

"I'm retired now. I live in the independent wing, room 103, if you need me."

She frowned. "If she doesn't take the strong pill, she's going to be awake a lot more and she'll cause trouble."

"Let's see how she does. She'll feel better and be more alert. But I have a favor to ask." He waited.

"Go on," Janice said. She seemed suspicious.

"Ask her not to use the N-word. You, either. I'll see if someone other than Roundtree can care for her. How does that sound?"

Janice shrugged with one shoulder. "Worth a try."

"Can you come earlier in the day? Help her stay calm?"

"Sure, I work afternoons and evenings at a Waffle House."

"Okay, good." He hesitated again. "This place must be hard to afford on Waffle House income."

Janice reddened. "I don't pay cash out of my pocket. When my uncle passed, we sold his farm to pay for Lucy's room here. It was my inheritance. Now, nothing."

"Well, let's see if we can make it worth your while." He slapped both knees with his hands. "I've got to get going."

"You think there are others being drugged at night?"

"Maybe."

"Are you going to search the other rooms?"

"Sorry, I don't have time to do it." In truth, he didn't want to get caught doing it. Sleeping pill abuse wasn't what he wanted to find.

Eddie stood to leave, then thought of one more question. "How long has Lucy been here?"

"'Bout six months."

"Do you have a record of her meds from before she came here?"

"I'll find it."

"Good. We need to know what else Dr. Banerjee has added to her treatment regimen."

"Yeah, we'll send that dothead and his nigger to damn jail." She gave him a fist pump.

"Keep your cool, Janice."

At the nurses' station, Eddie waited for Roundtree to finish a conversation with another nurse.

"She planning to sue us after all?" Roundtree asked.

"She wants to make a deal," Eddie said. "Her niece, Janice, will get here early and make her behave."

"And what do I have to give up?"

"Can you assign someone other than yourself to look after her from noon till your shift ends?"

"You mean a white nurse?"

Eddie shrugged. "She's too old to change, Letitia."

"She probably had slaves on that cotton plantation of hers."

"Just trying to solve a problem, Letitia."

"If that Cracker gives me one spot of trouble, I'm kicking her ass all the way back to Waycross."

"I'll help you do it. Put a note in her record for staff to call me in room 103 if she's any trouble."

"I'll do that."

"One more thing, Letitia. I need to see Dr. Banerjee. I have some prescriptions to fill."

"He only comes in once a month to update his patient records. You could make an appointment to see him in Savannah."

"It's not urgent. Let me know when he's here."

"Will do."

Eddie walked back toward Lucy's room, but that wasn't his destination. He eased through the door to the back staircase and trotted down to the third floor. He joined a group of seniors shuffling down the hallway until he saw Lilac Lady and Lipstick Lady emerge from the room with the handwritten Memory Care sign. Eddie waited for them to get into the elevator before he approached the room he assumed Gerry Matthews occupied. A worn-out brown shoe propped the door open. The gaggle of seniors blocked the view from the nurses' station, so he slipped inside, kicked the shoe out of the way, and locked the door from the inside.

"What do you want?" came a female voice, hoarse from years of smoking or maybe just as old and worn-out as the shoe.

It startled him. The voice had come from the bedroom where Eddie hoped to find Gerry, the last man on his list. He peeked around the corner and saw a woman sitting in an easy chair in front of the window. Through the blinds, the black-topped parking lot shimmered in the morning sun. An elderly man was propped up in the bed, thinning gray hair neatly combed, cheeks rosy after an early morning shave. His lower jaw made slow circles, like a cow chewing its cud, as his brain processed the arrival of an unrecognized visitor.

"I came to see Gerry," Eddie said. "Is that him?" Eddie gestured to the man in the bed.

"You a friend of his?" the woman said as though Gerry weren't right there in the bed.

"Yeah, we were Army buddies."

"You a tanker like Gerry? Germany or Fort Hood?"

"Must have been Fort Hood."

"He retired from the Army, ya know, and came back this way to work for my daddy. My family's money is why we have this place."

"You're Gerry's wife?"

"Yes, sir, I'm Lydia."

"And you live here too?"

"A course. Wouldn't leave him here alone."

"No, never."

"Did I see that Phyllis and Bernice came to visit?"

She waved, as though sending the women away. "Them two old bitties is always snooping around."

"Gerry's visitors have been restricted, so I had to sneak in."

"Ya shoulda kept the door cracked. This place needs fresh air."

She was right; the air smelled warm and heavy. Lydia was wiry and bright-eyed, but her mouth dragged low on the left side. *Probably a stroke*, Eddie thought. He estimated that the woman and Gerry were at least ten years older than he was.

"How did the, uh, ladies get in?"

"Same as you, through the door." Lydia cackled.

"Guess the security isn't too tight."

"It's just ta keep us from leaving. Those fools are holding us prisoner."

"They just want Gerry to stay safe while they treat his Alzheimer's," Eddie said.

"Gerry don't have no Alzheimer's. He has a touch of the madness, is all, but when he's thinking straight, he can tell you every World Series winner since 1948."

Eddie knelt beside the woman's chair. "Is that right? Has he been diagnosed with a mental illness?"

"Sure, Skitch-o-whatever."

"Schizophrenia."

"That's it," she said, as though she had answered a test question. "Has hallucinations sometimes, not often. Might tell you the sky is green, and the grass is red. Rest of the time he don't talk much. He could be an outpatient, but the Frog Doctor is holding us hostage."

"Frog doctor?"

"The French Jew."

"Cevert?" Eddie grunted as he rose, knees and hips rebelling.

"He's killing people," Gerry suddenly shouted. "I seen him do it."

Eddie moved to the bedside. "What did you see, Gerry?"

"People go in that office alive and come out dead."

"When did you see that?"

"Happened again yesterday."

"Was the day before," Lydia said.

Ah, Eddie thought. Jacob Hoffman. He wondered if Hoffman had been breathing when he reached Cevert's office. "I'll look into it," Eddie said.

"I told 'em about the murders, but they don't believe me," Gerry said, louder than necessary again.

"Gerry made me file a complaint, then they locked us in," Lydia said.

Gerry may not remember how to tie his shoes, Eddie thought, but he could remember what he had seen. Four paper pill cups, each with one medication in it, sat on the bedside table.

"Do you know which doctor prescribed these pills? Was it Doctor Cevert?"

"I don't know, sir. The nurses bring 'em."

Eddie looked up the pills in an online pill identifier. At midday, Gerry was being given SeroQUEL as an anti-psychotic and Clonazepam to suppress panic attacks. Eddie pulled his Joe Friday notebook from his pocket and flipped to the page on which he'd written the most common Alzheimer's medications—Aricept, Namenda, Namzaric, and Razadyne. None of the pills in the paper cups matched the typical Alzheimer's medications.

"Is he wearing a patch? On his arm maybe?"

Lydia shook her head. "We both quit smoking years ago."

Eddie suppressed a laugh. He had meant the Exelon patch for Alzheimer's patients. Whoever prescribed Gerry's medications heavily drugged him for his psychosis but knew full well he wasn't suffering from dementia. He did have another problem, however, indicated by the last two pills, immune system boosters.

"Gerry has cancer?"

"It's in his lungs. The asbestos in the tanks is what done it," Lydia said.

"I'm sorry to hear that. Does Gerry take painkillers?"

Lydia reached in the pocket of her dress and pulled out a vial. "He has these things but he won't take 'em. Says they're addicting."

Eddie read the label and suppressed another laugh. The vial contained Oxycontin, prescribed by Dr. Banerjee and filled by the River City Pain Management clinic. Gerry was dying of lung cancer but he feared addiction to opioids.

"He's right, they're a narcotic, but it's okay for him to take a pill when he's uncomfortable."

"What makes him uncomfortable is he don't want to die here, in this place. We have family in Statesboro. The nurses won't let them in 'cause they're my kin, not his."

That sounded to Eddie like a rule concocted just for Gerry. "Do you have a primary care physician?"

Doubt clouded Lydia's brown eyes. "I don't guess so. If we get sick, we go to the clinic. The pills come from the pharmacy, don't they?"

"I'm sure they do. Let me talk to the bigwigs and see if we can get Gerry out of Memory Care."

"We'd be most grateful. What was your name again?"

"Tommy. Gerry will remember me when he's thinking straight."

Peeking out the door, Eddie assured himself that the nurses were occupied and slipped into the hallway. A woman in a wheelchair waited for assistance outside her room, so Eddie pushed her down the hallway to the lounge.

"Are you a pink lady?" the woman asked.

"Yes, ma'am. They said they'd come get you here."

The woman gave Eddie a big smile and Eddie took the back stairway to the fourth floor.

He found Janice packing up to leave her aunt. Lucy had been bathed and was watching TV in the sitting room.

"I ran out and got the sleeping pills like you said." She handed him the packet. Janice had the flushed happy look of a coconspirator.

"Good job." He moved into the bedroom and sorted through this evening's pills in the organizer until he found the one he wanted, then showed Janice the tiny, round white pill. "That's the Rohypnol."

After replacing the Rohypnol with the over-the-counter pills, he pulled a small plastic baggie from his pocket and dumped the Rohypnol pills into the baggie. Eddie took a picture of the empty Rohypnol vial's label and placed the vial back on Lucy's nightstand. "If the over-the-counter pill isn't enough to help Lucy sleep, I'll find some Valium or Xanax, but let's flush the Rohypnol out of her system."

Eddie sat beside Lucy on the green plastic sofa and took her hand in his. "You have to be a good girl today. They'll come and get me if you have a problem, so no screaming or using bad language. Got it?"

He studied Lucy's broad face, featureless, as though it were missing pieces. Her eyes darted from Eddie to Janice and back to Eddie. Lucy gave him an almost imperceptible nod.

Eddie patted the old woman's hand and rose. He took Janice by the elbow and led her into the hallway.

"I'll see you in the morning?"

"I'll be here."

Eddie sauntered down the hallway and gave Nurse Roundtree a thumbs-up sign as he passed the nurses' station. Back in his room, he added a note to the Rohypnol baggie and placed it in the return vent.

✳ ✳ ✳

Eddie joined up with Donald at the top of the escalator and helped him to their table. The proud man seemed to have trouble maintaining his usual erect bearing and, strange as it sounded to Eddie's ears, appeared pale.

Cevert, Bobby, Susan, and Madeleine were already seated. Today Madeleine wore navy slacks and open-toed shoes that exposed stubby toes painted a matching blue. The first two buttons on her satiny gray blouse were undone and a string of pearls held the blouse together.

Eddie glanced around the room, disconcerted by so many small women and so many shrunken men staving off inevitable infirmity and looming death. He had already lost an inch off his once six-foot frame and his slacks puddled on his loafers. He averted his gaze and focused instead on Madeleine's scent, Michael's watery eyes, Donald's perfectly trimmed beard, Susan's distracted stare, and Bobby's overfed cheeks.

For lack of better options, Eddie joined everyone else in ordering the poached salmon and added his usual beer. He noted that Donald drank milk and picked at his food. Eddie listened without contributing to the flow of conversation and tolerated the good-natured bickering of close friends until the entrees were served.

"I really want to see my Army buddy, Gerry Matthews," Eddie said to Cevert. "Maybe I can talk to the doctor who made the original diagnosis. Who was that?"

Cevert set his utensils on his plate and slowly dabbed his lips with his napkin. "I don't recall the name. Probably his family physician. It would be in his records."

Eddie chewed the dry and tasteless salmon while thinking about that lie. "What was the basis for the diagnosis? Were there tests and so forth?"

"You're being rude, Eddie," Madeleine said.

"Yeah, leave Michael alone," Susan interjected.

Bobby watched the exchange carefully while Donald appeared ready to fall asleep at the table.

"It's okay, I'll explain it to Eddie," Cevert said, his manner condescending, laced with hostility. "Mr. Matthews has low levels of acetylcholine, which enables memory and high levels of cholinesterase in his brain, which erodes the acetylcholine. Matched to his behavior, the diagnosis was straightforward, and the prognosis was for an unfortunate and unstoppable decline in mental acuity."

Cevert leaned back in his seat, confident he had dazzled Eddie with incontrovertible medical science. But Eddie knew that Gerry was taking no cholinesterase inhibitors, the standard approach for husbanding the remaining acetylcholine in an Alzheimer's patient's brain. Cevert was lying.

Eddie gave them a theatrical sigh. "I can't eat this stuff. I'm going up to the grill." As he rose, he tossed his napkin on the partly eaten fish and started away.

"You're going to miss a great discussion tonight," Bobby said to Eddie's back. "About the Big Bang."

Across the table, Donald seemed more alert than the previous evening. "We've been there, done that," he said. "Try something new."

"This is new," Bobby insisted. "Scientists used to think that all the worlds' building blocks were compressed in a tight little ball when the Big Bang happened. Like someone put it all together. Now scientists realize that what existed at the moment of the Big Bang was Quark-Gluon plasma, a liquid, which when heated, expanded and provided the molecules that accidently combined to create the elements in today's universe. It's all an accident."

"It wasn't an accident," Donald said. "It was by design."

"You need a god in the same way that a wolfpack needs an alpha," Bobby said.

Donald recoiled. "Life has meaning only if there is a God. Greek gods, Roman gods, Viking gods, Hindu gods, Allah, Yahweh, and Jesus Christ; humans have always had gods. Without a god, life is too scary and meaningless."

Eddie knew that Donald had paraphrased one of St. Augustine's five proofs for the existence of God: there must be a god since humans want one.

The table was silent until Cevert filled the void. "Science will figure out what happened before the Big Bang."

"If you mean that science will prove whether there is a God, you're wrong because it isn't possible," Eddie said. "Science is limited to the observable realm, and, if there is a God, He isn't in that realm."

Cevert's fork of food stopped in midair. Bobby's mouth hung open.

"Tell me what existed before the Quarks and who lit the fuse on the Big Bang and you'll have the real answer," Donald said.

Bobby frowned in disappointment. "I'll bring a better topic tomorrow."

"Hope so," Eddie said.

Eddie turned away and ignored calls to return to the table. He had eaten half a steak burger when Crazy Karen Wykowski appeared at his high-topped bar table wearing a skirt that ended six inches above her knobby knees, spiked heels, and a scoop neck top out of which her breasts were being squeezed by a pushup bra like toothpaste out of a tube.

"Hey, sailor. Buy a girl a drink?"

Eddie waved a hand at the stool across from him and raised his other hand to signal a waitress. Karen ordered a vodka martini, extra dirty.

"Did you get tired of eating at Madeleine's table?" she asked.

"I got tired of eating dining room food."

The waitress brought the martini and Karen swallowed half of it. She stabbed an olive with her swizzle stick and spoke while she chewed. "Do you find her attractive?"

Eddie did not want to go down that rat hole. "What's the deal between you two?"

"We're running against each other for President of the Resident's Association."

"That's it? You want to be Queen of the Ball?"

"I have to beat her at something. She stole my man."

Eddie put two and two together and came up with five. "Jacob Hoffman?"

Karen downed the rest of her martini, coaxed the second olive into her mouth, and raised her hand for a fresh drink. "Jacob was in love with me and then Madeleine came along and stole him away. I can't imagine what she offered him. He got whatever he wanted from me."

"You baked him casseroles and cakes?"

Karen laughed so reflexively that the half-eaten olive shot out of her mouth like a bullet from a gun and landed on Eddie's hand. He offered it to her, and she slurped it up.

"He was a good catch, you know. Young and let's just say, virile." She gave him a sad smile. "I had no idea his heart was bad. She steals him and then he dies on her. Ironic, right?"

Eddie remembered the sparring between Lipstick Lady and Cevert. She had implied that Jacob had avoided barbaric treatments and Cevert had dodged the accusation by saying he wasn't an oncologist.

"Did Jacob have cancer?"

"What? No, there wasn't a thing wrong with him."

"Well, I'm sorry for your loss."

"Thanks. Dr. Cevert was kind enough to let me into his office to say goodbye to Jacob." A wistful look seeped into her eyes as she recalled the scene. "He looked serene, not anguished in his last moments on earth.

I don't know where Madeleine was taking him for lunch, but he looked great, all buttoned up in his best blue suit, a starched white shirt, and his fire-engine red tie." She gave Eddie a sad smile. "Jacob was an introvert, but he loved that tie."

Eddie made a mental note that Mr. Hoffman had been pronounced in Cevert's office and that his clothing hadn't been disturbed by resuscitation attempts or by the vomiting that typically accompanied an opioid overdose. And Cevert allowed Karen to say goodbye even though Hoffman was supposedly involved with Madeleine.

"Was Madeleine there? When you said goodbye to Jacob."

"No, she stepped out and gave me my privacy."

"Nice of her. How was she dressed?"

"Hunh?"

"Was she all dressed up like Jacob?"

"Oh." Karen stopped to think about it. "Something dark, I think."

"The little black cocktail dress?"

Karen hooted like a Barred Owl. "They don't make the LBD in her size. It was something you'd wear to a funeral. With pearls."

The waitress arrived at the table with Karen's second martini just as Madeleine strode up, her face flushed with anger or excitement.

"Go powder your nose or whatever you powder," Madeleine said to Karen. "I have something important to tell Eddie."

"Eddie doesn't want me to leave, do you, Eddie?"

Eddie hesitated and looked from one woman to the other. He needed to stay close to Madeleine and Dr. Cevert. "Let me see what Madeleine wants, Karen."

"I just need his ears for a minute," Madeleine said. "You can come back later for what's in his pants."

Crazy Karen went ballistic and threw her drink in Madeleine's face. Or tried to. Most of the clear liquid hit Madeleine's gray blouse. Madeleine grabbed the lighter woman's dress straps and yanked her off the stool.

"Catfight!" someone yelled.

Eddie jumped off his stool and wrapped his arms around Madeleine. He swung her away from Karen and took Karen's slaps on his back. Then a man slid off a barstool and locked Karen in his arms. Madeleine swiveled in Eddie's embrace to face Karen. They spat obscenities at each other like a snake and a mongoose squaring off. "Witch!" "Slut!" "Cunt!" "Whore!"

Back and forth they went until the bartender stepped between them and said, "Shut up. Both of you. I saw you throw the drink, Karen. Please leave peacefully and come back tomorrow."

Karen sagged in the arms of the man restraining her. "She always wins," she said and stumbled toward the exit. Over her shoulder, she fired a parting shot, "You don't know what you're missing, Eddie."

Eddie drew a clean white handkerchief from his back pocket and Madeleine used it to dry her chin and blot the wet spots on her blouse.

"Gonna leave a stain," Madeleine said.

"Want to go change?"

"No, everyone saw who was at fault. I'll keep the blouse on as a reminder."

"As a reminder to vote for you, not her," he said.

A raised eyebrow, a gleam in her eye, and a slight tug at the corner of her lips told him he had guessed right, and she didn't care. She hoisted herself onto the stool across from him and wiggled her butt to get comfortable.

"You shouldn't have stopped me. I have a wicked left cross." She made the motion in the air. "Did she tell nasty lies about me?"

"No," he lied. "She was just coming onto me."

"Of course, that's what she does."

"Want a burger, a drink?"

"I finished the salmon downstairs, but I do want dessert." She flagged down a waitress and ordered a chocolate shake. "Want to share?" she asked Eddie.

He shrugged a "yes."

"Two straws," she told the waitress.

Is that what she had offered Jacob? A shared chocolate shake?

"Where were you and Jacob going for lunch the day he died?"

She seemed dumbfounded by the question. "Why do you want to know?"

"You know I don't care for the food here. Thought it might be somewhere I should try."

Madeleine took a moment to examine his eyes. "The Bohemian Hotel. Very swanky."

"We should add it to our list."

She blinked once, twice, and said, "Okay."

"Will there be a memorial service for Jacob?"

"We don't do memorials. They remind us of our mortality."

"Don't need that," he said.

She smiled disarmingly, then got down to the reason she joined him in the bar. "Don't be so hard on Michael. Mr. Matthews isn't his patient. He was just asked to help, which he did out of kindness. He'll speak to the Palm Haven administrator and see if he can relax the rules."

Eddie knew when he was being played. Cevert had delegated Madeleine to soften him up with another stalling tactic. "I'll apologize to Michael. It's not his problem."

"Thank you."

He finished his burger as the chocolate shake arrived. Their heads bent close together as they sucked the sweet shake through matching straws. They looked like high school sweethearts at the malt shop.

As they left the grill, she took his hand and led him to the private elevator to her eighth-floor penthouse suite. When the doors opened, he had the distinct feeling that she'd have let him kiss her. He wondered how far Madeleine would go to protect Dr. Michael Cevert.

As he undressed for bed, he brought Sam up to date. "The leads I was given are total crap, as usual. Donna, who belongs in memory care, isn't;

Gerry, who shouldn't be in memory care, is; and Lucy is simply an ornery old lady who is being drugged to sleep. The only opioids I've found were prescribed for Gerry's cancer. That's legitimate enough."

"You have other persons of interest."

"Yep, Banerjee and Cevert. Nothing worse than shady doctors. Except dirty cops, as you know."

"That's not who I meant," Sam said.

Sam's insinuation annoyed him and he refused to figure out why.

"Madeleine is protective of Cevert but I doubt she's dealing opioids."

"Those two are up to something and other people are suspicious."

"I agree but I don't want to get distracted. Opioids are what I have to find."

"All right. Bore me with some more of the Vietnam story. Still sounds like you're on vacation, eating steaks and sipping cocktails."

"Be patient, my sweet. I'm about to meet the elephant."

CHAPTER SIX

... Then

Promptly at 0700 hours Carlyle picked me up in front of the BOQ where I had returned an endless string of enlisted salutes while waiting. At first, I felt like a fraud but that feeling dissipated with each acknowledgement of my fake rank.

Grinding gears, Carlyle cut through an enlisted residential area before turning left onto a primary road, putting the rising yellow sun at our backs. I felt like a gawking tourist as we passed a movie theater, a basketball court, a bowling alley, a dental clinic, a golf driving range, and the University of Maryland extension. Unarmed soldiers hustled to their places of work to cross another day off the calendar and get another day closer to going back to "the world."

"Doesn't seem like there is a war here."

"Oh, it's here, just beyond the wire. The VC attacked Long Binh during Tet to keep the troops here busy while they destroyed the ammo dump at the Bien Hoa airbase just a few miles to the north."

Soon we passed tennis courts where American women were playing in the relative cool of the early morning. When I did a double take and craned my neck to watch long after we had rolled down the street, Carlyle said, "Nurses from the hospitals on base. They only date colonels and above, so don't get your hopes up." He made air quotes around the word "date."

I laughed. "Rank has its privileges."

He grunted and said nothing else until we passed a two-story white building, two football fields in length, in the middle of the largest expanse of green grass I had ever seen outside of a golf course. "That's MAC-V Headquarters, 'Pentagon East,' where General Abrams hangs out," he said. "Rumor has it they have air conditioning and flush toilets."

Carlyle turned right onto another paved road that took us along the western perimeter, heading north. A chain-link fence topped by barbed wire and fronted by rolls of triple concertina paralleled the road. Inside the barrier, firing bunkers were dug every few dozen yards, the nose of an M-60 machine gun sticking through a firing slit in the sandbags and manned by a G.I. standing guard.

At the northern end of the street, we turned into long rows of wooden hootches on stilts, the Inventory Control Center of the Long Binh Army Depot. Beyond the offices, covered storage areas overflowed with crates and beyond them, fenced lots held vehicles whose headlights and windshields were still wrapped in packing paper.

Tucker pulled to a stop in front of the third building down from the road but didn't get out of the jeep. "They have a room ready for you with a computer terminal and a printer for your private use. Pull the computer records and analyze them. Got it?"

"Got it."

"Act like you own the place. Don't become chummy with anyone or tell them who you are. No matter what their rank, if someone asks a question, you say, 'Sorry, that's classified.' Got it?"

"Got it."

"I'll pick you up right here at 1700 hours."

"Got it."

❋ ❋ ❋

That evening, I plopped an eight-inch stack of green-and-white striped computer printouts on the back seat and got into Carlyle's jeep.

He glanced over his shoulder at the printouts and said, "You can tell me all about it at the club."

He drove back to the Quonset hut O-club, our secret rendezvous, where I ordered two beers, prompting a smile from Carlyle. Once again, we found an isolated table and took a seat. I chugged the first beer and enjoyed a slight buzz as the alcohol permeated my overworked brain.

"What's with all the computer printouts?" Carlyle asked.

"They're listings of all the transactions processed for the Special Forces teams we're investigating. I found no overages of equipment in the online accounts. A cursory look by an auditor would reveal nothing suspicious. So I pulled the transaction logs to crosscheck against the accounts and the activity level is through the roof. It's like you wrote a lot of checks that aren't recorded anywhere."

"Good job. You've confirmed that the illegal arms are coming through the Army supply system. What's your next step?"

"I'm going to note all the serial numbers of the equipment on these orders and the names of the people who signed off."

Carlyle smiled. "I like the way your mind works. It takes a crook to catch a crook."

"I guess that's a compliment."

"How long is it going to take to build my suspect list?"

"Another day should do it."

He finished his drink. "Instead of carrying all that paper in and out of the building, work from the BOQ. We don't need anyone to get curious about what you're doing."

"Okay."

When our sassy waitress appeared, Carlyle ordered another steak—"we'll be eating C-rations up north"—and I ordered a burger and fries. As nicely as a former altar boy could, I asked the waitress not to substitute a steak. When she delivered the food, she gave me a disdainful look. The burger and fries weren't as good as the steak. I took a six pack of Carling Black Label back to the BOQ to help me sleep.

✳ ✳ ✳

The next day, Carlyle came to my room at lunchtime to check on my progress. I sat on the floor with chunks of the computer printouts and sheets of paper encircling me. More paper was stacked behind me on the bed. Fortunately, I did not have a roommate to question my research. Tucker picked some papers off the bed, scanned them, and replaced them. He bent to look at the piles on the floor but clearly could not grasp the organization of my system.

"You know how they're cheating?"

"I know *that* they're cheating. "There are one hundred thirty-two illegal requisitions," I concluded. Some requisitions ordered multiple vehicles—one was for ten M-48 tanks—and some ordered cases or crates of M-16s and M-60 machine guns. "They've ordered enough equipment to arm a division of troops."

"Damn. They can't hide all this stuff."

"The computer isn't recording shipments when they're received and therefore it keeps ordering more and more equipment for the Green Berets. We need to interview the programmers."

He blew air. "No can do, buddy, the Green Beanies would know we were onto them before we ever got up there."

"Okay, there's another way. Get me a copy of the computer code and let me read it to see how the scheme works."

"You can read computer code?"

"I complained so much about the data processing support at the depot in Thailand that the data processing sergeant gave me a programming manual and time on the machines so I could code my own routines. The key to this scheme is in the computer code."

"You're like a kid trying to solve a puzzle, but that's not how you get a criminal conviction. You've found probable cause that justifies a physical inventory of equipment at the camps. Now we keep our eyes on the ball—find illegal equipment in the hands of identifiable men. Here are my orders: Make me a list of the officers in the Special Forces units who authorized all those transactions. That's my suspect list."

I had come to believe that I could survive this war at a peaceful camp like Long Binh, but this guy was an adrenalin junkie who was going to get me killed. "Yes, sir," I said, contemptuously.

As I compiled Carlyle's list of suspects, a pattern swiftly emerged. The commanders of the five A-teams had submitted a routine number of equipment requisitions that equaled the computerized account balances, while a Lieutenant Colonel William Barlow, the B-team commander at Dak To, had submitted requisitions that weren't recorded on the computer. I listed the serial numbers of the contraband that would be the object of Carlyle's camp searches. I wondered if a CID Warrant Officer could arrest a lieutenant colonel.

Late afternoon, my door swung open without warning, and Carlyle barged into my room lugging a stack of green-and-white-striped computer printout paper and an infantryman's rucksack. He dumped the printouts on my bed and set the rucksack on the floor.

"The computer code for the Long Binh supply system," he said. "A friend stole the printouts for me. Happy reading."

"Thanks. I have the list of illegal equipment and know who ordered it."

He gave me a high five. "I knew you could do it. We're leaving for the highlands tomorrow morning. You can only take what you can stuff into this rucksack. We'll pick up combat gear in Pleiku."

"I'll need another day, Tucker. I won't be able to get through the computer documentation until tomorrow."

"0700, Mister. That's an order."

This guy is going to get me killed for nothing, I thought.

He paused at my door. "You're doing great work, Kovacs. Could make a fine investigator someday if you're willing to learn from me. You should consider it."

Long after bedtime, I had a list of equipment that Barlow had ordered illegally for the B-team. Bone-tired, I picked up the computer documentation and began reading. Once I started, I couldn't stop.

✳ ✳ ✳

After sleeping for an hour, I showered and shaved and packed my rucksack. I stuffed it with as much underwear and as many pairs of socks and changes of uniform as the rucksack would hold, then added my shaving kit and Kodak Brownie camera. As an afterthought, I slid a copy of John D. MacDonald's *The Girl in the Plain Brown Wrapper* into a side pocket. I hoped I wouldn't need any of it.

Carlyle arrived on time, as usual. As I approached the jeep, I said, "We don't have to go up there. I figured it out."

"Where's your gear, Kovacs?"

"The computer system has been hacked. Barlow's equipment requisitions are fraudulent. Our investigation is over, and the MPs can arrest him."

Through gritted teeth, he said, "Get your shit, Kovacs, or we'll leave without it."

"We need to see your boss or some General and tell them the story."

"In ten seconds, Kovacs, I'm going to arrest you for disobeying an order and throw you in the Long Binh Jail. Move, trooper."

I slumped. I sighed. I turned and went back for my rucksack, my calculations, and the Barlow equipment list. I told the Charge of Quarters I'd be back for the rest of my things. The rucksack went into the back seat; the thick bundle of papers I handed to Carlyle.

"Jesus H. Christ," he murmured. He got out of the jeep, pulled my rucksack off the seat, opened it, and made room for the papers by tossing clothes onto the street. He buttoned up the rucksack, replaced it on the back seat, got into the jeep, put it in gear, and sped away from the safety of the Long Binh BOQ.

I have never forgiven myself for not being more persuasive, more forceful, more adamant about my evidence and my approach to the case. I never should have gotten into that jeep.

We hopped a C-130 transport from the Bien Hoa airbase to Pleiku, and I used the opportunity to ask if he had arranged my transfer to the States.

He smirked. "Where would the Warrant officer First Class like to spend his next vacation?"

I hoped he wasn't being sarcastic. After assignments in Virginia, Texas, Thailand, and Vietnam, I realized there were places where you didn't have to shovel snow. "Someplace warm, please."

"Lots of military installations in Georgia."

"Sure. That would be nice."

I closed my eyes and hoped for sleep, but the rocking of the plane, the noise and vibrations of the engines, and drafts of cold air kept me awake.

In Pleiku, we were issued helmets, M-69 flak vests, ponchos, twenty-round magazines of 5.56mm ammo, canteens, iodine water purification tablets, and C-rations. More of my clothing had to be left behind. To make room for the canteens, Carlyle pulled my John D. MacDonald novel from a side pocket of the rucksack and tossed it into a trashcan.

The flak vest was light and flexible. I tested it by bending it back and forth. "Is this thing bullet-proof?"

"It's just layers of ballistic nylon. It won't stop an AK-47 round, but it'll reduce the impact of shrapnel."

"Terrific." I slipped it on and put the helmet on my head. I was also issued an M-16 rifle and an officer's holstered Colt .45 pistol, which I strapped around my waist like an Old West gunfighter.

Armed to the teeth, we hitched a ride with a supply convoy headed to Kon Tum. Carlyle sat in the passenger seat of a ¾ ton truck while I sat in the open back of the trailing deuce and a half beside grunts loaded down like pack mules.

More Black than white, teenagers with pimpled cheeks and mossy-haired chins, these soldiers didn't resemble the rugged heroes of the World War II movies I had seen. These guys were America's youthful currency being spent by profligate old white men on a doomed quest to save a worthless domino. Several helpful kids told me to sit near the front so they could get out first if we were attacked. But, they said, if the shit goes down, do not stay in the truck bed. "It's a big target," somebody said. "An officer is a big target, too," somebody else said and everyone laughed.

We pulled out of the compound and followed Route 14 North into a countryside that alternated between jungle-covered hills, expanses of rice paddies, and barren fields burned by napalm. Swirling red dust, kicked up by truck tires, coated my face and my uniform. We made fitful stop-and-go progress, as though we were in California commuter traffic. We skirted bomb craters in the road, stopped to move damaged and disabled vehicles, stopped once to remove an intentionally prepared roadblock.

Stomach bile lurched into my throat. Muscles tensed, nerve endings dancing just under my skin, I could not relax, but we reached Kon Tum without incident.

At the Division base, Carlyle found a driver to ferry us to the helipad. We passed the flight line where a row of helicopters stood, rotors drooping lifelessly, looking to my eye like prehistoric, flying dinosaurs.

"Flight line gets hit with mortars or rockets almost every day," the driver said. "We have a different place for individual chopper flights and medevacs."

Beyond the flight line, the driver pulled to a stop beside a clearing surrounded by six-foot-tall elephant grass. The wrecked shell of a burned-out chopper lay on the clearing's far side.

"This is the LZ we're using. Stay on the other side of the wreck in case your bird draws fire."

We sat on the ground, our backs to the wreck, facing dense elephant grass in which enemy soldiers could be hiding, waiting in the suffocating heat for a chopper destined for Dak To, another twenty-five miles to the north. Carlyle talked and I listened. The fifty-five-mile stretch from Pleiku to Dak To, he said, demarcated the line between fighting the Viet Cong and fighting the NVA. In the lower half of the country, the VC waged guerrilla warfare in small unit engagements; up here, we had to fight the NVA in full-scale battles of battalion-sized forces in hostile terrain. The Special Forces A-team camps, he said, were basically operating behind enemy lines, and the Yards were our guerrillas harassing the NVA.

His honest description of our situation sent a new chill up my spine. After he finished scaring the shit out of me, I said, "I need to explain what I found in the computer code."

"Do I care?" He pulled his pouch of chewing tobacco from his vest, pinched a few strands, and stuck them in the side of his mouth. He offered the pouch to me, and I declined. All that spitting seemed unbecoming an officer.

"I think you should because Barlow isn't your only suspect. Requisitions with Barlow's approval bypass the portfolio manager at Long Binh and go straight to the computer programs that automatically reorder equipment. If Barlow requisitions it, the system fills the order. Some very sharp programmer at Long Binh has modified the computer system."

Carlyle spat out his chaw and wiped his mouth. He leaned back on his hands in the dirt and examined the hazy sky. As though talking to himself, he said, "Maybe I got this assignment because they didn't think I'd ever figure out the scheme."

He dusted the dirt from his hands and stood up. I felt it appropriate that I stand as well. He put a hand on my shoulder. "Fuck these people. I found a smart guy who knows how the supply system works. You're my secret weapon, Kovacs, and we're going to solve this case whether they want it solved or not."

I wished Carlyle had found some poor schmuck in Vietnam to do his dirty work. "Want me to write up a status report for your superiors?"

"No way." He shook his head. "When we're done, we'll drop our evidence in their laps like a turd in their punch bowl."

Carlyle heard it before I did, the unmistakable *thwop, thwop, thwop* of an approaching helicopter's blades. "Here comes our taxi," he said.

The Bell UH-1H "Huey" descended and flared over the camp, then darted over to the LZ like a wasp in a garden. It hovered several feet above the ground, blasting us with red dirt and stone pebbles that stung my cheeks. Head down, eyes covered with one arm, I couldn't hear the shouts of the chopper's crew chief over the roar of the engine. Carlyle grabbed a handful of my uniform sleeve and dragged me to the door of the Huey. The crew chief helped us aboard, sliding us past the door gunner manning an M-60 machine gun. We sat on the floor, backs to the pilot, as the crew chief gave a thumbs-up to the cockpit. The Huey rose a few feet, darted back over the camp, then banked steeply as it climbed to an altitude safe from ground fire. The Huey dipped its nose slightly and headed northward.

Flying at one-hundred-fifty-feet and one-hundred-miles-per-hour, the triple canopy jungle below us looked like a ragged shag carpet in a low-rent apartment. Every few miles, the crew chief pointed to something on the ground, and the door gunner responded with a burst from his machine gun. I never saw anything that resembled a target and we never received any return fire. When I pointed to the gunner and flipped my hand palm up in a silent question, he shrugged.

We approached a village and banked to the northwest, away from the camp marked on my map, which should have been to the east. The pilot raised the nose of the chopper to climb a jungle-covered mountain and cut the throttle as we approached the huge camp perched on top. I moved to the door opposite the gunner to get a view of our new base of operations and saw an eclectic collection of tents, bunkers, Quonset huts, and hootches, set in seemingly random configurations. Along the perimeter, rectangular firing positions ringed by sandbags were populated by rifle teams or mortar teams. Dozens of ammo boxes were stacked around the walls of the firing positions, ready for prolonged action. Wooden guard towers were spaced around the outer perimeter.

I'm in the serious shit now, I thought, as we landed on a helipad inside the camp. Head bowed against the rotor wash, I hustled away from the pad and bounced off an immovable object.

"Watch where you're going, Mister."

Standing a couple of inches shorter than me, he wore captain's bars and a name strip that read, "Baker" on starched fatigues. I tottered like a pin struck by a bowling ball. Rather than the trademark green beret or the ubiquitous boonie hat, this guy had an Australian bush hat on his head with the left side of the brim cocked up. *This guy is auditioning for a role in a movie.*

I started to apologize when Carlyle said, "We're the CID team, Baker. You our welcoming party?"

"It's no party, Carlyle. I'm Colonel Barlow's aide and that makes me your chaperone."

"All we need are directions to Barlow's office."

"Colonel Barlow is at group headquarters in Nha Trang. I'll take you where you need to go." Baker began walking away. We hurried after him.

"Who's second-in-command?" Carlyle asked.

"Major Daniels is at Ben Het," Baker said over his shoulder.

"Then we'll start with the A-team here."

"No, Carlyle, we have an itinerary mapped out for you. Tomorrow we go to Dak Seang and Dak Pek."

Carlyle didn't say anything, but for the first time, I saw anger on my easygoing partner's face. I snapped pictures as we followed Baker to an area where six olive drab tents had been erected in a semi-circle facing a wooden structure enveloped in sandbags stacked from ground to roof. A cantilevered roof left openings along the sides of the structure for airflow. Beside the building, a diesel generator spewed toxic smoke into the air.

"That's the team house," Baker said. "Team members only."

Baker pulled back the entrance flap on a tent perhaps fifty feet long and thirty feet wide with a wooden interior frame and two telephone pole-size center supports like the humps on a camel's back. Two Army cots, one metal desk, and one swivel chair with cracked cushions comprised our furniture.

"Our guest accommodations," Baker said. "We don't get many visitors."

Baker stepped back through the entrance flap and pointed to another tent. "Mess tent. They're serving now." He turned in the opposite direction and pointed to a small metal building with a black neoprene bladder on top. "Shower room. The latrine is just beyond it."

He waited for a response. Carlyle clenched his jaw, so I said, "Got it."

"If anyone asks, Colonel Barlow invited you guys to consult with our team leads about any legal issues they might have."

Once again, Carlyle failed to respond, so I said, "Got it." We were masquerading as lawyers. That's what I had thought I'd become when I was in school.

"Be at the helipad at 0700," Baker said. "Leave your packs here. This is your base of operations." He left us.

"I'm gonna hang his uppity Black ass," Carlyle said.

Images of a lynching I had seen in weekly news magazines, flashed through my mind. Perhaps Carlyle had unintentionally selected an unfortunate choice of words, but I reminded myself that Carlyle was of that geography and of that culture.

We stripped to our skivvies and walked to the shower room. Rinsing the red dirt from my hair, my face, and my arms felt as good as a spa treatment at a luxury resort.

In the mess tent, we were served hot food on metal trays like the ones at my grammar school. Carlyle walked to a table where a first lieutenant ate alone. The lieutenant noticed us and waved a hand at the seats on the other side of the table.

The lieutenant pushed his Army-issue plastic glasses up on his prominent nose and introduced himself as Paul Weber of Evanston, Illinois. "What are you guys doing here?"

Weber hadn't been let in on our little secret, so Carlyle gave him Baker's cover story.

"You came at a good time. Been quiet here since November."

"On the map, Dak To was to the east of the village so where are we?" I asked.

"You were probably looking at the old Dak To. That camp wasn't big enough to hold everybody we need up here, so they built this vacation spot and named it Dak To II. The old camp is now called Tan Canh. Not sure who's over there."

"Tan Canh isn't on our list of attractions to visit," Carlyle said, "so they're not Special Forces."

"What do you hear about Dak Seang and Dak Pek?" I said, wanting to know how much trouble we'd be in tomorrow.

"Just routine harassment. Ben Het seems to be the NVA's primary target now."

Maybe that's why Major Daniels had gone to Ben Het.

Back in our guest accommodation, I should have felt better after Weber's nonchalant description of the situation at Dak Seang and Dak Pek, but I didn't know the definition of "routine harassment."

Carlyle pulled his Army-issue Nikon camera from his pack and handed it to me. "Use this one. Your Brownie makes us look like tourists."

Carlyle stripped to his underwear, crawled under the covers, turned his back to me, and fell asleep in thirty seconds. *Can he not hear the sporadic explosions in the jungle?* I lay on top of the covers, fully dressed, wanting to be ready if we were attacked, wanting to die with dignity if a rocket came through our canvas ceiling. After a while, I removed my boots. The next thing I knew, Carlyle shook me awake.

"Get up," he said. "We're going to see the elephant."

"Huh? We're looking for elephants?"

"No elephants left in Vietnam, Kovacs. Victor Charles has killed the elephants so we can't use them as transportation. 'Going to see the elephant' is a saying that dates to the Civil War. Means you're going to war for the first time."

"Terrific."

CHAPTER SEVEN

... Now

Eddie skipped breakfast to complete his initial interrogations while most residents were in the dining room or in the gardens, heading to the beach, or leaving for day excursions. Lucy appeared alert and calm and managed a smile when Eddie entered her room.

"She feels better today," Janice said. "The new nurse is nice."

Eddie assumed the new nurse was a white woman.

Janice handed him Lucy's list of prescriptions from before she came to the home and Eddie compared it to the notes he had made about Lucy's current prescriptions. Dr. Banerjee had added only the Rohypnol to suppress Lucy for the overnight nurses. Roundtree had not gotten the doctor to write any additional scripts for the day shift.

"Nothing improper with Lucy's other meds," Eddie said.

A conspiratorial smile blossomed on Janice's face. "I have something to tell you," she said, and she nudged Eddie into the bedroom for privacy.

"I visited all the rooms on this floor and looked for that bad pill."

Alarmed, Eddie said, "Did the nurses see you do that?" He hoped Janice hadn't exposed his investigation.

Slightly abashed, Janice said, "The nurses all know me and they expect residents to visit to one another. Betty Stanford in 1417 has the bad pill. She's trouble too. Should I give her the good pills?"

"No, let's not fool with anyone we can't control." *No one can know what I'm doing.*

"Guess what else I found?"

He shook his head. "What?"

"Ten others had Xanax or Valium in their night slot. The names were stamped right on the pills."

"So, everyone is being sedated, just different amounts depending—"

"Depending upon how ornery they are."

Eddie chuckled. "Good work, but let's not give Banerjee and the nurses any reason to suspect we're on to them. Have you heard any rumors about residents dying of opioid overdoses?"

Janice looked shocked. "No. Is that happening, too?"

"I'm just checking, Janice." He paused and decided to go ahead with the one thing he could make right. "Can you take tomorrow off? I have a plan and I'd like your help."

"Tell me, tell me," she said like an excited little girl.

Eddie explained his plan and the reason for it. When he described Janice's role, she responded with a belly laugh. "That'll fry their asses," she said.

Eddie took the back staircase to the fifth floor and asked the orderly, Joey, where he might find Donna Roberts this morning. He needed to tie off a loose end.

"She's in her room," Joey said as he pushed another resident down the hallway. "Number 508. Has a visitor today."

A visitor? "Thanks."

Eddie walked through the open door to apartment 508 and found Ms. Roberts formally dressed and sitting primly on her couch. Eddie's arrival surprised a man in his fifties with a military-style crew cut.

"I was just leaving," the man said. "Hotter than hell in here."

"Old people have thin blood," Eddie said.

"Are you here to take me to Johnny?" Donna asked Eddie.

"Yes, ma'am," Eddie said. "Just have to find a wheelchair."

The man gave Eddie the once-over. "You family?"

"No," Eddie said, "just a volunteer."

The man nodded and left the room.

Eddie could smell a detective when he met one. This guy had been carrying a portfolio notepad. Did Lance have another guy undercover, a backup in case Eddie screwed the pooch?

Eddie quickly searched Donna's bedside table and bathroom medicine cabinet but found no medications. He surmised that nurses administered Donna's medications. He told Donna to wait patiently for Joey and he left her.

He stopped short when Madeleine emerged from a room up the hallway, her back to him as she consulted a slip of paper. He ducked back into Donna's doorway and watched her move to another room and enter. Was she campaigning for the Residents' Council, or just comforting the less fortunate? Either way, he couldn't be seen lurking in the assisted living wing. He took the back stairwell to the fourth floor and the elevator to the lobby.

In his room, Eddie stapled his note listing Lucy's current meds to her prescription record from before she came to Palm Haven and placed the papers in the return vent.

Three good leads, my ass, Eddie thought. With respect to opioids, he was beginning to feel he was on a wild goose chase. However, Banerjee was sedating unruly patients and Cevert was suspicious as hell. Cevert had an office in the building, had pronounced Jacob Hoffman who hadn't died of a heart attack, had been offended by questions about opioids, and had intentionally misdiagnosed Gerry Matthews. Eddie cautioned himself not to succumb to tunnel vision, but he had no other leads.

✳ ✳ ✳

At dinner, Eddie graciously apologized to Cevert, a tactic designed to disarm the doctor. Cevert accepted the apology and that put everyone at ease.

As they waited for their entrees, Eddie asked Madeleine what she had done to fill her day.

"Oh, I went into Savannah with a group of ladies and did a little shopping," she said nonchalantly. "What about you?"

"I did some reading out by the pool and called my brother and sister to let them know I'm doing well."

"Gotta stay in touch," she said.

I'm a better liar than you are and I know why I do it but I don't know why you do it.

Across the table, Susan, flushed with anger, whispered heatedly to Bobby while Donald made futile attempts to intercede. Bobby couldn't keep the argument with Susan to himself. He leaned away from his wife and said, "The Supreme Court has overturned Roe v. Wade and it has Susan in a tither. I'd love to know what y'all think about that."

"Dangerous topic," Cevert said.

"Somebody has to stop the Fascists," Susan said. "Women have the right to choose what happens to their own bodies."

All eyes turned to Bobby, waiting for him to pounce on his wife and he did. "A woman's right to choose ends when she spreads her legs."

Susan leapt to her feet and slapped Bobby across his face.

Bobby laughed at her. "You hate it when women are held accountable for their behavior."

"Before the Nazi's packed the Court, it was a Constitutional right to reproductive autonomy," Susan insisted.

Donald, the lawyer, rallied his energy and stepped thoughtfully into the ring. "Actually, Susan, abortion was never a Constitutional right. That's misinformation spread by politicians and the media. In 1973, the Court ruled that abortion is a private matter and therefore is protected by the due process clause of the Fourteenth Amendment. The ruling had nothing to do with abortions per se."

"But the Court went on to make rules about abortions and that has come back to bite them in the ass," Michael said. "As a doctor, I've always been conflicted about the viable fetus standard."

Susan sat down. "Until then, it's like another one of a woman's organs. The fetus is not alive."

Donald continued his lecture. "The idea that the Court's decision has outlawed abortions is also misinformation. The Court has simply said that abortions are not explicitly protected by Constitution so the Supreme Court can't rule on abortions. It's up to the states to pass abortion laws."

"Plenty of Fascists in the so-called Red states," Susan said.

Eddie could have let the argument die, could have remained hidden in the undercover role he was playing, but he couldn't resist making one logical point. "The viable fetus standard is illogical because there is a legal code that defines death."

"What's death got to do with anything?" Susan asked.

"The Uniform Determination of Death Act stipulates that all brain and cardiovascular activity must cease 'irrevocably' before someone can be declared dead." Looking at Cevert, Eddie said, "I presume that Mr. Hoffman met that standard."

Cevert was momentarily caught off guard before he said, "Of course."

"Logically," Eddie went on, "the opposite of death is life, so the presence of a heartbeat or brain waves means the fetus is alive. The taking of a life is murder, and we already have murder statutes. Ergo, if a state chooses to legalize abortion after a heartbeat is detected, it will have to amend its murder statutes."

"Bravo!" Donald said and he smiled for the first time in days.

"I had an abortion," Madeleine said in a hoarse whisper. "It was the worst day of my life."

Everyone turned to Madeleine.

"Must have been for a good reason," Cevert said, trying to console her.

"My husband, Bruce, had a son from his first marriage and he was cruel to the kid. I didn't want to have children with Bruce."

"You exercised your rights," Susan said.

Madeleine rose unsteadily, as though dizzy. "It was selfish. If you'll excuse me …"

Cevert hurried after Madeleine. Eddie jumped to his feet but Bobby stopped him. "Let Michael do it."

"Let's go to the dance," Susan said. "Maybe I can forget what you've done, Bobby."

"In the ballroom on the other end of the floor," Bobby said to Eddie. "Always good for a few laughs."

Bobby and Susan weaved through the tables, toward the ballroom. Donald struggled to his feet and Eddie took his elbow. "Let's get you home," he said.

He helped Donald to his room, number 616 facing the ocean in the independent living wing. As they walked down the long, carpeted hallway, Eddie noticed a plate covered in tinfoil outside one door, dry cleaning hanging from doorknobs, casserole dishes outside several doors, and a cake in front of another. He stooped to read a Post-it note stuck to a casserole dish: "From Angie" with a heart drawn in red ink.

"Bobby told the truth when he said the women would do anything to get a man."

"This floor is euphemistically called the 'Boys' Dorm' because there are more men on this floor than any other." He put a hand to the wall to steady himself.

"Surviving into old age is like winning the lottery."

"We are born alone and we die alone and, in neither case, do we have any say in the matter. In between, no one wants to live alone, Eddie."

They continued down the hallway and Eddie inquired about Donald's health. "Nothing serious, I hope."

"Nah, I just caught a bug or something."

Eddie was pretty sure that was a lie.

✳ ✳ ✳

The ballroom had been decorated to look like a '70s disco dance hall with dimmed overhead lighting and spotlights aimed at silver mirrored balls strung from the ceiling. Serving tables along one wall held punch bowls and snack trays. A DJ played Donna Summer's music. Women in dresses conversed in small groups or danced with each other. The few men in the room stood around the edges of the dance floor in their powder blue and salmon-colored sport coats and their gray nurses' shoes and waited for women to come off the dance floor. The scene reminded Eddie of the CYO dances of his high school years, and that triggered another thought: *These people aren't old, only their bodies are old.* Inside their failing shells, old people still housed the brains and personalities of the athletes, cheerleaders, students, junior executives, and young parents they had been in their teens and twenties.

Eddie moved to the refreshment table and caught Karen dumping a full bottle of vodka into one of the bowls. "You the bartender?" he asked.

She flashed him a mischievous look. "Gotta loosen up the boys, or it won't be fun," she said. "Wanna dance with me?"

Karen wore a tight-fitting floral print dress that accentuated her slender frame. Few women other than Karen had worn high heels.

"Sure."

Eddie took Karen's hand and led her onto the floor. After a moment, the DJ played the Bee Gees' "Stayin' Alive" and he found it easy to recall his disco moves. Karen's exaggerated movements weren't always in rhythm with the music, but she enjoyed herself.

Eddie started off the floor to give Karen a break, but she held him in place as "How Deep Is Your Love" began playing.

Karen leaned into him to steady herself and he wrapped an arm around her, fearing she may have had one too many vodka-spiked drinks from the punch bowl. Eddie was saved embarrassment when a handsome man with a full head of salt and pepper hair and a toothy grin cut in.

Eddie moved to the refreshment table and was joined by Susan who dipped a refill of her punch.

"You must have been a lady killer with your dance moves," she said.

"Sam and I liked to dance. Good exercise."

"At our age, women might mistake it for foreplay."

"Karen's partner looks like the lady killer."

"For sure. That's Ralph, the Palm Haven raconteur."

"Seems like a good target for Karen."

"Oh, she's already been down that path." Susan sighed. "I'd better find my husband. He'll get jealous if I go missing too long."

Eddie strolled to the drinks table and scooped himself a glass of the spiked punch. He winced as he took a sip. There was nothing subtle about the alcohol in the punch. He spotted Karen dancing with a spry fellow in a powder blue blazer. The lothario was nowhere to be seen, probably in some lucky girl's bed. As Eddie watched the dancers, he spotted the suspicious man he had run into in Donna Roberts's room. He wasn't very subtle as he worked the crowd—if it walks like a duck, swims like a duck, and quacks like a duck, it's a detective. The man interjected himself into groups and had brief conversations that typically ended with head shaking. He didn't dance with anyone.

Not wanting to be the detective's next target, Eddie slipped out the door.

He sipped a nightcap as he told Sam about the man who questioned partiers at the dance. "I think the DEA lied to Lance and put a guy in here undercover. Which means I'm in a race to break the case."

"When it comes to catching fish, my money is always on you," Sam said.

Tucker Carlyle's money had been on him in Vietnam. Eddie was struck by the similarities between that case and this one. Like his three useless leads at Palm Haven, Vietnam had started with fruitless visits to remote Green Beret camps. He told Sam about those camps now.

Chapter Eight

... Then

From the air, Dak Seang looked like my preconception of a Special Forces camp—a relatively small, square compound, perched on hilly ground in a valley overlooked by green mountains. However, the fortifications here differed from what I had seen at Dak To. Trenches dug "titty deep" and topped with sandbags lined the entire perimeter of the camp. Passageways led from the trenches to underground bunkers set into hillsides. On one side of the camp, the bunkers were large. On the other sides, they were small. Above ground, a gaggle of metal-roofed hootches fortified with sandbags huddled in the center of the camp. I saw an airstrip beyond the northern perimeter.

Our pilot landed in a clearing down a slope outside the eastern perimeter.

"Airstrip is too dangerous," he yelled over the engine noise. "I'll be back for you at lunchtime."

When the chopper touched down, I headed for the camp-side door, but the crew chief caught me and pushed me in the other direction. "Never exit a chopper uphill," he shouted into my ear. Then he twirled his hand over his head. The rotors! Of course.

The chopper lifted off and we waited for Baker to move. When he did, he ran full speed up the hill, slithered through the "safe spot" in the wire, and sprinted across an open field to a large bunker at the edge of the group of above-ground buildings. He dove into the bunker, and we hustled after him.

A laughing man, raw-boned, with hair that wanted to be blond and the beginnings of a legitimate beard, walked up to us and said, "Welcome to paradise. I'm Captain Schmidt. Carl."

Schmidt hadn't dressed for company. He wore a filthy army green T-shirt above fatigue pants. As I looked around the space, I noted that the other men were either bare-chested or wearing sweat-stained T-shirts. Most wore boonie hats. None of the Green Berets wore camo or a helmet or a flak jacket. Carlyle and I looked like kids playing war in our backyard. I removed my helmet and ran a hand through my G.I. haircut but kept the flak vest tight around my core.

The bunker smelled of male perspiration, cigarette smoke, and over-heated electronics. Desks had been built into one wall. Folding tables held radio gear, their antennae poking through holes in the roof of the bunker. No one stood guard at the firing slits that faced all four directions. The handful of men in the bunker paused from their duties to listen to our conversation.

"We're not under attack," Schmidt said, "but we are confined to the trenches and bunkers. The NVA drops about twenty rounds a day on us, odd hours, no rhythm to it. We're within range of the 152mm cannons at the NVA's Base Camp 609, just across the border in Cambodia."

"So we can't browse around the camp?" I asked, hoping his answer would be negative.

The heavyset, older soldier stood up and said, "I'm Master Sergeant Gordon. I'll take you around the perimeter in the trenches. You can see what you need to see from there."

"Maybe we can start with your property book," I said.

That prompted a chorus of laughter.

"A-teams don't keep property books, Chief," Gordon said.

A property book is a unit's onsite record of equipment balances, serial numbers, etc. I had thought every Army unit kept a property book. "Do you keep records of your orders and receipts?"

"All the orders are submitted by the B-team," Baker said. "They have the files."

"When the stuff gets here, we use it," Gordon said.

As I had surmised, Barlow, the B-team leader, submitted all the requisitions and maintained or hid all the files.

"Let's look around before our ride comes back for us," Baker said.

Baker took Carlyle by the elbow and ushered him toward the passageway to the trenches. Gordon stuck with me as we trailed behind the captains.

Gordon lit a cigar. "Can't smoke at night. Snipers in those hills zero in on the burning tip."

I put my helmet on and resisted the urge to stoop below the sandbag level. At the intersection with the perimeter trench, we turned left in front of a long line of the large bunkers. Before we had walked ten feet, I heard a baby cry. I stopped and gave Gordon a quizzical look. He just puffed on his cigar and walked ahead. A few feet farther along the trench, I heard the baby again. A passageway cut into the red earth led to the bunker's entrance. Turned sideways, I crab-walked to the bunker's entrance. I could now hear several low voices speaking a language I had not heard before. I stepped into the bunker and let my eyes adjust to the combination of ambient light from the firing slit and the red, white, and green Christmas lights strung around the ceiling. Women and children sitting on their haunches covered the floor of the bunker. A native man in camo fatigues leaned against the wall. The bunker smelled of raw earth and cooking rice. The Montagnards stared passively at me until I turned and left the bunker.

"That's the camp commander's bunker," Gordon explained.

"Captain Schmidt has a baby?"

Gordon laughed at me. "Captain Schmidt isn't the camp commander. Every base camp has a Montagnard commander. We're guests who train and advise them."

"It's full of women and kids."

"Of course. One of the perks of being a Montagnard soldier is that their families can live in the camps with them, get medical care and food."

"I heard that they eat snakes and dogs."

"The snakes are pretty good, but I draw the line at dogs. Their primary diet is fish from the river. They catch them by blowing them out of the water with hand grenades."

I gave Gordon a boys-will-be-boys chuckle. Carlyle and Baker were well ahead of us, so we began walking again. We passed a group of Montagnard soldiers standing in the trench, watching the countryside. Two of them held M-16 rifles.

"They're not supposed to have M-16s," I said.

"Left over from U.S. casualties. If the Yards were fighting for you, you'd want them to have M-16s."

Farther down the line, I smelled something rotten. A light-yellow blanket that appeared to have snakes slithering beneath it covered a shapeless lump tangled in the concertina. When I got closer, I realized it was a long-dead body covered with swarming maggots.

"This guy crawled around mines and Claymores, snuck through four rolls of concertina wire. Took all night and then we shot him. Next morning, we found he's the barber who's been coming to camp once a week. We leave the bodies in the wire to discourage the next guy who wants to fuck us up."

"That's disgusting."

"You ever kill a man, Chief?"

"No, and I hope I don't have to."

"Getting a kill out here is no different from shooting a deer back home. We're hunters and when we kill the prey, we celebrate. There's another interesting example just ahead."

The interesting example was two men in blood-soaked military uniforms side by side in the wire. They were tied together at their wrists. "What the hell?"

"Sappers," Gordon said. "They tie them together to discourage defection."

We passed more Yards standing guard with M-16s. This time I took out Tucker's Nikon and focused on the soldiers. The Yards smiled and posed for the picture.

"I guess you've had a lot of casualties," I said to Gordon.

Gordon was unfazed by my sarcasm. He gave me a one-shouldered shrug and moved on.

"Aren't you worried that arming FULRO will lead to revolt?" I said to his back.

He stopped. "FULRO? So that's what's got MAC-V's panties in a wad? There was a rebellion back in 1964, but the Yards have made peace with the government. Besides, the radical Yards are from the Bahnar and Rhade tribes. Ours are Xo Dang." He began walking again.

I hurried after Gordon and said, "Tell me about your mission. You seem like sitting ducks out here."

He paused to relight his cigar, giving it a couple of puffs to get it going. "We do recon patrols, looking for the NVA and their supply lines. We set booby traps and ambushes. We've mined all the roads leading to the camp. Of course, we do the whole psy-ops thing with Chieu Hoi cards and leaflet drops."

I knew that Chieu Hoi cards were Get-Out-of-Jail-Free cards for North Vietnamese deserters. "You drop the Chieu Hoi cards from helicopters?"

Gordon chuckled. "We do that, but a leaflet drop is when we toss dead NVA bodies onto NVA positions. It's bad for their morale."

I laughed along with him. "Are you winning the war?"

Gordon blew smoke and thought about my question. "We could win if we had U.S. infantry support. When our 4th Infantry Division was stationed at Ben Het, we were winning. We're supposed to get an ARVN Division as part of the 'Vietnamization' strategy but they haven't showed up. Nixon has caved into Jane Fonda. The Yards are really our last hope."

We moved from the end of the row of large family bunkers to a perpendicular row of small fighting bunkers facing the airstrip. Carlyle and Baker were halfway down the row, facing the airstrip and gazing at the sky. I asked Gordon why.

He checked his plastic Army-issue watch. "About time for resupply," Gordon said, chomping on the stub of his cigar.

The supply drop came in the form of a twin-engine C-7 Caribou that floated low over the airstrip and dropped netted bags of boxes hanging from small parachutes. Immediately there were shouts and cheers from the Yards in the trench and they climbed over the sandbags and through the wire to rush to the flight line. Mingled among them were a few Vietnamese soldiers in proper uniforms and berets, carrying M-16 rifles.

We watched as the uniformed soldiers formed a cordon around the supply bags and pointed their weapons at the Yards, who kept their distance. A couple of the uniformed soldiers then sorted through the supplies, setting certain boxes aside.

"What's going on?" I asked. "Who are those guys?"

"LLDB, the South Vietnamese Special Forces. They have a team of eight stationed with each of our A-teams and they operate a canteen on each Special Forces camp where the Yards can get a haircut, buy food, cigarettes, or beer."

"They're selling American supplies to the Yards?"

"Don't fret over it. We make sure the Yards get enough supplies and the LLDB get what they want and make a little money. It's the cost of doing business."

I did fret over it and took pictures of it. Soon the LLDB had completed its cherry-picking and the Yards humped the remaining boxes back to the camp while the LLDB carried their precious allotment of goodies.

We continued our tour past the firing bunkers where Yards opened and distributed supplies to the bunkers. On the western side of the camp, we had a good view of the aboveground buildings in the camp. Gordon played tour guide.

"Mess hall, team house, barracks, dispensary," he said, pointing with his cigar stub.

We caught up to Baker and Carlyle in the command bunker and thanked Captain Schmidt for his cooperation.

✳ ✳ ✳

The northernmost outpost of the Central Highlands defense, Dak Pek's circuitous perimeter encompassed seven hills just west of a shallow stream called the Dak Polo River. Three Special Forces A-teams, their battalions of Montagnards, plus an artillery battalion and an assault helicopter company occupied Dak Pek, each unit perched on its own hill.

In the command bunker, we ate a C-ration lunch, cooked over ignited chunks of C4 explosive, accompanied by cans of beer.

"Hamm's is the best beer because it comes in aluminum cans and can be cooled in the river," a Green Beret said. "The other brands are in steel cans, and you can never get them cold."

"Have to drink beer," someone said, "because the grape juice will give you the shits."

"Yeah, but the peanut butter will stop you up again," someone else said.

Everyone laughed. After lunch, we were shepherded to the artillery hill where we witnessed an outgoing firing mission that caused plumes of gray smoke to rise in the distance. An A-team captain said that an NVA Battalion had been spotted out there. Carlyle seemed aloof, distracted, and disinterested. While the rest of the retinue watched the artillery mission, I swung my binoculars around the camp to look for possible evidence. A long line of Montagnard wives and children waited patiently outside the camp dispensary, where the A-team medic had an uncontrolled pharmacy, complete with opiates.

At the front gate, two Army ¾ ton trucks, their beds canopied with canvas, rolled into the camp. They proceeded to a storage shed where they were loaded with supplies. The men on the trucks were natives with white-whiskered faces, too old for military service but not too old to load up on U.S. supplies. I read the trucks' serial numbers through my binoculars and found them on the Barlow equipment list. After loading, the trucks departed through the front gate.

I nudged an NCO standing beside me. "Have you had any FULRO activity on this camp?"

"Nah," he said. "FULRO is more a rumor than a real thing these days."

When we departed, the smiles and handshakes made me feel like a long-lost relative who had come from far away for a rare visit.

＊＊＊

Back at Dak To, Baker left us to ourselves, and we repeated the lukewarm shower and Army field chow dinner of the previous night. Although we had a table to ourselves, we ate in silence, and no one approached us to make friends. Too humid to stay inside our airless tent, we sat on ammo boxes and leaned back against a pile of sandbags as night fell over the camp. Carlyle stuffed his cheek with tobacco, and I wished I had borrowed one of Gordon's cigars. I wished I had a can of Hamm's beer too.

"Can we go home now? I took a lot of pictures of the Yards with M-16s, M-60s, unauthorized vehicles," I said.

Carlyle spat juice into the dirt. "Maybe ten percent of the Yards had M-16s. That's not a revolution, Kovacs. A few vehicles won't give any ARVN general a hard-on."

"At Dak Pek, villagers came into the camp in vehicles on Barlow's list and loaded up with supplies. They drove back out the gate."

"Bribing local village chiefs is routine. It's called 'civic action.' Today was a setup, Kovacs. They gave us an arranged tour of a theme park."

I absorbed my first day on an investigative team and concluded that I had a lot to learn. "They think we're really stupid."

"They think I'm stupid, but they don't know I have you."

He went inside the tent, but I remained seated on my ammo boxes. I tried to find words for how I felt. Naïve and gullible were obvious. Angry came next. Then I thought about how it felt to sit on ammo boxes in a Special Forces compound in enemy territory on the other side of the world. "Comfortable" and "relaxed" weren't right. I settled on "resigned to my fate" and "accustomed" to this place on the earth. A certain acceptance of my circumstance settled on my shoulders like a heavy wet blanket.

I compared my situation to that of my father in World War II. He had been trapped in a steel can hundreds of meters below the surface of the ocean hoping the next depth charge didn't gash a hole in his submarine while I was trapped on a couple of square miles of dirt hoping the next artillery shell didn't rip my guts out. I felt I had achieved some sort of equality.

The complexity and confusion and disorganization and political wrangling in this war were startling and fundamentally troubling. The men directing this war weren't exactly General Patton directing tank traffic around a quagmire in France. That war had been so simple—one paramount bad guy to defeat.

My head tilted back, I gazed at the sky. Out here, in the middle of the jungle, away from city lights and air pollution, the sky was a black backdrop for a dense array of brilliant sparkles. Millions or billions of stars that couldn't have gotten there by accident. I found it incomprehensible that death was the flick of a light switch and that my consciousness would simply cease to exist. There had to be a God. I asked Him to spare my life. That night I ignored the sounds of war and slept in my underwear.

✳ ✳ ✳

"This will have to be fast," Baker said. "In and out. Don't wanna be there if the shit hits the fan."

This morning Baker wore a helmet and flak vest which accelerated my adrenalin flow. Nine miles from the Cambodian border, our slick approached Ben Het low and fast, past the perimeter and over an open area where the pilot raised the chopper's nose to slow it down, like a rider jerking tight the reins on a horse. When the pilot had the chopper level and moving at walking speed, Baker jumped, so Carlyle jumped, and I got the hint and dropped out of the Huey. I tried to stop myself when my feet hit the ground, but my momentum carried me in the direction of the chopper's flight, and I toppled forward and rolled in the dirt. Before I got to my feet, the chopper had flown away.

Baker seemed to know where to go, so we followed him. We passed shell craters and hootches turned to kindling, buildings ripped into sharp blades of metal, and a collection of Asian men sitting on bunkers, cradling M-16 rifles. Instinctively I had categorized the men as "Asian" rather than Montagnard because they looked different facially and their uniforms were the first camo I had seen in Vietnam. Nearby two white men in jungle camo, one dark-haired with a long narrow face and the other blond with a square head, noted our passing with a look that said, "Don't stop and don't ask."

Farther along, Montagnards rolled wheeled carts loaded with artillery shells and boxes of ammo toward a bunker where other Montagnards were unloading the carts and taking the ammunition below ground. Beyond the perimeter, I saw fire-blackened tree trunks without branches standing on fire-blackened ground.

We walked into a collection of tents and bunkers, and Baker chose a bunker filled with desks and radio equipment. The earth smelled freshly dug. The A-team commander, Captain Tanner, and his executive officer, First Lieutenant Williams, were waiting for us. A Montagnard sat on an empty desk and an NCO wearing headphones sat at a desk heaped with radio equipment. Tanner wore a tattered uniform and looked like he hadn't showered in weeks. Williams had smears of camo paint fading into his dark skin. Tanner indicated that the Montagnard was his interpreter.

Three rolling desk chairs had been arranged in front of a flip chart. We were offered bitter camp coffee, which I regretted accepting. Tanner said we wouldn't be allowed to tour the camp as he expected incoming shelling to continue all day, so he had prepared a briefing. Carlyle asked if Major Daniels, the B-team executive officer, would join us, and Tanner reported that the major had left for Vu Dong, the camp just to the south that now seemed to be the NVA's primary target.

He walked us through the first page of the flip chart, which included a diagram of the camp and the NVA attacks. This briefing seemed better suited to a visit by brass than for a CID investigation.

A discussion ensued, led by Baker, about air support, casualties, remedial actions, and so forth. Having become a cynic, I interpreted the discussion to be a stage play at another theme park.

Tanner flipped to the next page, a list of his equipment: howitzers, recoilless rifles, mortars, anti-tank rockets, jeeps, trucks, and 4 M-48 Patton tanks.

Except for the tanks, Tanner's list contained no unauthorized equipment. Ten Patton tanks, formidable beasts with 90mm guns, were on the Barlow list. "Where did the Patton tanks come from?" I asked.

He shrugged. "They showed up one day and we used them."

"Do you have the serial numbers of the tanks?"

"No, why would I?"

"Where are they?" Carlyle asked.

"They're positioned along the northern perimeter guarding the approach to the airstrip," Tanner said. "NVA tanks would come that way. The Rangers are manning the tanks because the Yards don't know how to drive them. The tanks get shelled every day."

"Do your Yards have M-16s?" I asked.

Unperturbed, Tanner said, "Some. And now quite a few captured AK-47s. We're supposed to send captured weapons to Group HQ in Nha Trang, but then some clerk would steal them and take them back to the world as souvenirs, so we keep them and use them."

How were we supposed to investigate equipment abuses when weapons flowed from place to place without regard for the regulations cooked up by peacetime desk jockeys?

I asked for directions to the latrine. "This coffee goes right through me."

Tanner asked his interpreter to show me the way.

I followed the interpreter, thin as a whisper, past the A-team tents. I could feel myself changing after just three days in the boonies. I still feared a gruesome death, but the only way back to the world was to complete this investigation. When my guide turned left toward the latrine, I continued toward the strange Asians. The interpreter hustled after me and grabbed my shirt sleeve to stop me.

"No go. No go," he screamed.

I shook him off and walked up to three of the camouflaged fighters smoking and lounging on a bunker firing slit.

"Ask them who they are," I said to my interpreter.

He didn't have to ask the men. "They are Khmer Serei. Cambodians."

"Two white men are with them. Are they Green Berets?"

The interpreter hesitated. "CIA. They come from Tan Canh."

So CIA spooks and Cambodians had replaced the Green Berets at the former Dak To camp.

"Take me to the tanks."

Genuine fear appeared on the thin brown man's face. He made an X with his arms in front of his chest and then waved them back and forth, crossing and uncrossing them several times. "No go. Dangerous." Then he cocked his head as though listening for something. Next, I heard multiple shouts of "Incoming!"

The little interpreter grabbed the nape of my neck with surprising strength and dragged me toward the command bunker. A blast shook the ground and I heard the pings of shrapnel collide with metal. I didn't need any more encouragement. Running in a crouch, I followed the interpreter to the bunker and down its earthen steps.

"Took you long enough," Baker said as I entered the tent.

"Everything come out okay, Chief?" Williams asked.

That provoked a chuckle from Tanner.

These guys are either deaf or crazy, I thought. I couldn't speak so I pointed up the steps and asked a question with my facial expression.

"We relocated the command bunker to this location and they don't know it," Tanner said.

"It's artillery coming from their base camp in Cambodia, not rockets from the field, so not to worry," Williams said.

With each of the next four explosions, I flinched and ducked while the others remained composed. What followed was a surreal silence until the RTO, listening to his headset, reported, "No casualties."

After a couple of minutes, Tanner slapped his knees. "Guess that's it for now. Let's finish up so you guys can go home."

"You didn't mention the Khmer Serei," I said to Tanner.

"They belong to the CIA, not us," he said.

"What are they doing up here?"

Tanner shrugged. "Who knows? They come and go as they please."

Out of patience, with me as well as with Tanner, Tucker said, "Let's un-ass this joint."

Baker called for our chopper, and we made the short trip back to Dak To.

Chapter Nine

... Now

Once again, Eddie visited Lucy and Janice while most residents ate breakfast. As instructed, Janice had dressed for her role in today's activities. Her long blond hair now hung loose, covering her shaved sides, and softening her features. Dressed in khaki slacks and a black golf shirt with her Waffle House name tag on her left breast, she almost looked like a member of the staff. Lucy, on the other hand, sat on the edge of a living room chair with a worried look on her face.

"A man was just here, asking all sorts of questions," Janice said. "He frightened Lucy."

Eddie asked her to describe the man, although it was unnecessary. Janice described the man with the clipboard who had visited Donna Roberts, the man who had questioned Madeleine at the dance.

"What did you tell him?"

"Not a damned thing."

"Good. I don't know what that guy is up to."

"Are we going ahead with the plan?" Janice looked neither scared nor particularly confident.

Eddie guessed the detective would interview Gerry Matthews next, meaning he would be on the third floor. "Yes. Start your rounds now, while everyone is out of their rooms and the orderlies and nurses are preoccupied with transportation. Don't let Mr. Crew Cut see what you're doing."

Janice did her best imitation of a brave soldier ordered to charge a hill. "I'm on it," she said, and she left to visit the targeted fourth-floor rooms.

He stopped at the nurses' station and asked Letitia if she'd seen Dr. Banerjee around.

"Nope," she said. "The nurses generally let him know when a prescription needs to be changed. I'll let you know when he's in the building."

✳ ✳ ✳

Eddie hid in his apartment all afternoon, watching mind-wrecking daytime TV. He didn't want some nosey resident telling the authorities that he had been snooping around the assisted living wing before the fateful events that would unfold that evening. Before he left for dinner, he gave his good luck jar a healthy shake.

When he arrived at the dinner table, he absorbed some playful joshing from Madeleine for dancing with Karen. Susan or Bobby tattled on him.

"Just good exercise," he said.

Bobby's usual seat was unoccupied. "Where's Bobby?" Eddie asked Susan.

"He plays cards with his buddies in Savannah twice a month," Susan said. "That's what he says anyway. For all I know, he has a mistress."

"It's steak night, so Bobby is missing out," Madeleine said.

Once a month, the Palm Haven kitchen departed from its bland menu to reward residents for surviving another thirty days.

As they waited for their food, Eddie tested Cevert. He handed the doctor three pill vials. "You said you'd help with my prescriptions."

Cevert examined the prescriptions: one for a statin to control cholesterol, an antihistamine to relieve Eddie's grass and pollen allergies, and one for the painkiller Hydrocodone.

Cevert frowned. "I'll turn these two in tomorrow morning and you can pick them up at the pharmacy window," he said, holding the innocent vials in his right hand. "This one," he said as he shook the Hydrocodone vial at Eddie, "I can't fill for you."

"How come?"

"It's a narcotic and you're not my patient."

Eddie acted surprised. "It's for my back pain, the result of my auto accident."

"Michael is opposed to opioids so he doesn't prescribe them for anyone," Madeleine said.

"Take some Tylenol. It's safer," Cevert said.

Cevert stretched his hand and the vial in front of Madeleine, and Eddie had no choice except to take it back. His ploy to trap Cevert had failed. Cevert smiled as though he had won a chess game.

As they carved and chewed their beef, Susan said, "Bobby asked me to lead the discussion tonight. Is there life on other planets?"

"Nope. Homo Sapiens is God's only creation," Donald said. "He only sent His Son to earth. End of discussion."

"What about those Navy pilots in San Diego?"

"What about all the wackos who've been abducted?" Donald said with a smirk.

"Don't hold your breath waiting for clear video of flying saucers," Michael said.

"Airline pilots have seen them," Susan said.

"While their hands were up the skirts of stewardesses," Michael said and everyone snickered.

"We send radio signals into the ether and we never get an answer," Madeleine said.

"You'll see how wrong you are when the little green men get here," Susan said.

"The little green men will send androids—robots—on the long, dangerous missions to earth, just like we send androids to Mars and Jupiter," Eddie said to Susan. "We'll never meet the little green men because they'll come after the robots conquer us."

Without Bobby to organize the group, Michael and Susan wandered away from the table after dessert. Donald headed shakily to the independent living elevators.

Madeleine took Eddie's arm and said, "Walk me to the to my elevator." When the doors opened on an empty car, she leaned close and kissed his lips. She gave him a girlish laugh and danced into the elevator. Eddie felt like a bug caught in a spider's web.

He took the escalator down and walked out the front entrance onto a veranda the width of a football field. The entrance drive came from his right and ended in a turnaround under a columned portico. Uniformed young men—white jackets, black trousers—waited to assist arrivals and departures. Several six-seater golf carts loitered at the curb, ready to ferry passengers to shops, bars and restaurants on the island.

A wooden walkway led from the veranda to seagrass covered dunes and the ocean. To his left, a concrete path led to ten acres of palm trees, palmetto bushes, hibiscus, and bougainvillea. He walked through the gardens to a gazebo big enough to host a party and took a seat as a rising moon cast a dim glow on the black ocean.

✳ ✳ ✳

Eddie waited for Janice to text him that the night staff had completed bed check, then he started back to the main entrance. Marina lights lined the walkway but the garden had a creepy feeling after dark. It became creepier when Eddie heard someone running toward him. He didn't want to be noticed tonight so he stepped off the path into the bushes and waited for the jogger to pass. The young man with long, limp blond hair wore black scrubs. Maybe taking a smoke break far from the building, Eddie thought.

When the man was out of sight, Eddie walked back inside, climbed the back staircase to the fourth floor, and slipped into Lucy's room. At precisely 11:00 p.m., as Lucy Griffin snored peacefully under the influence of her mild sleeping aid, Eddie and Janice launched their assault of the assisted living wing. That morning, Janice had stolen the Xanax and Valium and Rohypnol from the fourth-floor residents, and during the dinner chaos, when residents were transported to the dining room, redistributed the sleep medications to patients' pill organizers on the third floor.

Eddie remained in Lucy's quiet room as Janice snuck into Betty Stanford's room, room 1417 near the lounge. In less than two minutes, Betty's emergency call button was activated, and Janice snuck into another room. Through Lucy's peephole, Eddie saw a nurse and the orderly run by in response to the fake emergency in Betty's room. From room to room on the fourth floor, Janice activated emergency call buttons and agitated residents who had not received their nighttime sleep medications.

Nurses and orderlies from other floors soon arrived to help quell the riot. When the third-floor nurses and orderlies burst through the fourth-floor stairwell door, Eddie and Janice trotted to the nurses' station, appropriated two wheelchairs from behind the station, and pushed them into the service elevator. They rode the elevator to the third floor and locked the doors open.

The third floor was eerily silent, its residents sedated by the medications intended for fourth-floor residents. With any luck, the third-floor staff wouldn't discover anyone missing till shift change in the morning.

Eddie and Janice rolled the chairs to Gerry's room, woke Lydia, and announced that they were escaping. Groggily and painfully slow, Lydia grasped the idea and became energized. Together, Janice and Lydia packed suitcases while Eddie lifted Gerry out of the bed and into a wheelchair. When they were ready to go, Eddie and Janice pushed Lydia and Gerry to the single back elevator. Down to the bottom floor they rode, Eddie constantly hushing Lydia, who was as thrilled as a high school girl on prom night.

Eddie left the three of them on the loading dock with the rear entrance to the home propped open and hustled to his car. This was the most dangerous part of the operation, the part where they could be discovered before they got away. He backed the Ford Bronco up to the facility's back entrance so Lydia could climb into the back seat as Eddie helped Gerry into the passenger seat, which Eddie coaxed into a reclining position. Before he rushed away, Eddie opened the Bronco's cargo door, folded both wheelchairs, and stowed them in the Bronco. *Don't give the bastards any help in figuring this out*, he thought. Janice removed the doorstop and moved back inside the building. In his rearview mirror, Eddie saw her wave as he drove away. Minutes later, she texted him that she was safely hidden in his apartment.

No one spoke until Eddie took the entrance ramp to I-20 West and headed to Lydia's sister's home in Statesboro.

Then Lydia blurted, "A man came asking questions today. Said his name was Stevenson."

Eddie had guessed correctly; the detective had the same list of names that Eddie had. "What did you tell him?"

With the conviction of her eighty-plus years, she said, "That the Jew doctor in the room next to us is up to somethin'."

That depressed Eddie. "What did Gerry tell him?"

"Nothin'. Gerry was asleep. Stevenson said he'd come back when Gerry could talk."

"I'da told him that the Jew is killing people," Gerry blurted. "Like the Jews killed Jesus."

Damn fortunate Gerry hadn't told Stevenson this whopper. "I think what you saw, Gerry, was Jacob Hoffman having a heart attack. He died in Doctor Cevert's office."

"He weren't having no heart attack. He was fresh as a daisy till the Jew killed him."

"Okay, Gerry, I'll check it out."

"Nobody believes me but it happened before. That woman, what's her name, was killed by the Jew last year."

"Celia Dawkins," Lydia said.

"Yeah, that one, same as this one. Them two old bitties know it, too."

Eddie decided to add Lipstick Lady and Lilac Lady to his list of leads to interrogate. But the sheriff had said, "The Drug Enforcement Agency suspects that a string of mysterious deaths at Palm Haven had been caused by opioid overdoses and then covered up." Jacob Hoffman exhibited no signs of drug overdose.

"Okay, Gerry and Lydia, this is important information but do not tell anyone else about it until I come back for you. Got it?"

"Yes, sir," Lydia said.

Gerry did not speak.

On the seventy-two-mile trip he tutored Lydia: find Gerry a good doctor; get a proper diagnosis; get appropriate medications; do not leave the sister's house. Lydia treated it like a game of hide and seek, promising no one would find them.

At the sister's house, he delivered a stern admonition to Lydia's relatives. "You haven't seen or heard from Gerry or Lydia. Don't respond to anyone but me." He wrote their names and address in his little notebook.

On the way back to Palm Haven, Eddie rolled the windows down and turned the radio volume up to keep himself awake. No matter the song on the air, the Allman Brother's plaintive "Statesboro Blues" played in his head. That he had outwitted Cevert, pleased him; that he had liberated Gerry so he could rest among family gave him a self-righteous glow; but he had to admit that his investigation was off track. He had found no opioids and identified no drug dealers. He could let Mr. Crew Cut waste his time chasing ghosts. He could go back to Florida, fish the Intracoastal Waterway and play golf at the Bellaire Country Club. But something else was going on at Palm Haven and his detective antennae were twitching.

At the parking lot, he repeated his trick with electrical tape and parked his Bronco back in slot 202 where it belonged.

He was about to text Janice to let him in the loading dock door when two blue-garbed nurses came out and stepped onto the loading platform. He had no choice but to wait for the nurses to disappear before he could reenter the building. Eddie stayed in the shadows and crouched between two cars. A waiflike nurse with a mass of strawberry blond curls lit a cigarette. The other nurse danced down the steps and hurried to the parking lot. Rail thin, with unruly black hair, the nurse weaved her way to a cheap silver compact car and fumbled with her car keys.

The overhead light came on when she opened her car door and got into the driver's seat. Moving as though he were dodging bullets in Vietnam, Eddie scurried past three car grills. Bent over the hood of the car next to the nurse, he watched her dig in her purse for what looked like a child's lollipop on a stick. Eddie recognized it immediately. Without hesitation, the nurse ripped the packaging open and shoved the stick into her mouth. She tilted her seat back, and closed her eyes, seemingly in newfound ecstasy.

Over his shoulder, he saw the redhead stub out her cigarette and reenter the building. On his smartphone he opened the camera app. He rushed to the nurse's passenger door and climbed inside. The nurse jerked toward her door, pulled the sucker out of her mouth, and held it away from him like a kid who didn't want a bully to steal her treat.

"Say cheese!" He snapped a picture.

"What the hell?" she screamed. "Get out of here!"

Eddie punched the door lock button and heard a satisfying pair of clicks. "Now with a smile." He snapped a second photo as she lunged at his phone. She missed but pummeled his shoulder.

He whirled around and grabbed her right wrist roughly and gave her an evil smile. "Where'd you get the Fentanyl?"

Her dark eyes glared at him from a face as thin as the rest of her. "None of your business." She made the mistake of waving the Fentanyl lollipop in the air as she spoke. He snatched it out of her hand.

"Hey! Gimme that."

He held it away from her, then slid it back into its packaging. "This," he said, indicating the stick she had sucked, "has your slobbering DNA all over it." He slipped it into a pocket. "Get me some Fentanyl or I'll report your ass to management. You'll lose your license, start buying on the street, and someday you'll overdose."

The nurse's eyes grew wide in astonishment. "You want to buy my drugs?"

"Oh, no, little lady. I'm not buying from an addict." He waggled a finger back and forth. "I want to buy from your connection."

The nurse began to cry. "I don't do this all the time. We just had a bad night."

"I imagine you did," Eddie said with a chuckle.

He grabbed her purse and rummaged through it. He pulled her driver's license out of its plasticine shield and snapped a picture of it. "My, my," he said when he found another Fentanyl stick. "Which floor are you on, Nurse Barbara Meacham?"

"Three."

"You work tomorrow?"

"Yes, we rotate two days on and two days off."

"Perfect. Tomorrow night you invent a reason to bring your connection to room 1409 at ten p.m. Got it?"

"I can't do that. He'll kill me."

"He won't kill you; you're bringing him a new customer." Eddie waved the unopened package at her. "Do me the favor and you can have your little sweet stick, but I do recommend that you wait till you're home to suck the lollipop. Too dangerous out in the parking lot where anyone could catch you."

Nurse Meacham went pale. "I can't."

"Aw. Hubby doesn't know. And the little kiddies would be surprised to learn that Mommy is an addict."

Nurse Meacham broke down and wailed.

Now Eddie had a better idea to protect Janice and confuse anyone who might check the electronic records to see who had entered the building. "Let me in the back door and you can have this one." He shook the unopened Fentanyl in Nurse Meacham's face.

Confused but willing to do anything for the fix, Meachum led him up the ramp and swiped her keycard to open the back door. He handed Barbara the Fentanyl stick and she scurried away like a sewer rat with a rotten apple core. "The Road to Perdition," Eddie muttered as he entered the building and crept to the safety of his temporary apartment. Janice swung the door open wearing one of his T-shirts and quite possibly nothing else.

"How did you get in?"

"A nice nurse opened the door for me."

Janice howled with glee. "We did it!"

"Keep your voice down," he shushed her, but he grinned too. Finally he had a real lead he could trace back to one of the two suspicious doctors.

She jumped into his arms for a hug and kissed him on the cheek. He eased out of her grasp and said, "Anybody come looking for me while I was gone?"

"Nope. Took them two hours to get everyone to sleep on Lucy's floor. Is Gerry safe?"

"Snug as a bug in a rug."

"You're a good man, Charley Brown."

He just smiled and imagined Janice as the daughter he never had. "I'll take the couch tonight and you can have the bed. First thing in the morning, whether I'm awake or not, go back up to Lucy's room as though you'd just arrived."

"Yes, sir." She saluted him, turned, and trotted to the bedroom.

After Janice closed the bedroom door, Eddie placed Meachum's Fentanyl lollipop in another plastic bag and sealed it. He wrote a note detailing the time and place of its seizure and rubber banded it to the plastic bag. Using his P-38, he opened the return vent and placed the Fentanyl inside. He tore off the notebook page on which he had written Gerry's new address and added it to his stash. The sheriff and the detective had followed irrelevant complaints and missed the real perpetrators—doctors and nurses.

Regretting that his earbuds were behind Janice's closed bedroom door, he kicked off his shoes and collapsed on the couch in his clothes. Unable to speak to Sam's picture he sent her a thought: "I've caught a minnow, Sweetheart. First the minnow, then the baitfish, and then the trophy fish." As he squirmed to find comfort on the lumpy couch, he told Sam that his Vietnam investigation could have ended with the whitewashed report MAC-V wanted based on visits to three staged Green Beret camps, but he let his ego get in the way. "This was the beginning of my downfall, Sam."

Chapter Ten

... Then

Early the next morning, Baker found us in the mess tent. "Get your shit and follow me."

"Vu Dong?" Carlyle said.

"You can give your final report to Colonel Barlow and then go back to Saigon."

As we stuffed our belongings into our rucksacks, Carlyle ordered me to remain silent during our interview with LTC Barlow. "Let me do the talking," he said. Excitement shone brightly in his eyes. "He's our suspect so we can't divulge what we know."

Barlow leaned back in his swivel chair behind a metal desk in the command tent and removed Army-issue glasses to examine us as we came through the tent opening. Carlyle marched to the desk, came to attention, and saluted. I moved beside Carlyle and copied his salute.

"Chief Carlyle and Chief Kovacs of CID reporting, sir," Carlyle said.

Younger than I expected, perhaps late thirties, with brushed black hair, dark blue eyes, and peeling skin on his sunburned nose, Barlow wore starched jungle fatigues with the sleeves rolled above his elbows. "At ease," he said. When he reached out his left hand and waggled his fingers, I noted the West Point ring where a man's wedding band should be. "Let me have your report."

Carlyle nodded to me, and I pulled a copy of our report from my rucksack. This copy contained our findings in military language with copies of the pictures I had taken of various equipment violations. The exposed rolls of film, our unadulterated notes, the Barlow equipment list, and excerpts from the stolen computer code listing were in a canvas satchel around Carlyle's neck.

We waited as Barlow read the brief report. He looked up and patted the report with one tanned hand. "Good work, gentlemen. I'll cover this with my plan to fix the violations and turn it in to the 5th Special Forces Group in Nha Trang. Colonel Vandenberg will endorse it and forward to MAC-V."

"This is an interim report, sir," Carlyle said. "We still need to visit Vu Dong."

"I'm afraid that won't be possible, Mister Carlyle. An NVA attack is underway. Medevacs only to Vu Dong. Captain Baker has arranged your transport back to Long Binh."

When Carlyle loitered, Barlow adopted a stronger tone. "Dismissed, Chief."

Baker moved beside Carlyle and grabbed his arm, but Carlyle stood his ground. "We're still looking for all the unauthorized equipment you ordered, sir."

"What? Get these buffoons out of here, Baker."

Baker tugged Carlyle away from the desk, but now I disobeyed Tucker.

"One hundred thirty-two requisitions for vehicles, small arms, and weapons systems—dusters, tanks, M-60s, recoilless rifles, Howitzers, and Ontos tracked vehicles—were ordered from Long Binh using your authorization code, Colonel," I said.

Barlow jumped to his feet. "Are you accusing me of a crime, Mister?"

My mouth went dry, and I couldn't speak.

Carlyle answered for me. "He's just reporting what the computer says, Colonel."

"The computer?" Barlow bellowed. "The computer is always wrong. We never get what we're supposed to have, and you want to talk to me about a fucking computer?"

"Let us clear this up by finishing our investigation, sir," Carlyle said.

"Your investigation is over, Chief. Get this trash out of here, Baker."

Barlow leaned on his desk and growled like an attack dog as Baker grabbed Carlyle and a Green Beret lieutenant grabbed me. We were dragged out of Barlow's tent and back to ours.

"You're confined to quarters until I come back for you," Baker said.

I sat on my bunk and removed my rucksack. Carlyle paced.

"Are you going to let them disrespect you like that?" I asked.

"What are the chances the computer is wrong?" Carlyle asked.

"Zero, Tucker. The code was hacked to process Barlow's requisitions."

"We've found less than ten percent of the equipment."

"The rest has to be at Vu Dong."

Carlyle stepped to the tent flap and peeked outside. "I hate guys like Barlow," he said, almost to himself. "They climb the ranks and after a while, they begin to believe they were chosen by God to be in charge."

I wondered if I'd get my ticket back to the world if we submitted an incomplete report. "He's committing crimes, but I don't know if he's gone rogue or if the Army wants him to do it since they can't convince the Vietnamese to come up here and fight."

"Either way, this disagreement with the Vietnamese should be out in the open so it can be resolved."

"We can't go to Saigon. We have to wait for the battle to end so we can finish up at Vu Dong." I couldn't believe I said that.

"We have to do our jobs and let the chips fall where they may." Carlyle said it wistfully.

Tucker gazed at the sky as though he might find answers in the clouds, then a "dust-off," a medevac helicopter with a big white cross on its side, caught his attention as it approached the camp. He stepped outside to watch it land.

He turned back to me. "Come on. I know how to get to Vu Dong."

We double-timed to the helipad, where men covered in blood and bandages were being unloaded and carried away on stretchers. Most were

Montagnards; one was an American but not a Green Beret. Carlyle cut through the medics to the door of the chopper and hopped on board.

"What the fuck?" the crew chief yelled.

"CID," Carlyle said. "We're going to Vu Dong."

The crew chief shrugged. "It's your funeral."

I stood at the door of the chopper and froze. "Maybe I should stay here, Tucker. Someone has to tell the story if …" I let my voice trail off.

"Help me with my buddy," Tucker said. He grabbed one arm and the crew chief grabbed my other arm, and they hoisted me onto the chopper. The crew chief whirled a finger over his head, a signal to the pilot he was cleared to go, and the chopper lifted off the pad.

I thought we had flown into a charcoal gray cloud, but the acrid smell of explosives carried on a westerly breeze burned my throat and made my eyes water. The dust-off hovered above the range of small arms fire, east of a camp dotted with columns of black smoke.

"They've cut a new LZ out here somewhere," the crew chief said. "Waiting for a marker."

Suddenly, the chopper dove and threw me against the bulkhead as my body tried to catch up to the plummeting chopper. I saw it then, a puff of yellow smoke dead ahead. Yellow meant caution—not guaranteed safe as green would have indicated, but not taking fire as red would have indicated. "We fly fast and without escorts, so the Commies don't know we're coming. Busby is good at it."

I assumed Busby was our pilot.

Montagnards with M-16s surrounded the flat LZ carved out of elephant grass. The crew chief pulled us close to shout over the sound of the furiously revolving rotors.

"It's a thousand meters to the camp. The Yards will take you there."

We jumped to the ground. Two Yards lifted one stretcher onto the dust-off. An American, his eyes staring blankly, lay on the stretcher. The voluminous blood on his chest concealed his name strip. We turned our backs and held our helmets on with our hands as the chopper lifted off and headed east. The two Montagnards who had carried the litter nodded at us and pointed in the direction of the camp. We nodded back and set off with them through the tall grass and into the dense jungle. One Montagnard led and the other trailed behind Carlyle and me. Sounds of concussive explosions and sporadic rifle fire, muffled by the jungle, grew louder as we neared the camp. My nerves felt like bugs crawling under my skin.

We emerged from the jungle fifty meters short of the camp perimeter, a chicken wire fence suitable for containing a medium-sized dog in a suburban backyard. The Yards yelled something, and Yards inside the fencing yelled back. Our escorts started running across the field and we hurried after them. The Yards in the camp swung a gate open and the four of us ran through it into a makeshift medical treatment area. A Green Beret medic tended to a man lying on a folding table. The wounded man, another American soldier, writhed and screamed in pain.

Green ponchos had been laid in a row on the ground and dead bodies, teaming with flies, lay atop them. All of the dead were Montagnards.

Carlyle asked the medic for directions to the command bunker and the medic pointed to the south with a bloody suture needle. To the north and west, incoming rounds exploded with the staccato cadence of the bass drum of a marching band. We jogged past bunkers crammed with Montagnard women and children, past hootches, scarred but still standing, past collapsed tents, past dead men, legs akimbo, surprise on their faces. The noise of war, a cacophony of shouts, screams, explosions, gunfire, and cries for help, left me disoriented and appalled.

I felt the blast before I heard it. One moment I was running and the next I was on my back, out of breath, a shooting pain assailed my lower back. After the sound of the blast receded, my head filled with white noise, like radio static. Dust swirled around me, the color of a thundercloud. Confusion gripped me and jumbled my thoughts. *Why am I on the ground?* My mind struggled to recreate what had happened and make sense of it. As I caught my breath, warm liquid sluiced down my forehead into my left eye. I wiped my eye and saw the redness on my fingertips. The blood coursed down my cheek and dripped from my jawbone, leaving red splotches on my flak vest. Tentatively, I probed my forehead with two fingers and found a flap of skin and raw meat, just below the hairline.

Panic triggered a rush of adrenalin. *I have to get out of here before the next shell falls!* My helmet lay a few feet away, the brim sliced in a V by the shrapnel that had gouged my forehead. I put the helmet on and stood on wobbly legs. I couldn't see Carlyle. I called his name and heard nothing in reply, my ears numbed to sound as though stuffed with cotton. Woozy, I staggered in a circle, trying to get my bearings, my nose and mouth in the crook of my arm to avoid breathing red dust. I chose a direction and emerged from the cloud behind a firing pit where two 105mm Howitzers were lobbing shells at an unseen enemy. A Green Beret supervised teams of Montagnards, who mindlessly loaded and reloaded the cannons like men on exercise machines at a gym. The Green Beret yelled at me, but I couldn't decipher what he said.

I veered away from the Howitzers, past more bloated and decaying bodies, and into a motor pool that had become a junkyard for dozens of mangled vehicles. The vehicles were parked in revetments, but direct hits had torn the revetments to shreds. On the far side of the wreckage, a raging fire fully engulfed a Quonset hut, the greasy, roiling black smoke of burning fuel oil billowing skyward. My head began to throb and I felt a stinging sensation in my right thigh. When I checked my leg, I found sticky, coagulating blood gluing tattered fatigue pants to the outside of my leg. *You're not in shock. Rest a minute and your senses will return to normal.* I dug in my rucksack and found that Carlyle's military Nikon had been the victim of random shrapnel, but my Brownie was intact. I clicked pictures of the damaged vehicles.

Beyond the motor pool, two dusters roared past me, moving to my right. I took a picture. Assuming the dusters were heading toward the attacking NVA, I turned left. A few minutes later I found myself behind a staggered row of firing bunkers, facing a perimeter of wire just fifty meters away. The dusters had run from the perimeter, run from the fight. The NVA had dug zig-zag trenches right up to the wire. I knelt beside the nearest bunker and peered around the corner. Inside an M-60 machine gun crew and two Montagnard riflemen with M-16s smiled, thinking perhaps, I was a combat correspondent. I snapped pictures of the unauthorized weapons. I turned away from the perimeter and crouched low, moving toward what I guessed was the interior of the camp.

I was wrong again. In a clearing, six M-48 tanks, the six tanks that completed Barlow's ten-tank requisition, were lined up facing the northern perimeter and beyond it, the airstrip. I had unwittingly circled the perimeter of the camp from west to north. Montagnard fighters with M-16s crouched behind the tanks. Montagnard heads poked through the hatches on top of the turrets. I crept closer and took pictures.

The Green Beret leading the armor defense spotted me and yelled, "You lost, sir?"

"Which way is the command bunker?"

"That way," he said and pointed away from the perimeter.

"How far?"

"Almost a mile."

I turned in the direction he had pointed and double-timed around scorched clearings, warped buildings, mangled vehicles, and abandoned firing pits. I took many pictures. The sounds of exploding rockets and cannon shells faded farther and farther behind me and that made me feel almost giddy. In the smoke and in my haste, I tripped over a body and fell to the ground. I skittered away from it as though I might catch some disease. An American lay on his stomach. A black oak leaf, the insignia of a major, stared at me like one-eyed cyclops from his helmet in the dirt beside him. I inched closer to the body and saw a bloody hole in the back of his head. With two fingers, I imitated scenes from movies by feeling around his neck for the pulsating signs of life. I felt nothing. The body was still warm but inert. I rolled it over and read the name tag: Daniels, the B-detachment XO. Never before had I touched a dead person, and my immediate instinct was to run away from the awful scene, but first I took a picture.

I had run another quarter of a mile when I saw an odd, elongated, grass-covered mound, like an Indian burial mound. On one side it had been struck by a shell which had blown away the earth to expose dented but unruptured armor plating. At the far end of the mound, a shell had landed just short of the mound creating a crater and knocking a reinforced steel door off its hinges. I climbed the side of the crater and entered the dark space through the open doorway. The beam of my flashlight lit the treasure that would solve the case. I took pictures. Lots of pictures, changing rolls of film three times. Case after case of M-16s, M-60 machine guns, bazookas, flame throwers and ammo—enough equipment to arm a division of soldiers.

Throwing caution to the wind, I double-timed southward. After another quarter of a mile, I rounded a Quonset hut that had been spared by the shelling and I saw Carlyle standing in front of the command bunker.

"Thank God! I thought they got you," Carlyle said as he came up to me. He grabbed me by the shoulders and looked me over, like a mother examining her son after a playground fight. That's when I felt my third wound, marked by a splotch of blood on my right shoulder. It hadn't hurt until Tucker had grabbed it. Carlyle, on the other hand, didn't have a scratch. I must have been on the very fringe of the cannon shell's blast area. Lucky me.

He saw the blood spatters on my flak vest and poked his fingers in two tears in the nylon. He lifted my helmet to examine my forehead. "Flak vest worked but the helmet saved your life," he said.

"I've got the evidence, Tucker. I took a million pictures."

"Don't say a word about what you saw. I had a big dustup with the A-team commander. He talked to Barlow who is pissed that we're here. Give me the camera and film."

I handed him my Brownie and five rolls of exposed film which he tucked it in his messenger bag.

He wrapped his arm around me and turned me toward a hole in the red earth beside sandbags stacked three feet high in a rectangle twenty feet by thirty feet. On either side of the sandbags, deuce-and-a-half trucks with four .50 caliber machine guns mounted in each bed were manned by Montagnards. They were pointed to the north.

"I think they're called 'Grim Reapers,'" he said.

We walked down mud steps into a huge cavern at least twenty feet beneath the surface. There were too many people and not enough air. The place smelled of fetid soil and fear. Everyone wore helmets and flak jackets. A box of gas masks lay open on the floor. Along the back wall of the bunker, tables held two Collins single-sideband radios capable of encrypted Morse Code transmissions as well as voice. An FM radio for short-range voice communications with squads in the field sat beside them. Antennae snaked up through the sandbag ceiling.

Everyone shouted at everyone else. A wiry Green Beret with flecks of gray in his hair shouted at two radio operators. The radio operators, guys built like NFL linebackers, shouted into their microphones. Two other NCOs paced as they shouted into the PRC-25 radio sets they carried on their backs. In the center of the space, a Green Beret shouted at two Montagnards. Three LLDB shouted at each other. A Montagnard with an M-16 watched the approach to the bunker through a small firing slit and shouted at his god.

Carlyle led me to the corner farthest from the stairwell, where we sat on the mud floor and leaned against the earthen wall. He said that the Green Beret with the broad German forehead, sparse blond hair, and restless blue eyes was the A-team commander, Captain Meyers. He was shouting at the senior Montagnard, ostensibly the base commander, and his interpreter. Two entire companies of Montagnards had fled the camp through a tunnel they had dug under the airstrip. The Montagnard commander claimed the two missing companies were fighting the NVA, but Meyers accused the commander of saving his "cousins" for an attack on the ARVN reinforcements, if they ever came.

Carlyle filled in the blanks. "The camp commander is from the Rhade tribe and he's the nephew of the man who started FULRO in 1958. The two companies he sent outside the perimeter are Rhade, and they are armed with the best weapons. The unauthorized weapons."

Carlyle identified the other players in the bunker. The three Green Berets at the radio table were the two communications specialists—Jenkins and Cowans—and the operations sergeant, Duncan. The blond NCO with a radio pack was the liaison to the artillery battery in the hills beyond the camp, and the brown-haired NCO with a radio set on his back was the liaison for the assault helicopter company that had pulled out of here after they lost too many choppers.

"He's trying to find us a ride back to Dak To," Tucker said.

"Listen up," Duncan yelled, and conversations stopped. He walked to the center of the room, strutting like a bantam rooster. "The ARVN Regiment at Dak To has been ordered to relieve us. The Rangers have set an ambush just north of the airstrip. Gunships and fast movers are on the way. Sit tight."

As he said it, the chopper liaison NCO walked up to us, shaking his head. "The slicks can't land in the camp until reinforcements get here. A slick only holds six people, so I'm looking for something bigger, but the big ones won't come closer than the LZ outside the wire." He turned away and started a new conversation on his headset.

What did I do to deserve this? I knew the answer: I had helped Danny avoid this very situation and now I had taken his place.

I feared I would lose control of my bowels. I leaned my head against the wall and willed the pounding behind my eyes to stop. To distract myself, I tried to recall happy memories from my childhood. What would I be missing if I died here? I couldn't think of a single sweet memory that included my father. No, I thought of one, my eighth birthday, when he found someone to bring a pony to our house. Dressed like a cowboy, I rode the pony around our yard. Oh, and Friday night fish fries. But those were family outings as we honored the Catholic prohibition against meat on Fridays. In every other pleasant memory, I was by myself: alone when I hit a Little League home run, alone when I scored twelve points in a high school basketball game, alone when Marcy stole a kiss. *I should be used to this*, I thought.

Four more LLDB interrupted my dreaming, scrambling down the stairwell, fear evident in their bulging eyes. Captain Meyers strode over to the LLDB team lead and went berserk, shaking him by the collar and screaming into his face.

"They've abandoned their posts," Carlyle said.

Before I could digest the news, the two CIA spooks I had first seen with the Cambodians at Ben Het, the ones I had dubbed Narrow Face and Square Head, spilled down the steps and into the room. The spooks had the menacing look of the rowdies you'd see in a South Boston bar fight. They spotted me and pulled Meyers aside for a conversation. Narrow Face whispered something to Meyers, who couldn't resist a glance at me. He took the headset from Cowans at the communications table and asked the sergeant to connect him with Colonel Barlow. During his conversation he stared at Tucker and me.

When he finished his conversation, Captain Meyers approached and stood over me. "Where have you been?"

"Nowhere. I got hit by a cannon shell or rocket or something and was knocked unconscious."

"Agent Fletcher"—he pointed to Narrow Face—"says you were taking pictures. Let me have them."

When Tucker hesitated, I dug the damaged Nikon out of my rucksack and showed it to Meyers. "With this?"

He frowned, then turned toward Fletcher and shook his head. Meyers decided to believe me and walked away.

As my protectors switched places, talked into headsets, peered through the firing slits, I imagined a graveside scene in which my mother was handed a folded American flag. I couldn't form a distinct image of my father's face. I saw a dark blur, a man without definition—emotionally unreachable, impossible to please, not a warm hug in his body. In his eulogy, he'd tell the mourners that it was karma that I had died. It was all my fault.

Duncan moved away from the radio table, took Meyers by the arm, and started a private chat. Narrow Face joined them. Carlyle, sensing important news, hopped up and insinuated himself in the conversation. When he returned, he was pale. He sat beside me and leaned close.

"The ambush has failed to stop NVA tanks. They are advancing on the camp."

"Oh my God, we're going to die." I was about to cry, and I didn't care.

"They've ordered the Rangers and the other Green Berets to come to the command bunker. The CIA guy says we're bait now, and MAC-V wants the South Vietnamese to step up and fight the NVA, but the ARVN Regiment has refused to rescue us because they don't want to be ambushed by the Rhade companies. The ARVN hope the NVA will wipe out the Yards."

"Jesus, how many wars are we fighting?" Anger welled up inside me again.

Duncan had another conversation with Meyers. They looked depressed. Meyers finally nodded and then wandered our way. He stood near us, cheeks bulging as though searching for the words to deliver an unsavory message.

"An NVA tank has broken through the wire and is headed our way. Our tanks can't chase it because they are either damaged or destroyed. Our best move is to get to Dak To and convince the Army to liberate this place. Gunships are on the way and when they get here, we're going to make a run for it. Stay right on our asses."

He moved to the radio bank beside Duncan. The LLDB huddled in their corner. The spooks stood to one side. A brief calm settled over the bunker. We had a plan—gunships and a run for it. The plan didn't last ten minutes. The .50 caliber machine guns on the trucks outside the bunker opened up and I had to cover my ears to deaden the greatest racket I had ever heard. Men crowded around the firing slits and shouted at one another. Over the sound of the machine guns, I heard a cannon blast followed by an explosion that shook the sandbags on our roof and dropped leaking sand into our already dense atmosphere. The machine guns went silent, and a truck engine started. Another blast came from the cannon, an explosion rocked the other end of the bunker, and the truck motor went silent.

Fletcher said, "It's a PT-76. Russian."

Duncan crossed himself.

Meyers said, "Sweet Jesus, he knocked out both Reapers."

The tank's machine gun opened up and the sandbags at the front of the bunker jumped and shimmied with the impacts. The Montagnard rifleman at the firing slit flew backward, dead before he hit the floor.

No one spoke. As Meyers and Duncan considered their next move, two grenades came tumbling down the steps and bounced onto the mud floor of the bunker. For a split second everyone froze, then everyone dove for cover. My head cradled in my arms, my rucksack turned to the grenades, I heard two pops and the shriek of torn metal. The Montagnard interpreter never had a chance. The artillery liaison NCO was also hit and lay on the floor, bleeding from his head and chest. The shredded radio gear was now silent.

Before anyone could react, the seven LLDB rushed to the stairs and climbed out of the bunker.

"They're surrendering," Fletcher said from his firing slit.

"Those cocksuckers!" Duncan said.

I wondered if I'd rather die than be captured. I heard it then, the sound of prop engines and Gatling guns.

Meyers and Duncan crowded around a firing slit, and Meyers said, "It's the Shadow. Come on, baby."

"The tank is backing away," Duncan said.

"The Shadow?" I asked Tucker.

"A Shadow is an AC-119 gunship," Carlyle said.

"This is our chance. Get ready to roll," Duncan shouted.

I popped to my feet so fast that I felt dizzy.

"Tell that chopper we're coming," Duncan said to the helicopter liaison. "Let's go," he said to the rest of us.

Duncan was first up the stairs, followed by the Montagnard commander and Meyers. I clambered up the stairs, and the others followed. Outside I couldn't see the tank, but the two Grim Reapers were smoldering hulks dripping with blood and charred bodies. I took a deep breath of air and choked on cordite and lingering tear gas. The sounds of fighting to our north weren't far away.

The seven LLDB deserters jogged toward us from wherever they had been hiding. The Montagnard commander stepped out of line as though welcoming them to our escape. When he had advanced within five paces of the Vietnamese, he opened fire with his vintage Thompson .45 caliber submachine gun, sweeping from left to right. By the time the first three had fallen, the others had turned to look for hiding places and the next two were shot in the back. The last two were running away, but the Montagnard knew how to use that "Tommy Gun," and he mowed them down.

The world stood still for a moment as each of us processed the scene. I'd have taken a picture of the war crime, but my Brownie was in Carlyle's satchel.

"Let's get out of here," Duncan said to the Montagnard.

"I stay and fight with my men," the Montagnard commander said, so we started toward the eastern perimeter in a crouching, jogging line: Duncan, Jenkins, the helicopter liaison NCO, me, Square Head, the wounded artillery liaison NCO leaning on the other Green Beret comms sergeant, Cowans, then Fletcher. Carlyle and Meyers brought up the rear.

Duncan led us between tents and hootches and bunkers, the route I should have taken to the command bunker, and passed the crater made by the cannon shell that nearly killed me. My blood marked the spot. We made it back to the eastern gate and the medical triage area without taking any fire. The Green Beret medic and the Montagnard riflemen were gone. The dead bodies on the ponchos remained.

As we ran across the open field, I heard the approaching helicopter. We ducked into the jungle, and I felt safer for the moment. We struggled through the underbrush, moving as quickly as the jungle allowed until we reached a patch of sunlight streaming through an opening in the jungle canopy. Duncan paused to watch the chopper high above us, waiting to dart down and pick us up.

Two shots rang out behind us and like deer spooked by a hunter, we sprinted across the clearing to the protection of the dark jungle on the other side. Now Square Head was also ahead of me, and I was at the end of the line until Cowans and Fletcher caught up with us and muscled past me. I found it alarming that Cowans was no longer supporting the wounded artillery liaison NCO. Captain Meyers arrived out of breath. There were no signs of the wounded artillery liaison NCO or Carlyle. As the line of soldiers began to move again, I hesitated, a cold feeling washing over me.

I turned back to the clearing and Meyers grabbed my arm and jerked me down the path. I tore away from him.

"Where are the others?" I asked.

"Forget him," Fletcher said as he hurried to catch up to the group. Meyers turned and ran.

Through the hole in the jungle canopy, I could no longer see the big H-19 Chickasaw rescue helicopter which must have been on the LZ, waiting. Suspecting that Carlyle needed help with the artillery NCO, I ran back across the clearing and plunged through the jungle. Ten meters down the path, the artillery NCO lay on the ground, moaning and taking rapid, shallow breaths. They had left him behind.

"Tucker. Tucker!" I called as I turned circles. No response. In a panic I crashed through the jungle and at a curve in the raw path I saw him, sprawled against a tree like discarded garbage, Tucker now a "thing," no longer human. The left side of Tucker's forehead had been blown away. His cheekbone stuck out sideways, in front of his ear. His left eye socket was empty.

"Oh my God, oh my God, oh my God."

The horror of the scene made me retch. I collapsed beside him, but I couldn't look at him. It wasn't only the grotesque carnage that repelled me; it was the proximity of unfair, uncaring death. Now this ugly war had taken a man I knew well. Independent, empathetic, duty-bound Tucker Carlyle had been stolen from me in one savage instant. I pinched the bridge of my nose to choke back my tears, holding a deep breath to staunch the rise of bile in my throat. Tucker Carlyle had been given an assignment his superiors expected him to bungle. He had been a pawn in a chess game. I couldn't let Carlyle die for nothing.

As gently as I could, I lifted the canvas satchel off Tucker's shoulder, snaked my hand through the strap so I could cradle Tucker's head, slipped the satchel off his shoulder, and slung it over mine. I rested his head against the tree once again and my hand came away smeared with reddish-gray slime. I wiped it on jungle grass, patted Carlyle on the leg, and said goodbye to my friend. I ran past the artillery NCO and tried to ignore his gasps for air and his gurgling. "Forgive me, God." I reached the clearing in time to hear the high revs of the chopper engine and watched in disbelief as my ride to safety ascended above the treetops.

"They fuckin' left me!" *You fool, they left the satchel of evidence.*

CHAPTER ELEVEN

... Now

Awakened by repeated knocking, Eddie opened his door on the chain and peered through the opening. Madeleine! "Hey."

"Come on, Cowboy. I'm taking you to lunch." She gave him a cross look.

"Now?" He hoped to hell Janice wasn't asleep in his bedroom.

"Yeah, now. It's eleven thirty already and the restaurants are busy this time of year."

He used a thumb and index finger to scrape sleep goop from the corners of his eyes. "You'll have to give me a minute to get ready."

"You sound like a woman. Don't leave me standing out here. Let me in."

He unchained the door and stood aside. Madeleine entered with her nose in the air, sniffed like a hunting dog, and raised one eyebrow as though she detected the scent of a woman. He couldn't let Madeleine wander into his bedroom. He took her by the elbow and eased her to the couch. With a snide smile, she threw his lap blanket onto the floor, and took a seat. Her yellow sundress rode above smoothly rounded knees and exposed shapely calves.

She noted his disheveled condition. "Did you sleep in those clothes?"

"I was watching TV and passed out, I guess."

"Uh-huh." She paused and stared as though waiting for him to crack. He stared back. He knew how to play the game—never add extraneous details or longwinded explanations when being questioned. "Change into something nice," she finally said and jerked a thumb over her shoulder.

"Swanky hotel?"

She blinked again and Eddie was becoming accustomed to her way of expressing surprise. "Casual. We're going to the Salt Island seafood restaurant."

Eddie surmised he hadn't reached Jacob Hoffman status. In the bedroom he made his rumpled bed in case Madeleine came snooping, then stripped and decided a shower would take too long. He tossed Janice's towels into the bathtub and pulled the shower curtain closed. The bathroom did smell like a woman. He gargled with mouthwash and used more deodorant than usual before dressing in shorts, a short-sleeved shirt, and sandals. He brushed his short hair and joined Madeleine in the living room.

"Okay, let's go," he said.

As he locked his door, a voice from behind him said, "You live right there?"

The suspicious man he suspected was a detective approached them with a toothy smile on his face.

"My permanent apartment isn't ready yet. I'm Eddie."

"The man who helps little old ladies." The detective said his name was Richard Stevenson. "I'm at the end of the hall on the right."

So, the detective had a perch from which to observe my comings and goings, like an eagle waiting for a rabbit to wander into view, Eddie thought.

Eddie introduced Madeleine and Stevenson said, "We met last night, during the bruhaha."

"Sorry, we have a reservation to get to," Madeleine said, and she whisked Eddie away down the hallway, leaving Stevenson flabbergasted by her rude behavior.

"That guy creeps me out," Madeleine said. "Snoops around everywhere. What is he looking for?"

Eddie shrugged. "Beats me." Eddie was pretty sure he knew what Stevenson was looking for. What he didn't know was whether Stevenson was FBI, GBI, or DEA. Not that it mattered all that much.

Car traffic was light, but residents in small groups climbed into golf carts for rides to places on the island. Madeleine asked the valet to hail a golf cart.

"Where are the others?"

"It's just you and me," Madeleine said. "My treat."

Madeleine didn't sound as though she was in an amorous mood. As they waited for a cart, Madeleine said, "I'll be right back." She walked to the valet stand and had a brief conversation with the attendant. He opened the car key box and then checked his clipboard. He shook his head and Madeleine returned to Eddie's side.

As they waited for their ride, Eddie saw Janice come out the doors and ask the valet to get her car. No doubt heading to work at the Waffle House. Although she wore the same clothes as yesterday, she looked okay to Eddie.

Janice noticed Madeleine with Eddie and gave him a thumbs-up and started toward him. Eddie shook his head—*don't approach us*—and she turned away.

Eddie watched a security guard at a podium checking the IDs of arriving residents and guests. The guard made notations in a large register on the podium.

Eddie ambled to the podium and asked, "Will I need some proof of residency when I get back from lunch?"

"Yes, sir. I have a roster I can check. We keep track of the guests." The guard leaned toward Eddie and used a hand to shield his mouth. "No priests or undertakers allowed. They have to do their business at the hospital or the morgue."

"Can't let those guys ruin paradise," Eddie said.

"Not on my watch, sir."

The valet signaled to Madeleine and she and Eddie climbed aboard a golf cart. Madeleine gave the driver directions to the restaurant. The restaurant was farther away than Eddie anticipated, through a residential neighborhood and into a commercial district known as Mid-beach. They sat close together, arm against arm from shoulder to elbow, her pliant haunches yielding to his hard, bony hip, but she said nothing and so Eddie remained silent.

The golf cart rolled up to the Salt Island Fish and Beer restaurant and Eddie felt as though he had returned home from a trip to a foreign land. The wooden building with its wide, planked deck resembled Eddie's favorite haunts in St. Petersburg. Madeleine tipped the driver and they walked into a casual, but clean dining room. The simple, minimalistic bar stretched the entire length of one wall, with dozens of plastic backless stools crammed in front of it. This was not a bar in which to relax; it was a bar for serious drinkers who left the place just before they fell off their stools. A simplistic back bar of narrow shelves featured bottles one deep in sections for liquor, wine, and craft beers.

Working age locals occupied most of the tables, but there was no waiting line. A waitress waved them to a table for four and handed them menus. For Eddie, reading the menu was exhilarating, like being at a carnival.

"You eat oysters?" he asked Madeleine.

"Did I grow up in the Carolina Low Country?"

"I mean raw."

"The only way."

The waitress bounced up to their table, paused only long enough to take their order, and flew away, like a touch-and-go landing at an airport. Madeleine ordered a Bloody Mary and Crab Cakes. Eddie asked for a dozen oysters on the half shell—with saltines and Tabasco sauce—a beer-battered fish sandwich made with sweet, deep-fried Flounder, and a Dortmunder lager.

"For a man from Wisconsin, you know your way around a Southern seafood menu." She gave him a questioning look.

Eddie had been tempted by the Shrimp and Grits—he considered himself a connoisseur and sampled them wherever he ate seafood—but didn't want to appear too expert at saltwater cuisine. "I've gotten around. Vacations in Florida."

"Uh-huh."

Against his better judgment—never lead an interrogator—Eddie said, "What did Stevenson mean by bruhaha?"

"There was some sort of mix-up in sleep medications on the fourth floor of the assisted living wing. Patients who should have been resting were awake and agitated. The nurses couldn't be sure that the residents hadn't gotten any sleep meds, so they couldn't administer more drugs. It took a whole bunch of staff to restore order."

"Dangerous mix-up for a place like this, for patients depending on the nurses to do a good job." Eddie felt almost guilty about residents who really did need sleep aids, and about residents on the third floor who didn't need the drugs, but the plan had worked and none of the drugs they used would cause permanent harm.

"They're going to fire the pharmacist's assistant who filled the weekly prescriptions for the fourth floor."

Now Eddie did feel guilty. Collateral damage. "I guess they'd have to do that. So why did Stevenson stick his nose in it?"

"I think he's a cop. Your Army buddy went AWOL last night." She canted her head as though searching for a better angle to see into his soul.

"What? He wandered away?"

"That's what they thought at first. The daytime nurses discovered his room empty at this morning's shift change but couldn't find him in the building or on the grounds."

"Jesus, Gerry could be anywhere on the island."

"I think about Mr. Matthews, wondering around somewhere and struggling with Alzheimer's, and it makes me sad."

That Madeleine was reinforcing Cevert's lie about Alzheimer's made Eddie sad. The oysters arrived on a slim tray, six to a side.

"Share them with me," Eddie said. He placed an oyster on a saltine, doused it with Tabasco, and inserted the entire cracker in his mouth. He smiled while he chewed.

Madeleine ate hers on a cracker with a sprinkle of horseradish and a dollop of cocktail sauce. *Perfectly acceptable*, Eddie thought.

"Have they searched the island?" Eddie wanted to know what the authorities knew about Gerry's disappearance.

"The local cops looked, but he's not here. Not his wife, either."

"His wife?"

"You didn't know his wife lived with him?"

"No, I never got in to see him."

Madeleine took a long draft of her cocktail. "They had help, Eddie."

"You're making it sound like a prison break. He could leave if he wanted, couldn't he?"

She tried for a chuckle and failed. "Of course, he could leave, but it would normally be with family checking at the front desk and getting a briefing on his health. It would normally be during business hours and not during a … a bruhaha, don't you think?"

"Well, I hope he's okay," was all he said.

The oysters had all been eaten. Eddie signaled the waitress for a refill of his beer while Madeleine fiddled with her glass.

Without looking directly at him, she said, "Michael wondered if you had something to do with it."

"That asshole! Is that why you brought me to lunch? To accuse me?"

"No, no." Madeleine reached for his hand. "I wanted you to know what he thought before you heard it from someone else, like blabbermouth Bobby. I'm talking behind Michael's back. As your friend."

Eddie never liked to hear someone insist they were his friend. Usually, they were trying to disarm him. "If Gerry wasn't his patient, why would Michael care one way or the other?" *Let her chew on that.*

Madeleine ignored his question and looked sheepish. "I checked with the valet, and he said your car keys never left the lockbox overnight."

"There ya go! I never even saw Gerry Matthews."

She patted his hand. "It's okay, Eddie. I just wanted you to know."

Eddie acted mollified.

The waitress cleared their table, then delivered their entrees. They made appreciative humming noises as they chewed their food. Madeleine speared a forkful of crab cake and offered it to Eddie. He was momentarily caught off guard, unsure of how to accept the offering.

Madeleine moved her fork close to his mouth, like a mother feeding a baby. "Here, try it."

He did. "That's really good. So is my Flounder."

After a few more bites, Madeleine turned pensive. "Here we are having fun and poor Mr. Matthews won't even know it when death slips up on him. You ever think about the end, Eddie?"

"Death? Sometimes. I look around the dining room each evening and think that in one way of scoring the game of life we're the winners—healthy and wealthy and still active—but in another way, we're the losers, slowly deteriorating as we face our inevitable end, and pretending it isn't happening."

"Doomed to wilt like unsold bouquets at the florist."

"Maybe we aren't God's favorite creations. His cruel joke on Homo Sapiens is that we know we're going to die. Animals don't know it's coming."

She leaned toward him. "Our pets live anxiety-free and when they face a tragic end, we euthanize them because we're compassionate. We encourage our loved ones to fight till the end and all we accomplish is extended suffering."

He grimaced. Was she referring to Sam's elongated battle? Had he encouraged her to suffer in the face of certain death? He had. "God also cursed us with an indomitable survival instinct."

She cracked a small, sad smile. "Unfortunately, hope is not a strategy, Eddie."

After they enjoyed one another's company and savored their food, Madeleine called the Palm Haven concierge for a golf cart. It seemed perfectly natural when Madeleine clasped his hand.

✳ ✳ ✳

Eddie knew immediately that someone had been in his apartment while he was at lunch with Madeleine. A drawer in the kitchen was slightly ajar. Sam's picture and his plastic jar were out of perfect alignment on the dresser. Clothes in drawers had been disturbed. He checked the return vent and found that his evidence was intact. Before screwing the cover in place, Eddie cut a barely visible gray hair off his arm and trapped it between the cover and the wall.

His first thought was that Stevenson had tossed his apartment, but a detective would have been more careful to return articles to their precise locations. Unless the detective wanted him to know that he was onto Eddie. His second thought was that Madeleine had taken him to lunch so that one of her friends could search his apartment. But what friend would have access to the apartment?

Before leaving for dinner, Eddie set a trap for anyone who attempted to enter his apartment. He grabbed a toothpick From a dispenser on the kitchen counter and bent it in half. As his door shut behind him, he wedged the bent toothpick into the space between the door and the jamb, a foot off the floor where he doubted it would be noticed.

That evening, Cevert arrived last at the table. As he approached, he gave Madeleine a barely perceptible shake of his head. Eddie assumed the signal meant that no one had found Gerry and Lydia. Cevert took his usual seat, seemingly lost in a world of his own. Madeleine seemed withdrawn.

As usual, Bobby thought it his duty to enliven the dinner. "Won big at cards last night. My treat in the bar after dinner."

When he received a muted response, he said, "I hate the term 'white privilege.' No one said, 'Here, white boy, take all you want.' I worked my ass off for everything I got."

"Like winning at cards," Susan said.

Some restrained laughter.

"It connotes the opposite of the Black experience, Bobby," Donald said. "Systemic racism is responsible for the underachievement of Black people."

Bobby huffed and puffed like a comic book dragon. "I'm just saying it offends me when my success is dismissed as something I didn't have to earn because I'm white."

"We're confused about this privilege thing because it's presented in a racial context when it should be thought of as a conflict between the elites and the commoners," Michael said, and everyone turned to look at the doctor. Cevert took his time, wiping his glasses with his napkin like a pedantic professor. "The elite, and they come in all colors of the rainbow, are the only people with privileges. They protect those privileges by setting the rules of the game, writing the laws of the land. The rest of us are lemmings."

"You're saying it's a class thing and not a race thing?" Madeleine asked.

"Exactly! The elite portray it as a race war to keep us from realizing it is a class war," Cevert said. "While we fight among ourselves, the career politicians and billionaires are safe and they laugh at us for being so stupid."

Everyone at the table took a breath to absorb Cevert's pontification. Eddie had a vision of Michael skewered by a peasant's sword but protesting, "No, really, I'm one of you." He coughed to cover a chuckle.

"Call it a class war if you want," Bobby said. "As I said, there's no such thing as white privilege."

The discussion could have ended at that point, but Eddie wanted to poke the bear and cause a scene. "Donald was on the right track, Bobby. It's about racism."

"You always agree with Donald," Bobby said petulantly.

"A brilliant Black woman once told me that white privilege isn't an economic phenomenon at all. It's the freedom to live without the fear of racial injustice."

"Ah," Donald said. "Well put."

Bobby jumped to his feet. "I'm going to the bar." He pointed at Eddie. "You're not invited."

"Breaks my heart." Before anyone could stop him or join him, Eddie hustled to the escalator and rode to the ground floor, as though heading to his apartment. He heard Madeleine above and behind him calling his name. He trotted through the lobby to the assisted living elevators and punched the button for the fourth floor.

A blonde with big Dallas hair loitered at the counter of the nurses' station.

"Going to check on Lucy Griffin in 1409," Eddie said as he passed the station.

"You the miracle worker who convinced Lucy to behave?" she said.

"Her niece has more to do with it than I do."

"Not what I heard."

Eddie gave her a wave and started down the hallway.

As usual, Lucy's blubbering could be heard as soon as he entered the sitting room. He eased the door to her bedroom shut and waited several minutes until Barbara entered with the wraithlike nurse who had smoked on the loading dock while Barbara sucked her Fentanyl lollipop. He had hoped for a doctor, but this nurse was no surprise. She had taken her smoke break while Barbara licked her lollipop.

"Why'd you bring me up here?" the redhead asked Barbara. "This old bag doesn't have anything you want."

"Just take a look at her meds, Peggy," Barbara said.

They spun around at the sound of Eddie throwing the bolt on the door lock.

"What's going on?" Peggy asked, fear evident in her eyes.

"We're going to have a little chat about drugs, Peggy."

"No, we're not!" Peggy started for the door.

Eddie blocked her way.

"This is a kidnapping." She swiped a hand at Eddie, trying to move him, and he put two hands on her chest and pushed her roughly. She stumbled backward.

"Hush or you'll wake Lucy," Eddie said.

Looking at Barbara, Peggy said, "What the hell is this?"

"I'm sorry, Peggy. He made me do it," Barbara said.

"Made you do what?"

"She told me where she gets her lollipops," Eddie said. He waved Barbara's Fentanyl stick at Peggy.

"She didn't get that from me," Peggy said.

"You see, Peggy, I caught Barbara *en flagrante delicto* you might say, licking this stick in her car while she was on duty and you were smoking on the loading dock. This has her DNA all over it, so you are her get-out-of-jail-free card."

"You fucking rat," Peggy hissed at Barbara.

"He just wants to buy drugs," Barbara said.

"Then sell him your drugs."

Peggy charged Eddie like a wounded bull in a rigged fight and Eddie gave her a shoulder, like a linebacker bouncing a receiver out of bounds. While behind her, Eddie slipped a zip tie out of his pocket, and in one practiced motion, as efficient as a cowboy roping a steer, grabbed her skinny arms, wrapped the plastic tie around her wrists, and yanked it tight.

"Ouch!" Peggy wailed.

Eddie dragged her to the couch and sat her down. Then he propelled Barbara into the hallway and made a choice. One of these two women was lying, and Eddie couldn't be sure which it was. In her car, Barbara had said, "*He'll* kill me," but she ensnared a woman in her predicament. That man was a level above these women. Eddie couldn't trust an addict to tell him the truth, but he could stash an informant out of the detective's reach.

"You can go," he said to Barbara. In fact, he didn't want her to witness the rest of his conversation with Peggy. "At the end of your shift today, resign effective immediately."

She recoiled and her eyes grew wide. "I can't do that. We won't eat."

"Get yourself some help for your addiction and find a new job. Nurses are always in high demand."

"Oh my God. My husband is going to kill me."

"You have a better chance with him than with the Fentanyl."

Barbara reached out a hand, expecting to get the Fentanyl stick.

"You've got to be kidding," Eddie said. "I'll keep this in case you're lying about Peggy."

"I'm not lying. She sold me those suckers and I've seen her take drugs from one patient and give them to another patient."

"Uh huh. I'll be back at you if she doesn't lead me to a source. Go and get yourself clean, Meacham."

Barbara looked defeated as she skulked away. Eddie reentered Lucy's room and closed the door.

"You going to rape me now?" Peggy said.

"Get over yourself," Eddie said. "I want opioids. What can you get me?"

Peggy looked confused. "Why are you doing this to me? I'm not a drug dealer," she said in the voice of denial Eddie had heard many times in his career.

"Barbara told me how you switch meds between residents." Whether Barbara had told the truth was immaterial. Cops told this sort of lie all the time, making suspects believe their cohorts had ratted them out.

She shook her head in disbelief and tried to explain. "All I did was help a resident who was very sick and in constant pain. The pill mill in Savannah overmedicates patients, so I took some from people who didn't need it and gave it to the person who did need it. Barbara caught me and then I had to get some for her—one damn time!"

Jackpot! Eddie had heard that nurses sometimes deluded themselves into believing they were angels of mercy. Then they killed people. "So, you're the new Robin Hood; steal from the rich and give to the poor. You should get yourself a green hoodie."

"Fuck you."

"Barbara stuck your tits in a wringer, and now I'm turning the crank." Eddie had a plan for the next rendezvous. "What floor do you work, Peggy?"

"Three, with Barbara."

"Handy. Bring the drugs tomorrow. Same time, come up the back stairwell and meet me on the landing between floors three and four."

"I don't work tomorrow."

Frustrated, Eddie said, "Fine, then the next day or you'll lose your license."

"Fuck." Was all she said. Tears began to drip from her eyes to her cheeks like raindrops from a clogged gutter.

Eddie pulled a jackknife from his pocket and slit the tie. While she rubbed her wrists, Eddie walked out the door. At the nurses' station, the cute blonde leaned against the counter. Barbara Meacham wasn't in sight. Whether she'd follow his instructions was anyone's guess.

He told the blonde that Lucy was fine.

"I really admire your devotion, sir," the blond nurse said.

He gave her a self-deprecating smile. "It's nothing, really."

At his apartment door he found the toothpick in its place. No one had entered his apartment while he was at dinner.

Walking around his bedroom with Sam's picture in one hand and a glass of bourbon in the other, Eddie told Sam all about Peggy. "She could be my baitfish."

"Peggy is a Red Snapper." Sam giggled. "Get it?"

Eddie chuckled. "Yeah, I get it. If Peggy is innocent, she won't show up for our next meeting and I'll keep fishing."

"There's a Grouper circling the bait."

A Grouper is a big fat fish. "No need for name calling, Sweetheart."

"Falling for a suspect is a no-no. You know better, Eddie."

"I'm not falling for her and she's not a suspect."

"She should be. She's mixed up with the Jew doctor your buddy Gerry and the two old bitties think is killing people."

"I'm here to find opioids, not chase wild theories. Aren't you the least bit interested in the fact that I'm stranded in the jungle?"

"You must have escaped. You're here."

"You miss the point—I convinced Tucker to go to Vu Dong and it cost him his life. It's the first of many things that haunt me."

CHAPTER TWELVE

... Then

The big chopper reached an altitude safe from rifle fire and then a streak of light, like God's finger, merged with the chopper and bloomed into a fireball. The chopper staggered and revolved like a butterfly with one wing, then plummeted below the tree line. After a thump, a black column of smoke rose above the trees.

Thoughts raced through my mind like a locomotive late for its next stop. *I'd have been killed on that chopper. The NVA will search the wreck and set up an ambush around the LZ. I have to get away from the LZ and the downed chopper.* Panic wracked my body and caused me to shiver in the heat.

Off the path, through the jungle, I fought my way around the artillery NCO so he wouldn't see me, around Tucker so I wouldn't see him. I crashed through elephant grass and banana plants, oblivious to the noise I was making, oblivious to the bloody slashes the grasses and plants left on my arms and face, until I was running without touching the ground and I crashed into the far bank of a dry creek bed. The collision expelled all the air in my lungs as I slid to the bottom of the creek bed. Dumbfounded, I sat on the red earth, taking deep breaths, in through my nose and out through my mouth to calm myself.

God had allowed me to believe I wouldn't have to pay for my sins. Now it was clear, He had reserved his worst punishment for me. I couldn't think of any fate less fair than to be all alone in the jungle, ten thousand miles from home, hunted like a deer by people who wanted to kill me. Then I laughed at myself for being so stupid as to think about fairness. This is my penance.

Stop it, Eddie! You're not dead yet. Think!

Should I hide or should I run? Should I make a futile last stand against the NVA in this creek bed, or should I hike ten miles through enemy territory and impenetrable jungle to Kon Tum? Was I even capable, physically, of such a hike? In the red dirt, I drew a map and placed myself two kilometers from the southeastern boundary of the camp. As a child, I had been taught that if lost, in a department store, for example, I should stay in one place and wait to be found by my parents. I could stay and wait, but that strategy presumed that someone would look for me. Colonel Barlow and Captain Baker knew I had come to this place but they wouldn't want me found. When they heard about the helicopter crash, they'd think I had died.

The battle to control Vu Dong raged on—small arms fire, tank cannons, and NVA shelling clearly audible—which I took to mean that the Montagnards and Rangers hadn't given up. Would the ARVN come to rescue the Yards? *No!* Would the U.S. Infantry come to save the Rangers? *Maybe. Duncan had communicated our situation before the radios had been destroyed.* If a rescue mission were to come, it would come from the east, and I'd be protected by it and I'd be found. *Stay where you are, Eddie, and hope for rescue.*

No, I shouldn't hope for rescue, I should pray for rescue. So I did. No sense of calm washed over me. I tried accepting my fate—God's will—but I couldn't stop my brain from racing to find a solution to my dilemma, couldn't stop my heart from racing on an influx of adrenalin.

I thought about Tucker. Two shots had come from behind me—only two—not a volley from trailing NVA ground troops. Tucker had been shot twice in the face—implausible accuracy had the shots come from a distance. He hadn't defended himself. His pistol rested in its holster and his rifle hung from his shoulder. The NVA hadn't attacked my fleeing comrades; they had waited for the chopper to get airborne before shooting it down with a B-40 rocket. They killed everyone at once very efficiently. I could reach only one conclusion: Tucker had been murdered. Captain Meyers had been the last man across that clearing. If Meyers shot Tucker, he did it under orders from Barlow. A good investigator would have taken a picture of the crime scene.

For hours, I hid in the creek bed, sweating in the cloying humidity, inhaling the moldy smell of the jungle, ignoring the dull throbs in my forehead. I rationed my dwindling supply of water. The afternoon passed slowly to the unrelenting sounds of the battle for Vu Dong.

I had given up hope for a miracle when I heard them. I couldn't see them through the jungle canopy—screaming jets, flying east-to-west over the southern perimeter. Minutes later, the breeze carried an eye-watering smell to my dry nostrils. The jets had dropped Napalm. After the jets departed, the jungle grew quiet while I grew increasingly excited. The planes had softened up the camp's southern perimeter and had not bombed the camp itself. That meant there were friendlies alive in the camp and it meant that a rescue mission would attack from the south.

The dry creek led to the south, so hunched over, I jogged in that direction, tripping over rocks, senses tuned to any sign of the enemy. After trekking for half a mile, I had yet to find a break in the jungle that yielded a view of the southeastern corner of the camp. I waited what seemed a lifetime before I heard the deep-throated growls and felt the powerful downwash of approaching choppers. They came from the east, flew above me, and headed to the camp's southern boundary.

I climbed out of the creek bed and cut through the jungle toward the camp. Dense foliage slowed my progress and thick shrub limbs bruised my arms. I crept onward as quietly as possible, conscious of the possible presence of the fleeing enemy, but it was impossible to advance soundlessly. I tripped and fell. I got whacked in the face by tree limbs.

Before long, the flame of elation was extinguished by a flood of fear. Several helicopters had already made the trip to the southern LZ and I feared all of them would disgorge their troops and return to their base before I could catch up to them. Birds in the treetops squawked their annoyance at what humans were doing to their habitat. Perhaps they knew what was coming. I knew I could be cut down by NVA at any moment, but I couldn't help myself. I plowed forward without concern for the noise I was making.

I stopped when I heard two, no three, men shouting in what I assumed was Vietnamese. Still as a heron fishing along the banks of a river, I listened to the men hack at the jungle. They were heading straight toward me. I turned to run and smashed into a wall of bamboo. I slithered under a banana plant and held my breath. For a fleeting second, I thought about placing the muzzle of my M-16 under my chin and pulling the trigger to avoid capture, imprisonment, and torture. Shame swept over me at the cowardly thought.

Then a voice—an American voice—from less than ten meters away, said, "Leave your weapon on the ground. Stand up and don't move. We'll come to you."

Men emerged from the jungle on all sides of me. Montagnards. And then a Green Beret. "We heard you coming from a mile away, so there was no way you were NVA."

"I haven't seen any NVA, but I'm sure glad to see you."

"What were you doing out here, Chief?"

I had to be careful with my answer. "I'm from Long Binh, expediting arms and supplies for the Special Forces camps. Several of us escaped from the camp, but we came under fire and got separated. There may be other survivors near the medevac LZ on the east side of the camp."

The Green Beret canted his head and sighed. "We saw the crash site on the way in. That's where we're headed. Let's get you out of here."

He spoke into his radio and detailed two of his Yards to escort me to the LZ.

"The last chopper will wait for you."

Hallelujah! The Yards led me through fifty meters of jungle—that's how close I had come to saving myself—and then sprinted across a clearing to the massive, Marine CH-47. More Montagnards poured out of the twin rotor beast. The Marines were only providing transportation.

"Who are you guys?" I asked a Green Beret who was supervising the dispersal of the Yards.

"We're the rapid response unit from Kon Tum, called a MIKE Force. Our Yards want to save the Yards in the camp. No one else would come."

So, the South Vietnamese Army refused to stand up to the NVA.

"Thank God for Yards."

He propelled me through the disembarking Montagnards and up the rear loading ramp of the chopper. There I stood with blood oozing from scrapes on my arms and face, dried blood down the left side of my face, on my shoulder, my right leg, and flak vest. I must have looked seriously wounded because the crew chief said, "We'll get him to the hospital."

Soon we were airborne, heading back toward the east side of the camp, retracing my escape route. The jungle seemed less ominous from above, serene even, until we approached the medevac LZ where I had first touched down and from which the escaping Green Berets and CIA spooks had taken off. I moved next to the crew chief at the open door of the helicopter and surveyed the sight. Arms and legs protruded from an unrecognizable tangle of scorched metal. Beside the wreckage, five oblong charcoal briquets lay in a row.

"No one survived that crash," the young Marine crew chief yelled over the roar of the chopper's engine.

Two of the NVA soldiers milling about raised their rifles and took aim at us. The door gunner swung his machine gun in their direction, but I grabbed his arm to stop him. "Let me." I switched my M-16 to fully automatic and emptied the magazine at them. One of the NVA toppled to the ground and didn't move. I remembered a line from a Beatles song: *Happiness is a warm gun.*

"Oorah!" the Marine said. "You wasted a gook!"

"Hooah!" I responded with the Army battle cry. Master Sergeant Gordon was right: Killing an NVA was as easy as stomping on a cockroach.

The chopper motored away without taking a hit.

"Where are we going?" I did not want to sound ungrateful, but I didn't want to be trapped with Barlow and Baker at Dak To.

"Rocket City, sir."

"Where's that?"

"Kon Tum. Our camp is called Rocket City because we get rocketed every day."

"Terrific."

When we landed, the crew chief directed me to the medical tent.

✳ ✳ ✳

Her name was Krueger and her eyes were the shimmering color of water in a swimming pool after dark with the underwater lights on. She may have been a nurse or maybe she was a doctor; in either case, she was a first lieutenant with a sweet bedside manner and talented hands. Using tweezers, she plucked shrapnel from my shoulder and thigh, charred and twisted bits of metal half an inch long, and asked if I wanted them as souvenirs.

"Sure, why not?"

She placed them in a small plastic jar with a screw top. She swabbed the blood from my face and said, "Head wounds bleed a lot. Look worse than they are." She frowned as she stitched my forehead. "Sorry, that's going to leave a mark."

She pressed patches over my three wounds and handed me a vial of painkillers. "If you have any concussion symptoms—headaches, blurred vision—come back and see me."

Hemingway fell in love with his Italian nurse. I could fall in love with Krueger. "I might just do that."

She smiled dismissively. She had probably been propositioned by every G.I. on the base and I wasn't a colonel. She typed a form and handed me a copy. "You're good to go."

I hung my flak jacket and helmet from my rucksack and slung my M-16 over my shoulder. Carlyle's messenger bag I strapped around my neck. I put on my soft cap, its visor bent from being crushed in my rucksack, and strutted to an Officers' Club. It felt natural to walk in unchallenged and claim a table. I ordered a Crown Royal and ginger ale—Tucker's drink of choice—and silently toasted my mentor. Then I sipped the drink as I carved a steak.

The bartender directed me to a tent with an open bunk. After a shower, I dumped Carlyle's messenger bag on the bed and found a sweet surprise: orders to transfer one Spec. 5 Edward C. Kovacs to Hunter Army Airfield, Georgia, with a reporting date that allowed for thirty days leave. Tucker had kept his word.

I collapsed into a fitful sleep interrupted by gruesome nightmares about a corpse with half a face and a discarded body struggling to breathe. I tossed and turned until I realized I'd never find peace until I decided what to do with our evidence. I weighed my choices. I could shitcan the evidence and let Barlow and MAC-V decide what to do with the Yards and the Central Highlands. That was above my paygrade. If Barlow continued to arm the Yards, the Yards might revolt against the South Vietnamese. That, I concluded was a South Vietnamese problem, not mine. On the other hand, Barlow had ordered Tucker's murder, so it fell to me to bring Barlow to justice. It was also my duty to complete Tucker's mission. The choice was easy. In Tucker-speak, I would dump a stinking turd in Barlow's punch bowl.

✳ ✳ ✳

I didn't roll out of bed until 9:00 a.m. the next morning, feeling as though I had been run over by a dump truck. After asking around, I found the Military Intelligence unit in a pair of trailers tucked in a clutch of

Quonset huts. In the technical operations trailer, I flashed my CID badge and ordered my rolls of film to be developed ASAP. Then I borrowed a typewriter and wrote a report alleging that Special Forces LTC William Barlow had systematically defrauded the Army supply system with the assistance of a Long Binh programmer who had hacked the First Logistical Command computer system to facilitate the fraud. Then I added the accusation that I hoped would spur action on the part of my secret audience: I had personally witnessed the cold-blooded murder of seven LLDB by the Montagnard commander at Vu Dong. That commander, I alleged, had plotted an ambush of ARVN troops scheduled to deploy to Vu Dong. FULRO is real, I wrote, and operating surreptitiously. I urged the readers of my report to investigate the suspicious death of Chief Warrant Officer Tucker Carlyle. Although he was dead and couldn't defend himself, I listed Captain Meyers as the suspect who had carried out the execution at the behest of LTC Barlow.

When my film was developed, I collated the pictures with the written report, added the listing of the altered computer system code, and made two copies of the original. I asked the company clerk how they communicated intelligence with the Green Berets at Dak To, and he said they had a courier who carried paper documents up there every other day. "You just missed him," the Spec. 4 clerk said. "He'll make his next run the day after tomorrow."

"Perfect." I wanted time to get the hell out of Dodge.

I sealed one copy of my report, nearly an inch thick, into an envelope, and wrote, "LTC Barlow, For Your Eyes Only" on the envelope. Then I stuffed the envelope into a mail routing pouch addressed to First Lieutenant Paul Weber, the B-detachment intelligence officer at Dak To. I hadn't saved Tucker's life, but I could save his reputation.

"Day after tomorrow, right?"

"Yes, sir," the clerk replied.

Most of the afternoon I spent waiting to see officers at the ARVN Regimental headquarters. First, I saw a junior officer who asked me to wait while he spoke to his superior officer. After telling my story to that officer, I waited while he spoke to people up the chain of command. And so it went until I finally had an audience with the man responsible for regimental intelligence. He spoke to someone in Saigon and accepted a copy of my report with a conspiratorial smile. He had his minions arrange my transit to Bien Hoa Air Force Base.

I thought Tucker would have been proud of me. When I landed, I appropriated Tucker's jeep, returned a snappy MP salute as I drove through gate nine at Long Binh, and reclaimed my room and duffel bag at the transit BOQ. The charge of quarters remembered me and handed me a stack of my mother's letters that had been forwarded from Thailand. It frightened me to realize that the Army knew where to find me.

✳ ✳ ✳

The next morning, I showed the Charge of Quarters my orders and asked how I could hop a flight back to the States.

He frowned. "Only two ways to get back to the world. Well, three if you count a body bag. You get a voucher from your company clerk and fly a cushy charter from Ton Son Nhut to a civilian airport, or you fly standby from Bien Hoa on an Air Force plane to some Air Force base. I'd bet on the voucher, Chief. Your company clerk can fix you up."

I thanked him and tossed my duffel bag into Tucker's jeep. My orders were for Spec. 5 Edward Carl Kovacs, a man I hardly remembered having been. Reluctantly, I removed the Warrant Officer's bars from my uniform and pinned my Spec 5 insignia to my collar. I was once again a fungible asset of the U.S. Government.

Maybe my paranoia was unjustified, but the last thing I needed was to be detained by some Military Police clerk. I drove to the Bien Hoa airbase, parked Tucker's jeep where I hoped it wouldn't be found for months and humped my duffel bag into the passenger terminal. Past flights bound for bases at Yokota, Japan, and Incirlik, Turkey, I found a flight heading to Elmendorf Air Force Base, Alaska—almost the same as The World. Military men and women from all branches of service milled about, stood in subdued groups, or sat in the few plastic chairs available, their energy having been sucked from their depleted bodies months before this monumental date of rotation stateside. An Air Force guy with three stripes on his arm stood behind a podium.

"Any space available on this bird?" I asked.

"Nope. One standby seat left and it's going to that captain over there." He nodded in the direction of an Army Airborne Ranger, a man who had no doubt survived a harrowing tour.

"What would it cost to bump him?"

The Air Force guy blinked a couple of times and moved his mouth around as though swallowing the last bite of a meal. "Let me see your orders."

I handed them to him, and he took a quick look. He wrote my name on his notepad. "You've got plenty of time to get to your assignment."

"When's the next flight to Travis?"

"Tomorrow. Arrives in the morning with new cannon fodder and departs in the afternoon as the 'Freedom Bird.'"

My shoulders slumped. "Tomorrow will be too late. My grandmother is dying."

"They should have put 'expedite' on your orders."

"I know. Typical Army snafu. Give me a break and let me see my nana one more time."

He rubbed his clean-shaven chin and glanced around the area to see if anyone was paying attention to us. "It'll cost you."

"Sure. Tell me."

"A Benjamin," he whispered. "Meet me in the latrine." He pointed to the restroom door on the other side of the waiting area.

One hundred dollars would buy a lot of pot and pussy in Saigon. I exchanged five twenties for a boarding pass in the latrine, then tried to act nonchalant as I lost myself in the crowd.

When I boarded the plane, I watched the Ranger captain walk back into the terminal. He would have to survive Vietnam for another day.

At the Elmendorf passenger terminal, I paid the exorbitant price of $1.75 for a beer, so I had just one. I arrived in Appleton thirty-six hours later after a hop to Scott AFB, Illinois, and two Continental Trailways buses.

Chapter Thirteen

... Now

When the pharmacy opened, Eddie stood in line to pick up the meds Cevert had filled for him.

A pharma tech named Jameson, like the Irish whisky, said, "Always busy on Monday morning. You can pick these up later today."

"I'll just wait for them. Thank you."

Jameson flashed a cross look at him. "Suit yourself. Have a seat."

Eddie didn't sit down in the plastic chairs with the other residents waiting for their meds. He smiled his thanks and leaned against the wall, watching the activity through the wide glass fronting the pharmacy. Behind the counter, a young, fresh-faced blond pharma tech named Flanagan and a stout Black woman named Gilliam shuttled between racks of drug containers and two worktables, where they read prescription orders, counted pills, loaded the vials, and sealed them in individual paper bags with a pricing receipt stapled to each bag. They worked with speed and precision, loading the sealed bags into plastic tubs by floor for the assisted living residents, and in named slots in the pharmacy to await pickup by independent living residents.

Flanagan noticed Eddie watching them and gave him what he thought was a nervous smile.

A fiftyish man with gray hair and spectacles occasionally emerged from the rows of shelves to smile ingratiatingly at the residents. Eddie took him to be the head pharmacist who watched the proceedings like a pit boss in a Vegas casino. If Flanagan and Gilliam were stealing residents' drugs during the Monday morning rush hour, they were as good at the sleight-of-hand as a card shark dealing from the bottom of the deck.

Flanagan again noted that Eddie was scrutinizing the operation and came to the window. "I'll take care of your prescriptions for you."

He had been allowed to cut the line. He wondered why.

She went to her worktable, deftly filled two vials, and returned in a flash, waving a paper prescription bag at him. "They're all ready for you."

"Thanks, Ms. Flanagan."

"Shauna," she said and gave him a big customer service smile.

Eddie couldn't help thinking Flanagan wanted him to stop watching and go away. He didn't go away. He stayed to watch one floor nurse from each assisted living floor pick up the appropriate tub and deliver the meds to his or her floor. He recognized two of the floor nurses, Sandy from the third floor and Roundtree from the fourth. When the floor nurses departed, the waiting residents queued up at the window like caged animals at feeding time to get their pills. Eddie deduced that the pharmacy had been restocked over the weekend so that the weekly or monthly prescriptions for residents could be distributed on Monday mornings.

The morning drama over, Eddie went back to the fourth floor and walked through Lucy's open door. He found her slapping cards down on the coffee table and laughing uproariously.

"She beats me every time," Janice said.

He asked Janice for another favor, and she readily agreed to help him, basking in the excitement of Eddie's detective work.

Waiting for the elevator, Eddie saw her again, Madeleine, casually moving from one room to another. *What is she doing?* Thankfully, the elevator arrived before she spotted him.

He carried his bag of medications to his room and placed the filled prescriptions in the bathroom. He thought about how opioids could get into the complex through the pharmacy and how the operation might work. A doctor, either Banerjee or Cevert, could prescribe the drugs for residents and then a floor nurse like Peggy could intercept them, and then someone with easy access to residents, like Madeleine, could distribute them. It was slick and difficult to uncover, but it required a lot of people to participate and keep their mouths shut. It pained him to admit that Sam could be right about Cevert and Madeleine. Peggy was the most likely connection to the pair.

✳ ✳ ✳

Once again, Eddie rigged his door with a bent toothpick before heading to the dining room.

Bobby dropped a book on the table as he took a seat. Donald appeared frail and more fragile than ever, moving gingerly to his dinner seat. His tablemates watched him in silence until he nodded that he was ready, like a dignitary at the head of a conference table. Madeleine waved a hand and a waitress appeared to take their orders. Against his better judgment, Eddie ordered the old-folks-home macaroni and cheese, made with non-fat cheese and non-fat milk. Donald's deteriorating condition cast a pall over the table.

Trying to improve the mood, Michael said, "I didn't know you're a reader, Bobby. What's the book you brought?"

Bobby swallowed and dabbed his lips. "I'm a member of the book club. There are only a few guys in the club, so the women dictate what we read. This month they chose the worst book ever written." He held up the book.

"That one's on all the bestseller lists," Michael said. "Young Irish woman, her third bestseller in a row."

"Tells ya something about the people who compile those lists," Bobby said. "In this one two millennial women email each other and cry in their energy drinks. They're throbbing with anxiety."

Madeleine howled. "Throbbing? You must have read that in a dirty book."

"Bobby reads all sorts of books," Susan said.

Bobby ignored Susan. "Their jobs suck, they aren't paid enough, politics are fake, the earth is dying, and their lives have no meaning. They blame Baby Boomers for handing them a screwed up world."

"I guess they don't know what the world was like before we made it better," Eddie said.

"That's right," Susan said. "We blew up our parents world and stopped a war with flower power. If Millennials don't like the way it is, they need to get off their asses and do something instead of complaining."

"Once upon a time we were revolutionaries, Susan," Cevert said. "Then we morphed into soulless, establishment lackeys. I can't explain how that happened."

"That's not fair, Michael," Susan said.

Encouraged, perhaps, by Michael's pessimism, Donald said, "It's true. In the name of commerce, we gave the world smartphones and the Internet and got Millennials hooked like heroin addicts and that's the poison that's destroying them."

"Millennials invented social media. They poisoned themselves," Madeleine countered.

"Do you know the biggest difference between millennials and Boomers?" Bobby asked.

"We tuck in our shirts and they don't?" Eddie offered and Michael chuckled.

"No!" Bobby leaned into the table to throw his strongest punch. "They hate meritocracies, want everyone paid the same and treated the same no matter their performance level. They don't want to work hard to get ahead."

"That's the definition of Socialism," Michael said.

"We did it to ourselves. It's like feeding a wild animal," Donald said. "They became dependent upon us and pretty soon they couldn't fend for themselves."

Baby Boomers, Eddie thought, were trapped between the fatalism of "The Greatest Generation" and the nihilism of millennials. "It's the natural devolution of empire. Our parents were tough as cowhide but they made it easier for us, so we are softer than they were. We made it easier for Gen-X and they are softer than us. And then Gen-X produced millennials, who are softer than overcooked macaroni. It's our fault."

Susan sniggered.

"The Roman and British Empires lasted four hundred years before they collapsed," Bobby said. "Ours will die in less than a century if we leave it up to millennials." He tossed the book into the middle of the table. "This one goes on the burn pile."

Bobby leaned back, satisfied that he had supplied the table with an excellent discussion topic. He challenged the table with translucent eyes, a color that didn't match Bobby's florid complexion, like a tie that didn't match a suit.

Eddie picked up the book and read the back cover. "Maybe this is too sophisticated for you, Bobby."

"She's a fucking Communist!"

"Doesn't mean she can't write a good book."

Bobby stood and tossed his napkin in his chair. "I can't figure you out, Eddie. Sometimes you sound conservative and then you turn around and sound liberal."

"I'm not a can of peas, so I don't have a label. Whether you lean red or blue, you've been scammed," Eddie said.

Bobby's cheeks puffed and turned red, like an overheated boiler. "He's not normal." Bobby pointed at Eddie, like Pontius Pilate condemning Jesus.

"No, he's not," Madeleine said with a sigh and a hint of admiration.

Before Bobby could fire another salvo, Peggy, Eddie's putative baitfish, rushed up to the table, breathless. She recoiled when she noticed Eddie. She had lied about her work schedule.

"What is it, Peggy?" Cevert asked.

"Doris has overdosed!" she wailed, "Doris has overdosed!"

Doctor Cevert's face went pale.

"Doris Christenson on four?" Madeleine asked.

"We've gotten her down to your office," Peggy said to Cevert.

"Sorry," Cevert said. He stood and started after the nurse. Madeleine hurried after them.

Bobby jumped up and said, "I'll help."

Cevert waved him back. "No. We've got plenty of hands."

Bobby dropped his napkin on his plate. "I gotta see what's happening." He bumped into waitresses and diners as he hastened to catch up to Cevert.

"You better keep him out of the way," Eddie said to Susan.

Reluctantly, Susan rose and started after her recalcitrant husband. Donald coughed into his white handkerchief again. Eddie thought he saw a spot of blood on it. Donald excused himself, leaving Eddie alone.

Eddie walked back to the assisted living elevators. He took a crowded car full of overly perfumed women to the fourth floor, where two young nurses in blue scrubs were waiting near the service elevator behind the nurses' station. They looked nervous.

"What do you need?" asked a nurse with sleepy brown eyes.

"Good evening. I live in the other wing, and I promised Nurse Roundtree I would look in on Lucy Griffin," Eddie said.

"She's down for the night."

"Out like a light," the chubbier nurse said, and she tittered.

"Well, she's been a problem for Nurse Roundtree, and I promised to keep tabs on her." He pulled his law firm business card from his pocket and flashed it at Sleepy Brown Eyes. "I'm Ms. Griffin's attorney and I'm just trying to keep things from escalating, if you get my drift."

"You a troublemaker?" the chubby nurse said.

"It's okay," Sleepy Brown Eyes said to the chubby nurse. "I've heard about this guy. He's the guy who makes old lady Griffin behave." To Eddie, she said, "Make it snappy."

Eddie put his card away. "Thanks." The floor was ethereally quiet. On the way to Lucy's room, he checked nameplates on the rooms he passed. No Doris Christenson. He cracked Lucy's door and peeked inside, then looked over his shoulder to note that Sleepy Brown Eyes was watching him. He slipped into the room, careful not to wake Lucy, and heard her soft blubbering with each exhale. After ten seconds, a quick look out the door confirmed that the nurses weren't at their station. Probably in some other patient's room, Eddie guessed.

Eddie left Lucy's door cracked and eased farther down the hallway. He found Doris Christenson's room two doors down and across the hall, room 1412 facing the ocean, its door unlocked. The nurses hadn't thought to secure the room as Cevert tended to Doris one floor below in his office. He pulled a penlight from his pocket and scanned the sitting room. The coffee table had been pushed up against the couch, probably to allow passage of a gurney that had carried Doris away. Through the open blinds, he saw the glow of marina lights that lit the paths through the garden.

In the bedroom, the nauseating odor of the vomit that covered the disheveled bedsheets made him catch his breath. Two trickles of blood stained her pillow. A red emergency call button hung beside her lamp. Doris's pill organizer sat undisturbed on the bedside table.

Eddie sorted through the pills and found none of the usual overdose suspects—Vicodin, OxyContin, Oxycodone, Hydrocodone, or Fentanyl. If she had been prescribed an opioid, she had taken all of them this evening. He looked through drawers in the bedroom and the medicine cabinet in the bathroom and found nothing unusual. However, in the bathroom wastebasket, among crumpled wads of paper, ear swabs, and used tissues, he found an amber plastic pill vial. The part of the pharmacy label naming the doctor, the drug and the dosage had been ripped off, leaving a residue of paper backing and glue, but big letters across the top declared the source of the pills to be the River City Pain Management Clinic. *Pain management. Opioids.* The vial was empty except for a dusting of pill powder at the bottom. Using a tissue from a box on the vanity, Eddie picked the vial from the refuse and slipped it into his pocket.

Quickly, he moved to the door and peeked down the hallway. The nurses huddled in front of the service elevator with their backs to him. Eddie crept back to Lucy's room and reached it just as the elevator doors opened. The limp-haired orderly Eddie had seen in the gardens exited and whispered to the nurses. Eddie pretended he had just emerged from Lucy's room by closing her door.

"What's he doing up here?" the orderly asked the nurses.

"He's okay, Randy," Sleepy Brown Eyes said. "He's old lady Griffin's lawyer."

The lanky orderly loped up the hallway and approached Eddie. "You done in there?" He meant Lucy's room. Randy made Eddie think of the movie *Deliverance*.

"Yes, Ms. Griffin is fine," Eddie said.

Randy grasped Eddie's bicep, pointed Eddie down the hallway and gave him a little shove. "Back to your room, buddy."

"I'm going. I'm going."

Eddie shuffled down the corridor, then glanced over his shoulder to see Randy run down the hallway and disappear into Doris's room. As he reached the public elevator, the service elevator doors slid open to reveal a uniformed female cop, a burly security guard dressed in a black uniform, a lumpy, middle-aged man Eddie immediately classified as a detective, and the ubiquitous Stevenson. Sleepy Brown Eyes and the cops exchanged a few words.

When the doors on the public elevator opened, Eddie stepped inside and flattened himself against the wall, hidden by the control panel. He held down the door open button and watched the entourage scamper up the hallway to Doris's room. The fact that the authorities had been called indicated to Eddie that Doris had not survived her overdose.

Eddie exited on the third floor and pushed through a crowd of gawking seniors. Peggy shepherded two paramedics and their gurney into Cevert's office, then emerged to keep the crowd at bay.

Eddie sidled up to her and whispered, "Tomorrow night. In the stairwell. Don't fuck with me."

Peggy's face dissolved and she began crying. "I really don't work tomorrow."

Eddie patted her back as though consoling her for Doris' death. "I don't give a shit. Wear scrubs so you look like you're working."

He went to the fourth floor of the central building and entered the dimly lit bar. After his eyes adjusted, he spied Madeleine at a small cocktail table along the far wall. Eddie took a seat across from her. Madeleine's lips were turned down at the corners and her eyes were glassy and red-rimmed.

"Thought I'd find you here."

Madeleine stared at her empty cocktail glass. "Doris Christenson is gone."

"Was she one of Michael's patients?"

Madeleine's hand covered her mouth. "Yes," she mumbled between her fingers.

Eddie signaled a waitress and ordered drinks.

He remembered a curious detail. "The night nurses wear blue scrubs but the day nurses wear black scrubs. Is there a reason for that?"

"The day nurses in black are employees, but the night nurses in blue are contractors from a staffing company," Madeleine explained.

The nurse who had helped Cevert with Jacob's body had worn green scrubs, neither an employee nor a contractor. "So what happened?" Eddie asked her.

"Michael administered Naloxone, but it was too late."

The "save shot," Eddie thought. Naloxone is a rapid-acting antidote to opioid overdose. *Finally evidence that the DEA was right about opioids at Palm Haven.* "Want me to leave you alone?"

"No." She reached for his hand and held it a moment. "I need to have company."

He covered her hand and held it gently. When the drinks arrived, their intimate moment was disrupted when Bobby stumbled up to their table. "I'll have a drink with you guys. Eddie and I need to make friends," Bobby said.

"Sorry, Bobby, I need to be alone," Madeleine said as she rose from her seat.

Eddie stood and said, "I'll help Madeleine to her room."

"Okay, I see how it is. You're the new Jacob" Bobby slid into Eddie's seat and snapped his fingers for a waitress.

As they walked away, Madeleine said, "Tomorrow night let's skip the dining room and go into town for dinner."

"All right." Eddie escorted her to the penthouse elevator. He waited for the elevator doors to close, then went down to the lobby in the public car and back to his apartment.

The bent toothpick lay on the hallway carpet. Eddie eased his door open and called, "Anyone home?" No one responded. He paused on the threshold and surveyed the vacant kitchen and sitting room. He considered retrieving his pistol from the return vent but didn't want to reveal his hiding place. He tossed the book on his table, picked a candle holder off the TV stand, and crept to the bedroom. No one there. He checked the bathroom and found it unoccupied. He checked drawers, closets, and his dresser top and found nothing out of place. Stevenson was preoccupied with Doris' death so this intruder was someone else, someone looking for Eddie and not evidence.

Satisfied that he was alone in the apartment, Eddie sealed the pill vial in a quart-sized plastic bag. He made a note of the time, date, and place where he found it and rubber-banded the note around the plastic bag. He found his hair clipping in place on the air conditioning vent and replaced it after storing the vial in the duct.

Tonight, his brief to Sam was longwinded as he recapped what he knew about Jacob Hoffman, Dr. Michael Cevert, Dr. Banerjee, Gerry Matthews, Barbara Meacham, Doris Christenson, Peggy, Madeleine, two old bitties and an intruder. Two people had died at Palm Haven in the space of a week, one of an obvious opioid overdose. His last case was now a murder case and Eddie felt increasing pressure to catch the trophy fish before the ubiquitous detective did.

"You're going on a date with a suspect? What's happened to you?" Sam asked.

"It's not a date. I'm disarming her."

A guffaw was Sam's response.

"Banerjee is dirty and Cevert is up to something but I have to think the drugs would get here easier if brought in from the outside."

"You don't think Cevert prescribed opioids for his patient, Doris?"

"Too obvious and incriminating." It did cross his mind that the pharmacy label had been torn off Doris pill vial.

"Then you have to look at people who leave the building in cars, not golf carts."

"Yeah."

He poured another shot from the nearly empty Bourbon bottle. He was drinking too much.

"Let me continue the Vietnam story."

"Why? You'd already come back from Vietnam. I know you feel guilty about Tucker."

"There's a lot more to feel guilty about."

Chapter Fourteen

All my friends were off to war against the Viet Cong or protesting the war on college campuses, so I spent three weeks playing cribbage, grilling brats, drinking local beer, and enjoying the company of my brother Danny and his circle of friends.

Sitting at Danny's backyard picnic table in the weak Wisconsin fall sun, I said, "When I get discharged, I'm going to the University of Wisconsin in Madison."

"Sounds like a plan. Dad asked me to pass along his offer to you: you come back home, live with him and Mom, commute to the college in Green Bay, and work the dry cleaning machines nights and weekends."

We had quite the laugh over that. "I didn't know you were on speaking terms with him."

"He communicates through Mom. I don't visit him. He asked about your service experience."

I glossed over the North Vietnamese attack on an unidentified Special Forces camp and showed him the shrapnel Nurse Krueger had removed from my leg and shoulder and the scars on leg, arm, and forehead.

"Jesus, Eddie, you're a war hero and I'm a draft dodger. Now that it's over, I'd rather be you."

I probed Danny about his future and he deftly danced around questions about romantic interests.

He watched the national news on television every evening but the intravenous drip of hideous atrocities in Vietnam juxtaposed with racial riots and anti-war demonstrations in America sickened me.

I didn't need a ticker tape parade to welcome me home and thank me for my service and I didn't need a shrink's shoulder to cry on. I just wanted to forget where I'd been and what I'd done so I could live in peace. Whether I had done the right thing by serving my country or the wrong thing by enabling imperialism was a riddle I had lost interest in solving. To help me forget, I purchased an amazing new toy, a Sony Walkman, and that chased the nightmares away.

As the days of my leave passed, I became less apprehensive about MPs knocking on our door to haul me back to Vietnam, but then the fear returned when it came time to report to my next assignment. I trusted the local recruiter's instructions to fly to Augusta, Georgia, where he assured me, Hunter Army Airfield was a "big-ass" base. MPs in the Augusta airport, placed there to be on the lookout for deserters from Fort Gordon—Augusta's big-ass base—informed me that little known Hunter Army Airfield was in Savannah, 138 miles southeast of Augusta.

"You're lucky," the NCO-in-charge said. "No one even knows about the place." The airfield had been activated, he said, when Fort Rucker, Alabama, couldn't train helicopter pilots as fast as the Viet Cong could shoot them out of the air.

Was it fate that I'd be stationed where Tucker's family lived or had he gotten me this assignment in his hometown so we could be buddies?

The NCO noticed the medals on my chest denoting my tour of duty in Vietnam and decided to be helpful. "Stand by, Sarge, while I find someone who can take you to the bus station. It's a long ride to Savannah on back roads with about a dozen stops."

A scrawny PFC showed up a minute later. "Let's go, Sarge. Bus in thirty minutes."

He drove me to the Continental Trailways terminal in a jeep and yacked the whole way. In a stereotypical New Jersey accent, he regaled me with insights based upon his six months in the South.

"You won't like it here. They hate Yankees, still fighting the War of Northern Aggression."

"I was stationed at Ft. Lee, Virginia so I know a little bit about the South."

"Then you should have known not to wear your Class A uniform."

The Class A uniform is the dress uniform, a green suit-like jacket and pants over a drab beige shirt with a skinny black tie. This combination had not been dreamed up by the fashion industry.

"Everybody knows you're Army. They see those Vietnam service ribbons on your chest and they'll call you a baby-killer and a war criminal. They hate Vietnam vets worse than they hate niggers. They're used to the niggers down here."

At the bus terminal, I noted how southerners had come to accommodate former slaves: bathrooms for whites only; water fountains for whites only. I had seen pictures of segregated facilities and had dismissed them as a sort of fairy tale. Now, I couldn't dismiss the signs of America's racial divisions. Was this the "freedom" for which I had risked my life?

As I bought a ticket and walked to the loading ramp with my duffel bag slung over my shoulder, I averted my eyes, avoided contact with my fellow travelers, bracing for attacks that did not eventuate. I stowed my bag in the hold and climbed on board the bus.

A fortyish woman guarded the last available seat. With the private's warnings echoing in my head, I hesitated in the aisle until the woman surveyed my uniform, nodded her assent, and slid over to the window seat. From my accent—I thought I had no accent—it was obvious to her that I was from "Up North," but rather than ignore me, she became my tour guide, describing the sights of interest along the way.

Using secondary roads paralleling the Savannah River, the bus drove through small towns razed by General Sherman during the Civil War and past shotgun houses, plantation manors, oak trees as tall as a house, and magnolia trees as wide. Through shadows so dense the headlights could not penetrate them, the bus passed mile after mile of cotton fields where I imagined slaves had once toiled.

That modern-day Southerners are burdened with this history is the fabric of Southern culture, she told me. When she learned I was single, she added a piece of advice, "You're a nice young man, so if you want to meet good girls, go to church."

Church wasn't on my itinerary. I moved into a bottom-floor apartment in an old, white, two-story frame house on West Gwinnett Street, two blocks from Forsyth Park, in the heart of Savannah. My roommate's name was Greg, an oversized hunk of gregarious manhood from Battle Creek, Michigan, whom we called "Corn Flakes." Olivia, a pale flower child of about thirty, lived in an upstairs apartment with her young son. She would put her child to bed, then come downstairs and put me to bed. It was a satisfactory arrangement for both of us.

Our house was on the dividing line between the white residential neighborhood to the south and the Black residential neighborhood to the north. The neighborhoods did not mix. Once a week, the street sweeper would clean one side of the street and all cars had to be parked on the opposite side of the street. When he parked on the Black side of the street, Greg's car was broken into, and his 8-track cassette system was stolen.

The mom-and-pop convenience store on the corner was robbed so regularly it might have been a part of the social welfare system. The robbers escaped by running down the alley behind our house. It was not the sort of neighborhood where good girls would hang out with G.I.s.

Nonetheless, we avoided living on base with the grunts who bragged about their time in Vietnam and the crybabies who moaned that they'd soon be sent to Vietnam. I just wanted to forget.

Hunter Army Airfield did not have a supply depot, but it did have a warehouse full of helicopter parts. A fiftyish, alcoholic staff sergeant named Owens was nominally in charge of inventory, but he spent his days at the NCO club, so I managed the inventory from a glass-walled office I shared with a chubby secretary named Loraine, who constantly made googly eyes at me.

Two weeks after arriving on base, the officer in charge of the warehouse, a Captain Rogers who rarely graced us with his presence, called me into his second-floor perch above the warehouse floor. There stood a major named Burns with Judge Advocate General insignia on his collar. My knees buckled. I was sure he had come to take me back to Vietnam to be court-martialed for going AWOL.

He dismissed Captain Rogers, telling him our conversation was classified. He sat in Rogers's chair and waved me into a visitor's chair.

"Neat trick you pulled over there," the major said.

"What do you mean, sir?"

"Giving your report to the ARVN. They sent copies everywhere and the shit hit the fan. Why'd you do that?"

"Chief Carlyle told me to do it, sir." Mentally, I apologized to Tucker's spirit for throwing him under the bus.

"But you didn't give a copy to Colonel Barlow. The report he sent us didn't include your soiree at Vu Dong."

"He got the same report as the ARVN, sir. You can check with Lieutenant Weber, the B-detachment Intelligence Officer. I sent Colonel Barlow the final report, care of Lieutenant Weber."

"Nice. That way you'd have another witness, right?"

"In case I needed it."

"Your plan didn't work. Lt. Weber was killed in an attack on Dak To. So maybe the colonel was telling the truth."

Maybe Weber didn't die at the hands of the enemy, I thought. *Maybe I got him killed by involving him.* "Then check with the Military Intelligence detachment at Kon Tum. They know I couriered that report to Dak To."

"No need for that. The ARVN disseminated your report and your pictures of Vu Dong to everyone at MACV. You had your ass covered, so why go AWOL from Vietnam?"

"I didn't go AWOL, sir. I had orders to report here."

"You didn't process out of MAC-V."

"I never processed in."

"You're pretty slick, Kovacs. Tell me what happened to you at Vu Dong."

I gave him an abridged story.

"Did you see Chief Carlyle after you got lost?" the major asked.

"Yes, sir. He was dead. Shot in the face."

"Did you see it happen?"

"No, sir. I found him after he'd been shot."

"The MIKE Force found Chief Carlyle and Sergeant Callaway," he said. "They recovered the bodies at the crash site, too."

Callaway must have been the artillery liaison NCO. "Did Callaway make it?" *If Callaway had survived, he may have told them who shot Tucker. And he may have told them I ran off and left him.*

"No. Callaway was dead when the MIKE Force found him," Burns said. "He might have survived if he'd been found sooner." Burns waited for a reaction, but all I gave him was a poker face. "Barlow's been court-martialed, demoted, and summarily retired. You got your man and we tied a pretty ribbon on his sorry ass."

"He should be in prison for ordering Carlyle's murder."

Burns sighed. "There's no proof of that."

"What about the Montagnard commander who murdered the LLDBs?"

"The ARVN are searching for the Montagnard commander, but he and his Rhade renegades have vanished in the jungle."

"Well, I hope the ARVN find him. I still have nightmares."

"I can imagine." The major slid a sheet of paper across the table. He handed me a pen. "If you had witnessed Carlyle's death, I'd take your statement, but since you didn't, I just need you to affirm that you were not a witness to the chief's death. Simple statement of fact."

I read the document and had to admit it was simple—I did not see what happened to Tucker. The document did not speculate on how Carlyle had been killed. I got it then—Barlow was their sacrificial lamb and the rest of the atrocity would be swept under the rug. The only possible witness to Tucker's murder had died before he was rescued. Captain Meyers was dead. So, after getting Tucker killed, I betrayed him by whitewashing his murder.

"And one more." Burns slid another sheet of paper across the desk. "Confidentiality agreement. Everything you saw or did while in Vietnam is classified. You aren't authorized to speak to anyone or disclose any information about your mission in Vietnam. Not to your current commander, not your girlfriend, certainly not to the press. You'll go to jail if you do. Understood?"

"Got it. Sir." I signed the document and became an accessory after the fact to murder and fraud, all with the good wishes of my government.

Burns didn't give me a copy of either document. He dug in his briefcase and pulled out a blue leatherette folding case and a black portfolio with gold engraving on the cover. He handed me the blue case and I opened it. A Purple Heart medal was pinned to some satiny material on one side and an Army Commendation Medal was pinned to the other leaf.

"The Kon Tum Dispensary nurse filed the wounded-in-action report for you. Had your rank wrong, though, listed as Chief Warrant Officer First Class Kovacs."

"Don't know how she got that wrong, sir."

Burns gave me a conspiratorial smile. "I filed the recommendation for the Army Commendation Medal but this one came from a different source." He handed me the larger portfolio. It had the seal of the Republic of Vietnam on the cover. Inside on the left was a document written in Vietnamese and facing it, a bronze cross with a metal circle around it hanging from a ribbon with yellow stripes and on a red background.

"What's this?"

"The South Vietnamese government awarded you their Gallantry Cross for solving the case of the illegal arms. The citation says something about courage, valor, and justice."

So I'm being bribed to keep my mouth shut. The shame is that I accepted the bribe. "I'll wear them in honor of Chief Carlyle."

"Sorry, Kovacs, you can't wear the medals. In fact, you can't even tell anyone that you won the medals. Your mission is still classified, and you're bound by your confidentiality agreement."

"I understand, sir." *Fuck the confidentiality agreement,* I thought. *My father needs to hear about these medals. All he ever received were Presidential Unit Citations for the subs' war patrols.*

I stood and saluted the major.

Burns just nodded. As he walked out the door, he said, "Don't reenlist Kovacs. You're not our kind of soldier."

I excused myself for lunch and went home to take pictures of my medals and write my father a note: "Compare these whoppers to your trinkets, old man." A week later I received his reply: "I won my war, sonny boy."

✳ ✳ ✳

I suppose it was inevitable given our proximity in the office, or maybe it was her peaches and cream complexion—a Southern specialty—hooded blue eyes, and bee-stung lips. When I accepted Lorraine's invitation to join her at church, her smile spread slowly, like a milkshake spilled on a flat surface.

"I always thought you were a nice boy," she said.

After the church service, Greg found Lorraine cuddled up to me on the couch, my arm around her shoulders. "Excuse me, don't mean to interrupt," he said and scuttled off to his bedroom.

"I'd better be going," Lorraine said.

I walked her onto the front porch. Before she took the steps to the yard, Lorraine whirled and kissed me on the lips.

I hadn't tried to seduce her. I had proven myself "a nice boy."

Lorraine became a regular at our apartment. Made it a habit to cook us dinner. "You boys don't eat right." Lorraine and I sat on the couch and

watched TV with a little touching and making out during commercials.
I enjoyed her companionship but wasn't serious about her.

✳ ✳ ✳

The medals I had received haunted me until I worked up the courage to call
on Tucker's father, Royce, and offer my condolences. While on leave, I had
skipped Tucker's military funeral, possibly the most shameful thing I had
done to that point in my life. In truth I had wanted to avoid the emotions I
would have experienced. I looked up the detective agency in the telephone
directory and found that it was still listed as Carlyle & Sons. Royce hadn't
stopped hoping Tucker would come home to the family business.

I located the Carlyle office on Abercorn Street in the old Victorian
section of town, just south of Forsyth Park. The building was a red brick,
two-story structure, studded with sunburst windows topped by white
eyebrows, the kind you might see in a cathedral. A half flight of concrete
stairs that led to double doors reminded me of small-town courthouses.
Completing the eclectic mashup of architectural characteristics, a tall
palm tree stood in front of the building. I parked in the back lot and
made my way into the dimly lit foyer. The ground floor was subdivided
into offices with pebbled-glass doors. John D. MacDonald wrote novels
about offices like these.

I opened the door of the correct office and entered a reception area
only big enough for one desk, a worn love seat, and a potted ficus tree.
An elderly lady with glasses on a chain resting on her bosom asked, "Can
I help you?"

"I'm Eddie Kovacs. I'd like to see Royce Carlyle."

"Do you have an appointment?"

"No, but I think he'll want to see me. If he's busy, I can wait."

She disappeared for less than a minute before a man with a broad smile
on his tanned face burst out of the inner office and said, "By the will of

God, you made it home!" He walked right up to me and wrapped me in a bear hug. To the elderly lady he said, "Darlene, this is Chief Warrant Officer Kovacs, Tucker's partner in Vietnam."

I was wearing civilian clothes, so Mr. Carlyle—that's who he had to be—didn't know my legitimate rank. Darlene gave me a nice smile and said, "Good to meet you, sir."

Carlyle stepped back and extended a hand. "Pleased to meet you."

I shook it. "Likewise."

"Darlene, when Beau gets here, have him join us."

He motioned me into his private office, all dark wood and bookshelves, with one sunburst window overlooking the parking lot. Like his son, Royce was an inch or two taller than me, with dark features and salt-and-pepper hair. He had to be about sixty-five years old but seemed energetic and healthy.

He sat behind his desk, and I sat in a visitor's chair. From a bottom drawer, he pulled a bottle of Old Grandad bourbon and two sipping glasses. It was not yet lunchtime, but it would have been rude to decline his offer. We clinked glasses and took a sip.

"This demands a celebration. Tucker told me all about you," he started. "He liked you a lot."

"I liked him, too. How did you hear about me?"

"He called from the MARS station at each base you visited so we could exchange information about the investigation. I think I gave him good advice."

The investigative approach Tucker was adamant about following had come from his father. If Tucker had followed my advice, he'd have lived through the mission.

"The mission we were on is still classified, so I can only tell you that it was a success. We got a corrupt lieutenant colonel relieved of his command and kicked out of the Army. Tucker was relentless in his pursuit of evidence no matter where it led him."

"He gave his life for that mission. What can you tell me about that? The Army was vague about the circumstances."

I steered clear of the truth, afraid of what Major Burns might do to me. It was another shameful act. "At the last camp we visited—I can't reveal its name—we found the evidence we had been seeking. The camp came under a full-scale attack by the North Vietnamese Army; tanks, artillery, men through the wire, everything."

Royce sipped his drink and nodded for me to continue.

"The Green Beret commander decided we couldn't wait any longer for reinforcements and had to abandon the camp, so ten of us left the command bunker and slipped out of the camp into the jungle. We headed to a landing zone where a helicopter was supposed to pick us up. I was near the front of the group and Tucker was at the back. Before we reached the LZ we came under fire and Tucker and another man at the back were killed."

My voice choked up and the grief that had been staunched by fear for my own life swept over me. I began crying as I should have done at Tucker's funeral and that triggered new tears in Royce's eyes. He pulled a silk handkerchief from a pants pocket, but he didn't offer it to me. He wiped his tears away, then came around his desk and put an arm around me.

The door opened and a young man found us in an awkward embrace. "What's going on?"

"This is Chief Kovacs, Tucker's partner, who managed to escape from the attack. He was just telling me about how it happened." He didn't need to explain what "it" was.

"They never told us there was a survivor."

"Chief, this is my son, Beau."

I rubbed my raw eyes, embarrassed at having been caught in exactly the emotional situation I had wanted to avoid, then turned my reddened face to Tucker's younger brother. Two or three years older than me and a bit shorter than his older brother, Beau more closely resembled his father, broad at the shoulders with laser-sharp blue eyes. "Eddie Kovacs," I said.

We shook hands and Beau took a seat. "When the Army notified us of Tucker's death, they said that everyone who tried to escape the camp had been killed. But here you are," Beau said.

I refused to let this guy make me feel guilty for surviving. "We came under fire from behind where Tucker was bringing up the rear. Everyone ran, but I went back to look for Tucker. The other guys got on that chopper and lifted off without me."

"They left you behind?" Royce said, anger welling up in his voice.

"They thought I was dead," I lied. "The helicopter got shot down and they all died. If Tucker and I had made it to the chopper, we'd have died in that crash."

"God spared you for some special purpose in your life," Royce said.

Beau made a derisive blowing sound with his mouth. "Tucker's death saved your life."

I had never thought of it that way but Beau was right. "I prefer to think God spared me."

"Did you find my brother?"

"I did. He was about thirty meters behind the group. He and an NCO were dead."

"How did you manage to escape?" Beau asked.

"I hid in the jungle and was rescued by reinforcements who came later. We'd probably all have survived if we hadn't tried to escape. That's the tragedy of combat decisions—fight or flight—you can't predict which will save your life."

Beau snuffled impolitely. "Well, you got lucky, but Tucker didn't."

"That's not Eddie's fault, Beau." To me, Royce said, "You going to stay in the Army?"

"No, the Army isn't for me." *The Army doesn't want me around.* "My father wants me to come home and work in the family business—dry cleaning. But that's not for me, either. So, I'm not sure."

"When do you get out?"

I told him.

"That's great. Why don't you come to work for us? We've got an opening."

"Yeah, Tucker's spot," Beau said. He didn't hide his animosity.

Royce ignored his son. "Tucker said you were a crackerjack detective and know all about computers. We'll need that skill as computers become more prominent in our lives. He said I should give you a job."

Beau made another impolite sound as he rose from his chair. "Fine. He can take all the night surveillance jobs," he said.

Royce tried to lighten the mood. "It'd be like starting in the mailroom." He smiled.

So Tucker had orchestrated the whole situation—an Army assignment in his hometown and a job at his father's firm as he continued his Army career.

I glanced at Beau, who glowered at me. Fuck Beau Carlyle. I had been bitten by the investigative bug and I needed a reason not to go back to my toxic family. "Okay, I'm your new mailroom boy. I really appreciate this."

CHAPTER FIFTEEN

... Now

Eddie slept in. Told himself he deserved it. He made scrambled eggs, toast, and microwave bacon that he ate at his round dining table. He threw open his drapes on an overcast day, cool enough under the clouds for residents to take breakfast at tables around the pool. About half male and half female, the diners seemed to be paired off like Cardinals in the spring. Beyond the pool, two couples in tennis whites were chasing a yellow ball around the court. He watched for a while, concluded that none of the women were ever going to make the *Sports Illustrated* swimsuit issue. He wondered if Madeleine had recovered from last night's emotional events and what she was doing with her day.

The sheriff, Tucker's nephew, Lance Carlyle, had said, "The DEA promised to give me first crack at it, but they'll take the case over if I can't solve it soon." After seeing Stevenson with the local authorities last night, investigating a drug overdose, Eddie was certain the DEA had lied and put their own man inside. *So I'm in a race,* Eddie thought, *but I have the evidence.*

He showered, dressed in shorts and a polo shirt, and grabbed the book Bobby hated, thinking he might find a spot to sit and read for a while. He rigged his door to alert him to intruders and headed up to what had become something of a second home for him—the fourth floor in the assisted living wing.

There was no crime scene tape across the door to Doris's apartment and no authorities tossing the room. Either a manner of death hadn't been determined yet or her death had been ruled an accident or suicide. He stopped at Lucy's room and reminded Janice of their plan for the evening.

He crossed to the fourth floor of the central building. Through stained glass windows, the sun streamed in from the east, lighting six rows of empty pine pews in the chapel. In the arts & crafts room, one woman was painting with watercolors while two others were trying to get the pottery wheel to spin. In the game room, two women played pool and two men played foosball.

When he peeked into the card room, he was surprised to be hailed by name. Lipstick Lady—Phyllis Candler—and two companions were at a card table. Eddie recognized Lilac Lady, Bernice MacMillan, but not the other woman. Phyllis graciously invited him to be the fourth for bridge and Eddie accepted. His partner was a woman named Gladys Van Camp from Marietta, whom Eddie found to be witty and reckless with her bids. While Eddie gently probed Phyllis and Bernice for information about Michael Cevert, he and Gladys lost two rubbers.

Phyllis offered one succinct opinion: "People die in Cevert's office. Gerry and Lydia Matthews saw it and now they're gone. I don't let my friends become Cevert's patients."

He thanked the women for a pleasant afternoon and left the card room. Before returning to his apartment, Eddie ducked into the library to complete his fourth-floor tour. Five rows of bookshelves were crammed into the room along with a checkout desk and the magazines and DVDs that were also on loan to residents.

Eddie browsed down one row and up the next and was disappointed to find that the book selection was very much like that at a large chain store—books by celebrities and formulaic sequels by tired, overhyped bestselling authors. Eddie continued into the fourth row and found the shelves that held legal and military thrillers. He had heard the story of the eight-year-old boy who had become famous when he snuck his handwritten book into a library. Eddie squeezed the novel Bobby hated between Grisham and Clancy where the story so throbbing with anxiety might just be found.

He felt like a schoolboy who'd been caught doing something shameful when he heard voices from behind the last row of books, nearest the back wall. A man and a woman. She hissed and the man tried to shut her up. Eddie removed two books from a shelf at eye level so he could see who was arguing in the library. *My, my, my,* he said to himself, *if it isn't my reluctant helper, Peggy, and Randy, the nasty fourth-floor orderly.* Randy gripped Peggy's arms and shook her. After a bit, Peggy slumped into Randy's chest and he gave her a comforting hug, patting her back. Randy tipped her face up to look at him and kissed her. *Boyfriend and girlfriend.* He pulled a plasticine bag from his pocket and stuffed it in the pocket of Peggy's scrubs. With his thumb he wiped a tear from her eye. Then the pair started for the exit end of their row, so Eddie slipped around the other end of his row and waited for them to walk toward the door.

✳ ✳ ✳

When they alighted from the taxi under the portico, Madeleine handled the fare and the tip for the driver. She had also paid for dinner at the Pirate's House restaurant in Savannah. The choice of restaurant had been left to him.

In their salad days, Sam had kept a plain white cookie jar on a kitchen counter into which they dropped their pocket change at the end of each day. She contributed more than Eddie did—tips from her job at the hair salon—and the jar filled at a satisfying pace. Once every two months, Eddie dressed in jacket and tie and Sam donned a dress and heels, and they spent the cookie jar money on a romantic dinner at the Pirate's House. The house, built in 1754, had made an appearance in Robert Louis Stevenson's

"Treasure Island" and is said to be haunted by the ghosts of rum-swilling pirates and intrepid sailors. Typical of its day, the ground floor is chopped up into many small rooms that create an intimate dining experience. The cold tingling in his chest and the blockage in his throat were caused by Sam's spirit, which surely lurked in this building.

Tonight, he was disappointed to find that the other patrons of this once fine restaurant were classless tourists clad in shorts and tank tops and flip flops. The tourists stared at them, at their semi-formal dress and date night demeanor.

"You go through life admiring elderly couples who've kept their love alive for decades and then one day you realize you've become the old couple and everyone is looking at you," Madeleine said.

"Well, we are adorable," Eddie said.

Madeleine smiled.

Initially, Eddie had thought dinner in town was a ploy by Madeleine to keep him away from his apartment or Cevert, but as the evening progressed, they gorged on seafood, traded spars, and laughed at each other's bad jokes.

A couple of times during their dinner, he had scrambled to keep his lies intact when she asked about his childhood. He told her how it felt to grow up in a state often confused with Minnesota or Michigan, a place ignored by the national press, a place whose only identity was the Green Bay Packers and the moniker "frozen tundra." He told her how, as a child, he had lain awake under the bedcovers, listening to clear channel radio stations on his transistor radio—Milwaukee, Chicago, Pittsburgh, New York, Boston, and Atlanta. He told her that he knew there was a bigger world out there and he desperately wanted to be part of it. He wanted her to know him and he wanted to know her. There could only be one reason for that.

To buttress his cover story, he told her that after his discharge, he had complied with his father's wishes to work in the family dry cleaning stores and his life became a mundane succession of working days and sequestered winters.

"After he passed, the stores were ours and I was trapped." That was a lie. His father had passed while Eddie was living in Florida. His mother's passing had been a different story. He was at her bedside to witness an event as gruesome and horrifying as finding Tucker's disfigured body.

Madeleine took a deep breath and swallowed hard. "I felt trapped too. I was raised as a proper Charleston debutante but married a rough, coarse man against my parents' wishes. Then Bruce made more money than my parents and we snubbed our noses at them."

"You got the last laugh."

"No, they were right about Bruce."

Holding hands, they entered Palm Haven's lobby and she pulled him toward her private elevator. He wondered if this was the night they go beyond a stolen kiss, and he wondered if he could refuse to follow her upstairs. He had things to do, but that wasn't the only reason for his reluctance.

After she pushed the call button, Madeleine wrapped both arms around him and kissed him. "Want to come up for a nightcap?"

Eddie should have been prepared for this, but he wasn't. "I'm not ready for this," he stammered.

Her face darkened, like a storm cloud on the horizon. "How long has it been since your wife passed?"

"Six months."

The storm cleared. "Should be long enough, Eddie, but I won't push you to get over Samantha."

Eddie wondered if he'd have accepted Madeleine's invitation if he didn't have work to do. "Thank you."

✳ ✳ ✳

At the appointed time, Eddie took the back stairwell to the landing between the third and fourth floors. No Peggy. He was about to give up on Peggy and default to tracking down Barbara Meachum when the squeak of door hinges alerted him to someone in the stairwell below him. He peered over the railing and saw Peggy climbing the stairs reluctantly, as though she were climbing onto a gallows. Eddie surmised that Randy had convinced her to show up for this meeting.

"You're late," Eddie said.

"God, how I hate addicts."

Eddie had experienced this reaction in his past: There is no touchy-feely, warm and fuzzy customer service relationship with a drug dealer; dealers have nothing but contempt for the addicts who produce their profits.

He waggled his fingers at her—*hand it over*—and she handed him a plasticine baggie containing three white pills. A photo flash went off above them.

"What the fuck?" Peggy exclaimed.

"Smile. You're on candid camera."

Standing on the fourth-floor landing, Janice checked the picture on her phone and gave Eddie a thumbs-up. Then she disappeared through the door to the fourth floor.

"Got ya," Eddie said. Randy hadn't counted on Eddie's ploy.

"Fuck you. Entrapment, that's what this is. It will never stand up in court."

Eddie marveled at the incongruity of this delicate flower of a young woman having such a foul mouth. Whether his approach was entrapment or not didn't concern Eddie. Peggy was just a link in a chain.

"The cops would call it a sting. For me it's just security." He held the bag in front of eyes and shook it, probably the bag Randy had stuffed in her pocket. "Three pills? I'm embarrassed for you, Peggy."

"It's all the Hydrocodone I could get today," Peggy said. "You'll have to wait till next Monday to get more."

Sure. Shipments from the pain clinic arrived on Monday mornings.

He handed her a sheet of notepaper. On it he had written the names of one current and four former residents—Donald McCabe, Gerry Matthews, Doris Christenson, Celia Dawkins, and Jacob Hoffman—and the names of two doctors—Michael Cevert and Arjun Banerjee.

"Now what do you want from me?" she asked.

"I want you to pull the prescription records for the patients and the drug orders for the doctors."

"Why?"

He got straight to the point. "I want to find a connection for opioids so I can sell them."

"No one will buy from you." Peggy scoffed. "The old fogies in here get all they want from the pain clinic."

"I'm not going to sell here. I want to use the connection to sell down in Florida."

"Holy shit! I can't help you with that." She ran her hands through her luxuriously curled hair, then ran her nails roughly over her right shin bone. *Mosquito bites or Meth addict?*

"Well, Peggy, I've got your picture dealing drugs so you're my connection."

"No, no, no. Ask the bimbos up there." She pointed to the fourth-floor door.

"Sleepy Brown Eyes and Chubby on the night shift up there?"

She nodded. "Gail Osborn is the chubby one. Melissa Sanders is the one who looks like you could snap your fingers and get a blowjob. They're connected to drug dealers for sure."

Eddie was certain that Sleepy Brown Eyes and Chubby were conspiring with Dr. Banerjee on the sleeping pills, so maybe he was the opioid source.

"Yeah, they're on my list but first I need the prescription records."

"I don't have access to the pharmacy."

"Don't lie to me. Someone has a key for overnight emergencies. Bring them right here tomorrow at ten p.m. sharp."

Peggy rubbed her eyes with her fingers. "Can I go now?"

"Wait for me to get out of the stairwell first."

Peggy sat down on the steps and sniffled.

No one had broken into his room while he was away. Eddie wrote another note attached to Peggy's baggie of three Hydrocodone pills and placed it in his return vent.

"The Red Snapper is gill-hooked," he told Sam. "Now I troll it past the two sharks and see which one bites."

"I'm warning you, the Grouper is the third shark."

She just wouldn't let it go, but he had to admit that Sam was rarely wrong. "That's why I'm pumping her for information."

"Is that what you call a date at our restaurant?"

Eddie blushed. "Sorry, I should have taken her somewhere else."

"McDonald's or the Dairy Queen would be her speed."

He laughed in spite of himself. "I want to tell you about how we met and married."

"I was there you know."

"Be patient, our story links my Army experience to my biggest regret of all. Besides, I like the story."

Chapter Sixteen

... Then

My roommate, Greg, and his girlfriend, Marion, planned a party to be held at our house on the weekend. Lorraine hung out with us, of course, and Olivia had wandered downstairs uninvited, and then Marion arrived with a girl with long, straight, auburn hair, an eggshell white face dotted with freckles and eyes the color of the Caribbean Sea at dawn. Marion introduced her as Samantha.

Like a cat stalking a bird, I chased Samantha from one knot of partiers to another, insinuating myself into conversations, showing off like a buck deer in mating season. Lorraine figured it out and stayed glued to my side. Samantha figured it out and avoided me. Olivia figured it out and went shopping for someone else to love.

I detached myself from Lorraine and found Samantha dancing with other girls, so I joined the group. Samantha gave me a cautionary look but kept moving to the beat of Pink Floyd, her head bobbing, her unfocused eyes aimed at my knees as though she were in a trance. When the song ended, I tried to move her to the couch, but she resisted, holding me in place for one rock song after another. When Deep Purple started "Smoke on the Water," I insisted I needed a drink and she relented. I mixed one for her—rum and Coke—and we found an unoccupied corner in which to lean and talk.

Her father was indeed a major and preparing to retire. He had bought a fruit farm between Dothan, Alabama, and Panama City, Florida.

"It's called Watermelon Alley," she said. "All the watermelons and cantaloupes you've been eating come from that area."

She had a married older brother already living in the Florida Panhandle, and a younger sister, Raelene, still in high school. Samantha worked as a licensed cosmetologist in a salon downtown. She made it clear that she did not intend to become a farm laborer in Watermelon Alley.

I told her about growing up in Wisconsin and that I was "short," just three months till my discharge.

"You're lucky you made it back from Vietnam," she said. "What are you going to do with the rest of your life?"

"I've accepted an offer to join a private investigative firm here in Savannah."

She laughed as though a young boy had just told her he wanted to grow up to be an astronaut. "You mean like Barnaby Jones?"

The Jones character was a milk-drinking, geriatric P.I. "No, like Mannix." That guy was handsome and debonair.

She laughed at that.

"Can I have your phone number?"

She looked dubious. "Aren't you dating that round girl?"

"No," I lied. "She's a secretary at the base. Greg must have invited her."

She canted her head. "What about the one who looks like a ghost?"

"Somebody Greg knows." I didn't want to reveal that Olivia lived upstairs.

Innocent Lorraine charged up to us and hissed, "Take me home! Right now!"

Samantha snickered as she sauntered away, knowing I had lied. I called Lorraine a taxi. I felt bad about that at the time.

The crowd thinned and soon Marion prepared to leave with Sam.

"I can drive Samantha home," I said.

Marion scoffed. "You drop the major's precious daughter at her house at this hour and you'll get a face full of buckshot. She's staying the night with me, or she'd have had to be home hours ago."

They started for the door, and I said, "Wait!"

Samantha smiled over her shoulder. "Check out the bathroom."

After they left, I went to see what she meant by her cryptic remark. On the mirror, in bright red lipstick, she had scrawled her telephone number.

✳ ✳ ✳

I waited a day before I called her. A gruff voice answered, "Williams' residence."

"May I speak to Samantha, please?"

A grunt, then a shout, "Sam! It's the damned Yankee." The phone clattered onto a hard surface. She had told her parents about me. That was a good sign, wasn't it?

I asked Samantha for a weekend date, dinner at a Chinese restaurant downtown. On Saturday night, I drove to her home, a sprawling white brick split-level in the Windsor Forest section of Savannah and parked next to a big black Buick in the driveway. I rang the doorbell and held my breath. As I feared, the major answered the door. He was my height and thick as a side of beef on a meat hook. His blond hair was shaved into short spikes and his jowls sagged from the edges of his jawline.

"Hi. I'm the damned Yankee."

An irrepressible smile tugged at the corners of his mouth. He walked away, shouting, "Sam! The Yankee is here."

He hadn't opened the door or invited me in, so I waited on the porch. Samantha's mother was next to make an appearance. An attractive redhead with a nose so straight and sharp it could slice cheese, stared at me through the screened door, unabashedly giving me the once-over. She swung the door open and said, "Wait here." She walked away without introducing herself.

It seemed a long time but was probably a couple of minutes before Samantha appeared in a go-to-church-on-Sunday dress and a touch of lipstick. She wore a scowl. Raelene, a carbon copy of Samantha, traipsed after her sister. They walked past me and straight out the door.

"What's the deal with the kid?" I asked.

"She's our chaperone," Samantha said.

"Mama made me go along," Raelene said. "Keep you guys from doing something dirty."

On the way to the restaurant I learned that Samantha's father's name was Samuel and that her older brother was Samuel Junior, but they called him Sammy. When Samantha was born, they did it again, in the feminine form, and Samantha was known as Sam.

"What about your parents?"

"Mama is Mama. You can call my father Major Williams. We call him Big Daddy."

Wow! Straight out of a Tennessee Williams play. "And Raelene?"

"Big Daddy heard it in some country song."

I turned to the young girl and said, "They call you Rae?"

"Hell no," she said. "That's a boy's name. Like Sam." She gave Sam a superior look.

We laughed at Raelene's attempt to eat Lo Mein with chopsticks, but our conversation was constrained by her presence.

✳ ✳ ✳

After three weeks of picking her up at home and dropping her off—sober—before curfew, I gained the major's trust. Mama was a different story, cold as a cadaver on a slab. Then I received the invitation I dreaded: dinner with her parents at their home.

As scared as I had ever been in Vietnam, I arrived at their door in my dress uniform holding a spray of flowers. The major chuckled. Mama put the flowers in a vase and set them on the dining table, but I could tell by her demeanor that she wasn't about to be scammed by a Yankee.

She served smothered pork chops and black-eyed peas and biscuits, followed by peach cobbler for dessert. We drank iced tea so sweet my teeth ached.

Major Williams pointed to the ribbons on my chest. "You were in Vietnam?"

"Yes." Contrary to Major Burns' orders, I had worn all my medal ribbons to impress Big Daddy.

"Korea was my war. Every generation should have a war. Thins the herd and accelerates evolution. What did you do over there?"

"I'm afraid that's classified, sir. It involved the Special Forces."

"I have a Purple Heart, too. Hope you weren't wounded anywhere important." His laugh came straight from a men's locker room.

"No, sir." I tapped my forehead. "Just my head."

He chuckled. "I don't recognize that medal," he said, pointing to a deep red ribbon with dark yellow stripes down the center and a bronze palm leaf device. "What is it?"

"It's the Vietnamese Gallantry Cross, sir."

His face scrunched up in confusion. "Never heard of it."

"It's awarded by the Vietnamese government, not the U.S. military."

"What for?"

"Valor. Courage."

He decided to be impressed. "Well, when your mission is declassified, I want to hear all about it."

Unhappy that Big Daddy was impressed, Mama changed the subject abruptly. "Where do you go to church, Eddie?"

Sam's family were Southern Baptists who didn't believe in dancing or drinking or fooling around before marriage. Sam knew I had been raised a Catholic and said that was the worst possible thing to admit. A Protestant of some sort would be acceptable. Methodist was the neutral answer Sam said I should give. Now she clasped my hand under the table as a reminder.

Since I was doing so well with the major I decided not to lie. "My family is Catholic, but I gave that up long ago."

Sam covered her mouth to stop spitting her food onto the table. Mama sucked in her breath as though punched in the stomach.

The major found a diplomatic solution: "You can go to church with us on Sunday. See if you'd like to join our congregation."

✳ ✳ ✳

As the retirement of Major Williams neared, he planned a full week at their house in Florida to check up on Sammy, who had gotten the farm started. The major invited me to come along and experience rural Florida life. Since we'd all be under one roof and under her watchful eyes, Mama acquiesced, and I accepted.

A former boarding house in a tiny town, their house sat on the main highway twenty miles north of Panama City. Raelene, Sam, and I each had a room upstairs, while Mama and Big Daddy slept in the master bedroom downstairs.

That first night, I sat up in bed, wondering if I should tiptoe to Sam's room, then decided against it. With Raelene on the same floor, it was too risky.

✳ ✳ ✳

In the morning, pickup trucks full of day laborers arrived at their house, and Mama chose the ones she wanted to work that day. They left with Sammy for the fields.

The rest of us set up a fruit stand on the road in front of their house. Vacationers from Tennessee and Alabama passed by on their way to the sugar sand beaches and every family needed a watermelon or a couple of cantaloupes. Big Daddy expected Sam to run the fruit stand.

All day long, I lifted, carried, pushed, pulled, and humped wooden racks on which we stacked an endless supply of cantaloupes and watermelons. Sam met the cars as they stopped, explained the difference between the round melons and the oblong melons, laughed at the people who thumped the melons with their fingers, took the cash and made the change.

At the end of the day, I relaxed on the wide country porch sipping iced tea as the farmworkers gathered to be paid for their day's labor. The workers were Black, itinerant Mexicans, and dirt-poor whites. Mama paid them in cash.

In the middle of the night, a warm body slipped into my bed. Although Sam was five-foot-nothing in her bare feet, she was far from fragile, her loose, casual clothing hid the surprising fullness of her contours. She was uninhibited and adventurous, and I was chagrinned to learn I wasn't her first rodeo. She was dangerously noisy and I had visions of Major Williams storming into the room with a shotgun. Afterward, she giggled as she returned to her room.

✳ ✳ ✳

The second day, my job became easier as I only had to replenish the stock of melons as Sam sold them. Sam complained often and bitterly, saying she refused to leave her life in Savannah to become a farmer. She asked leading questions about my plans. What will it be like to be a private investigator? How much money would I make? I had the idea I was being interviewed for a job.

That evening, Mama and Sam prepared a meal of fried chicken, fried corn, fried okra, collard greens swimming in pork fat, biscuits, and white gravy. Sammy and his pretty wife, Patti, came over as well as Big Daddy's two younger brothers and their families. The children played outside while the men sat in recliners in the living room, listening to Waylon Jennings records. Big Daddy told his brothers that I was a war hero and that my exploits were so important they were classified. At first, I was embarrassed, then I basked in my little bit of glory. "Just doing my duty," I said, faking humility.

I didn't contribute much to the conversation after that. The three brothers and Sammy talked about local happenings and local politics. The word "nigger" was thrown around as casually as a baseball on Sunday afternoon.

Before the visitors left, Sammy asked if I liked to fish. I said I did.

"Cool. I'll take you to the wildlife refuge on Saturday and we'll catch a mess."

As we climbed the stairs to our bedrooms, I mentioned to Sam my discomfort at hearing the term nigger used so blithely.

She bristled. "You going to lecture me on racism? When Big Daddy was stationed at Fort Shafter, Hawaii, Sammy and I were in elementary school. The Polynesian kids called us Haole, shark bait. In elementary school! Everybody is prejudiced against somebody, Eddie."

✳ ✳ ✳

The boat ramp was nothing more than a dirt road that sloped gently to the water's edge. Sammy launched the sixteen-foot aluminum camp boat—just a hull with three flat crossbeams for seats—and we were enveloped by wilderness. Twenty to thirty yards wide, the river was flanked by cypress trees whose limbs overhung the water and provided welcome shade. A thirty-five-horsepower outboard engine was mounted at the stern, but Sammy drove the boat from the bow with an electric trolling motor. Barefoot, he stood upright, perfectly balanced, and steered with his toes, guiding us around cypress knees and in and out of narrow sloughs. I sat on the beam closest to the stern so we both had room to rig our poles and cast. Positioned in the center of the boat was a large cooler filled with ice. Close to me, a smaller cooler held drinks and snacks. A single shot .22 caliber rifle lay alongside my seat.

Around a bend he said, "This is the spot. They're bedding right here. Laying eggs and fertilizing them. Can you smell it?"

All I smelled was mildew and cypress pollen, but Sammy had chosen a good spot.

I caught the first fish, the size of my hand. "Blue gilled Sunfish," I announced.

"Maybe you call it that up north, but down here that's a Bream," Sammy said.

We quickly caught twenty fish, some bigger than hand-size and silver-sided instead of green. "They're the granddaddies," Sammy said.

He pulled up anchor and we floated slowly downstream. We floated, we stopped, we fished, until Sammy estimated we had caught one hundred Bream. Sammy cranked the outboard motor and drove us back upstream against the current. The last line of *The Great Gatsby* flashed through my mind: "So we beat on, boats against the current …" According to Fitzgerald, we are who we are and there are no second acts in life. I wondered if I could be a different person down here.

✳✳✳

"You going to marry Sam?"

We were on the long road back to Sammy's house. The blunt question caught me off guard. "Don't know that Sam would say yes."

"She told me she's in love for the first time in her life. She's never brought any other boy home."

Well, she's known other boys, I thought, but I didn't say it. "I doubt your parents would approve."

"Big Daddy likes you. Mama could be a problem."

"What's she have against me?"

He laughed. "You *have* been planning it. Mama wants Sam to marry a God-fearing, church-going Southern gentleman, an Ashley Wilkes type.

To her, you're Rhett Butler. She's dragged a herd of young lieutenants past Sam like a fisherman dragging a lure past a bass, but Sam never bites."

"So, she dislikes the fact that I'm a Yankee enlisted man."

Sammy nodded. "And you have 'Catholic' tattooed on your lost soul. She told Big Daddy you'll keep Sam barefoot and pregnant." He gave me a conspiratorial look. "If you want to marry Sam, you have to get Big Daddy on your side."

"That's what I'll do."

"You'll make a good brother-in-law, Eddie." He clapped me on the shoulder.

So, the fishing trip had been a test, an adventure concocted by the major and Sammy, to bypass Mama's objections to me.

＊＊＊

When I entered the kitchen door of Big Daddy's house, I heard an argument raging between Big Daddy and Sam in the living room.

"Clean yourself up for dinner," Mama said to me and turned back to work at the stove.

I started up the stairs and heard father and daughter shout indistinguishable words at each other.

After I showered, I found Sam and Patti sitting at the dining room table. Sam's eyes were puffy and red. I wasn't sure if Patti was comforting her or guarding her in case she tried to escape. I moved toward her, and she shook her head.

"Sammy and Big Daddy are on the front porch," Patti said.

"I hear you're good with a fishing rod," Big Daddy said.

"Did a lot of fishing with my father."

"You'll fit right in," Big Daddy said.

He excused himself and when he was out of earshot, I asked Sammy what the fight was about.

"Your girlfriend refused to work the stand, busiest day of the week. She hopped in your car and went to the beach."

"She need permission to do that?"

"She's got a job to do for the family," Sammy said and that ended the discussion.

Mama and Raelene had fried the Bream whole in a cornmeal batter. I had never eaten fish more delicious or sweeter corn on the cob. While the rest of the family pretended nothing was wrong, Sam shot me angry glances and said not a word.

When our big catch had been reduced to a pile of bones and fins, Sammy and I went to the porch to relax with more iced tea and Sam headed straight upstairs to her bedroom. I heard Big Daddy yell at her, "Church at ten o'clock sharp. Don't make us late."

✳ ✳ ✳

I was sound asleep when Sam slithered under the covers beside me. "Do you love me, Eddie?"

"Yes." I was sure I did.

"Let's get married and get out of this place," she whispered.

That brought me fully awake. "I think the man does the asking, even in the South."

"So, ask me now."

I felt as though I was on a rubber raft, racing downstream on a raging river, heading for roiling rapids and steep waterfalls, at the mercy of fate, destiny, or perhaps, God's will. I had been swept off my feet by a small, redheaded dynamo. As though I were raising my hands in the air at the top of a roller coaster, I succumbed to the exhilarating freedom of total helplessness.

Kneeling beside the bed, I said, "Will you marry me, Sam?"

She squealed, wrapped her arms around my neck, and fell on top of me. We sprawled on the floor, her lips all over my face.

I put a finger to my lips. "Are you trying to get us caught?"

She straddled me and we sealed the deal right there on the floor. An image of Big Daddy with a shotgun flashed through my brain. Was that her plan?

We slid back into bed and whispered under the covers. "What the hell do we do now?"

"In the morning you ask Big Daddy for my hand in marriage."

The gentlemanly thing to do filled me with dread. "Do we need his blessing?"

"You have to be twenty-one to get married in Georgia. Florida, too. He'll have to sign for me."

But sixteen was the age of consent for sex. Seemed a contradiction to me. "And, after that?"

"You catch bad guys in Savannah and we live there happily ever after."

✳ ✳ ✳

We sat on the couch and waited for Mama and Big Daddy to emerge from their bedroom. My knees bounced and my hands sweated. They came out together, dressed in their Sunday best.

"You're not ready for church," Mama said.

"Eddie has something to ask Big Daddy," Sam said.

"We're going to be late," Mama said. "Get upstairs and get ready. Both of you."

"Let me have a word with the boy," Big Daddy said with a twinkle in his eye. "Won't take long."

Mama slammed her purse down on the coffee table, but Big Daddy ignored her. I followed him onto the porch. He sat in a rocker and waved me into another. He squinted into the morning sun and said, "Well?"

I hadn't slept at all after Sam left my room last night. Over and over, I practiced this speech, choosing precisely the right words. "Sam and I are in love. I think you can see that."

"Uh-huh."

"And I've come to love the South."

"Uh-huh."

"And I've come to love your wonderful family."

"Spit it out, son."

I swallowed bile to keep from spitting it out. "I'd like your blessing to marry your daughter."

He smiled. "Uh-huh. And how will you support my daughter?"

He expected me to say we'd both work on his melon farm, but I didn't want to start married life on a lie. "I've accepted an offer to join the Carlyle Detective Agency in Savannah."

He whooped, reached over, and slapped my knee. "I was right. I guessed you were CID in Vietnam." He jumped to his feet and motioned for me to stand. He gave me a bear hug."

"Here's how we'll do it. We'll have a military wedding, dress uniforms at the post chapel. Maybe the day before my retirement ceremony. The chaplain is a Methodist and a good friend, so he'll perform the ceremony. How's that sound?"

"Sounds good," I lied.

He put a meaty arm around my shoulders and led me back into the house. "Say hello to your new son-in-law, Mama."

Without a word, Mama picked up her purse and walked toward the bedroom.

"What about church?" Big Daddy asked her back.

She didn't answer, kept walking, and then slammed the bedroom door behind her.

Big Daddy said, "I'll see about Mama." He waved a finger back and forth between me and Sam. "Tell her the plan, son."

I took Sam by the arm and led her toward the porch. Raelene followed until I showed her a one-handed stop sign. "Not you, little one."

She turned up her nose. "I have to be maid of honor. They won't let that big nigger do it."

She was referring to Dominique, Sam's best friend. As I related Big Daddy's wedding plans to Sam, we overheard the fight in the master bedroom.

"How could you let a damned Yankee marry my daughter?" Mama said.

"You want her to marry some redneck cracker down here?"

"I can find someone appropriate."

"You had your chance to marry her off and you failed. Now it's my turn," Big Daddy said.

✳ ✳ ✳

"We're screwed!"

"What did you do, Eddie?"

I had driven straight to Sam's salon, dragged her away from her station where she had been coloring a woman's hair and into the supply room. "The post chaplain found out I'm a Catholic and he refused to perform the ceremony."

"How did he find out? It's not tattooed on your forehead."

"Your mama snitched on us."

"That bitch! I can't move to Florida."

I had been leaning against the door to prevent unwelcome intrusions. Now someone was pushing on it roughly, barging their way into the supply room. Dominique, the tall Black shampoo girl, peeked around the door. "That woman's hair is going to fry if you don't get out here right now," she said to Sam.

"Shut the damned door," Sam hissed.

Dominique misinterpreted the command, slipped into the cramped space, and closed the door behind her. "What's wrong, child?" she asked Sam.

Sam's nose and eyes crinkled up like a crushed paper towel and she cried, loud bawling wails of anguish, as she soaked the front of my uniform. I explained the situation to Dominique.

"You don't have to be twenty-one to get married in South Carolina," Dominique said. "Eighteen's the law. All you need is a driver's license and two witnesses."

Dominique lived just across the border in South Carolina. She told us that there was a Justice of the Peace in Ridgeland who was known as "the marrying judge" because he performed all the marriages for kids who had to get married without parental consent. Ridgeland was just thirty miles north of Savannah.

Sam stopped crying. Her face unfolded into a calm mask, like the smooth surface of a glacier lake. Not a ripple on that water, but her eyes glowed like fireplace embers.

"Let's elope," Sam said.

"I'll be a witness," Dominique said. "And I know just the man to be the second witness."

We followed Dominque onto the salon floor, where she whispered to a skinny young man wearing earrings and a ponytail. He laughed and congratulated Sam. Then the entire staff joined in the celebration.

We climbed into my car and barreled across the state line into South Carolina, committing the Federal offense of transporting a minor across state lines.

As though it were no big deal, the Judge performed a ceremony that lasted less than ten minutes. The clerk printed an official marriage certificate for us.

✳✳✳

The next morning, I drove Sam to work at the salon where we found Raelene waiting for her on the steps of the shop. "You better be married," Raelene said to her sister.

Ironic, I thought, how the euphemistic shotgun could be used alternately to deter a marriage or coerce a marriage.

"Come get in the car, Raelene," I said. "We're going to your parents' house."

That they were expecting me says something about my character, I think. We wound our way between moving boxes stacked nearly to the ceiling so they could sit side by side on the couch in the formal living room. I took the closest easy chair. A feeling of a life abandoned permeated the room. The pictures that had hung on the walls, the keepsakes and mementos that had sat on shelves and side tables, were now packed in boxes in a vain attempt to take their memories with them to a new world.

I handed Big Daddy the marriage certificate and he studied the South Carolina state seal carefully in the way that bank tellers examine large denomination bills to detect forgeries. He held it for Mama to read, but she slapped his hand away. She jumped to her feet and swung her open hand, striking me flush on my left cheek. The splat sound echoed through the hollow room. I rocked back in my chair, stung as much by shame as by the slap.

"Now we're disgraced," Mama said.

Big Daddy restrained her, gently forcing her onto the couch. "What's done is done," he said.

✳ ✳ ✳

We attended Big Daddy's retirement ceremony and the day after that, he and Mama and Raelene left for Watermelon Alley. At my request, Greg reluctantly moved out of our ground-floor apartment, leaving Sam and me alone and married in Savannah.

With Royce's tutelage and sponsorship, I earned a private investigator's license and worked at the Carlyle & Sons Agency while Sam worked at the beauty salon. For us, "happily ever after" lasted nearly five years.

CHAPTER SEVENTEEN

... Now

Eddie borrowed a beach umbrella and a chaise lounge chair from the Concierge and bought a small cooler and canned lemonade at the convenience store. He dragged the supplies to the beach, one hundred yards south of Palm Haven and away from the residents who galumphed along the sand behind the condo complex. He setup behind lavish homes whose values had been crushed by Palm Haven's construction, among a few carefree mothers and their unencumbered children frolicking in the sea. He hoped his instructions had been clear.

Battered by gritty wind, his baseball cap pulled low over mirrored aviators, he pretended to read *Leaving Berlin* by Joseph Kanon but he wasn't comfortable. Sam could sit on the beach all day, but Eddie hated the sand in his shorts and the salt on his skin. He wanted to be *on* the water, not in it or beside it.

Finally, a young man in walking shorts and a blue windbreaker approached from the north, meaning he had come through the Palm Haven lobby. Sloppy! Eddie sincerely hoped the windbreaker didn't have a police shield emblazoned on it. As the man passed by, Eddie handed him Doris's pill vial still wrapped in a tissue and the man slipped it into his pocket. The man continued down the beach about ten yards, gazed at the ocean for a minute, then reversed and walked past Eddie again.

"Prints and analysis of contents," Eddie said.

Eddie gave him fifteen minutes to leave the area, then humped the chair and umbrella indoors,

✳ ✳ ✳

After a shower, Eddie joined his friends in the dining hall but he didn't sit down. He needed a plausible reason to dump his tablemates before meeting Peggy this evening. "Who wants to eat in the grill tonight?"

"Too noisy. Can't have a discussion up there," Bobby said.

Eddie had guessed they'd prefer the dining room. "Do we need another discussion?"

"Have a seat, Eddie," Madeleine said.

"What's the topic tonight? The sex lives of bees?"

Bobby cleared his throat. "Donald thinks the Bible is an accurate historical record of—"

"We can do the Bible some other night," Susan said. "Finally, we have a victory to celebrate—the new gun control bill. Let's drink to that."

"Hear, hear," Donald said as he raised his glass in a toast.

"More Americans have died from gun violence than in all the wars in American history combined," Susan spat at Bobby.

"It's harder to adopt a rescue dog than it is to buy a gun," Madeleine said.

Flustered by the attention and his loss of control of the conversation, Bobby stammered, "Guns don't kill people, the crazy people pulling the trigger do it."

"There's some truth in that," Michael said gently. "After every mass shooting, we find that the parents knew their kid was sick, teachers suspected it, and no one did anything about it."

Bobby gathered steam. "The bill didn't overturn the Second Amendment. It's my Constitutional right to own a gun."

"Have you even read the second amendment?" Donald asked. He tapped on his phone, then held it in front of him as he read. "'A well-regulated Militia, being necessary to the security of a free State, the right of the people to keep and bear arms, shall not be infringed.' That's all of it. The Amendment passed at a time when a fledgling nation, sparsely populated and agrarian, needed everyone to own a weapon if called upon to defend the country against foreign aggression."

"Or against Native Americans," Susan added.

Donald flashed a solicitous smile at Susan. "The Supreme Court made a mistake when it decided that gun owners didn't have to be members of a militia."

"All those poor kids in Texas had to die before something was done about assault rifles," Madeleine said.

"Assault weapons aren't the biggest problem," Eddie said, standing above the others. "Mass shootings horrify us, but they represent just 1.2% of all gun deaths. Politicians ban assault weapons to curry favor with voters but handguns cause more than 89% of all gun deaths. They're the problem."

"Where did you get those numbers?" Bobby asked.

"*The New York Times*," Eddie said.

"Sure, a Commie newspaper. Are you just a contrarian or do you enjoy screwing with me?" Bobby said to Eddie.

"Both," Eddie said with a shrug.

Susan cackled.

"Sit down, Eddie," Madeleine urged him.

Michael ignored the spat. "I'm sorry Susan, but the bill is pretty weak. Background checks routinely miss people with mental health issues."

"That's right," Madeleine said. "That crazy kid who shot up the Fourth of July parade passed several background checks." Madeleine turned to Susan. "If you ever feel unsafe, Susan, come to my apartment."

"Oh, I'm not afraid of Bobby, but y'all should be," Susan said.

Eddie was no longer listening to the discussion. He was watching Stevenson take a seat at a table with Phyllis and Bernice, Lipstick Lady and Lilac Lady. He showed them a piece of paper.

Eddie nudged Madeleine and pointed to Stevenson. "What's he doing?"

"He's already been here. Showing everyone a picture of Gerry Matthews."

Stevenson had become an impediment, like a pebble in Eddie's shoe. Only a matter of time before Stevenson tracked down Gerry's next of kin.

"Hope he finds him," Eddie lied. "I'm eating in the grill," he announced. No one followed him, so he went to his apartment.

✳ ✳ ✳

Eddie drank a beer and watched TV news until the appointed time to rendezvous with Peggy. On the fourth floor, Sleepy Brown Eyes and Chubby were reading magazines behind their counter. With the residents drugged to sleep, they had little to do. Randy was nowhere in sight. Both nurses assured Eddie that Lucy was asleep, but Eddie insisted he have a quick look.

"You two are the poster children for active seniors, aren't ya?" Chubby said, and she grinned.

Eddie gave them a wave as he walked down the peaceful hallway.

Lucy was not asleep. She was watching a talk show on TV and eating chocolates out of a heart-shaped gift box.

"Hey," Eddie said. "You're up late." Checking on Lucy had been a ruse. He didn't have time for chitchat.

"Want one?" Lucy asked as she extended the box of truffles.

He didn't want to be rude, so he accepted. He gave her a "Hmm," as he took a bite.

"I feel good. Janice says to thank you."

"Yeah. Glad to see you're doing well, Lucy."

"Take a load off and stay for a while."

"Sorry, got to run. I'll see you tomorrow." He left before she could cajole him into staying. No one paid him any attention as he scampered down the hallway and through the stairwell door. Peggy was on the landing holding a manila folder full of documents. He hesitated on the floor above her, waiting to be sure that Randy wasn't lying in ambush.

"You want it or not," she said, annoyed with him.

He hurried down the flight of stairs and grabbed the folder.

"Did you have to get help from anyone else?"

"No, I found the key to the pharmacy."

Cevert was the doctor on call for emergencies. The key was probably in his office.

It was time to turn the screws on Peggy. "When you were playing Robin Hood, did you help Celia Dawkins?"

Peggy gasped and cupped a hand over her mouth.

That shot in the dark hit home so he followed with another wild shot. "You gave Celia some pills and accidentally killed her."

"No!" she said too loudly, and Eddie shushed her. In a whisper, she added, "She was alive and feeling better. Two days later they whisked her away and no one ever talked about it."

"They" whisked her away. Just like Jacob Hoffman. "Did you help Doris Christenson, Room 1412?"

She threw her head back and took a deep breath. "I didn't have anything to do with that."

"The cops think she was murdered," Eddie said, although he had no such information. The cops hadn't strung crime scene tape on Doris' room door.

"What!?" Her right eyebrow climbed up her forehead and looked like a question mark that had fallen over. "No. I heard it was an accident. Ms. Christenson had a lot of pain from her brain tumor. No one would want to murder that nice old lady."

"Well, somebody killed that nice old lady."

Peggy's head sank to her shoulders like a turtle retreating into its shell. She collapsed on the stairwell steps, scrunched up in a protective ball. "I swear I didn't give it to her."

"Well, Peggy, I don't care who gave the Fentanyl to Doris Christenson. I want to meet the doctor who brings it into Palm Haven. He's the source who can get me a large quantity of opioids. I prefer Fentanyl in pill form. Nothing that's been cut with heroin or other shit."

She looked like the Cobra that the mongoose had offered to befriend. She scratched the back of her left calf. "You're going to get me killed," she said as though it were an obligatory line in a play.

"Make it fast before the cops figure out who overdosed poor Doris Christenson."

A door squeaked open on a floor below them, stirring panic in Eddie's gut. Someone trudged up the stairs. Neither this stairwell nor Lucy's room were safe any longer.

"Tomorrow, at midnight, meet me in the women's restroom by the loading dock entrance and tell me how I can meet the doctor. Don't let anyone follow you. Got it?" Eddie stuck the pharma records down the front of his pants and covered them with his shirt. He grabbed Peggy's arm above the elbow and propelled her down the steps toward whoever was climbing the stairs.

"Go back to your floor and don't let anyone up here."

As he reached Lucy's room, he opened and quickly shut her door loudly to arouse the attention of the nurses, hoping they'd think he had just exited Lucy's room.

He heard Lucy yell, "What?"

Casually, he walked toward the nurses' station and the elevator. Behind him, Lucy peeked out her door, saw him walking away, and called his name.

"Tomorrow, Lucy," he said over his shoulder.

Leaning against the nurses' station, Randy gave him the evil eye. *He knows what Peggy is doing.*

Sleepy Brown Eyes said, "Took ya long enough."

"You didn't do anything nasty in there, did ya?" Chubby said.

The nurses laughed. Eddie reddened and decided to play along. "She's worn out now and going to sleep."

"Good job," Chubby said and she winked.

When he stepped out of the elevator onto the first floor, he was chagrined to see Stevenson leaning against the opposite wall in the darkness of the pharmacy waiting room. The detective looked down the hallway toward the back stairwell, then back at Eddie. Eddie's heart skipped a beat. Stevenson was waiting to see who emerged from the ground floor door. But if Stevenson was watching the stairwell door, who had been coming up the stairs?

Eddie decided that offense was the best defense. "Are you a pervert or something?"

"What?"

"What are you doing lurking in dark corners? You make people nervous."

Stevenson checked the back stairwell door again, and seeing no one emerge, pushed away from the wall and approached Eddie. "Are you nervous, Eddie?"

"Why would I be nervous? I was visiting Lucy Griffin on the fourth floor. Ask the nurses up there. They love me."

"You're the one who sneaks all over the building, in places you don't belong. What are you up to, Eddie?"

Eddie looked him up and down. "If you're pretending to be a resident here, get rid of those polyester jackets and slacks that make you look like a cop."

Dumbfounded, Stevenson said, "What?"

Eddie turned and walked quickly into the lobby with Stevenson in his wake. "I'm going to my room," Eddie said. "I'll let you in with a key this time if you want to tuck me in."

"Hunh? Stay on your own side of the building," Stevenson said.

Eddie took a beer from his tiny refrigerator and chugged half of it. He opened the folder of pharma records on his little dining table and devoured the files like a starving man rescued from a desert island. and rifled through the documents.

He started with Dr. Banerjee and quickly confirmed that the doctor had prescribed potent sleep aids for most of the residents on the fourth floor, although he prescribed the strongest medication, Rohypnol, only for Lucy and Betty, the worst troublemakers. Several residents on the other floors, including Donna Roberts on floor five, were receiving sleep meds as well, leading Eddie to surmise that the conspiracy to anesthetize residents went beyond the lazy night nurses on the fourth floor.

Gerry's primary care physician was listed as "Veterans Administration Hospital – Atlanta." Banerjee had written the scripts for Gerry's cancer and anti-psychotic medications. Cevert had not prescribed any drugs for Gerry Matthews, and Gerry had not been prescribed any Alzheimer's medications by any doctor. Cevert had remanded him to Memory Care to shut him up.

Cevert's patients were Celia Dawkins (deceased), Jacob Hoffman (deceased), Doris Christenson (deceased), Donald McCabe, Madeleine, women named Beverly Johnson and Alice Walton, and a man by the name of Albert Pulenko. Eight patients, three dead. Celia Dawkins had passed six months ago after a long battle with ovarian cancer. Jacob had been diagnosed with Pancreatic cancer, a disease that can kill within weeks. But Karen never knew. Doris had a brain tumor, and Donald was struggling with a lung tumor. All of Cevert's patients had been prescribed large doses of Fentanyl despite his denials. Why was the label torn off Doris's pill vial?

Michael Cevert wasn't an oncologist, so what was he doing for his patients?

The pharmacy records went into the return vent, which was now overflowing with Eddie's treasures. Eddie teased himself with the thought that he should buy a corkboard and pin his evidence to it so he could pace in front of it and scrutinize the papers ad nauseam like the playacting detectives in movies and on TV shows who thought the clues were hiding among the pixels.

He didn't need props to think it through. Doris Christenson had no Fentanyl in her pill organizer, just residue at the bottom of an unlabeled vial. The person who had provided the pills in that vial was a murderer, and the person who delivered the pills to Doris was an accessory to murder.

He raised his beer bottle to the ceiling in a silent toast to Tucker Carlyle. "I'm going to find the drugs in the hands of the perpetrator, just like you taught me, Tucker."

He walked into his bedroom and spoke to Sam's picture. "Cevert is the shark. He's not an oncologist but he's supplying his patients with enough opioids to kill an Army." He realized that all Cevert's patients had cancer. Did Madeleine have cancer?

"Don't get tunnel vision, Eddie," Sam said. "That man has help from you know who."

Madeleine's defense of the doctor and repeated touring of the assisted living wing did distress him.

"Let me tell you about my worst regret. It's the end of that story."

CHAPTER EIGHTEEN

... Then

We were working a homicide that had happened at one of Savannah's disreputable riverfront bars where merchant seamen often tangled with rowdy locals when Royce sent me to the Ralph H. Johnson Veteran's Administration Medical Center in Charleston, South Carolina, to question a survivor who had taken a bullet in the back. The survivor, an Army veteran, was rehabbing at the expense of our tax dollars.

The interview didn't add anything to our evidence against the shooter. The survivor had been running from the fight when struck by a stray bullet and couldn't say with any testimonial certainty which seaman had fired the gun. The fruitless interview didn't disappoint me very much as I had planned to make the best of this wild goose chase by having lunch at Pearls' Oyster Bar before returning to Savannah.

Notes in hand, I made for the elevator and a hasty retreat from the depressing place. I stopped short when someone shouted "Hey, you!" as I passed an open doorway. Probably some patient who thought I worked at the place.

I started away again, then stopped when the voice said, "Don't walk away, Chief!"

There were few people in the world who knew I had once impersonated an Army Warrant Officer. I returned to the doorway and peeked around the doorjamb.

"Thought that was you," came a voice from the shadows.

The man in the wheelchair had lost his right leg below the knee and his left arm below the elbow, giving his atrophied body an odd symmetry. He had long red hair pulled back from his scarred face and knotted in a ponytail, but I recognized him. "You're the communications sergeant from Vu Dong."

"You win the prize. Sergeant Jeffrey Jenkins, sir."

"I thought you were dead. I saw the chopper crash. I saw the burned and mangled bodies."

"Would have been better if I had died." He swept a hand around his emaciated body to illustrate life worse than death. Soldiers in Vietnam often declared they'd rather die than be maimed; fighter pilots claimed they'd rather die than be captured. But when faced with the reality of their circumstance, nearly everyone chose a debilitated life.

"How did you get away?" I gestured to the cripple's missing extremities.

"The CIA spook, David Fletcher, saved me so I could live like this."

Fletcher. Narrow Face! "Anyone else escape?"

Jenkins shook his head. "Just the two of us."

"You guys left me to die."

"We didn't know where you went, and we waited too long for you to show up."

That's not how I remembered it. Fletcher knew I had gone back to check on Carlyle. "I was rescued when the MIKE FORCE from Kon Tum took the camp back."

"And you couldn't leave well enough alone. Had to make a report to the fucking ARVN."

I shrugged. "Only way to ensure the fraud wasn't covered up."

"Fraud, my ass." Jenkins's voice cracked. "You have any fucking idea what you did, Chief?"

"I stopped a revolution and I hung Barlow's ass for arming FULRO." *And I hung him for ordering the murder of Chief Tucker Carlyle.*

"You got the wrong guy, you dickhead. Barlow was a piss-ass martinet, a figurehead."

I had considered the possibility that Major Daniels had been the ringleader; he had prepared all the camps before we could get to them. Since Daniels had died at Vu Dong, I hadn't accused him of any crimes. "Then Major Daniels did it for Barlow. Same thing."

"Daniels?" Jenkins coughed up a derisive laugh. "Daniels thought FULRO was planning another revolt, wanted to stop it, but FULRO was over and done with. The Yards just wanted to keep their territory. Daniels blew the whistle on the arms operation and was the reason you and your partner were snooping around. He got what was coming to him."

Daniels had been shot in the back of his head. Not a freak bullet from the NVA, but an execution. "You guys killed him."

"Green Berets didn't kill him. We were happy to get the weapons, I can admit that, but Fletcher ran that operation." He canted his head and raised his eyebrows, wondering if I could figure it out.

Fletcher had crossed the clearing just ahead of Captain Meyers. "Did he shoot Chief Carlyle, too?"

"Fletcher said the NVA got him."

"Bullshit! Who hacked the Long Binh computer system?"

"Have you been listening to me, Chief?"

"You're saying the CIA undermined MAC-V and broke the agreement with the South Vietnamese government, hacked the computer system and killed Americans to keep the operation going."

"I don't know what MAC-V or the CIA knew. Fletcher and his buddy, Simon, were civilian contractors, mercenaries, and they had help at the Long Binh depot."

"Why did they do it?"

"To make the folks at home feel good, MAC-V pushed for Vietnam-ization, but the ARVN were cowards who were never going to take over the war. So, Fletcher came up with a better way to arm the Yards and save the Central Highlands."

"And I exposed the conspiracy. The American people deserved to know that Vietnamization was a political stunt."

"You self-righteous asshole. The Army made Barlow the scapegoat. His wife divorced him. His kids won't speak to him. He lives in a trailer park in Florida."

"Dereliction of duty. It all happened right under his nose."

"Shee-it. Barlow was too stupid to know what was going on. But ruining a man's career wasn't all you did. The Yards and their families were kicked off the camps. The CIA recruited the Cambodian Khmer Serei but they weren't as tough as the Yards and all our camps fell. The South Vietnamese resettled North Vietnamese refugees in the Central Highlands and forced the Yards to flee to Cambodia and Laos where they were systematically annihilated. Two hundred thousand Yards lost their lives in the war. Hell, Chief, you destroyed an entire culture."

That's why Major Burns prohibited me from talking to the press, to cover up the fiasco. I struggled to mount an adequate defense. "I did the right thing for my partner," was all I could think to say.

"You never saw the big picture, Chief. Your job was to win the war and the Yards were our only hope!" he shouted. "You lost the whole damn war!"

With his good arm, Jenkins wiped spittle off his chin. He suppressed his anger as he recollected the end of the story. "The last four hundred Yards surrendered to UN forces on the Thai border and were relocated to the area around Fort Bragg, North Carolina, Special Forces headquarters. We took care of them. Of course, I spent most of my time in VA hospitals up there."

I bolted from the room, as though running away could erase the past, but I heard what Jenkins said, "You can't run from the past, Chief. We'll make you pay for what you did."

I sat in my car, sweating despite running the air conditioning on maximum, wondering how in the world doing the right thing had turned out to be the wrong thing to do. Rationalizations came swiftly to mind: The blame for the demise of the Montagnards lay at the feet of the corrupt

South Vietnamese government; The Yards wouldn't have stopped the North Vietnamese incursion into the Central Highlands, no matter how well armed; The Montagnard culture never would have survived a South Vietnamese victory. The fateful tactic I couldn't excuse was our failure to trace the computer system changes while at Long Binh. We could have exposed the scheme without traveling to the Central Highlands. Tucker had died for nothing. And David Fletcher was alive.

My stomach roiling, I skipped lunch at Pearl's Oyster Bar and drove straight home. The medals I had proudly displayed in a shadow box, I threw in the trash can. They were a bribe to keep my mouth shut. I panicked. I changed my name to Karl Novak, in honor of my grandfather Karl, and Sam became Mrs. Samantha Novak. Royce vouched for me, and Big Daddy lent a helping hand, and I landed a job as an investigator for the District Attorney in Pinellas County, Florida. Sam was livid—Savannah had become home in a way that no transient posting had ever been home for a military brat.

"Can't you stand up to them instead of running away?" Sam asked.

"Not these guys, Sam. They'll slit my throat while we're sleeping and you'll never even know they were here."

Our new home was St. Petersburg, four hundred fifty-seven miles from Charleston, the last place the Green Berets had located a man named Eddie Kovacs. Sam quickly adjusted, as military brats do, and I completed a degree in Criminology at night and on weekends. Happily ever after lasted until Sam got sick. No, that's not true. Happily ever after ended when I did the right thing again.

Chapter Nineteen

... *Now*

He was brushing his teeth when Sam said, "You never told me the whole story. I thought you just accused a bad guy of the wrong thing. I understand it now, your obsession with Vietnam, your need for redemption."

"I should have told you. I didn't want to scare you more than necessary."

After dressing, Eddie stepped into the assisted living elevator and rode it to the seventh floor. He consulted his little notebook and asked the day nurse for Beverly Johnson, Alice Walton, and Albert Pulenko. The nurse gave him Albert's seventh floor room number and told him that Beverly and Alice lived on the sixth floor.

Eddie found the door open to Albert's room and stepped inside. A man sat in a wheelchair with his back to Eddie, gazing out the window at the gardens and the ocean. A tall oxygen concentrator stood beside the chair. Eddie called hello, but the man didn't stir, so Eddie moved to the window and into the man's peripheral vision. Still no reaction. A face as craggy as the Rocky Mountains stared sightlessly through the window. The clear plastic oxygen line ended in the man's nostrils.

Hands on knees, Eddie positioned his face directly in front of the man's blank eyes. "Can you hear me?" Nothing.

"Can you speak?" Nothing.

Eddie remembered that Sandy, the third-floor nurse, had opined that most of the assisted living residents belonged either in Memory Care or a nursing home. Eddie hated himself for thinking it, but Albert was better off dead.

Eddie sighed and searched the bedroom and the bathroom and found no opioids in his pill organizer, no vials in the bathroom cabinet. But Cevert had prescribed large doses of Fentanyl. So, where?

On the sixth floor, the day nurses were scurrying from room to room, delivering necessities, but the orderly, a slender young man with a toothpick in his mouth, told Eddie that Beverly Johnson lived in room 1614 and Alice Walton had the apartment next door, 1616. The door of room 1614 hung open, so he called out for Beverly and crept into the sitting room. A stooped Black woman wearing a short, salt-and-pepper wig and rust-colored glasses shuffled out of the bedroom. She moved slowly and carefully but used neither a cane nor a walker.

"Did you bring my medications?"

"No, ma'am," Eddie said. "I'm here to check if you're getting the right ones. Today's meds should come soon."

"I don't always get what I need. The candy sticks are what I like."

"Ah, the Fentanyl sticks?"

She squinted at him and made an indecipherable noise. "Fent-what?"

"The candy sticks, ma'am."

"Oh, they ease the pain, you know."

"Sure. How did you come to be a patient of Dr. Cevert?"

"Donald introduced me. Worked for his law firm for years."

"Donald McCabe?"

"Yessir. He's helping me out in here, too."

"I have dinner with Donald every night. Wonderful man."

A light rap on the door alerted them to the presence of a nurse carrying Beverly's drug bag.

"Haven't seen you before," the nurse said. Her name was Martha. She didn't enter the room, stood at the threshold, examining Eddie with lively green eyes.

"Friend of Donald McCabe. Miss Beverly used to work for him."

"Yes, I know *that*," the nurse said, still sounding unsure of Eddie.

"Donald is having health problems of his own, you know, so he asked me to check on Beverly for him."

"Oh. I'm just bringing Miss Johnson's medications. Y'all visit while I load her pill organizer."

Eddie moved to the bedroom doorway and watched the nurse unpackage the vials and a couple of Fentanyl sticks. "Can you check and see if she's getting the right number of those sticks? She says she should get more."

The nurse turned back to Eddie, suspicion clouding her distinctive eyes. "That's what they all say. Has two of them here for when she's in the greatest pain. You can ask the pharmacy or contact her doctor."

Eddie remembered that Beverly's pharmacy record listed three Fentanyl suckers plus dissolvable Fentanyl pills because she suffered from Leukemia. The meds were going missing before they reached the floor nurse. Someone, maybe Shauna, was shorting Beverly so someone else could sell the drugs.

He shrugged. "I have dinner with Dr. Cevert every evening."

Martha gave him an odd look. "I meant her oncologist in Atlanta."

Cevert isn't an oncologist, so why is Cevert prescribing her pain medication?

"I meant that Dr. Cevert could do a better job of speaking to Beverly's oncologist."

Eddie turned back to Beverly in the sitting room and said, "The nurse is taking good care of you, Beverly. I'm going to check on Donald now."

"Let me know how he's doing," Beverly said.

"I will."

Eddie left the room and walked next door to Alice Walton's room. The door was closed, so Eddie knocked and received no response.

From behind him, the slender orderly said, "Down the hall at a party."

"Okay," Eddie said. "I'll come back later."

Eddie waited for the orderly to enter a room, then tried Alice's doorknob and found it unlocked. He slipped inside and began a careful reconnaissance.

A scream came from behind him, and Eddie jerked around to see a Black woman waving a long black umbrella at him like a medieval knight challenging him to a sword fight. He had been caught pawing Alice Walton's pill organizer. He held his hands in front of him in a defensive posture and spoke soothing words, but that didn't mollify the woman, who screamed again. Behind the angry woman, the sitting room began to fill with other residents looking at the suspected thief who had been caught red-handed. Eddie feared nurses and orderlies would arrive soon and call security. Then Beverly Johnson squeezed to the front of the gawking crowd and said, "He's all right. Just checking the medicine."

"That's right," Eddie said to the umbrella wielding woman. "Making sure you get what you need. You are Alice Walton, aren't you?"

"Yeah, that's me."

Eddie had worn a tie and navy blazer to look official for this adventure. "I'm so sorry I came right in, but I have to check all the meds, so …"

Beverly shooed the other onlookers away, but she stayed to help Alice. Eddie was relieved that no nurses had turned up to quell the riot. Then he was dismayed that no nurses had responded to the emergency.

"He's a friend of Donald," Beverly explained to Alice.

"That's right. Did you work for him, too?" he asked Alice.

"No, no, we met when I was on the Atlanta City Council. He was a donor to my campaigns."

Alice gave him a wide berth as she moved to her bed stand and looked at her pill organizer. Seeing nothing disturbed, Alice asked, "Am I getting the right stuff?"

"Do you get pain pills that you put in your cheek and let dissolve in your mouth?" Fentanyl pills worked that way, like the cold remedy Zicam.

Alice squinted through silver-rimmed glasses. "No, no, the pain isn't bad yet."

"Don't get mad at me for asking," Eddie said, "but do you have cancer, Alice?"

"No, no, I have ascites, from cirrhosis of the liver. Never drank a drop of alcohol in my life, yet here it is, killing me." She patted her abdomen. "Have to drain the fluid every two weeks."

Eddie noticed then that Alice's abdomen was distended as though she were five months pregnant. "I'm sorry to hear that," he said.

"It's okay. I'm gonna live till I die. If you're done here, we'll go back to the party."

"Let me have a quick look at your pill organizer." She didn't whack him with the umbrella so he moved around the bed and quickly determined that no Fentanyl rested in her organizer.

"Looks good," Eddie said. "Thank you."

The three of them walked out of the room. Alice closed her door behind her. He followed the women down the corridor until they entered a room where the earlier onlookers were having a party.

"William's birthday," Beverly explained.

A birthday cake rested on the coffee table, trails of black, waxy smoke rising from four candles. William was seventy-four or eighty-four. Or maybe even ninety-four. "Give him my regards."

And there she was again. Madeleine. He recognized her chestnut hair shimmering in the light like the mane of a thoroughbred horse as she chatted with Alice. He ran to the back stairwell and walked down to the fourth floor. As he swung the door open, he saw the detective walking down the hallway toward the nurses' station. Eddie ducked into the lounge and walked around the back of the fish aquarium to watch the detective. A pair of elderly women watching the television from the couch gave Eddie a questioning look. He picked a container of fish food off the stand and shook some flakes onto the surface of the water.

"It's my job to feed the fish," he said.

The women looked doubtful.

Stevenson stopped at the nurses' station and had a conversation with nurse Roundtree. She shook her head a couple of times and nodded a couple of times. Then Stevenson got into the elevator car.

Anticipating Stevenson's next move, Eddie trotted down to the third floor and slipped into the lounge as Stevenson waylaid Sandy near Cevert's office. Sandy tried to disengage and Stevenson pulled her back to ask more questions. Finally, Stevenson let her go free, and headed to the elevator.

Eddie ducked into the stairwell and, assuming Stevenson was going down in the elevator, climbed to the fourth floor. He did not want to be caught coming out of the stairwell. By Stevenson or by Madeleine. At Lucy's door, he peeked inside and found the apartment empty. He stopped at the nurses' station and asked Roundtree if she'd seen Lucy or Janice.

"They went to the grill for lunch. Said they were going to grab an ice cream before Janice has to go to work." Roundtree wore a big smile and Eddie returned it.

"Miracles do happen, Leticia."

"Did your friend catch up to you?"

"Which friend?" Stevenson? Madeleine? The deputy from the beach? He felt surrounded.

"That younger guy with the crewcut."

Shit! "Oh, I know who you mean. He's on my floor. Any sign of Banerjee?"

"Not a trace."

He took the elevator to the lobby and saw Karen coming through the front entrance. She wore a beach cover-up, sand stuck to her toes, and her hair was windblown. He greeted her and asked if she had a good day out there.

"Not good enough. Too many women and not enough men." She started away, then turned and said, "Let me know when you're ready for something better."

∗∗∗

When he opened his apartment door, he found that someone had slid a sealed envelope under his door. The message was short and sweet:

Fentanyl. Smudged prints. DNA from an unidentified female and Randy Tibbetts, a petty thief.

All of Cevert's patients had been prescribed Fentanyl that had gone missing. Doris's pill vial had no label but carried Randy's DNA. Eddie got rid of his tie and headed to the dining room.

That he was walking into an ambush was obvious to Eddie. Bobby rose from his seat, a wicked sneer on his face. Madeleine leaned against the window, her arms folded across her chest. Susan and Cevert leaned forward in their seats, as though anticipating a good show.

Eddie smiled disarmingly. "Y'all look like a sheriff and his posse. Who we hanging?" He skirted Susan and pulled out his chair.

"Don't sit down," Bobby said. "You've been voted off the table."

Eddie raised his left arm and ducked his nose to his armpit. "Was it my deodorant?"

Susan laughed and Bobby shushed her. "Half the time you're not here and the other half, you're an asshole," Bobby said. "The vote was three to one."

Eddie looked at Madeleine and she shook her head. "Donald voted for you, and I abstained," Madeleine said. "I want to hear what you have to say for yourself."

"Won't matter," Bobby said. "It will still be three to two."

"Unless you let Susan vote for herself. Where is my one friend, Donald?"

"He didn't want to be here for this," Cevert said. "I think he's walking in the gardens."

"Enough chitchat," Bobby said. "I Googled you, Eddie, and found all the dirt. You don't own dry cleaning stores in Wisconsin."

"You're talking through your ass again, Bobby. When my father passed, my sister and I sold our shares to my brother, Danny."

"There was one store and your brother inherited it. You were cut out of the will."

Madeleine loudly sucked her breath. A rare smile appeared on Cevert's face. Eddie blushed. Dad had spent his whole life trying unsuccessfully to get Danny to work for him, so his dying revenge was to bequeath the store to his favorite son.

"You lied to us about your name. Samantha Williams married Eddie Kovacs in Ridgeland, South Carolina, but she turns up as Karl Novak's wife in Florida five years later. She never divorced Eddie Kovacs because Eddie Kovacs and Karl Novak are the same person. You." He jabbed a finger at Eddie.

"You have me mixed up with someone else. Ask the IRS how many taxpayers are named Samantha Novak."

"You're lying again. I have the Social Security records." Bobby waited and so did Eddie. "Four years ago you were an investigator for the Pinellas County District Attorney in Florida, and you got fired."

"That's not me."

"Lies on top of lies." Bobby waved a sheaf of paper at Eddie, news clippings. "It says here that Karl Novak went to the media behind the DA's back and hung a cop for murder. The cop went to prison and here's the kicker, was murdered by inmates."

Eddie chanced a glance at Cevert. The normally taciturn doctor sat erect and attentive.

"I remember reading about that in the newspaper."

"You played God and destroyed people's lives. The cop had rid the world of a very bad man. The DA lost the election but his successor fired your sorry ass."

"As usual, you're wrong, Bobby. I'm just a regular guy."

"You're not Eddie so what are you doing here? Get out of here, Karl, or whatever your name is."

Madeleine walked away from the table.

"Fine," Eddie said. "You've saved me the trouble of eating this crap and correcting your bullshit theories."

The worst mistake an undercover detective can make is to be stripped of his cover story. The second worst mistake is to lose touch with his suspects. Eddie followed Madeleine to the private elevator for the eighth-floor penthouses. When she saw him tailing her, she held up a one-handed stop sign, and he slowed his pursuit. She got into the car and let the doors close without looking at him.

Eddie took the public elevator to the ground floor and strode across the deserted lobby to the independent living elevator. On the sixth floor, he rapped on Donald's door and was surprised when it was opened by a nurse in green scrubs.

"I eat dinner at Donald's table," Eddie said. "Just came to check on my friend."

The nurse was slender, with brown hair in a ponytail, hazel eyes, and a nice but somewhat sad smile. It took a moment for Eddie to realize she was the nurse who had escorted Jacob Hoffman's dead body to the loading dock. She was Dr. Michael Cevert's mystery nurse.

The nurse stepped aside, and Eddie crossed the threshold.

"He won't be very talkative," the nurse said. "He's getting an IV. He's usually invigorated afterward but it will take a while."

Eddie noticed that the nurse wasn't wearing a nameplate. He moved through the sitting room to the bedroom doorway. Donald lay on the bed, propped on pillows, eyes half-closed. A clear liquid dripped from a bag on a hook beside the bed, through a tube, and into Donald's arm. Cevert had lied about Donald's condition.

"I should have known," Eddie said. "Donald insists he'll be okay, but that's not true, is it?"

The nurse shook her head. "The tumor is inoperable, wrapped around a major blood vessel in his left lung. Has he been hiding that?"

"He never complains."

"We'll be moving him to assisted living pretty soon."

Eddie crept to the bed and whispered Donald's name. Donald's eyes moved to Eddie's face.

"I voted for you," Donald said. His voice was hoarse.

Eddie took Donald's hand in his and squeezed. "I know you did, buddy."

Eddie straightened and gave the nurse a pained smile. "If he forgets, remind him that I was here."

"Sure thing."

✳ ✳ ✳

Expecting Stevenson or his mystery stalker, he threw his apartment door open, and there stood Susan, dressed like a '60s flower child-version of a femme fatale in a sequined silver dress and holding a magnum of champagne and two crystal flutes. She had brushed her hair and applied eyeshadow and lipstick. Eddie looked up and down the corridor and saw no one.

"No one followed me. Bobby is out somewhere, probably with his mistress," she said. "I came to apologize for voting against you."

She leaned into him to keep her balance and Eddie grabbed the champagne and glasses before she could drop them. "No apology necessary. I know Bobby twisted your arm."

He thought that in her somewhat inebriated condition she might be easy to pump for information, so he swung the door open and let Susan into his apartment. She wobbled to the couch and did a half pirouette before flopping down. A come-hither look in her eyes, she threw an arm over the back of the cushion and crossed her left leg over her right. The side slit in the dress exposed her ivory thigh.

Eddie uncorked the champagne as though a visit from Susan was routine. The wine bubbled over, and Eddie poured their drinks.

"Bobby wasn't the only one who wanted to vote you off the table." She tittered.

Eddie did the math. "Michael wanted me off the table."

Susan guzzled her champagne and held her glass out for a refill. "He insisted, said you had ruined the dinner conversations."

I've fucked up again. Now Cevert knows who I am and he won't bite the baitfish but I know who his delivery boy is. I can get to him that way.

"And here I thought I had added a touch of humor to the boring discussions," Eddie said.

"You're smart, see things differently. Bobby thinks Michael has an ulterior motive." She tried for a cat-who-ate-the-canary look and failed. Susan had obviously drunk her limit in the bar before Bobby left her.

"What could Michael be up to?" Eddie asked in an innocent voice.

"He's broke." Susan reached for the champagne bottle and poured her own drink before sloshing the wine over the rim of Eddie's glass. "Has three ex-wives and six kids who are taking him to court for not paying alimony and support. One of them—Gloria, I think—wants him to move out of here so he can afford to pay her." She tried to toast Eddie but spilled wine into her lap. She didn't seem to notice.

So, the opioid business pays the doctor's rent but isn't enough to pay his alimony. "What does Bobby think the doctor is doing?"

"Bobby thinks Michael is swindling Madeleine. And maybe Donald. He's seen them give money to Michael. Then you come along and get in the way."

One rich asshole swindling other rich assholes disappointed Eddie. He had hoped Susan would tell him the inside story of Cevert's drug dealing.

Susan had trouble keeping her eyes open and her head upright. She stretched out on his couch, her dress riding up to expose her diaphanous white panties. Her eyes closed, she said, "I think I need a nap before we have fun. Don't let me sleep through it."

Susan passed out, her breathing rhythmic and peaceful. Eddie couldn't let Susan spend the night on his couch. He had to be in the ladies' restroom at midnight to meet Peggy. He called the front desk and asked that they bring a wheelchair to his room to transport a resident. He was told it would take a while.

Eddie paced the small room and mentally diagrammed the mechanics of a drug business: Cevert prescribes drugs for his patients; the pill mill fills the prescriptions; the drugs are siphoned off by Shauna in the pharmacy; and someone, maybe Peggy, sells the drugs to the residents. The flaw in the business model was lack of demand. Peggy had said it herself: the old fogies got all the opioid they wanted so how many other elderly addicts could be at Palm Haven?

A knock on the door interrupted his ruminations. *All I need is Bobby come to save his wife*, Eddie thought. He peeked through the eyehole and saw a large Black man in a black uniform. Back to the couch, he yanked on Susan's dress down to cover her crotch. She smiled, maybe dreaming, maybe thinking Eddie was starting something. He let the man in.

"Oh, it's her," the security guard said.

"This has happened before?"

"Coupla times."

"I thought I had bored her to sleep."

The guard laughed. "You and a few others."

"Like who?"

"I don't kiss and tell," the guard said.

"'Course not," Eddie said.

Eddie was going to help lift Susan, but the huge guard waved him off, levered lightweight Susan off the couch as though he were a magician levitating his beautiful assistant, and gently parked her in the wheelchair.

Eddie dug a twenty out of his wallet and handed it to the guard. His name tag read, "Wallace." "Thanks for helping, Mr. Wallace."

The guard gave Eddie a crooked smile. "My first name is Wallace." He pushed Susan toward the door, her head lolling from side to side. Over his shoulder, he said, "Last one was that guy Ralph. He sleeps with all the girls."

Susan thought Bobby was having an affair so she had revenge sex. "I'll be darned."

"When I took this job, I thought y'all would be playing bingo out here, but it seems like y'all want one more roll in the hay 'fore ya meet your creator."

Eddie laughed and opened the door for the guard. As she was rolled away, Susan, half awake, said, "See ya later, Eddie."

Eddie caught just a glimpse of a man dressed in black who closed a door across the hallway from Stevenson's room.

"I moved too slowly and gave Bobby time to figure me out," Eddie said to Sam. "If Cevert believes him, he'll never bite. I may have to give up the race and cooperate with the undercover cop. That wouldn't feel like victory."

"Are you worried about beating the detective or about which shark he'll catch?" Sam asked.

✳ ✳ ✳

Eddie hated having to dodge Mr. Law Enforcement; fooling the residents was hard enough. At midnight he peeked out his door before exiting. The guest room hallway was dark, all doors closed. He surveyed the lobby before slinking along the wall in the shadows, past the escalators, to the restroom alcove. No Stevenson in sight.

He cracked the door to the women's restroom and glanced inside. Peggy was leaning against the sinks, her face drawn and pale, her eyes clouded with worry. Despite his unmasking at dinner, Peggy had shown up for this meeting. That almost certainly meant she wasn't connected to Cevert. Were there two dealers? *Banerjee!*

All the stall doors hung open. He looked inside the stalls to see if anyone was waiting to ambush him. He had thought Peggy might bring Randy to the meeting as a bodyguard, but she was alone.

"How do I meet the dealer?" Eddie asked.

Peggy stood up straight, took a breath, and delivered her lines like a stage actor in a play. "He has eight cartons of what you want. Original packaging, dissolvable form. Twenty large."

The shark couldn't resist the bait! Eddie translated Peggy's message: Fentanyl pills, twenty-eight to a carton for a total of two hundred and twenty-four doses for twenty thousand dollars. Original packaging meant the dealer stole directly from pill mill shipments which meant that Shauna wasn't siphoning the pills for floor nurses; she was walking them straight out the back door. Peggy's connection was a serious criminal and this bust would put a gold star on Eddie's resume. He switched to the calculator app on his phone and did some quick math—eighty-nine dollars and change per pill.

To sound like a street-wise buyer, Eddie said, "That's outrageous! He's thirty dollars higher per pill than the usual wholesale."

Peggy smiled and nodded her head. "He said if you were legitimate, you'd know what the price should be."

"Maybe we should start with a smaller batch that I can sell in Savannah for a small profit."

"He can't subdivide this, ah, batch, but he's willing to sell at market price, seventeen, you know, large."

Peggy didn't sound comfortable with criminal slang. Eddie did another calculation. "Still high."

"It's a big shipment. He says you'll make it up on volume."

Eddie figured he had earned his bona fides by price haggling so he said, "Sounds like a deal. Not a great deal, but a deal."

"Awesome. He'll need a gesture of good faith from you, too—a deposit of twenty-five hundred."

Who's scamming who? "Your guy is an amateur. You show me yours and I show you mine. I need to see a sample."

Peggy grinned. "He said you'd say that. Tomorrow night, loading dock at 9. That's when I take a smoke break."

"Okay." *Why not? I'm gambling with house money.*

"No fucking pictures!"

He turned to leave and stopped with his hand on the door handle. "Give me a couple of minutes to get away before you go back to work."

Down the hallway, Eddie sidled up to the wall like an escaping prisoner evading the searchlights and guard towers and scanned the shadowy spaces for Randy. Apparently, Randy didn't want to be around if his girlfriend screwed up the deal.

Eddie slipped into his apartment, grabbed a beer, and slouched on his couch as he thought about drugs in original packaging.

He went through the evidence for Sam. Cevert had to be the shark because he was prescribing large doses of Fentanyl that never reached his patients, while Banerjee was prescribing sleep aids. Some of Cevert's patients had been prescribed Fentanyl lollipops, but most had been prescribed Fentanyl in pill form. Randy, the small-time thief, and Peggy, the angel of mercy, may have sold some pills inside the complex, but they made their bulk sales off the premises. Eddie offered them a chance for a windfall without the risk of getting caught by cops in Savannah and they couldn't resist.

"A lot of sharks in the water, Eddie. Blowing your cover may have been a good break. If Madeleine doesn't kiss and make up with you, she's one of them."

"You could be right but knowing who the sharks are is useless unless I can catch them at it."

CHAPTER TWENTY

... Now

First thing in the morning, Eddie made another trek to the fourth floor of the assisted living wing. Before he could reach Lucy's room, he heard a commotion behind him. Out of the elevator came a gurney pushed by an orderly, followed by a string of Black women: one elderly, two middle-aged, and three young. The well-dressed women dabbed at their eyes with silk handkerchiefs. They rolled in Eddie's direction, with nurse Roundtree in tow. Eddie moved against the wall to give them room as they passed. They stopped outside room 1412, Doris Christenson's former room. Donald McCabe flashed Eddie a wistful smile and a weak wave from his perch on the gurney. Roundtree unlocked the door and the entourage entered.

Eddie continued to Lucy's room and found it empty again. Lucy out and about, a virtual social butterfly. Roundtree came out of Donald's new room and saw Eddie in Lucy's doorway.

"She went to the beach," Roundtree said.

"The beach? She and Janice?"

"Janice didn't come this morning. Ms. Griffin is doing so well that Janice doesn't have to come every day. Ms. Griffin went with another resident. They'll be fine."

So the baby bird had left the nest to try its own wings. Lucy's amazing transformation made Eddie feel good about what he was doing at Palm Haven. "Okay, call me if you need me, Leticia."

Eddie wanted to see Donald, but his family was with him. He had no legitimate reason to wait in Lucy's empty room. If Cevert was stockpiling undistributed drugs, they may be in his office. That would mean Sandy was involved.

Eddie whirled around, went out into the stairwell, and bounded down to the third floor. He burst onto a floor bustling with activity and dodged food carts and wheelchairs. Eddie hid in the lounge and watched Cevert's office. When no one entered or exited the office after fifteen minutes, he conceded that he'd have to meet Peggy tonight to take the next step.

He climbed back to the fourth floor and watched Donald's family emerge from his room. Eddie waited as they silently but tearfully walked down the hallway and entered the elevator. He eased open the door to Donald's room and found the man asleep. Eddie walked around the hospital bed and checked for drugs. There were no vials on the nightstand, but in the top drawer he found one Fentanyl lollipop, still in its wrapper. He wondered how many Donald was supposed to have.

At 8:30 Eddie made sure he wasn't being tailed and snuck into the men's restroom near the loading dock entrance. He propped the door open and stood around the corner, listening for footsteps. Nothing happened until 8:50 when someone came squeaking and swishing past the alcove. He heard the loading dock door swing open and then click as the bolt slid home. He moved into the gloom near the assisted living service elevator and watched Peggy huddle under the narrow overhang. She lit a cigarette with her back to the door and fidgeted but did not look around. Through heavy rain falling straight from low clouds, Eddie couldn't see if anyone was hiding among the cars in the parking lot. He had no choice but to take a chance. At precisely 9:00, Eddie looked back toward the lobby, saw no one approaching, and opened the loading dock door.

She whirled around. "Quick, give it to me."

Eddie stood perpendicular to her so he could watch the parking lot and the interior of the ground floor at the same time. He pulled his wad of bills from his inside jacket pocket and held it away from Peggy, like tempting a dog with a treat. "Show me."

Peggy reached into a pocket of her scrubs and retrieved a pill vial. The label had been ripped off, like the vial Eddie had found in Doris's room. Several white pills rattled around inside the vial. She made a grab for the money and Eddie jerked it away. "When and where?"

"Dr. Cevert's office, two o'clock in the morning. Not tonight or tomorrow. The day after tomorrow."

The day after tomorrow would be a Monday when Cevert would have a fresh shipment from the pill mill. I knew it all along.

"Means the Grouper is a shark," Sam whispered.

"What about the nurses?" Eddie asked Peggy.

"I'm on duty and I'll get rid of Cheryl."

Eddie sensed shadowy movement in the interior hallway—the Doppler effect. He grabbed the vial and shoved the bills into Peggy's hand. "Get rid of him if he comes out here." She looked confused.

He hurried down the ramp to the parking lot, slipped around the gate and hid behind his car. Drenched by the rain, he watched the loading dock. Peggy flicked her cigarette butt onto the road and retreated through the loading dock door, effectively locking him out. A shadow soon appeared at the back door. The overhead lights on the loading dock went dark. A man, tall and slender, emerged from the building into the darkness. Had Cevert planned to rip him off? The man scanned the road and the parking lot while Eddie shivered in the cold downpour.

Eddie would have to sneak around the building, but he couldn't chance carrying the pill vial through the front entrance. He reached around his rear tire and stood the pill vial on the inside wheel rim, then crept behind cars toward the far end of the lot. Eddie thought about those signs on eighteen wheelers: If you can't see me, I can't see you. He could no longer see the loading dock, so the man couldn't see him. Eddie awkwardly scaled the chain link fence and when he dropped to the ground, the top prongs snagged his shirt and ripped it into two flapping pieces. After traversing the soggy, shifting sand dunes on the far side of the building, he pushed through bushes that scraped his arms and face and left green debris on his shoulders. He stepped onto the paved walkway and into the path of Randy, hurrying toward the gazebo under an umbrella.

Randy halted. "Do I need to call for a straitjacket, old man?"

"Got lost, I guess," Eddie said. He brushed leaves and twigs off his scalp, squeegeed water out of his hair and eyes, and had no trouble appearing stupid. "What are you doing out here in the rain?"

"Trying to find another old coot who got lost. The home is that way." He canted his head in the direction of the building.

"Sure. Thanks."

Randy waited for Eddie to start walking so Eddie couldn't follow him. Eddie walked the pathway back to the main entrance, half expecting Detective Stevenson to pop out of the shadows.

Instead, Eddie bumped into Wallace as he walked through the front entrance doors. Wallace's eyes grew large as he regarded Eddie's disheveled appearance. "You look like you've been in a fight with a sea monster."

"Mermaid," Eddie said. "She was too fast for me."

Wallace laughed. "You see the man was looking for ya?"

"Middle-aged man, crew cut?"

"No, this man been burned bad. He said in a house fire."

Not Randy or Stevenson. Who? Eddie rubbed the gray stubble on his chin. "Doesn't sound familiar."

"Well, have a blessed day." Wallace shook his head as though to say, "There's no way to understand the behavior of rich white people."

Eddie smiled and nodded. Without looking back, he walked to the temporary housing corridor and stopped out of Wallace's vision around the corner, between the indoor pool and the gym. He waited for five minutes before Randy returned from the gardens. Randy wasn't guiding some lost old coot. He carried a brown paper lunch sack in his free hand.

Eddie waited another five minutes but no one came through the front entrance. Hoping he hadn't caught pneumonia, he hurried to his room, dried himself off, changed clothes, and poured himself a stiff bourbon.

"Told you the shark is Cevert. I set the hook, Sam. He can't get away now."

Sam nagged him: "If Cevert is the shark why is he selling to a guy— you—that he knows was an officer of the law?"

"Disgraced officer of the law."

"Bullshit."

"Susan said he's broke, desperate for cash."

"Bullshit, the shark is someone you don't want it to be."

✳ ✳ ✳

The knocking on Eddie's door startled him, and his first thought was that Detective Stevenson had procured a search warrant to unmask the irksome resident in guest room 103. He peeked through the eyehole. It wasn't Stevenson; it was Madeleine, dressed casually and holding a bottle of white wine. *Come to kiss and make up? She isn't the shark.* Eddie opened the door but barred her entry until he checked up and down the hallway—no Stevenson. Then he let her in.

"I have a bone to pick with you, Cowboy," she said.

"I suppose Bobby and Michael are gloating over getting rid of me."

Hands on hips, a scowl on her face, she said, "Are you Karl Novak or not?"

The possibility that Madeleine was checking to see if it was safe for Cevert to sell him drugs, crossed his mind, then was blown away like trash on the wind. "I was born Eddie Kovacs. A long time ago I changed my name to Karl Novak and moved to Florida because some bad guys were after me for what I did in Vietnam. I was an investigator then, too. Now I'm back to my original name because I want to leave my past behind me. I just want to be an ordinary Joe."

"There are no ordinary Joe's at Palm Haven." She snickered as she set the wine bottle on the round dining table. "You have a corkscrew? Glasses?"

He went to a drawer in the kitchenette and found the corkscrew. From the bathroom, he brought a pair of water glasses. He uncorked the bottle and poured.

Madeleine raised her glass for a toast. "To the truth."

They clinked glasses and took a sip. With a penetrating look, she said, "Why did you lie to me about being a cop, Eddie?"

Ah, he thought, *a woman might tolerate a man's boorish or childish behavior, but never a lie.* He had rehearsed an answer to this question.

"I wasn't ever a cop. A DA's investigator helps the prosecutor prepare cases."

"Like police involved shootings."

He nodded. "Yes."

"And you made a mistake that could happen to anybody."

He moved into the living area and cleared the room service debris from his coffee table and sat on the couch. Madeleine sat a respectable distance away. "It was no mistake," he finally said in answer to her question. "The cop killed an unarmed man simply because the man didn't comply with his orders."

"You must have made a mistake. You got fired."

"I didn't get fired. I had reached mandatory retirement age—six-ty-six—and the DA wouldn't approve an exception." Of course, he had been fired but the DA forced him into retirement rather than face an age discrimination lawsuit.

"Bobby says the dead man was a bad guy."

"Rap sheet as long as your arm, but it was still murder."

"Was the victim a Black man?"

"Of course."

She moved closer to Eddie. He could feel her warmth. "And then inmates beat the cop to death. Doesn't that bother you?"

The DA had withheld evidence to protect the cop so Eddie ratted him out and the DA was convicted of Violation of Oath by a Public Officer. At the time, Eddie had been influenced by a John Locke quote: 'Wherever law ends, tyranny begins.' Eddie thought Locke had gotten it backwards; tyranny thrives when it is sheltered by the law.

"Yes." He hung his head. "I've never gotten over it."

"Maybe I can make you feel better." She laid a hand on his thigh. "You've had a rough go of it as Mr. Novak. I'm glad you're Mr. Kovacs again. I prefer Eddie to Karl."

She leaned in and kissed him. He returned her fervor, and her lips parted. Her tongue teased and dueled with his. In the back of his mind, a little voice said, "Don't do it, Eddie," but that little voice was not in control. He was stirred physically in a way he hadn't experienced in years. He responded passionately and they tilted over on the couch, him on top. He gently bit her provocative lower lip, something he had been aching to do since he first met her. She recoiled and pushed him off her. He took a deep breath and sat up. She swung her legs around and stood.

He thought he had been too anxious, moved too fast, but she took his hand and led him to the bedroom. "I don't do it on couches."

In the muted glow of the pool area floodlights, snaking through the closed blinds, she ran her hand across the dresser and stopped at the picture. She picked it up and turned it toward the dim light.

"Is this Samantha?"

"Yes, about ten years ago."

"Pretty." She laid the picture face down and picked up the small plastic jar. She shook it and the charred metal shards rattled. "What's this?"

"That's my good luck charm. Two pieces of Chinese-made shrapnel they pulled out of me."

"The scar on your forehead."

"No, that one hit my helmet first and bounced off my thick skull. The pieces in the jar were embedded in my arm and leg."

"My God, they nearly killed you."

"Forrest Gump would say I had million-dollar wounds."

"You lied about Vietnam. Why hide it? Did you make a mistake then, too?"

No matter how many times Eddie had replayed the events in Vietnam and rationalized his behavior, he couldn't shake the weight of shame that had cloaked his shoulders for forty-five years. He had hung the wrong man. He had provided the South Vietnamese with an excuse to crush the Montagnards. And then there was Sergeant Callaway, the artillery liaison NCO who lay dying near Tucker. Shouldn't he have at least comforted the man in his last minutes on earth?

"For decades we were all ashamed of having been our government's pawns in a futile and unnecessary war. Today Vietnam is a vacation destination. All the dying was for nothing. For decades, the soldiers who had been there didn't talk about it with anyone who wasn't there."

"Any other lies you need to confess? Did Sam really die of breast cancer?" She waited.

"Yes, six months ago like I told you."

"Then you won't be shocked by what happens next."

She lifted his T-shirt over his head and stroked his chest. He unbuttoned her blouse, and she slipped her arms out of it. His heart raced. When he reached around her back to undo her bra, she stopped him. "Not yet."

She undid his pants, and he stepped out of them. He tugged at her slacks, and she helped him. They felt no adolescent rush, just a slow appreciation of the moment. In their underwear, they lay down on the bed and kissed again, each of them exploring bare skin. Hers had the feel of luxurious cloth, smooth as still water and gently contoured like an English meadow. His was coarse and knotted with ropey muscles. She shimmied out of her panties so he removed his boxers. Her hand paused at the scar on his shoulder, moved to his thigh, and found the other scar.

"I've been wounded, too." Her eyes met his with a fiery intensity as she decided who he was, and he decided who she was, and things could never be the same after that. She undid her bra and tossed it on the floor.

Eddie immediately knew what he was looking at. He laid her back and bent to kiss the X-shaped scar where her left breast should have been. She stroked the back of his head as he kissed the scar again.

He reached for her other breast and caressed it, tweaked the nipple and made her shiver. "This one is beautiful."

"The other one was, too." She gently stroked his manhood and found him ready. He moved a hand to the mound between her legs and caressed her, causing a sharp intake of breath and an involuntary movement of her hips toward his pressure.

"Now, Eddie. Please."

He rolled atop her and eased inside. She followed his lead instinctively and soon they found a comfortable rhythm. When they reached the end of their journey, she raised her hips and braced her pelvis against his. A look of intense concentration formed on her face, her brow furrowed and her eyes scrunched tightly closed. Then the air rushed out of her lungs in a single long blast and her hips dropped to the mattress.

They remained loosely coupled for several minutes. Nothing but clichés came to mind, so he remained silent. Then he began moving again.

Her eyes popped open and her lips spread in a wide smile. "You scoundrel!"

He laughed and when it was over, he rolled to her side and slid an arm under her neck.

They rested for several minutes until he touched her scar and said, "How long ago?"

"Nearly five years."

Eddie knew what that meant: Madeleine was approaching the life expectancy for most women after a mastectomy. "You didn't have reconstructive surgery."

"I didn't know I was going to meet you."

He chuckled. "Do you see an oncologist?"

"I go to Charleston every six months for a checkup. In between, I don't think about it and I don't talk about it. If it happens, I can deal with it."

Brave talk, but when faced with impending agony and certain death, everyone grasped for straws. "If it happens, there are amazing advances in treatments."

"All that desperation is so undignified." She sat up, one gorgeous breast and one ugly scar six inches from his eyes. "Now that you've seen the damaged goods, do you still like me, Eddie?"

He ran a hand thoughtfully down her spine, gently pressing each vertebra as though he were playing a piano. "All my cells are producing butterflies. Do you have butterflies?"

She held his face in her hands and gave him a lover's kiss. "You're an acquired taste, Eddie."

"Like pickles."

"More like anchovies. You're not everyone's flavor of the day."

She rolled off the bed, stepped into her panties and pulled up her slacks, then picked up her blouse. She gave him the same girlish smile as when she had stolen a kiss on the escalator, set Samantha's picture upright and walked to the door. "Can you check the hallway before I leave? No one needs to know I was here."

When Madeleine was gone, leaving a faint, spicy scent in her wake, the innately suspicious investigator in him considered the possibility that she was playing him to insulate Cevert. No, the lovelorn man in him decided, her affection for him was real and he was hopelessly and giddily infatuated with her. She had kissed and made up, so she's not a shark.

Sam faded out of his consciousness like fog dissipating under a warm sun. He placed her picture in a drawer.

Chapter Twenty-One

... Now

Eddie wasted the morning piddling around his apartment and waiting for the residents to be out enjoying the sunny day. Then he went to the loading dock door and stuffed two crumpled business cards in the hole in the doorjamb to prevent the locking bolt from seating when the door closed. He casually retrieved the pill vial from his car, reentered the building, and shuffled back to his apartment. The pill vial with its five Fentanyl pills—his $2500 deposit should have bought a box of twenty-eight—went into the return vent.

He was dressing for dinner when Madeleine knocked on his door. Unlike millennials who would have texted each other, Boomers did their business in person. She squeezed past him into his room with the entitled insouciance of a girlfriend.

"We have to get you back on my table," she said.

Eddie thought that having a girlfriend might be more trouble than he needed. It was against all the rules to get romantically involved with suspects. More importantly, Eddie had no desire to socialize with Cevert before tonight's drug buy—drug bust—and didn't want to make Cevert playact, either. A slipup was all too possible.

"Let's go to a restaurant for dinner."

"No, I can't let Bobby run my table." She started for the door, clearly in charge of their relationship.

Her insistence upon eating at her table made Eddie nervous. Maybe she was part of Cevert's cabal and was luring him in.

They took the escalator to the second floor and stopped short of the threshold, shocked by what they saw. Detective Stevenson was taking Donald's empty seat at the table with Cevert, Bobby, and Susan. The detective was closing in on Dr. Michael Cevert. Eddie started toward the table, but Madeleine rushed ahead of him.

"Let me handle this," she said.

Madeleine stormed off toward her table, gesticulating as she went. Diners at other tables took notice and paused their conversations to watch the action. Eddie followed in her wake.

She stopped behind her vacant seat and pointed to Stevenson. "Who invited him?"

Stevenson tried for an innocent look and failed. "I invited myself. Seemed like there was plenty of room."

"Only I can invite people to *my* table," Madeleine said imperiously.

"Sorry, I didn't know there were reserved seats," Stevenson said as he made a halfhearted attempt to stand.

"She's in charge," Bobby said to the detective. Then he turned to Eddie. "You're voted off this table. Get out of here."

"I've changed my vote," Susan said. "Eddie can stay."

"You vote for who I tell you to vote for," Bobby said.

"If Eddie goes, I go," Susan said, and she stood.

Bobby tried to grab Susan's arm and she jerked it away. Bobby turned red as a McIntosh apple while Stevenson smirked as he watched the argument. Eddie knew that a favorite tactic of detectives was to get suspects to turn on each other.

"I'm voting now," Madeleine said. "Eddie stays."

"It's four against two," Eddie said with a grin. "I stay no matter how Mr. Stevenson votes."

The detective held his hands up, palms outward, feigning concession.

Cevert stood. "I'm tired of all this bickering." He threw his napkin onto his plate and pushed his way through the crowd toward the escalators.

Stevenson rose and followed him. Eddie jumped to his feet and hustled after the two men.

"Where are you going?" Madeleine said to his back.

As he clambered down the escalator, Eddie watched Cevert walk out the front entrance with Stevenson trailing at a discreet distance. Eddie hurried to the porch and looked left and right for the two men. Fearing they had taken a golf cart into town, Eddie squeezed through crowds of seniors lollygagging on the veranda and dodged cars offloading residents and being driven away by valet boys. To his left, he spotted Stevenson on a footpath, disappearing into the gardens. Eddie jogged after him.

The marina lights on either side of the footpath reminded Eddie of the safety lights along the aisles of airplane cabins that came on when a plane crashed. Eddie could see the outline of the paving stones but could see nothing straight ahead. Cevert and Stevenson had walked deeper into the gardens. Whispers alerted Eddie to the couple sitting close together on a bench beside the path. He couldn't see their faces. Slowly, he moved forward, ears attuned to voices and hearing nothing.

Underwater lights in the pool beneath the rock waterfall cast wavering shadows across the footpath, but there was no sign, audible or visible, of either Stevenson or Cevert. Eddie glanced at the orange and silver koi swimming in the pond and immediately regretted his temporary loss of awareness.

From behind him, someone looped a steel rod over his head and yanked it back against his throat. Eddie squirmed like a hooked fish, but his attacker was wiry strong and kept his light-footed balance as Eddie thrashed left and right.

The man grunted as he pulled harder on the rod, cutting off Eddie's oxygen and threatening to crush his windpipe. The attacker shifted his right foot forward and turned his right hip to brace himself as he bent Eddie backward, increasing his leverage and the pressure on Eddie's throat.

A darkness deeper than night flooded Eddie's eyes. He knew that the instinct to grab the rod and push it away was exactly the wrong thing to do. He threw his right elbow into the man's gut, then stomped on the high ankle area of the man's left foot, his back foot on which the man was balanced. As the man tottered, Eddie threw all his weight to the left. The man stumbled into the rock wall beneath the waterfall and toppled into the koi pool, pulling Eddie with him. The fall loosened the man's grip on his rod and Eddie used two hands to push it away while his attacker scrambled to get atop Eddie's back. With amazing speed and agility, the man circled Eddie's throat with knobby fingers and pressed Eddie's cheek to the gritty bottom of the pond. Eddie tried to push himself off the bottom of the pool, but his attacker held him in place with the full weight of his body. The last pocket of air in Eddie's lungs bubbled to the surface.

Underwater, Eddie couldn't understand what was being said, but there were shouts. And then there was splashing, and the weight was lifted off his back. Eddie lay still, exhausted, forgetting to rise up and breathe, so someone grabbed his shirt and pulled him into a sitting position. Now there was yelling and tussling all around him, but Eddie didn't care. He gulped air and heaved into the pool, retching again and again, first stagnant pond water, then green slime inhaled from the bottom of the pond, and finally his lunch.

"Aw, Jesus, what a mess this guy made."

Eddie glanced over his shoulder and saw Randy approaching from the direction of the gazebo. Stevenson, wet from his struggle with Eddie's attacker, was handcuffing a tall, ropey man. Wallace, the security guard, shuffled into Eddie's vision and announced that the cops were on the way. Several residents had gathered around the bizarre scene to soak up the excitement. Lilac Lady, her hand over her mouth to prevent a gasp, and Lipstick Lady, wearing her fiercest scowl, were in the front rank.

From behind Eddie, someone placed hands on his shoulders and said, "Let's get you out of there and inside where I can get a look at you."

Cevert helped Eddie to his feet and over the rock wall onto the foot-path. Unsteadily, Eddie bent to retrieve the attacker's rod—a black steel walking cane. Embossed on the handle was the logo of the CIA. Wallace grabbed the cane as two uniformed cops arrived—one tall and gangly, the other short and barrel-chested.

"You know this guy?" the short cop asked as he pointed to Eddie's attacker.

Eddie examined the man. He was both older and taller than Eddie. The left side of the man's face looked like melted cheese as did his left arm. Eddie guessed that the man's torso bore similar scars. The long, narrow face was missing its left eyelid, left eyebrow, and left ear. The hair that remained above the burn line on his head was coarse and white. He looked like an ogre from a nightmare.

Eddie sensed an opportunity to dismiss his past, like uncoupling boxcars from a moving locomotive. He forgave himself for what he had done in Vietnam and for what he was about to do.

"No," Eddie croaked, his throat ragged as hamburger from a meat grinder. "I've never seen him before in my life."

Narrow Face suppressed his surprise and gave Eddie a questioning look. A silent conversation ensued, Eddie and the man speaking only with their eyes. Eddie told Narrow Face that he'd forgive him for Tucker's murder if Narrow Face would forgive Eddie for disrupting the CIA's mission to win the war. One life for many.

Narrow Face caught on and gave Eddie an imperceptible nod of agreement. "I thought he was someone else," Narrow Face said to the cop.

The cop ignored the handcuffed man and said to Eddie, "He roughed you up pretty good. Want to press charges?"

"No," Eddie said. He cleared his throat again. "Just get him off the property."

"Have it your way," the shorter cop said.

The cops took Fletcher from Stevenson and led him away, with the onlookers in tow.

Wallace flipped a couple of pages on his clipboard and ran an index finger down a row of names. "Signed in as David Fletcher. You don't recognize that name?'

"No, I don't," Eddie lied.

"He's the guy was looking for you last night. Knew your name."

Eddie realized that Narrow Face had chased him off the loading dock and into the gardens the night before. "It's some sort of mix up, Wallace," Eddie said.

Eddie tried to move away, but Wallace wouldn't leave it alone. He read from his clipboard. "That Fletcher guy was staying in one of the temporary apartments on your floor. I'm sure his application to reside here will be rejected now."

Wallace's revelation solved the riddle of the break-ins. Narrow Face had tossed Eddie's apartment during the first break-in and had come back a second time to assassinate him. Becoming Eddie Kovacs again had nearly gotten him killed. "Good, the incident is over."

Eddie hopped in place on his right foot, having turned his left ankle when he had stomped on Fletcher's foot, so Cevert offered to be Eddie's crutch. Like partners in a three-legged sack race, they hobbled up the path, water squishing from Eddie's boat shoes. He nodded to Stevenson and said, "Thanks."

Stevenson stopped him with a rough hand on his arm. "You know I'll figure it out, Kovacs."

Eddie snorted. "No, you won't."

"We need to finish our conversation, Doctor," Stevenson called after Cevert.

Eddie and Cevert ignored the detective and shuffled away, but Eddie was shaken by the thought that Stevenson was now questioning Cevert overtly.

As they emerged from the gardens, Madeleine approached them. "I'll take it from here," she said. She slid under Eddie's left arm, replacing Cevert.

"I should really have a look at him," Cevert said.

"I've got this, Michael," she said.

"His hyoid may be broken. His windpipe may be damaged."

"We'll call you if we need you," she said with more intensity.

Loitering residents watched as they limped to the driveway and traversed the wheelchair ramp to the veranda. Speculative whispers trailed them into the lobby.

"Thanks." Eddie tried to disengage from her grasp, but she held him tight around the waist.

"You're coming with me."

"I need dry clothes."

"You don't need clothes where we're going. These will dry overnight."

She urged him to the private elevator, and they rose to the penthouse floor. Her apartment was in the middle of the floor, overlooking the ocean. Through the foyer, they passed the fully equipped kitchen and hallways that led left and right to bedrooms with en suite bathrooms. One bedroom could be converted to a hospital room to combat a terminal illness. A breakfast bar and four stools separated the kitchen from the living room. Straight ahead, cushioned window seats underlined a broad expanse of glass. From this height, Eddie thought Madeleine could see all the way to the Mediterranean. A large sectional on the right faced a wall dominated by a wide screen television.

Madeleine unbuttoned his shirt, then said, "Drop 'em." He kicked off his shoes and unbuckled his belt. Madeleine did the rest.

"That's the way I like you. Go take a shower." She directed him down the hallway to the master bedroom, feminine but not frilly, a room in which her male companions could retain their masculinity. He couldn't contain his curiosity, so he took a quick tour. There were no human faces in the framed pictures of beaches and parks on the dresser, as though Madeleine had no past she wished to remember. Sliding glass doors led to a balcony and wicker furniture. He found everything he needed in the bathroom, including a toothbrush still in its packaging, but no bathrobe for male guests. A good sign. He wrapped a towel around his waist and emerged in a cloud of steam, like a saintly aura, and found her waiting for him.

"Let's get you fixed up." She sat him on her king-sized bed and went into the bathroom for supplies. She handed him a package of cough lozenges and said, "These might help." She secured an icepack around his ankle, swabbed a knee abrasion with an antibacterial ointment, rubbed a smelly salve into his aching shoulder, and caressed his cheek where a red splotch had blossomed, like a basketball floor burn.

"I have just the thing," she said and went into the bathroom again to retrieve some face moisturizer. She smoothed it on, and Eddie feigned distaste with a loud sniff.

"It's okay to smell nice," she said. "Lie back and relax."

Madeleine went back to the kitchen and returned with a chilled bottle of Pinot Grigio and two glasses. She poured the wine, removed her blouse and slacks, and climbed into bed beside him.

He sucked on a soothing lozenge and deadened his throat pain with the wine.

She took a deep breath. "What was that all about out in the gardens?"

"Vietnam."

"The reason you changed your name."

"Yes."

"So long ago. It's time we got over it."

"America won't get over Vietnam until the last Baby Boomer is dead."

She sat up, a look of disappointment on her face. "Tell me the truth, Eddie: Did that man attack you because you did something shameful over there?"

Can the right thing be shameful? "Everything about war is shameful."

She gave him the look a mother gives her young son when he's told her half the story, so he concocted another half-truth. "I uncovered an illegal arms operation he was involved in. He wanted revenge."

She sucked air in fear. "Oh, dear God. Why did you let him go? You should have had him arrested."

"He won't be back." *We made a deal. I forgave him for Tucker's murder and he forgave me for the slaughter of 200,000 Montagnards.*

She took a sip of her wine, buying time to compose her thoughts. Then she said, "Were you scared when he was strangling you underwater?"

He stared at the tray ceiling for a bit and decided to tell her the truth. "I feared the embarrassment of losing the fight. Reminded me of the fights I lost in grammar school."

She smiled. Several heartbeats passed before she said, "What I hate about death is that it comes when and how it wishes. I will lose control and that is definitely not me."

"Definitely not you."

She gave him a demure smile and poured more wine. "It's easier if you go through it with someone … ah, close to you." She paused again.

An image of two people tiptoeing through a minefield crept into Eddie's consciousness. They were both wondering how vulnerable they were willing to be.

"In Asian and Native American cultures, the aged are venerated and cared for. In our culture the elderly are warehoused and forgotten," Madeleine said.

"Out of sight, out of mind. Young people don't want to acknowledge what awaits them."

"So, we take care of ourselves. I've been thinking about how we can take care of each other."

"How's that?"

"You could move in with me, save yourself a lot of money." Madeleine fixed her deep brown eyes on his and tempted him to submit, to step off the ledge into those eyes and fall into a bottomless abyss. A childish thought crept into his consciousness: Jacob Hoffman had had an apartment of his own, so he wouldn't be moving into another man's space.

He gave her a cocky smile. "I think I'm next up for the 'Boys' Dorm,' Donald's apartment. All the cakes and casseroles a guy can eat."

"Men are such pigs. Maybe I can change your mind." She swung a leg over his. "Let's enjoy our last days together."

Even as children, we recognize that life is a story with an unhappy ending, so we insulate ourselves by inventing imaginary friends and kinder, gentler worlds. Then as seniors on our last laps, we try to recapture the comfort of those childhood fantasies.

Eddie felt as though he were back in the second story bedroom at Big Daddy's house with Sam asking him to marry her. To disarm Madeleine, he said, "I'd like that."

CHAPTER TWENTY-TWO

... Now

The convenience store sold a selection of canes. Eddie rejected the ones with handles at the top and tripod legs. *Let the old fogies have those.* He selected the sturdiest of the offerings, a cane with a steel center post encased in burled maple. From a rack of paperbacks, he chose *Rum Punch* by Elmore Leonard. As she rang up his purchases, the middle-aged cashier frowned at his disheveled clothing, and he returned an impish smile—*I'm not a hobo; I had a good night. You should be so lucky.* For the first time in decades, he had slept without the crutch of Vietnam-era music in his ears.

After showering and dressing in pressed clothes, Eddie limped to the pool and sat at a table under an umbrella. He ordered breakfast and a pitcher of Mimosas and imagined himself on holiday at the French Riviera. A deeply tanned couple in tennis garb sidled up to his table and asked after his injury. They had been in the gardens last evening and witnessed Narrow Face's attack.

"Minor ankle sprain. Case of mistaken identity, apparently," Eddie said.

Eddie offered them a seat and a drink, but they declined, saying they had an impending tennis date. The woman, her name was Audrey, opened a can of tennis balls and set one on the table. "Cut that open and stick it on the bottom of your cane. You won't make a racket and the cane won't slide out from under you on the tile floors."

Not on your life. "Thanks. I often wondered why people put them on their walkers."

She smiled at him, and they walked toward the courts.

Eddie sipped his second Mimosa but couldn't recapture his jovial mood upon waking in Madeleine's bed. She had excused herself from dinner this evening saying she was accompanying Michael Cevert on a trip to Atlanta for an arbitration session with his ex-wife. They wouldn't return until tomorrow, she had told him. Eddie remembered Susan telling him that Cevert might be leaning on Madeleine financially, but Eddie knew where Cevert would be at 2:00 a.m. the following morning—selling Eddie drugs in the doctor's office. He had gone back and forth on Madeleine's possible involvement with Cevert, and now he had to admit that Sam may have been right all along—Madeleine could be a shark, or at least Cevert's Remora. As he turned her lame excuse over in his mind, like a jeweler examining a diamond from every angle, he wondered if he could be cold-hearted enough to condemn her to die in an 8' x 8' cell. Would he walk away from Palm Haven with a final victory, like a retiring quarterback winning the Super Bowl? Would her arrest make up for Vietnam? Would it make up for St. Petersburg? Sadly, he concluded that arresting Cevert and Madeleine would deliver all the redemption he had sought for so long.

He finished the pitcher of Mimosas and limped through the door that led past the gym. The day passed quickly as he read his novel. Elmore Leonard always did that for him. Then he took a long nap so he'd be fresh for the big bust.

At 1:45 a.m. Eddie threaded his belt through his holster and clipped his deputy sheriff's badge to the left of his belt buckle. Lance had insisted upon deputizing him to give Eddie the power to make arrests. After noisily clicking around his apartment all day, Eddie took Audrey's advice—using

a serrated knife, he punctured the tennis ball and stuck it onto the bottom point of his cane.

Eddie slipped out of his apartment and crept across the deserted lobby. *Quiet as a mausoleum*, Eddie thought. Through the entrance doors, he saw two security guards on the veranda, Wallace and another man, thumbs in their police duty belts, staring at a black sky. No moon over the water tonight. His pulse racing, Eddie took the public elevator to the third floor of the assisted living wing. He had never experienced anxiety as a young man. Now he wondered if his anxiety was the product of old age or something more personal. If anyone other than Peggy was on duty at the nurses' station, he would call the bust a failure and retreat.

No one walked the floor. No one seemed to be awake. Peggy had sent her shift partner—Cheryl—on some wild goose chase. He thought it odd that Peggy wasn't keeping watch for unwelcome intruders. Perhaps she was in the office. He tried Cevert's office door and found it locked. Had he beaten Cevert to the rendezvous, or were the crooks waiting for him to announce himself? On the back of the nurses' station, he found the key to the office and drew his pistol from its holster.

He tilted his head back, as though praying to the heavens, and said, "Don't be in there. Please, don't be in there."

The key slid soundlessly into the lock and turned smoothly. Eddie eased the door open. What had been designed to be the sitting room of an assisted living apartment contained a desk, visitors' chairs, filing cabinets and wall shelving. Cevert's diplomas hung behind the desk. The sounds of music and voices came from the bedroom. Eddie crept around the desk and stopped on the bedroom threshold, bewildered by the sight. The words "Hands up!" hung in his throat.

Cevert organized instruments on a rolling cart. "You're late, Peggy," he said with his back to the door.

Madeleine turned and gasped. The nurse in green scrubs, the one who had attended to Donald in his apartment, the one who had escorted

Jacob Hoffman's body out of the building, looked askance at Eddie but kept working. The six women who had come to visit a couple of days ago were dressed for a funeral and sitting on folding chairs. They all wore the same question on their faces: What's the gun for? Cevert, wearing a lab coat, turned and blanched. He regarded Eddie with caution but said nothing.

Two tall, thick candles, the sort seen on altars in Catholic churches, were topped by gently swaying flames. Above the bed hung a crucifix. A sad Sarah McLachlan song played on a portable speaker and one of the younger girls softly sang along. Propped up on the hospital bed lay Donald McCabe, a serene look on his face as he watched the nurse plug IVs into his veins.

As though awaking from a coma, Eddie fathomed what was happening. He closed the door and slipped the gun into its holster.

"I'm glad you came, Eddie," Donald said. "Gives me a chance to say goodbye."

"You can't do this, Donald. You're a God-fearing man."

Donald gave him a weary, doleful smile. "If it's a sin, I'm prepared to pay for it."

Eddie turned to Cevert. "You're committing a crime, Doctor."

Cevert pushed his glasses up his nose. "I'm curing cancer the only way it can be cured."

"Isn't it lovely to know you won't suffer, to know your life will end peacefully?" Donald asked Eddie. "Michael has promised no gasping for a last breath, no fear of suffocation."

"Assisted suicide is illegal, Donald," Eddie said.

"Assisted suicide is legal in Switzerland, Germany, Canada, Belgium and Luxembourg," Cevert said.

"But not in Puritanical America," Eddie said.

Madeleine approached Eddie, a string of pearls starkly accenting her black dress.

"Something you'd wear to a funeral," Karen had said. Eddie wondered if Jacob Hoffman had had a Star of David hanging where the cross now hung.

Madeleine put her hands on his shoulders and gazed into his eyes with intensity and sincerity. "Nine states have death with dignity laws and Montana has no law against it. The others are backward."

"You're in a backward state."

"Some states will legalize abortion so that women can control their own bodies, but we don't allow intelligent adults to control their own bodies, decide when and how they will die." Madeleine drew a breath. "Our laws are ridiculous, illogical."

"No more people die, but fewer suffer," Cevert said.

"This isn't suicide," Donald pleaded. "I'm acknowledging the inevitable and choosing how to deal with it."

Donald's two daughters began sobbing, hiccupping back their grief.

"Is he terminal?" Eddie asked Cevert.

Cevert looked at Eddie the way Bill Belichick looked at reporters who asked stupid questions. *Everyone is terminal.*

"There's no hope for me," Donald said.

Donald's ex-wife gave Eddie a sorrowful look, then a slight nod of her head. Too many jagged, partial thoughts competed for space in Eddie's brain to think clearly: He had sworn to uphold the law; he was in love with Madeleine; Donald was his friend. He wondered if all Cevert's dead patients had been suicides. *No, there had been no ceremony for Doris Christenson.*

Eddie swept his jacket aside to display the badge pinned to his belt. "I'm an officer of the law. I can't let you do this." He pulled out his phone and snapped pictures of the surreal scene.

"Let me go, Eddie," Donald said. "A compassionate God wouldn't want me to suffer any more."

Eddie struggled to sympathize with Donald's predicament and his heretical resolution, but he pushed those thoughts aside to consider Peggy, the nurse who had set up a phony drug buy, the nurse who was absent from the room.

Eddie's thoughts were interrupted by pulsing red and blue lights. He limped to the window and parted the curtains. Two large black SUVs, the sort favored by the Feds, were rolling down the lane toward the loading dock, grill lights flashing but no sirens.

Peggy had double-crossed him. Why would she do that? To stop Cevert's practice? No, she'd be implicated. To rip him off for twenty-five-hundred-dollars? No, he had pictures and other evidence. Peggy did not want to get caught.

Eddie rapped his knuckles on the window to draw everyone's attention. "It's not up to me, anymore. Stevenson, the guy who imposed himself on our dinner table, is a federal agent and he just arrived with a raiding team to arrest Michael."

"You can't let that happen," Madeleine screamed.

"I can't let this happen," Eddie said. "Take Donald back to his room and get her the hell out of here." He pointed to the nurse in green scrubs.

Madeleine pressed the heels of her hands to her temples. "Okay, okay, we'll postpone this but we need time to clean up."

"Postpone? No little lady, it's game over. After you move Donald, bring Michael to my apartment for a little chat."

Angry at having been deceived by Peggy and wanting to stop Stevenson, Eddie cut through the dark third floor mall and rode the escalator to the lobby. A horde of men in black riot gear flowed through the loading dock doors like a malevolent river. Comically and pitifully, Eddie limped toward them.

"Get him," someone shouted.

The sound of troops double-timing, gear bouncing and leather stretching, echoed in the cavernous lobby.

"Put him on the ground!" Eddie couldn't see the man but he recognized the voice as Stevenson's.

Two men grabbed Eddie's arms and threw him to the floor, bruising his knees and elbows. His cane clattered away. A rough hand on his head pressed his cheek to the cold tile. His arms were jerked behind his back and his hands cuffed.

"I'm a cop," Eddie said. "Badge on my belt."

"Roll him over," Stevenson said.

Eddie's captors turned him over as easily as flipping pancakes on a griddle.

Stevenson examined Eddie's badge and tapped it with his fingers. Talking to the men around him, Stevenson said, "That dumb-ass sheriff put another man inside."

That brought chuckles from the other cops.

Standing over him, Wallace said, "I knew it. I knew it. Mr. Kovacs is a cop."

"What are you doing, old man?" Stevenson asked.

"Peggy double-crossed us."

"Peggy? What?"

"They're in Doctor Cevert's office," a woman said. Lipstick Lady. Phyllis.

"Peggy gave you the wrong information," Eddie said.

"I don't know what you're talking about," Stevenson said. "We got our information from two nice ladies, Phyllis and Bernice."

A wave of icy doubt enveloped Eddie. "They're wrong. I've already been up there and no one's there."

Guilt brought a flush to his face. *I'm doing this to catch a drug dealer,* he said to himself.

Don't lie, Eddie, Sam said.

Stevenson's brow furrowed. "If they're not in his office, where are they?"

The clues crawled across his brain like maggots on a corpse. Randy had been at the gazebo the night Eddie waited to rescue Gerry Matthews. Randy was in the gardens in the rain when Eddie eluded Narrow Face.

Randy had returned with a brown lunch bag he had gotten in the gardens; a bag large enough to hold one box of Fentanyl pills. Randy was in the gardens when Narrow Face assaulted Eddie. Eddie gave Stevenson the logical answer. "They're at the gazebo on the beach end of the walkway through the gardens."

"What's the doctor doing out there?"

"It's a big drug deal, Detective."

"They're upstairs," Phyllis insisted.

Eddie gave a slight shake of his head. "Hurry before they get away."

Stevenson decided to trust a cop. He barked commands at his men: "Two men block each stairwell. Two men guard every elevator. No one leaves the building."

Stevenson pulled Eddie's revolver from its holster. "I'll hold onto this so you don't have an accident, old man. Stay here till we get back."

Stevenson waved an arm at his troops like an Army sergeant assaulting a machine gun nest. "Follow me, men."

Eddie's captors uncuffed him and helped him to his feet. As the officers exited the building, Eddie disregarded Stevenson's order and trailed behind. The cops took the paved path through the gardens so Eddie covered their flank. He hobbled down the wooden walkway toward the beach, keeping pace with the flashlight beams flickering through the garden foliage.

He heard yelling and screaming and shouted commands. A gunshot rang out and Eddie ducked. Out of the shadows around the gazebo a man waving a gun ran down the summit of the dunes to the beach. On the hardpacked sand, the man sprinted toward the walkway. Eddie climbed the dunes, the going difficult for a one-legged man, the deep yielding sand reminding him of snowdrifts in Wisconsin. In his long career as an investigator, Eddie had never fired his weapon, but now he wished he had it.

He slid down the side of the dunes into a patch of sawgrass and crouched like a baseball catcher. As the running man neared, Eddie gripped his cane in two hands. Like timing a fastball, he swung the bat right-handed and struck the man's right shin bone. The man screamed and crash-landed onto the sand. Moaning, the man scrabbled away on his hands and knees. Dragging his own damaged leg, Eddie shuffled to the man's side and switched to a left-handed grip. Eddie cocked the bat and struck the man over the head, and the man lay still. Eddie had always been a switch hitter. He lifted the man's nose and mouth out of the sand and turned the man's bloody head to see his face. Randy.

Wallace, out of breath, stumbled up to them and picked Randy's pistol off the sand.

"Hold onto this guy for Stevenson. Got it?" Eddie said to him.

"Got it," Wallace said with a grin.

Federal agents were emerging from the gardens, so Eddie slogged through the soft sand to the walkway. His silencing tennis ball had been lost in his assault on Randy and his cane made a disappointing clicking sound as he limped to the entrance. No one chased him. The agents were preoccupied with their trophy—Randy. The Feds' SUVs now blocked the entrance drive, sealing the crime scene.

Apparently aware that an arrest had been made outside, the Feds had abandoned their posts at the elevators and the lobby was filling with spectators. He hurried to the assisted living elevator and waited for the car to disgorge a knot of elderly rubberneckers in bathrobes and house slippers. Even while asleep at 2:00 a.m. the old fogies had sensed the excitement in the building like squirrels sense a circling hawk. On the third floor he hesitated when he saw a withered woman leaning on a walker in her doorway across the hallway from Cevert's office. He held up the key to Cevert's office so she could see that he was authorized and stepped to the door.

"They're gone," the woman rasped from behind. "Made a racket and woke me up."

"Sorry about that. A patient emergency."

He slipped into the dark room and locked the door behind him before he found a light switch. The bed was dressed in fresh linen, the chairs folded and propped against the wall. The IVs and the instrument cart had been stored in a closet. The smell of extinguished candles hung in the air. Relieved, he locked the door and returned the key to the back of the nurses' station.

The woman hadn't moved. "Can I go to sleep now?"

"Yes ma'am, it's all over."

Eddie got back into the elevator and rode it to the fourth floor. Unlike the third floor, residents were gathered in small clumps, talking about what was happening downstairs. No one questioned Eddie as he made his way to Donald's room to commiserate with his friend. When he threw the door open, he saw that it wouldn't be necessary. Donald's bed was empty.

CHAPTER TWENTY-THREE

Gail and Melissa—Chubby and Sleepy Brown Eyes—huddled near the assisted living corridor. Chubby mouthed "Up yours" to Eddie and shot him the bird. In the lobby a throng of seniors had gathered to watch the show. Near the registration desk, a DEA agent barked in Cevert's face, lobbing questions at him like mortar shells. Cevert wore pajamas and a bathrobe, as though he had been summoned from sleep, but his face betrayed his loss of composure.

Officers shepherded residents toward elevators, clearing a path to the front doors. Eddie flashed his badge at an FBI agent and was waved through. He stepped onto the veranda and paused. An ambulance with its red lights flashing pulled away from the curb and threaded its way between the Fed's SUVs. Eddie assumed Randy was in the ambulance. Through the tinted back windows of the Fed's SUV, Eddie could see a shadow rocking forward and back, forward and back. *Peggy got what she deserved.* Stevenson leaned against the rear of the SUV, speaking on a cell phone. Casually he tossed a slashed tennis ball into the air, caught it, and tossed it again.

Eddie retreated through the entrance doors and into the crowded lobby. He searched for Cevert but couldn't find him. Eddie's shoulders slumped as despair swept over him. *Have I lost that race, too?*

He went to his apartment and opened the return vent. Into his canvas satchel—the one Tucker had carried in Vietnam—Eddie placed the evidence he had collected: Doris's empty pill vial; the unlabeled pill vial containing five pills, reputedly Fentanyl, that Peggy had given him as a sample; the pharmacy records of Cevert's patients; his notebook; Barbara Meacham's Fentanyl lollipop; Gerry Matthews's address; Lucy's old prescription record; Lucy's Rohypnol; pictures of Peggy handing him drugs; and the three Hydrocodone pills Peggy had given him.

He limped back through the lobby and the entrance doors to the veranda. Federal agents in slickers with yellow initials on the back—some FBI, some DEA—were questioning selected residents. Donna Roberts gesticulated as she spoke to a Fed. Probably asking where they had Johnny, Eddie thought. Lucy Griffin saw him and waved. Stevenson still leaned on the back of his SUV, arms crossed, a look of satisfaction on his face.

As Eddie approached, Stevenson tossed him his slashed tennis ball.

"You have Peggy in the SUV?" Eddie asked.

"Who's this Peggy you're trying to hang? I don't recognize that name."

"Peggy Crawford, a night nurse. Randy's accomplice."

"There was no accomplice. Randy Tibbetts had the gun, tried to rip off Bobby Claiborne. But you knew where they'd do their drug deal."

"Bobby Claiborne was selling drugs?"

"Yup. A crook ripping off crook is pretty funny."

Eddie feared the next answer, but he had to ask the question. "Anybody else involved?"

"We have a team chasing a nurse named …" he checked a slip of paper, "Sandy Hanson. Bobby Claiborne rolled over on her before we could even break out the bright lights and rubber hoses. He says she stole Dr. Cevert's scripts and he forged them. That's how the drugs got here. I guess you hadn't figured that out."

Of course! She had access to Cevert's office and his script pad. "Sandy was on my list," Eddie lied.

Eddie now had a clear picture of Bobby's drug business. Bobby wanted a deposit for a test buy of Fentanyl, so Peggy wrangled the deposit money from Eddie and Randy used it to buy one box of pills. Peggy had been in a hurry that night because she had to transfer the deposit money to Randy for his meeting in the gardens. That good faith purchase encouraged Bobby to bring seven more boxes of pills for the big sale tonight, but Randy intended to steal the drugs at gunpoint. As cover for the rip off, Peggy told Eddie the deal would happen in Cevert's office. She knew that would embroil him in a different crime. Maybe she guessed he was a cop.

He pointed to Bobby rocking in the back seat of the SUV. "Can I talk to him?"

"Nope. He's mine."

"Did he say why he did it?"

"The usual: money. His stores went bankrupt and he's struggling to pay off State and Federal tax liens, but he wanted to be with the rich crowd."

Just like high school when we'd do anything to get a seat at the cool kids' table in the cafeteria."

Eddie slipped the satchel off his shoulder. Like a defeated knight surrendering his sword, Eddie handed the satchel to Stevenson. "You win."

"What's this?" Stevenson asked.

"All the evidence you'll need to hang Shauna Flanagan, Randy Tibbetts, Peggy Crawford, and a doctor named Arjun Banerjee who drugged old people so they were easier for the night shift to control."

Stevenson sifted through the contents, examining the items and reading the rubber banded notes. He took special interest in the pill vial Eddie had found in Doris's trashcan.

"Randy Tibbetts's DNA is on that vial. He murdered Doris Christenson."

"You've been a busy little beaver. The ladies had this all wrong but you got most of it right. We should have worked together. You made me for a Fed, right?"

"You stuck out like a zebra at a rodeo."

Stevenson tried to stifle a chuckle but couldn't manage it. "And yet here I am with the grand prize," he said as he jerked a thumb over his shoulder at Bobby in the back seat.

"Don't tell the sheriff where you got the evidence in the satchel. Say you collected it."

"Hunh? Why?"

"The sheriff is a family friend and he has political aspirations. He won't be pleased that you made the collar and not me."

"Fuck that dipshit." Stevenson pulled Eddie's pistol from the small of his back and handed it to Eddie. "Don't shoot your pecker off with that thing."

CHAPTER TWENTY-FOUR

... Now

Eddie pushed his way to the hallway to the guest apartments and he saw her then, loitering under the escalators, her head on a swivel until she spotted him. Her face was pale with fear, one hand clutching and wringing the other. She hurried after him as he turned into the hallway and walked past the gym and the indoor pool.

"Wait," she called. "Let me explain, Eddie."

He didn't wait or look over his shoulder. Madeleine quickened her step to keep pace. He slipped his keycard into the lock on his apartment door, and she caught up. He looked up and down the hallway, which was clear of people, and he let her into his apartment. He went straight to the kitchen counter and poured a shot of bourbon for her and one for himself. He handed her the drink. They didn't sit.

"Where the fuck is Donald?"

For the first time since Eddie had met Madeleine, she appeared frightened and vulnerable. "He's gone. His last words were, 'Thank Eddie for keeping the cops away.'"

"You went through with it?" Eddie turned away and tried to control his rage.

"Michael said it was too late to stop. I knew we could count on you."

"I didn't stop the cops," he shouted. "They were here to make a drug bust." His excuse for deflecting Stevenson's attention did not ring true to his own ears.

Madeleine wrapped an arm around him from behind, leaned her head on his back. "Why would you want your friend to suffer? Donald was ready to die."

Eddie shrugged her off. His friend was gone, the space Donald had occupied on earth now a vacant hole. And now Eddie possessed unwanted information about a capital crime. "Where is he?"

"At the morgue."

"How did you manage that?"

She canted her head, like a dog that doesn't understand its master. "When the DEA moved their SUVs around to the front, we snuck Donald out the back into the vet's van."

"What vet?"

"The woman in the green scrubs is Michael's daughter, Sarah, and she owns a veterinary clinic in Savannah."

Cevert's mistake was using Peggy. He should have kept it all in the family. "Where's Donald's family?"

"In my apartment."

"Keep them there until the Feds leave."

If Eddie was going to arrest Michael Cevert, he wanted the Feds out of the way and he wanted Donald's family as witnesses. "What does Donald's death certificate say?"

She gazed into her glass. "Respiratory failure."

Hard to contest that. "I told you to bring Michael. Where is he?"

"I think he's hiding under his bed. He's always been afraid of you." She sloshed the bourbon around in her glass, as though she were aerating a fine wine. "You lied. You're still a cop."

"Not really. I'm just doing a friend a favor by having a look at what's going on here."

"A friend at the DEA?"

"The local sheriff."

"Did he ask you to watch Michael?"

"No, but Stevenson was on his trail. Maybe he still is."

She walked to the kitchen counter and poured herself another drink. She motioned with the bottle—did he want a refill—and he shook his head. She gulped her drink and poured another.

"No one influenced Donald. He signed a contract stating he was submitting to death of his own free will. Self-determination is the ultimate freedom, isn't it?"

"He signed a contract?"

"Donald wrote the contracts for the suicides. He was a lawyer, you know?"

Smart. Death with Dignity laws typically required a signed contract. "Did Celia Dawkins sign a contract?"

She suppressed her surprise. "You are a good investigator."

"And Jacob?"

Her lower lip quivered. "Yes."

The DEA had mistaken assisted suicides for covered-up overdose deaths. Eddie walked to the kitchen counter and accepted two fingers of bourbon. "Are all of Michael's patients candidates for assisted suicide?"

"Yes. Candidates is a good word. They don't have to go through with it."

"Is Albert Pulenko a candidate?"

Tears poured from Madeleine's swollen eyes and rolled down her puffy cheeks. "He waited too long and now it's too late. He'll be moved to a nursing facility and eventually to hospice care. His life savings will be drained by medical bills although nothing can save his life. He'll technically be alive but he's already dead. Is that the ending you wish for us?"

Eddie couldn't allow Madeleine to distract him with emotions. "Did Doris Christenson sign a contract?"

Madeleine stared at the floor for several moments. "She hadn't decided yet, hadn't committed."

If Doris hadn't committed to dying easily, Eddie doubted she had intended to overdose. "Did Michael give her the Fentanyl that killed her?"

"No, of course not. Michael insisted that his patients be lucid when they signed the contract. She was clean before her death."

Clean, but couldn't stand the pain. So Randy sold her some painkillers.

"Gerry Matthews wasn't Michael's patient so why did Michael get involved with him?"

"Michael made a mistake when he signed that order for Memory Care. He was afraid of what Mr. Matthews had seen. He was afraid of Sandy, too. She wanted Mr. Matthews off her floor."

Sure, Gerry suspected something was happening in Cevert's office and Sandy didn't want to be caught stealing prescription scripts. Eddie's head bobbed as he thought about it. Gerry had been right: He had seen residents go into Cevert's office alive and come out dead. Celia Dawkins. Jacob Hoffman.

The pieces of the puzzle were falling into place: "Sandy stole Michael's scripts and Bobby forged them and Shauna redirected them to Bobby when they arrived in the pharmacy. Bobby went to Savannah twice a month to sell them because he couldn't afford this place."

"It's so sad," she said.

"Did Michael know his scripts were going missing and were being forged?"

"No. Sandy kept the books for him."

"Did Bobby know what Michael was doing?"

She spat a derisive laugh. "Maybe. He kept trying to become Michael's patient. If you want the world to know your secrets there's telephone, telegraph, and tele-Bobby. That's why Michael wouldn't take him on as a patient."

Eddie had no time for jokes. "So, Michael is just an angel of mercy."

Her hands flew around, and her whiskey sloshed out of her glass and onto the carpet. "Yes, that's it." He took her glass and led her to the couch.

"How does Michael get the drugs to do, ah, what he does? I'm sure they're controlled substances."

She gave him a questioning look. "You haven't figured that out? Sarah supplies the drugs from her veterinary clinic. We're compassionate toward our pets but not to our relatives. It's crazy."

Apparently there were many things he hadn't figured out. As though he were thinking out loud, he said, "Michael puts people down like dogs."

"Sarah administers the drugs, just uses Michael's office. This whole thing was her idea in the first place."

"Handy. Why not do it at the vet clinic, away from watching eyes?"

"She needs Michael to sign the death certificates. And she needs the deaths to happen where they are likely to happen—at a community full of retirees and not at a vet clinic."

"So, Michael's daughter used her father's office and his status as a doctor, and he was compensated, I'm guessing, so he could pay his bills."

She nodded.

The "candidates" were the last piece of the suicide puzzle. "I saw you roaming the halls of the assisted living wing, calling on the residents closest to heaven's pearly gates. You recruited Michael's patients, didn't you?"

A single tear coursed down her cheek beside her nose. "'Recruit' is such a distasteful word. I talked to people, made friends with them, understood their circumstances."

"And offered them options."

She nodded again.

"Was this your way of making up for a life wasted on a marriage to Bruce?"

"You want to hear me say it?" she screamed. "I stayed with Bruce for the money. I loved the money. I loved it!"

He blew air, then paced back and forth between the kitchen and the couch. He ran a hand through his wiry gray hair. "Are you a candidate?"

She composed herself. "Yes, of course. Donald prepared a contract for me before ..." She let her voice trail off.

"Was I a candidate?"

Confusion contorted her face. "No. Why would you ask?"

He shrugged. "After Jacob took the easy way out, you needed someone new to warm your bed."

Her lower lip quivered. "That's disgusting! Jacob and I weren't lovers. He was just a candidate who decided to go through with it."

"You still needed someone to change your diapers when your time came and you found me. I had been through it with Sam, so I was qualified."

She started crying, as she might have done as a young girl. "Don't worry, I won't put you through what you went through with your wife. I can have any man in this place to keep me warm at night, but I want you, Eddie. I love you." Her words died in the air, like smoke dissipating on a breeze.

He stared at her, his best detective stare that had melted the resolve of many a criminal suspect. Madeleine didn't flinch and didn't waver. Eddie could imagine the future Madeleine had planned: The two of them immersed in a love affair, pretending it would never end, but inevitably, a date with Dr. Michael Cevert and his daughter.

"You can't … Michael can't do that any more."

"You'd deny me death with dignity? Maybe I don't love you."

"The old bitties are onto Michael and Stevenson won't forget the tip they gave him. Go back to your apartment."

"Now you have everything you need to arrest us. What are you going to do, Eddie?"

"I don't know."

"This is going to happen to you one day, you know?" Madeleine said. "You'll become ill like the rest of us and then you'll know the terror of impending death. Doctors will offer you sad alternatives and you won't have this one."

"I need some space, Madeleine!" he said and was sorry his tone had been so harsh.

Madeleine recoiled, then calmed herself. "Sam wouldn't want me to suffer the way she did. She wouldn't want you to suffer."

"Sam has nothing to do with this."

"Don't lie to yourself; she's all that stands between us."

Eddie roughly showed her to the door.

She resisted his push into the hallway. "Come live with me so we can enjoy the rest of our lives. Give yourself permission to be happy, Eddie."

"Get Donald's family out of here." He gave her a shove and closed the door.

He poured another double shot of bourbon and retrieved Sam's picture from his sock drawer. He slumped on the couch and stared at the picture.

Sam said, "Why so glum? You've solved a case bigger than opioids. This is redemption for Vietnam."

"I've made peace with Vietnam."

"Then make up for St. Petersburg and become a star again."

Chapter Twenty-Five

... The next afternoon

Eddie hadn't been in the Carlyle & Sons offices on Abercorn Street in over forty years and the air tasted that old. Beau's wife, Rosemary, now greeted clients and she seemed happy to see him. She ushered him into what had been Royce Carlyle's office decades ago. The furniture had been changed, but the dim interior had not. Beau sat behind the desk in jeans and a golf shirt. The tall sheriff, in a brown and tan uniform, looked out the grimy back window at a litter-filled parking lot.

Without turning around, Lance spoke first. "I guess I should congratulate you for cleaning up my messy little island. A pharmacist, a nurse, a killer, and a drug dealer is quite a haul. Harry-fucking-Bosch couldn't have done better, but you let the DEA beat you to the collar. What the fuck, Kovacs?"

"You were too late getting me in there. The DEA already had a guy inside and he jumped the gun," Eddie said.

Lance rapped his Smokey-the-Bear hat on his thigh, as though shaking off trail dust. "The DEA is taking credit for the arrests with the 'instrumental' cooperation of an anonymous citizen. You going to tell me that wasn't you?"

Stevenson thought he was throwing me a bone, but he just got me in trouble. "The DEA figured out who I was and confiscated my evidence."

"Feels like I paid for the DEA to make a score." Lance's hands began flying around as he spoke. "Seven thousand five hundred dollars for a month at that place. And two thousand five hundred dollars in drug buy money."

Eddie blushed. Had he been a younger man, he'd have punched this spoiled kid's lights out.

"The least they could have done is identify you as working for Lance," Beau said.

"No, the least Eddie could have done is tell me about the witnesses he stashed."

"He stashed witnesses?" Beau exclaimed.

"Yep," Lance said. "Exfiltrated one to Statesboro like a damned Special Forces operation."

"I was trying to win the race with the DEA. I moved him to keep the DEA from questioning him."

"The DEA gave me his address but the old gent has died."

"Gerry is dead?" Eddie asked. "What did his wife tell you?"

"That old hag is looney tunes," Lance said, "but she had a piece of the puzzle. Pointed a finger at Dr. Cevert, whose scripts were written for the drugs. If we had that information, we'd have made a case."

"Against whom? An innocent doctor?"

Lance heaved a sigh of disgust, as though deciding whether to accept the outcome. "There's also the perp you let get away."

"Huh?" Beau grunted.

Barbara. "She was my confidential informant and had to be protected," Eddie said.

"Your C.I., huh? Well, we've picked her up, so we got at least one arrest out of the mess."

You asshole! "She's a witness, not a criminal. She belongs in rehab."

"She can dry out in jail. I'm going to the press with my story," Lance said. "It was my undercover cop who worked with the DEA."

"Please don't use my name," Eddie said. "Either of them. Let it look like your local team helped the DEA."

"Don't worry, I'll take as much credit as possible."

"You can add to your glory, Sheriff. Two nurses conspired with Dr. Banerjee to sedate patients to make their jobs easier at night."

"That's been resolved. Dr. Banerjee has resigned his position and Palm Haven has agreed to replace the contractor nurses with full-time employees."

Palm Haven covered up medical malpractice to protect its reputation. "There's one more. A nurse named Peggy Crawford was Randy's girlfriend. I caught her stealing drugs from patients and then she gave me false information about the drug deal. She's in the wind."

"I don't know who that is," Lance said. "Two little old ladies snitched on Bobby. You should have been talking to them, you old fool."

Eddie *had been* a fool, but the ladies hadn't snitched on Bobby. They had accused Cevert of murder.

Scrambling to salvage one shred of dignity, Eddie said, "I built a case against Randy for the murder of Doris Christenson. His DNA was on her pill vial."

"Doesn't matter. They can't prove her death wasn't an accident or a suicide so it'll end up a drug charge. Randy was a minnow. Bobby is the big fish you screwed me out of," Lance said. "Your only job was to catch the dealer."

Eddie had to chuckle at Lance's use of a fishing metaphor. The humorous moment passed quickly as Eddie thought about how he had overlooked Bobby as a suspect. The buffoon had sidetracked him with boorishness. Bobby hadn't been going to Savannah to play cards. Susan had it wrong, too—Bobby didn't have a mistress—he had a financial problem he solved by selling drugs.

"Look, until Randy offered Bobby Claiborne the chance to move a large quantity of drugs in a single deal—the carrot I dangled in front of him—he was selling small quantities to street dealers in Savannah. The DEA never had it right."

"But they made the arrests," Beau said. "We can't let it look like all this stuff was going on under Lance's nose, so we'll make a big deal of our assistance."

"Like I said, leave me and my name out of it."

"Did you find anything else out there that I can publicize?" Lance asked.

Eddie took his time answering. He had taken this job to end his career in a blaze of glory, to erase the stain of his ignominious firing in St. Petersburg, and to offer a mea culpa for Vietnam. Instead, he allowed Tucker's murderer to go free, befriended and fell in love with a morally ambiguous doctor's alluring accomplice. Since Stevenson was unaware of Donald's suicide, Cevert's crime was still ripe for the picking, like a juicy plum on the low hanging branches of a tree.

In Vietnam, Eddie had done the right thing and the consequence was a life of fear and regret. Now Eddie had been given another chance to do the right thing: Arrest Cevert and Madeleine and let the justice system sort it out. Perhaps their case could be a test of the Georgia law. He imagined himself on a podium, surrounded by reporters, basking in glory while an arrogant and inept sheriff ate humble pie.

The image faded. America's Founding Fathers strove to separate church from state, and yet, many laws, including bans on assisted suicide, owed their provenance to religious teachings. Was it his place, was it any man's place, to judge the mature, intelligent adults who availed themselves of Cevert's services? Or did that power belong only to God?

Eddie had discarded his religion, his family, and his hometown; jettisoned his birth name when expedient; exchanged his career dreams for Sam's love as easily as he changed his underwear. Picking up and leaving it all behind was his special skill.

"I'll see you in heaven, Sam," he whispered silently.

"Till then, I'll miss you," she responded.

Eddie tossed his badge on Beau's desk. "Nothing else to report. I just wasn't done."

"Well, now you're done. Move out of that place today. Maybe I can get a refund for the time you didn't need to screw me." Lance put his smokey-the-bear hat on his head. "If y'all will excuse me, I gotta do police work." Lance left the room.

Beau leaned forward, elbows on his desk. "I'm sorry you didn't get a career-crowning bust. Lance wasted too much time sending his own men in there. By the time you got here, the DEA had connected the drugs to pill mill records. All they needed was the missing link at Palm Haven." He slid an envelope across the desk.

Eddie assumed the envelope contained a check for his services. "You don't have to make me feel better. Glory and redemption aren't all they're cracked up to be."

Beau frowned, confused.

Eddie wasn't about to explain that remark to Beau Carlyle. "If I hadn't helped the DEA, they'd have arrested the wrong man."

"Sure. Of course."

Eddie slipped the envelope into a breast pocket. The two men stood and shook hands.

"So, it's back to Florida to fish and play golf as Karl Novak."

"No, I'm staying here as Eddie Kovacs. That's who I am."

"Here in Savannah?"

"Out at Palm Haven. I like it out there."

"You can afford that place?"

Eddie shrugged. "I got a special deal."

Beau walked around his desk, clapped Eddie on the back and gave him a roguish smile. "I know what's going on here, you sly devil. You've met someone to take care of your ragged ass."

"Yeah, you could say that."

~The End~

Acknowledgments

A big thank you to Emily Lawrence (Lawrence Editing) who helped me turn a rough draft into something readable.

A shout out to Donna Black, Mike Brown, and Sharon Marchisello of the Hometown Novel Nights writers' group who served as beta readers and offered highly valuable criticism of early drafts.

And a special thank you to Lisa Weldon who exclaimed, "It's not only a detective story; it's a love story!" That revelation provided the polishing wax for the story's final version.

About the Author

Mike Nemeth, a Vietnam veteran and former high-tech executive, writes mystery novels that deliver a message about America's prevailing social ills. He is the author of three previous novels including award-winners *Parker's Choice* and *The Undiscovered Country*, which inspired songwriter Mark Currey to compose the song *Who I Am*. His short pieces have appeared in *The New York Times*, *Georgia Magazine*, *Augusta Magazine*, *Southern Writers' Magazine*, *Deep South Magazine*, and the *Writers' Voices* anthology. *Creative Loafing* named him Atlanta's Best Local Author for 2018. Mike lives in suburban Atlanta with his wife, Angie, and their rescue dog, Scout.

www.ingramcontent.com/pod-product-compliance
Lightning Source LLC
Chambersburg PA
CBHW050821190726
48286CB00007B/1953